Bridle

Christine Thomas

HEADLINE

ISBN 0 7472 3246 6

Typeset in 10/12½ pt English Times
by Colset Private Limited, Singapore

Printed and bound in Great Britain by
Collins, Glasgow

HEADLINE BOOK PUBLISHING PLC
Headline House
79 Great Titchfield Street
London W1P 7FN

Prologue

'Theresa O'Neill 1882–1918. May her soul rest in the peace of the Lord.'

Bridie knelt on sharp, prickly grass, churned round the edge of her mother's grave. It stung her bare knees as she carefully held her skirt out of the dirt. Her mother would have scolded if she had got grass stains. She gazed intently at the words on the plain headstone, put in place only yesterday. Leaning forward across freshly heaped soil she traced letters with her finger on pale grey stone warm with early summer sun. The newly chiselled shapes still had their first sharp edges. They'd slowly wear away with rain and frost until the words mellowed into a mossy little memorial like most of those on graves surrounding it. That would suit her mother better, thought Bridie. She'd been a gentle, soft-voiced woman, always with a kind word and loving touch for children. Bridie, sixteen years old and her eldest child, loved her dearly.

As she stroked her fingers over the letters a light breeze touched her, and Bridie thought for a moment that she felt her mother's hand rest tenderly on her unruly red hair. In longing, she bowed her head on her knees and began to to weep. For the first time since the village priest left, solemn-faced, and her father had come lumbering down the narrow cottage stairs to tell her brusquely that Mam and the baby were passed away, she realised that it was true. Tears came at last.

Doubled over with sudden pain, she crouched on her elbows in dry, rough clay, rocking back and forth until her clothes were stained and her face was streaked with mud. She shook her fists towards the empty blue sky. With swollen eyes Bridie searched its high pale brilliance and found nothing. No angels, no God, no spirits. Nothing. Rage and betrayal shook her so, her teeth chattered, until at last exhaustion began to steal over her, loosening her fists, hanging her head, calming the painful sobbing.

Beside the small wooden hut where the gravedigger kept his spades, Father Robert, the parish priest, paused on his way out of the churchyard to look at the little figure sitting motionless on the ground. His lined face softened as he watched. He was fond of Bridie. He'd christened her, taken her first communion and supposed he'd marry her one day. He'd been to the cottage many a time and found her helping her mother when she should have been at school. Mrs O'Neill had looked anxiously at her husband when the priest told him bluntly that he was breaking the law, but she depended on her daughter and so mostly Bridie stayed at home, looking after the three little ones. Now, he supposed, she'd take her mother's place. He sighed, knowing that wisdom didn't always come best from books. His hand strayed automatically into the sign of the cross, and, respecting her need to be alone, he turned on his heel and went on his way.

The sun grew warmer, and from all sides birds sang and called from the dense yellow-green May foliage. They hopped and squabbled and busied above paths white with early daisies. Bees hummed. Clover grew in pink and white clumps along the bottom of the grey stone wall enclosing the church and its graveyard. Pale grass as fine as hair covered a recent grave; a child had died of scarlet fever. Many did. Bridie brushed listlessly at her skirt. It only made things worse so she gave up and, cupping her chin in her fists, sat gazing at the quiet place until she felt quite empty inside. Quite scoured out.

It was noon when she got stiffly to her feet, stretched, and tried to run her fingers through her hair, to separate the tangled mass glued to her face by tears. She turned back to the grave and was at last able to do what she'd come to do hours earlier. She began to repeat her favourite psalm, under her breath. 'The Lord is my shepherd, I shall not want,' she whispered. When she'd said it through she crossed herself and half lifted her hand as if to wave goodbye, then walked slowly along the grassy path to the church gate. It always squeaked. Pushing her way through, Bridie ran her hand up and down the smooth wood, full of memories of long Sunday Masses listened to drowsily from tall pews bathed in shifting shafts of red, blue and gold sunlight as it shone through high stained windows. Bridie had thought the light came from Heaven; God's candles. She half smiled at her childish idea and let the gate swing slowly shut behind her. On her way back along the lane to the village, she vowed to herself that she'd do her very best to look after them all, Maire, MaryEllen and May, because her mother would want her to. So would her Dad.

Sean O'Neill was as rough and ready as his wife had been gentle. They'd married when both were just sixteen and had loved each other despite poverty and sickness, just as their wedding vows had said they should. Sean had been stoical about the many stillborn babies, and even about his four daughters and no sons. Theresa, who'd actually had to bear all the pain and loss, was not so much stoical as resigned to suffering. Often she looked at her four daughters and her eyes were full of sadness.

Watching them around the tea table, Mam had wondered how Bridie could be so different. Maire, MaryEllen and Little May had dark hair and pale cheeks, black curls and deep, deep blue eyes. Their faces never tanned, even when they worked the fields in high summer. Alabaster faces, smooth, delicate and round. Most of the village girls looked like the O'Neill girls; it was the local genes. Bridie stood out like a flame in darkness. In church, of a Sunday, the priest's eye would be drawn again and again to her bright head glowing coppery above the highbacked pews. In the rows of dark heads, Bridie's was startling. Her red curls grew in a mass and no amount of brushing or hairpins would make the wiry hair lie flat.

'Botticelli,' they'd have said, if they'd known. Her long, fine-featured face was as fair as the others', except for freckles which faded and darkened with the seasons.

'Don't know where she gets it from,' Sean would growl. 'I never heard of no colouring like that in my family.'

Theresa felt accused. 'I don't know, either, I'm sure,' she'd say, looking again at her unlikely daughter.

'Well, now,' Aunty Aileen who lived in Dublin said, 'that's Kerry features she's got. Down round Dingle Bay you'll see ever so many of the young women with our Bridie's looks. There's Kerry blood there, to be sure.'

'Must be way back, then,' Theresa had answered, 'None of my relatives ever said anything about Kerry.'

'I don't know of none, either,' agreed the old woman, 'but you can take my word that's what it is.'

Bridie would look at herself in the tiny mirror above the scullery sink. She liked the way she looked. Her freckles crinkled together on her nose when she laughed. Sometimes she pulled a face into the mirror, just to watch them. Light could change the colour of her eyes from grey to green to the whitish sheen of a stone on a dull winter day. Bridie liked being different.

Her mother's sudden death brought changes that meant much less time for peeping in mirrors. Cleaning, washing and cooking saw to that.

'I know we always helped her,' she told her sisters, 'but sure and I didn't know how hard she worked. How she did it with all them babbies as well. . . .' She shrugged.

But she took over cheerfully and chased her sisters into doing their chores so that they got on good-naturedly instead of grumbling. Little May, though, got away with murder. She was everyone's favourite, including Sean's. She wound him round her finger, Theresa used to say. He didn't spend a lot of time with his girls, as he called them. Never had done. So long as they helped out, and got in no trouble, Sean was content to leave the girls to their mother.

'Woman's work,' he'd say to the other men leaning on the bar in O'Donnell's, down in the centre of the village. 'They're best left to it.'

The men nodded agreement, and ordered fresh pints of dark, nutty-flavoured Guinness. Women were for leaving at home, except on holidays and Saturdays when the fiddles and squeeze boxes and penny whistles would come out and the bar burst with joyous playing and singing and banging of beer mugs until one o'clock in the morning. Since his wife's death, Sean had been spending more time than usual with his elbows on the bar. O'Donnell's open, generous face sobered in sympathy and he was ready and willing to advance a few pennies of credit to a fellow in distress. Sean O'Neill was a bit of a layabout, but no one held that against him since it was generally agreed that most of the village men were tarred with a touch of the same brush. Women clicked their tongues when they went into the main street in mid-afternoon, and heard their men's voices murmuring deeply from O'Donnell's. But it had always been that way and they had always been poor. And tomorrow didn't always come. Almost every man in the bar had lost more than one child. They knew about death, so they watched with understanding when Sean's big stubbly face would get redder and redder from unshed tears and Irish whiskey; by the end of the evening he would be snoring on the pitted, scratched wooden bar top until someone going that way propped him up and half carried him home to his front door.

One Saturday evening, about six weeks after Theresa died, Sean was waxing maudlin around midnight. O'Donnell had chalked up a lot more than usual, and he was still going strong.

'God save us, she's gone. God rest her. T'resha. Know?' He raised a watery, bloodshot eye to the room. 'God rest her shoul, buried shix weeks. My T'resha.' Sean began to mumble and a tear dripped into his beer glass. He hiccoughed several times, then started to cry loudly.

O'Donnell cast an experienced eye over his customer.

'Be better off at home, I reckon,' he said to several of the drinkers who were watching Sean's maudlin tears with interest. 'Anyone goin' his way?'

Two men sitting at a small table put down their dominoes.

'We can leave it and finish the game later. Don't no one interfere. We'll carry him between us. Reckon he deserves it, poor feller. Give 'im here.'

Between them they hoisted his weakly resisting frame between them. He was a tall, heavily built man with a belly bulged by years of beer. Taking his dead weight, the two men staggered as they hitched his arms up, one over each of their shoulders.

'Come on,' they said, impatient voices rough with sympathy. 'Let's get yer home.'

Feet dragging between his two minders, Sean's voice could be heard fading into the distance, singing disjointedly about Irish Eyes and hiccoughing steadily until the listeners in the bar could hear no more. With customary discretion, he was propped against his front door and left. He slid down the door-jamb and sat, stupefied, on the ground. He mumbled incoherently and the word 'Theresha' was audible from time to time. Half sitting, half lying, on the warm earth, he alternately talked to himself and dribbled tears that smelled of ale.

Upstairs Bridie started to worry. It was the first time her father hadn't come in and gone to sleep almost at once. She wondered what Mam would have done; he hadn't usually got as drunk as this when she was alive. Bridie bit a fingernail and listened to the sounds outside. When he started crying again she felt tears rise, stinging, to the back of her nose.

'Oh, poor Dad,' she said aloud. The jagged, drunken sobbing brought back her own grief in the churchyard and her heart ached. She slipped off the bed she shared with Little May and put her fingers to her lips for the small girl to be quiet. May's dark eyes watched her sleepily over the thick blanket of knitted squares Theresa had made. Maire and MaryEllen were silent in the tiny third room, fast asleep. Going quietly down the stairs in bare feet, Bridie opened the door at the bottom that led into the main room. Light from a full moon poured through the uncurtained window and the white walls gleamed dully. Her father's voice sounded even louder. She opened the door carefully, in case he was propped against it, and found him lying on his back staring up at the brilliant stars, his face working as tears welled over stubble unshaven for several days. He looked ghastly in the bright moonlight, his eyes watery holes above blotched patches that the moon made stains. Bridie caught her breath and stood staring at him.

'Come on, Dad,' she said eventually.

She bent to help him sit up, and suddenly Sean noticed her.

'Eh?' he said out of a mouth that hung slack.

'It's me, Dad. Bridie.'

'Terry.'

'No, it's not Mam. It's me. Come on, Dad.' Bridie's voice began to have an edge to it as she verged on panic. It wasn't clear she'd be able to get him inside the house at all.

He rolled back, stargazing. 'Oh, God help us,' his daughter muttered. She put her hands under his armpits and began to pull. He didn't move. She dropped him and his head hit the ground with a thud. He let out a roar of pain and surprise. Bridie bent again and took a firm grasp on the coarse stuff of his jacket.

'Come on, help me,' she said crossly, and pulled

harder. The sleeves began to ride up round his neck but he didn't move an inch. Exasperated, Bridie deliberately let his head bang again. Sean clutched his churning skull and moaned.

'Jaysus, girl, you'll kill me.'

'You've no call to get so drunk you can't get inside your own house,' snapped his daughter. Her sympathy evaporated and she waved a hand to dispel the fumes that rose in waves every time he moved. She'd just have to get help. In the distance, towards the village, doors banged and men's voices shouted goodnights. O'Donnell's was shutting up at last. Bridie leant against the edge of the door and watched the lane that ran past the front of the cottage. It was light enough to see anything that moved. After about ten minutes she heard slow footsteps crunching along the gravel at the edge of the lane. She screwed up her eyes and saw a new labourer from one of the farms further outside the village trudge past, humming to himself.

'Mister.'

The man stopped and looked around.

'Mister. Can you lend me a hand getting me Dad inside? I can't move him.'

The farmworker came to the low gate that led straight into the lane. He leant over the gate, thin as a hayrake, his nose a sharp spike in the shadows. 'Oh, it's O'Neill. Yes, he's the worse for wear. I saw him earlier, down O'Donnells. You got your hands full, darlin'.'

'Will you help me drag him in?' Bridie repeated.

The young man opened the gate and came down the path.

'You take his feet so they don't drag too much, and I'll pull him this way.'

Between them they hauled a semi-conscious Sean over the threshold into the whitewashed room. The labourer looked round and nodded towards the space in front of the blackleaded range that took up most of the longest wall in the room.

'Put him there?' he asked, raising an eyebrow in the gloom.

Bridie couldn't see anywhere else where there'd be enough room for her father to stretch out on the floor, and he was beyond being put up to bed.

'Yes,' she whispered. They half carried his inert body across the floor and dropped him, spread-eagled, on to the rag mat before the range.

'It's not cold at night, this time of year. He'll be warm enough,' remarked the young man.

'You've been real kind, Mister.' Bridie looked critically down at her father. 'I know he'll be grateful to you in the morning, though he's in no state to thank you now.' She giggled, suddenly seeing the funny side of it, and put her hand over her mouth apologetically.

The young labourer grinned and put his hands in his pockets. 'Glad to help you. Let him sleep it off, and he'll be all right tomorrow. Can you manage now?'

She nodded, and he thought how pretty she was in the dim light. He felt sorry about her father, it was hard on her.

'I'll be off, then.' He turned and ducked out of the low door.

Bridie watched him vanish into the night air, and went to put down the latch after him. She looked at her father, who was snoring massively, and shook her head at his inert body. Closing the stair door quietly behind her, she crept back upstairs and into bed with Little May.

Silence fell again, that dense, pressing hush that brings the rushing blood loudly to the ears. Bridie, tired after the struggle with her father, slept deeply and when a touch came on her hair she dreamed again the loving touch in the graveyard. Her mother had come. Bridie smiled and turned her face to the gentle kiss. Mam stroked back the thick hair and bent to kiss the dreaming lips. The touch grew bolder and the kiss hurt. Mam's mouth became scratchy and menacing. The dream began to change. A nightmare, a hand pulling her head roughly backwards so that she half woke in fear. The hand buried itself in her hair, turning her head, and as she fought to wake up she found her father standing over her, one hand pulling at his trousers and the other pulling her mouth towards his.

Bridie lay paralysed. Staring, she watched Dad finally get his belt and trousers undone and dropped round his knees.

'T'resha. Darlin',' he whispered.

Bridie shook her head wordlessly.

'Come here.' Dad began to pull her towards the edge of the bed. The clumsy movement helped Bridie find her tongue.

'No, Dad. No, no! I'm not Mam. Dad, what are you doing?' Her voice rose in terror as her father took no notice, and slid his hand under her back and down, clutching her buttocks. He began to pull her night-gown clumsily from under her.

'Stop it,' she cried.

She opened her mouth and took a deep breath, to shout at him, but his mouth was on hers, tongue thrusting violently, stinking of whiskey. Her stomach heaved. She struggled to drag her face away, to draw breath. He lurched, knocking Little May sideways, so that she woke with a violent start and began to cry. Her tears stopped abruptly and she held her breath as she took in what was happening a few inches away. Dad and Bridie were having a fight. Little May froze. She crept backwards to the very edge of the bed and lay clutching the coarse grey sheet to her with both hands. Eyes round and unblinking as saucers stared at the shadowy heap of bodies writhing, thrashing and very nearly knocking her to the floor. Bridie's strength was of sheer terror. She pushed her father away and clawed his face.

'No, Dad! NO. Please, don't. NO.' The plea came out in a voice so thin and shrill it cut into his throbbing head. He shook her off and, with a grunt of effort, put his leg across so that she was pinned beneath him. Bridie began to moan. Her lips drew back in a snarl and, raising her head with an effort that made the tendons stand out in her neck, she bit her father hard. The girl heard a hoarse gasp of surprise and rage and felt him raise himself on one hand. He pulled himself right up, drew back one arm and struck her full across the mouth. Bridie half screamed and Little May whimpered. Then the kissing started again. Helplessly, Bridie mewed in the back of her throat while her father forced her knees apart and was in her. A sharp pain came again and again, and then, with a sort of coughing noise, he pushed in her slowly once or twice, and fell forwards. His face slid limply down into her neck, and soon after he began to grunt as he sank into a dead sleep.

Little May took her hands off her ears when the bed stopped bouncing up and down and opened her eyes, which she'd kept squeezed tight shut after her Dad had hit Bridie. Her mind was still repeating HolyMaryMotherofGod like a frantic talisman while her eyes, adjusted to the darkness, took in the sight of her father lying quite still on top of Bridie, who was hidden underneath him, not making a sound. She wondered what Bridie would do, and lay holding her breath until something more happened. Nothing did. Bridie lay quite silent and still. Her father snored as usual.

After a while May lifted her head cautiously and whispered into the darkness, which was now dense as the moonlight faded. 'Bridie?' There was no answer. May went cold with fear. What if Bridie were dead? Her mother had lain in bed all still and silent when she was dead. Little May felt trembly. She didn't want Bridie to go away like Mam. She stuck her thumb in her mouth and sucked hard as she decided that Bridie couldn't be dead, because if she was her father would know. He wouldn't let Bridie lie there dead. Just before dawn the little girl fell asleep, thumb in mouth, curled up against her father's warm, comfortable back. Lulled by his presence and his rhythmic snoring, she slept an uneasy, fearful sleep.

Bridie heard Little May call to her as if from some faraway place. She lay very still and wide-eyed, staring into the dark. She tried not to blink because each tiny moment that her eyes closed, the horror flashed before her. All of it. Blink. The touch on her hair; the kissing; the awful pain.

Blink.

She swallowed and her throat hurt. Her lip was aching and stiffening as it swelled. She felt sore, bruised all over, but numbed by Dad's weight. Cold and squashed, she couldn't move, and it wasn't just because of Dad. She had a strange, awful feeling that went through and through her mind as she lay in the cold wet misery of her bed. She somehow wasn't inside herself like she had been only a few hours earlier, when she stood with the young labourer and they'd smiled at each other over Dad's sad, drunken body. Blink. Oh dear God. Blink.

Bridie knew when it was dawn, even though the first faint patches of grey had not yet tinged the horizon. With the most delicate care, she rolled Dad off on to his back. She slid her cramped, aching legs from beneath his, and gently unclasped his arms from around her. He lay right up against Little May, who did not move. Bridie put her feet carefully over the side of her bed on to the chilly floor. Even in high summer the cottage got damp and chilled in the dewy mornings. Her thighs were slippery and her night-gown clung to her, sodden with her blood. She screwed up her nose in disgust then stood up quickly. There was only one thought in her mind: to get to the water tap in the scullery and wash. Wash. She must wash. And wash. And wash.

She tiptoed to the bedroom door and opened it just enough to slide through. The hinge grated if it was opened all the way. Creeping down the narrow stairs, she began to shiver wildly as she opened the door at the bottom. The cottage suddenly seemed full of doors, creaking, squeaking hazards to bring Dad roaring after her. She lifted the wooden latch on the scullery door silently and stood bemused by shock and fear in the earthen-floored lean-to where they did their washing. A single tap stuck out from the wall. Below it a wide, shallow sink and above, the tiny mirror that had once reflected a girl who seemed now to belong to another lifetime.

Under the sink stood what she wanted. Moving like a sleepwalker, she bent down and lifted the metal bucket up to the tap. Using both hands, she put it gently into the brown crock sink. It filled slowly as she ran the cold water in dribbles that wouldn't make too much noise. As the tinny sound of running water plinked in her ears, she listened, stiff with dread, for any movement from upstairs. Commonsense would have told her that once her father went to sleep after drinking, the Apocalypse itself wouldn't waken him. But commonsense and the Dad she loved had vanished

16

in the night, bringing God knew what along with the beginning of a new day. With the bucket half full she lifted it down and set it in the middle of the tiny room. She looked at the cold clear water uncertainly, then decided to bathe her face first. She put her head under the tap so the water wouldn't make such a noise running straight into the sink, and turned it on. She was lucky it was summertime; in midwinter the water, if it ran at all, would have been nearly ice.

She gasped nonetheless as it ran over her head and down her face, pouring off her nose into the bowl of the sink. Her long hair hung in a sodden solid mass over her face; the darkening bruise on her mouth stung. She turned her head to one side and caught several mouthfuls, rinsing and spitting. Finally, she reached up blindly and fumbled for the tap. When it was off, she wrung her long hair out like a sheet and twisted it into a tight coil. It was wet enough to stay put, more or less, while she prepared to wash. The puddle she'd lain in so long had made her night-gown stick to her. She took it by the hem and carefully rolled it up until she could pull it over her head without having to let it touch her face. Naked, she trembled as she straddled the cold bucket. Squatting as best she could, she began to splash water over her legs. When all trace of blood was gone, she emptied the bucket down the sink and refilled it. This time she took a piece of rag from a collection under the sink and, standing over the bucket again, scrubbed and scrubbed and scrubbed where her father had soiled her, until her skin, white and chilled, began to break and bleed. Half sobbing, she still dipped and rubbed, dipped and rubbed, until the pain broke through her trance. It was enough.

Once more Bridie emptied and refilled the bucket. This time, with fresh rags, she washed, then dried herself from top to toe. She made another effort to wring out her dripping hair and rummaged in a basket that lay on the floor. It held dirty clothes waiting for washday when she'd scrub them on the bleached wooden washboard, in hot water from the range. She managed to find enough of her own clothes and borrowed a woollen jumper of Maire's which was a bit tight, but she was so cold she had to wear something. Creeping into the other room, she fetched the comb from the shelf above the range. It stuck and dragged in her wet hair but she persevered until it hung in strands round her shoulders and could be tucked back behind her ears.

Bridie stacked the bucket and rags back under the sink. She opened the scullery door and walked down the path with its bright geraniums and phlox to the little gate. She didn't care now if it squeaked. Pushing it open, she turned into the lane and walked towards the village.

The early rays of sun shone white gold above sparkling fields. The first birdsong had shrilled into the soft air when Bridie was filling her bucket. Now the dawn chorus had faded into daytime chattering and shrilling. Birds rustled and started in the hedgerow as she passed and a mouse caught up late ran across the lane ahead of her. Bridie was dully aware of creatures around her. She wanted to run, hurry hurry hurry. But pain slowed her and she hobbled slowly, as if prematurely aged. The sun rose higher by the minute. It dried her hair and its warmth seeped through and comforted her. She felt Maire's jumper grow warm on her back and with that, the deep inner shivering was calmed.

Morning voices drifted from the village. A door banged and a woman's voice called something and laughed. At the crossroads just before the village really began, she turned right. Not wanting to walk down the main street like she was, she took the long way round. A track led through hedgerows thick with nettles, buttercups and heavy, sweet heads of cow parsley which made her sneeze. The little lane wound ahead. Bridie didn't see it. Her eyes didn't leave the path in front of her. She plodded awkwardly, hurting.

At last she came to the church. Resting her hand on the gate to the churchyard, she stood and looked across to her mother's grave. The flowers were still fresh from yesterday. Bridie closed her eyes.

'I'm sorry, Ma. I didn't mean it. Please know I'm sorry.'

The words fell emptily. Her mother had gone. She couldn't be reached. Bridie's heart ached worse than the rest of her. She went up to the heavy church door. It was never locked, and swung open smoothly as she pulled the big iron ring of a handle and went in.

It was a small village church with a tower but it always seemed vast to Bridie and the village children. She loved the holy feeling of the still air hanging under the high roof. At Mass voices rose up and up until they reached the fairytale cloud city of Heaven, where God listened and knew if you were singing or not, and could see you if you'd played about, giggling with the O'Donnell boys instead of paying attention. Bridie had long since outgrown her childhood ideas of Heaven, but she loved the church for its peacefulness. She breathed in the scent of dust and lavender polish. Stale incense hung in corners; dusty spirals lazily danced in sunlight reflected off the high polish of rows of old, blackened pews. Bridie held on to the curved, carved back of the first pew while she genuflected painfully to the altar. Then she walked slowly down the aisle to the very front pew where the priest's very very old mother sat when she visited, all alone in her worn widow's black. Her feet trod indifferently the polished brass set into the floor to mark the graves of two former British landlords. Village women took it in turns to come each week with cloths and a bottle of Brasso, to polish the brasses until they shone like pure gold. Bridie sometimes wondered how rich you'd be if it was real gold, and you could prise it away and keep it. This morning she didn't wonder anything. She slid silently into the pew and sat with her head bowed. She didn't pray. She didn't do anything. She just waited.

Father Robert came in by the side door. He genuflected in the direction of the altar and strode briskly down the side aisle to the vestry. He carried a pile of new catechisms under one arm and was tucking a packet of Players into his trouser pocket with his free hand. He enjoyed his first smoke of the day on the short walk from the presbytery to the church. He bustled about for five minutes and then emerged into the front of his church to check the candles. Small white ones were kept on a shelf above the branching metal holder where there were usually at least half a dozen burning at any time. The day Bridie's mother had been buried all the little holders had been full the whole day.

The stout little priest's black gown rustled round his ankles. His boots had steel tips to make them last longer, so whenever he stepped off the carpet, he clattered loudly. Bridie listened unseen. She heard him cough and blow his nose on a big linen handkerchief before he opened a fresh box of white candles and began to stack them on the narrow shelf just to one side above the candleholder. He was balancing the last three carefully on the top of a pyramid of white tallow when a movement caught his eye. He turned to look and recognised the crown of the red head bent almost out of sight in his mother's pew.

'Bridie O'Neill?' he called quietly. 'Is it you, Bridie?'

The head raised itself and a very pale face appeared out of the shadow.

'Yes, Father.'

He stuck the last of his candles, which wouldn't fit on to the pyramid at all, into one of the holders and came over to the pew. As he came closer and could see the girl more clearly, his heart sank. She'd been beaten.

21

'What is it, Bridie? Why are you here so early? What has happened?'

Bridie shook her head dumbly.

'Your face is bruised. Has someone hit you?'

'Yes, Father.'

There was silence.

Bridie dropped her eyes and stared at the hassock hanging on a nail in front of her. It was embroidered with lots of tiny red crosses in thick wool that prickled your knees when you knelt on it for the prayers. She made up her mind.

'I'd like to make my confession, Father. If you wouldn't mind. It's early, I mean. I could wait here. . . .' Her courage began to fail her.

The grey-haired man nodded. 'Surely you can. Go on in. I'll be a few moments.'

The steel tips rang across in front of the altar, paused as he turned to bow and stopped as he walked on to the carpet in the vestry. When he came out he had the blue and white stole over his shoulders that he always wore when he heard confession. Bridie heard him sit down in the other side of the tall black box where he listened to the day to day sins of the whole community. A bit of stealing, quite a lot of fornication and lust, sometimes adultery and a great many people feeling guilty that they didn't even try to be very good. He opened his worn black book and began to read aloud, inviting Bridie to confess her sins and ask God for His forgiveness. They both knew the words by heart. There was a long pause.

'It was Dad.' The words came out finally in a

whisper so low that Father Robert had to strain to hear them. He was helped by the fact that he'd guessed already what had happened to Bridie in the course of that dark night. He'd looked at her pallor, the spreading bruise and the unconsciously twisting hands, and knew that, in all likelihood, she would tell the story she was about to utter through dry, white lips.

'I couldn't stop him, Father. I would have but he was too strong.'

'All right, Bridie.'

'Father?'

'Yes?'

'I think I'd have killed him if I could have. Is that a mortal sin? Will I go to hell for that? I wouldn't want to have hurt me dad, but when he . . . he . . . I would've killed him.'

Anger stopped Father Robert answering at once. He rubbed a weary hand over his face and turned towards the grille through which he could faintly make out the shape of Bridie's head.

'Bridie, listen to me carefully. You have done wrong through no fault of your own. You are your father's victim. He has done you the wrong. You have sinned, Bridie, but you are not responsible. But you will want me to give you a penance for the things you have felt and thought.'

There was a long silence while Bridie felt the words hang in her mind. She couldn't make anything of them.

The elderly priest stifled a deep sigh. He knew she

would carry the guilt and also knew from experience how futile it would be to say more.

'Me penance, Father?' Bridie prompted.

'Ah, yes. Let us see. Which psalm do you know best?'

'The one hundred,' she answered without hesitation.

'I want you to repeat it each day before you go to sleep, and think about what it means. For one week. Will you do that?'

'Yes, Father.'

'Good.'

There followed the lovely ritual of the absolution – for a sin, reflected the priest wryly, it flew in the face of commonsense to say she had committed. He left the confessional quickly, discreetly leaving her to take her time. He pottered in the vestry, then went out to see what she was doing.

Bridie was sitting on the steps of the altar with her chin in her hands. He stood in front of her, hands behind his back. After a bit she said apologetically, 'I'm sorry, Father, but I can't go back. I can't go home, because he . . . he's there, and. . . .'

The priest stared at her. 'Have you any idea what you can do instead?'

This was a matter that had occupied Bridie in the night. She'd made a plan.

'I'll go to England, Father.'

Robert looked surprised. He knew his parishioners well, and he'd not heard of the O'Neills having kin on the mainland.

24

'Have you family over there?'

'No, Father.'

'Ah.'

'I can get work. I'm old enough to go into service or something like that.'

He looked at her gravely.

'Fifteen?'

'Sixteen.'

The priest swung round on his heel and marched slowly halfway up the aisle and then back down again.

'I've an idea. I have an old friend, Francis Holmes, who lives in London. He's a good man, and kind. If I call him, he might help you find a position in service and keep an eye on you when you arrive. Its not like the village, Bridie, London is like nowhere you've ever been. Do you think that would be of help?'

Her face looked all eyes.

'Yes, Father. Thank you, Father. Oh, yes, please.'

'We will do that, then. Is there any other way in which I can help you?'

Bridie hesitated.

'I'm ever so sorry, Father, to be a nuisance, but I'd be so glad if you could ask Maire to bring me my clothes and things.'

The priest realised that he'd overlooked the most important question. What was she to do for money?

'How will you buy your ticket?'

Bridie had thought of this.

'I've me mother's ring. I don't want to, but I'll pawn it.'

The priest nodded again. She was sensible. She'd survive.

'I've to go down to your end of the village later, and I'll see Maire.' I'll see your father, too, he thought grimly, but said nothing of that to her. 'Just now, will you go up to the presbytery and ask Mrs O'Sullivan for some tea and jam. Tell her you've been on an errand for me and I told you to come. Tell her I said you were to lend her a hand with the kitchen until I come in. Will you do that, Bridie?'

For the first time a small, lop-sided smile brightened her face.

'Be off with you, now,' he answered sternly.

She walked stiffly away up to the church door and across to the priest's home, where his housekeeper clucked with disapproval when she saw the girl's bruises, but held her tongue and expressed herself instead by way of hot sweet tea and a large plate of bread and greengage jam. Bridie had to eat slowly, though she was ravenous. She was saving the last deliciously jammy soft bit from the middle of the bread for last, while topping and tailing gooseberries for Mrs O'Sullivan, when there was the ringing sound of metal on the flagstones in the hall, and the priest came back from the village. Father Robert smiled at Mrs O'Sullivan.

'I'm afraid I have to take your helper away,' he said across the big scrubbed table, helping himself to a ripe gooseberry.

He beckoned to Bridie, who followed him down the hall to his study. He gestured to her to sit down and, hitching up his cassock, perched on his desk in front of her.

'I've seen Maire and MaryEllen,' he began. 'They are putting your belongings together and will bring them up here as soon as they can. They are, of course, completely puzzled and upset by the idea of your going away. They really do need you, Bridie,' he raised his eyebrows at her, 'now your mother's gone. Would you not be able to stay if you were quite certain that your father would never touch you again? I believe that if I spoke to him in the strongest possible words about what has happened, he would be very contrite indeed. You said he'd been down in O'Donnell's drinking unusually hard. I doubt he may even remember what he did. He'd not a bad man, your father, Bridie, and I believe he was probably too drunk to know what he was doing.'

Bridie stared at him, appalled. Was he changing his mind? He'd seemed all understanding and sympathy in confession, and now he was talking as though it had all been just a bit of a mistake. She shook her head speechlessly.

'You're bent on going to England?'

She found her voice as anger overcame her disappointment.

'Yes, Father. I couldn't stay, no matter what. I know the others will be upset, and it upsets me to leave them. But I have to go. I think Maire would understand if ever she knew what's happened.' Her voice sounded stronger, more decided. The priest realised that he was dealing with a young woman, not

27

a child. He looked at her thoughtfully and finally nodded.

'Very well. What are we to tell them? They have to have a reason, and I doubt you want to give the truth?'

Bridie felt astonished. Father Robert was inviting her to lie? The world had indeed turned upside down since yesterday. She thought rapidly.

'Well,' she said at last, 'there's no easy explanation comes to mind. Would it sound all right if I just said I wanted to go away to find work? I know it won't make them feel happy, but it's a kind of reason.'

The priest pursed his lips doubtfully.

'It'll have to do,' he said, 'because I can't come up with anything better. It's what I'll tell Frank Holmes as well, all right?'

'Yes, please. Nothing about the . . . the . . . you know?'

'That's confession, Bridie. It can never be repeated. Now then,' he continued, 'you'll be needing money, and tickets and instructions where to go and how to get there. It's a long way you're going, young woman, and on your own. Think you'll manage?'

'I'll just have to, won't I?'

The priest looked at her seriously.

'I think that is just what you're going to have to do. The Good Lord will watch over you, you know.'

'He didn't last night.' Bridie put the bad thought into words before she could stop herself. In front of Father Robert, too. She flushed with shame and picked at her skirt nervously. The priest went round to open a drawer of his desk, taking out an envelope which he handed to Bridie. 'Here. I've put Mr Holmes's address in this, and some money. That is for your ticket.' He raised a hand at Bridie's protest. 'I don't like the idea of your pawning your mother's ring. It belongs to you and you should keep it. This is from the fund I have for helping people in trouble; the poor box, if you like.'

Bridie took the envelope. The priest saw her turn it over before stuffing it into her pocket. Ah, the Parish daughters, he thought sadly. If the Good Lord doesn't take better care of them, then the poor box must, I'm afraid.

He knew all too well how many village girls could tell tales not much different to Bridie's. Mostly they stayed, though, not saying much. Few had the kind of outraged determination that the little O'Neill girl was showing. The money was partly a gesture of respect. The elderly man liked people who stood on their own two feet; he met too many altogether of the other kind in his line of business.

'The first step is to go to the train station in Dublin,' he began to explain the journey. 'I heard old Barney say he was taking a sheep over to a fellow just outside the city, and he's willing to let you ride on the cart. He'll see you get there. Then from Dublin you take the train to Dun Laoghaire. There you take the steam packet to Holyhead on the other side of the water. You buy your ticket straight through to London from Dublin. That way you needn't spend time looking for one ticket office after another. All right? One ticket, Dublin to London. Then in Holyhead you'll have to find your way to the train station again, and ask for the train to Euston. Then you just sit tight until you get to the end of the line. At Euston the train stops. Goes no further. So you can't go wrong. Dublin, Dun Laoghaire, Holyhead to Euston. Got that?'

It might just as well have been Jerusalem to Istanbul. Bridie, who'd only been to Dublin two or three times in her life, nodded and clutched the envelope in her pocket tightly.

'And I've telephoned Frank Holmes on your behalf. He tells me you are welcome, and he will do everything he can to find you some work. He has very generously offered to let you stay in his house until you've come to some arrangement about a job. You're lucky to have such an offer, and I hope you do his kindness justice, Bridie.'

'I will, Father. Oh, I will.' She was so relieved to have somewhere to go that she'd have promised anything.

'Time is going to be tight,' the priest went on. 'There's a night ferry goes, I think, around ten o'clock. If you can get the train at five, that should give you time enough. Old Barney wants to go at midday. Can you be ready to leave then, if Maire and the others bring your things over here?'

Bewildered by the speed with which it was happening, Bridie nodded. What had been a plan born of a nightmare was now being calmly discussed in terms of timetables and train stations.

'All right, that's how we'll do it then. I'll ask Mrs O'Sullivan if she'll be good enough to put some sandwiches together.' He went towards the kitchen, but turned back as the doorbell rang. Outside stood Bridie's three sisters, with a suitcase on the step in front of them. Little May, seeing Bridie in the study doorway down the hall, ran forward with a cry and flung her arms round her sister's waist. She held on tightly while Maire and MaryEllen came in with the case. They all stood uneasily in the hallway looking at Bridie, waiting for her to say something. She did her best, making up the story she'd suggested to the priest. They all looked blank.

'What on earth do you mean?' asked Maire. 'We manage well enough. There's no call for you to go away to work. Who'll look after us? It'll have to be me, won't it, and I'm not sure I could manage without you.' She looked round for help from her younger sisters. 'We need you much more than we need more money, Bridie. Please don't go away.'

Bridie felt as if she were being steadily torn in two. She shook her head. 'I know. I really do know, but I have to go anyway,' she said in a low voice.

Maire put her face close to her sister's and looked at her hard.

'Why?' she demanded. 'I don't believe what you are saying.'

Trapped, Bridie looked furtively at the priest, who took no part in the discussion.

'Who give you that lip?' The question wouldn't

brook evasion. Maire confronted her sister angrily, demanding to understand.

Little May suddenly gave a shriek and buried her head in Bridie's skirt.

'What's she on about?' Maire was getting more baffled by the minute.

'I dunno,' muttered Bridie, who could feel the situation sliding completely beyond her control.

'You do. You do, so.' May pulled her head out of its hiding place and looked up desperately at the big girl's face. 'I'm going to tell if . . . if you don't.'

'Tell what?' Maire's voice was shrill with frustration and curiosity.

Bridie, harassed and hopeless, gave up. 'Dad gave me the lip,' she said, and hoped they'd leave it at that.

Maire looked sceptical. 'You planning to go away because of that? It's not the first black eye or whatever we've had, and you never wanted to go away on account of nothing thing like that before. Tell the truth.'

Bridie shook her head in misery.

'I can't.'

'Bridie O'Neill, you're lying to your own sisters. You should be ashamed.' Maire was hopping mad.

Then May shocked them all into horrified silence.

'It was Dad. He came last night and had a fight with Bridie. And he hit her and made her cry and cry. He lied right on top and squashed her.'

Three pairs of eyes swivelled downwards to the little girl's pinched, furious small face.

'He hurt Bridie something bad. Didn't he?' she

32

turned to Bridie fiercely, demanding honesty.

'Oh my Lord,' whispered Maire, in spite of the parish priest standing there. 'Is that it, Bridie?'

Shamed beyond any words, Bridie nodded numbly.

Her sister gazed at her with fascinated pity. She was way more precocious than the older girl and had a good enough idea of what May was describing.

MaryEllen, always shy and diffident, began to cry quietly.

'Shut up, MaryEllen,' snapped Maire impatiently. 'There's nothing wrong with you. It's Bridie.'

Chastened by the lack of sympathy, MaryEllen subsided into silence again.

Maire pushed the case with her foot, edging it towards Bridie.

'Here. I think you'd best go after all, though I'll miss you badly, I really will. I wish you could stay at home, but I don't believe you can, can you?'

With the terrible feeling that her boats had just been burnt so there'd be no turning back, Bridie looked her sister straight in the eye.

'No, Maire love, I can't stay at home again. I'm glad you've found out why, because now I don't have to go away feeling I left you with lies. I never wanted to do that, but I didn't know what to say.'

Maire suddenly pushed Little May aside and threw her arm's around her elder sister.

'Oh, Bridie, it's awful. I'm sorry. I'll kill Dad.'

'No!' cried Bridie, alarmed. 'You mustn't talk like that. He probably doesn't even know what he did, he was too drunk.'

The priest intervened for the first time.

'Leave your father to me, Maire. I'll talk to him, and he will know exactly what he did, and he will grieve for the rest of his life for it. You might come and see me later on, when Bridie has gone. Would you like to do that?'

Maire looked around at the other two. 'We'll all come, Father.'

Mrs O'Sullivan opened the kitchen door and stuck her head into the hall.

'Old Barney's coming up the path. His cart's outside the gate.'

The priest looked at Bridie.

'Are you ready?'

'Yes, Father.'

Little May, realising what was about to happen, began to shriek. A tantrum erupted that forced the others to put their hands to their ears. Bridie prised May's fingers off her skirt only to have the little fingers clutch tightly at her hair. They hurt enough to bring tears to Bridie's eyes. Maire went to pull her away, but May kicked and struggled and screamed. Her hair torn almost from its roots, Bridie pushed her small sister desperately at Maire. 'Take her, for Heaven's sake,' she gasped.

The priest stepped forward, and picking up the howling child, held her away from him at arm's-length. May fought furiously to be put down, but he held her easily and in a few moments the yells diminished into sobs and she put out her arms to Bridie in appeal.

'You won't start screaming again?'

May shook her head.

Bridie took the little girl into her arms and kissed her. 'I love you, little one,' she whispered, 'and I will come back and see you one day. Perhaps you'll come to see me. Be a good girl and do as Maire tells you.'

The small dark head nodded. Bridie turned to Maire and MaryEllen.

'I love you, too, and I won't forget you. I'll think of you all the time and I'll miss you so much.' Her voice began to shake. She hugged them, first MaryEllen and then Maire, swallowing back tears. She gave a passive May into Maire's arms and picked up the case.

'Is Barney wanting to go?' she asked.

Father Robert nodded. She carried the case through the kitchen and out of the back door.

'Goodbye, Mrs O'Sullivan,' she said.

The housekeeper thrust a packet at her.

'Here. I've made you some sandwiches. You take care and be a good girl now.'

Case in one hand, packet in the other, Bridie pulled herself on to the back of Barney's cart, along with a large unshorn sheep that shied away from her. The wizened old man grinned at her toothlessly, his faded brown eyes quizzical as he asked was she ready to go. Bridie nodded.

Barney settled himself at the reins and gave them a jerk. The cart jolted forward. Bridie waved and waved until the cart rounded a bend, and then sat watching the road slowly unfold beneath her dangling feet.

The dirt track turned to stones, the stones to paving and finally they were on the streets of Dublin. 'Here we are, coming up now,' said Barney. It was the only time he'd spoken throughout the drive. 'Station's along there.' He gestured with the end of the reins. 'Let you off here then?' he suggested.

'Yes. This'll do nicely, thank you, Barney.'

She heaved the suitcase down and stuffed the sandwiches in her pocket. ' 'Bye Barney. Thanks.'

The old man grunted and jerked his reins again. He and the cart lumbered off down the road and Bridie, completely alone, turned into Dublin Station to begin her long journey, to leave everything and everyone she loved and with a place she didn't know for her journey's end.

Chapter One

Bridie had lost all sense of time as, by the blind walls of the Bank of England, she came to a halt. The great intersection – Cheapside, Cornhill, Threadneedle Street, King William Street, with Princes Street and Victoria Street – bemused her completely.

'I can't follow me nose in a circle,' she said under her breath, echoing the advice of the policeman who had given her directions earlier, and looked round for likely help. The heavy buildings closed in on her, a frightening foreign country. It was all so grey and black, bricks and stones crusty with soot and dirt. Pigeons, whole flocks of them, scavenged and squawked on the sills and in the street, their droppings making whitish smears against the soot. Fearless, arrogant birds. Bridie tried to skirt round them, alarmed by the quick, poking beaks. She bit her lip agitatedly and the pigeons suddenly scattered.

One of the biggest of the doors across the way swung open. A bucket and mop were followed down the steps by an impressive figure. Encased in a floral pinny and firmly rooted in carpet slippers, it wheezed its way to the gutter, where the woman wrung out the greasy strands of the mophead before chucking the filthy contents of the bucket into the road. As she straightened up she met Bridie's eyes. The girl smiled and two button black eyes almost vanished as the City cleaning woman beamed back.

'All right, duck?' she asked companionably.

Bridie shook her head slightly.

'I'm lost.'

'Where did you want to get to, love?'

'Stratford.'

'Yes? I'm from Bethnal Green meself. Out the same way.' She clanged the bucket down and pointed a red, chapped hand down the road.

'Over there, see? Down Cornhill and Leadenhall. Straight over Aldgate until you come into White-chapel. Then it's just straight on until you see Stratford High Street. You're there, then. T'ra then, love,' she called cheerily as Bridie turned to go. 'Take care.'

The carpet slippers slopped their way back up the steps and the bright pinny disappeared into the high gloom of the interior as the door swung shut behind her.

Bridie tramped into the Bow Road at eight o'clock that evening, badly footsore and sweating in the skirt and jumper that were too heavy for the warm day. The case felt fit to break her arms and she longed to stop and put it down. She didn't dare. As she'd moved steadily eastwards, away from Euston and through the great City, the grand buildings had tailed off. For a long way now houses and people became poorer and rougher with every street she passed. On and on she walked. When the sole fell off her shoe where Bow

Road turns to Stratford High Street, she began to cry. Tears made tracks in her dirty face as she slumped in a heap at the edge of the road, put her head into her aching arms and wept.

She'd stopped near a crossroads. On the corner of four mean streets stood a public house whose double doors gave directly on to the road. Although it was hardly dusk, the gaslights had been lit, and the lighted windows looked cosy. Bridie wiped her nose, runny with tears, on the hem of her skirt as the doors opened on a gust of good-natured laughter, and the familiar smell of beer and tobacco spilled out. A young woman in a green cotton dress had started to turn up the road away from Bridie when she stopped and looked back.

'You in trouble, love?' she asked.

Bridie, embarrassed, bent as if to show her foot.

'I've broken me shoe. Me feet are all over blisters,' she complained, poking at her toes, half to show the blisters, half to avoid looking up.

The girl was used to seeing children run barefoot. 'Oh, yes,' she said vaguely.

She went to move on when Bridie, in desperation, said, 'Miss, can you tell me how far I've still to walk? To Stratford?'

Miss looked round.

'You're nearly there. Up the road, at the top, and you're in the High Street.'

'Oh, thank God,' Bridie cried in relief.

The girl looked at her curiously. 'You going any-where I know?'

39

'Tredegar Square.'

A surprised expression came over the girl's face. 'Really?'

Bridie was nonplussed. 'Yes, I'm going to a friend of a friend. I want to go into service, and he's helping me.' She felt so low, the urge to confide overcame discretion.

'Oh, I see.' The young woman pointed the other way. 'Well, you've come past it, then.'

Bridie felt tears brim over at the very idea of going back again.

'You go back, about halfway down Bow Road. Tredegar Square is on your left, going that way.'

Bridie looked back and shook her head in despair.

'Look, it ain't far. I'm going that way meself. Want me to show you?'

'Oh, yes.' That was different. Bridie bounced to her feet, blisters forgotten. Hastily dragging off the other shoe she left it lying in the road and hurried barefoot after the green dress in case it wouldn't wait. Hopping and and skipping to avoid stones, she caught the girl up.

'I know some of the people in the Square, 'cos me sister's in service near there. You going to anyone in particular?'

'Yes. A man called Mr Holmes.'

'Mr Holmes? Are you – honest?'

'Why?' asked Bridie anxiously. 'Do you know him?'

'Oh, not personal like. But everyone round here knows about him.'

Bridie felt dismayed. Was this good or bad? The girl chattered on.

40

BRIDIE

' 'e's on the Council, or works for the Council, or summat. Anyway, 'e gets things done . . . like water taps. It was partly him that made them give us taps with clean water. He's always on about dirt, and tries to make 'em clean up, like. And scarlet fever, and the diphtheria, and the consumption. That kind of thing. He tries to do something to stop it. I think that's what he does, anyway.'

She looked at Bridie with new respect. 'If you're going to work for him, all I can say is, you're lucky. By all accounts he's a lovely man.'

Bridie digested this news in silence. 'Is he old?' she asked at last.

'Well.' The girl waggled a hand back and forth. 'So-so. Not old exactly.' She laughed. 'But 'e ain't no spring chicken neither.'

'Has he got a wife?'

'He did have. She died quite a long time ago. I've heard that that was what got him going on his work. She died of the consumption, come to think of it. I think me nan said that's what happened.'

'Oh,' said Bridie. Mr Holmes was turning out fascinating.

'This is your turning,' said the girl suddenly.

Bridie looked down the tree-lined street. Plane trees rustled lazily in the summer dusk. At the far end the little street opened out into a square filled almost completely by a green and overgrown garden. Black iron railings barely contained the rambling roses that, covered with tight buds, climbed everywhere. Rhododendrons made a dark mass at one end, and

41

beneath a spreading magnolia tree a long wooden bench sheltered a sleeping cat. Tall houses stood round the sides of the square, their windows open to the soft air.

'Oh my,' said Bridie softly.

'Nice, ain't it? A lot of nobs live round here. I told you you was lucky. Anyway, I'll love you and leave you. What did you say your name was?' The girl had half turned to go, and asked the question as an afterthought.

'Bridie O'Neill.'

'Mine's Daisy Davids. Might see you again. T'ra then.'

'T'ra,' echoed Bridie.

She walked beneath the plane trees to the end of the little road and looked round the square. The cat looked up lazily as she perched on the edge of its bench, dragging a comb through her hair. Tugging at her curls as best she could, until the comb went through them, she hoped she looked a little neater. She bent down and hastily wiped her face with the edge of her skirt, and ran her hands down her sides to try to get off the worst of the dirt. She knew she probably looked like a tramp, but making the effort was something.

'Bridie's such a sensible girl.' Her mother's voice seemed to come from nowhere. She sighed and pocketed the bit of comb.

'Number twelve,' she said aloud, and picked up the case for the last time. Scanning the front doors in the gathering gloom, she found number twelve at the far end, in one corner of the square. A garden ran round the front and side of the house, tree-lined and private. Heavy curtains not yet drawn let the glow of gaslight, recently lit, spill on to the area and steps. Bridie could see a brown, booklined room with a high white ceiling. She squared her shoulders, clenched her fists and climbed the steps. Lifting the heavy brass doorknocker, she let it fall.

Footsteps approached, the brown-painted door opened and a spare man of middle years, with a thin, lined face and penetrating grey eyes, smiled at her.

'You must be Miss O'Neill. Come in, my dear, I've been expecting you.'

He bent to take her case and welcomed her in so warmly that Bridie burst into tears. Hot with shame she turned away but he reached towards her and touched her arm. They stood awkwardly in the doorway.

'Please, Miss O'Neill, please do come in. It doesn't matter at all.'

As he spoke there was a furious yowl and a large tabby flew over a garden wall two doors down and tore up the front steps of number twelve. The cat dodged frantically around Bridie's feet and sent her stumbling. Tripping over herself in agitation, she sat down heavily on her suitcase.

'Vermin!' exclaimed Mr Holmes.

Bridie looked up, startled, and both hands flew to her hair.

'Oh goodness, no!' cried Mr Holmes. 'I meant the cat. Vermin Ermin. He was christened that as a kitten.

He was so flea ridden, you see, and because of his markings. Ermin, you understand. Oh dear, it's not what it seemed.'

The gesture dismayed him dreadfully and Bridie stared at him distractedly. Her will to go anywhere ebbed away. This London was a mad place. Sniffing, she let herself be helped up and led down the hall to a room at the back of the house. In front of an open kitchen window a table for two was laid and ready. Fragrant bread, a big chunk of yellow cheese, a small bowl with pats of butter, and two covered dishes in the middle holding something that steamed.

Bridie's mouth began to water.

'I was just about to eat myself, not knowing when you might arrive. This is excellent, we can eat together now.'

She looked longingly at the food as he beckoned her through the door.

'Come with me, and I'll show you where you can wash. You must be so tired and hungry. Mrs Goode has got things ready for you. You'll see her in the morning. She's my housekeeper.'

Talking all the way, he took Bridie upstairs to a small room at the back. It overlooked the garden and here again the window stood open. A small bunch of flowers had been placed on the washstand, and folded towels lay on the counterpane of a high wooden bed.

'The bathroom is there.' He indicated along the landing, where a door stood open.

Bridie's face dropped in astonishment. A bathroom!

'If you take your towel, you'll find soap and water there. Come downstairs when you've finished. The door to the kitchen will be open.'

He left her standing there, and went back to make a pot of tea. The girl was filthy but for all that he had been struck by how pretty she was. Mrs Goode would have her scrubbed in no time. Tonight, the poor child must be close to exhaustion. Francis Holmes sat down, poured himself a cup of tea, and waited. He waited so long that he put the hot dishes back in the range to keep warm, and after a while brewed a fresh pot of tea. He began to wonder if he shouldn't go up and see what his guest was doing, but, being patient by nature, he picked up the evening paper and let Bridie take her time.

Upstairs, his guest was paralysed. She stood rooted to the spot where he'd left her. The room she stared at was tall and square. The long window, by now quite dark, was framed by deep blue velvet curtains reaching all the way to the floor. Varnished boards made a narrow edge round a patterned carpet, soft under Bridie's bare toes. Looking down, she stepped hastily off into the bare space by the door. A bowl with fluted edges and tiny forget-me-nots around the edge stood on a marble-topped washstand. There was a mirror above the washstand and by the wooden bedhead hung a crucifix carved in pale wood.

Poor Bridie had never in all her life felt so utterly out of place. Overcome by misery and embarrassment, for two pins she'd have fled and never, ever, come back. Staring at the towels folded on the end of the bed, she suddenly knew what to do. Straining her ears to try to tell if Mr Holmes was anywhere near, she could hear nothing but the sigh of leaves outside. Slowly she undid her skirt and stepped out of it, unbuttoned her blouse and screwed the two into a bundle.

She tiptoed on the carpet until she could reach the towels. The largest fell open into a big oblong that would wrap round her. She took the other and cautiously opened the door a crack. No sound. No movement. Her heart beating painfully with fright, she crept to the open bathroom door and looked in. A great white bath tub stood on curly legs, inviting her. Closing and locking the door, she first pulled the blind down over the window, then took off all her clothes. Teeth clenched with desperation, she took the first bath of her life. Plug in, taps on full, cold water and soap. Grey scum. Fingering it with disgust she pulled the plug and began again. The next bathful wasn't so bad, and the third stayed quite clear. At last she felt clean.

Looking in the mirror, she saw her face was drawn and wan. The swelling round her lip had blackened and the flat wet hair clung to her head. Her heart began to bang again as she faced the return journey. Sliding round her bedroom door, she jumped. Vermin Ermin gazed at her from the middle of the counterpane. He stretched a languid paw and picked at his claws with sharp yellow teeth, watching her with great black, dilated eyes. Bridie stared back. He was a huge tabby with white whiskers.

'Vermin?' she asked.

The dark ears pricked forward.

'You arrived filthy, too, by all accounts. Friends?'

The cat turned and began to wash his tail.

'All right. You can keep me company.' Opening the suitcase she'd carried such a very long way, she squatted down and considered. None of its contents were suitable for this grand house, but they'd have to do. She took out the dress she'd wear to go to Mass of a Sunday. With fingers that trembled clumsily she buttoned the dark blue bodice fitted close to the waist. It gathered into the long folds of skirt that fell almost to her ankles. Her mother had been a skilful needlewoman. Fully dressed, Bridie scrabbled in her discarded heap for the bit of comb. Her curls would spring back round her head as they dried. She had no shoes. Anxious to leave the room tidy she stuffed the filthy things she'd taken off behind the washstand and the closed case underneath the bed. Downstairs, a door opened and closed. He was still there. Her throat tight with nerves, she tiptoed out of the little blue bedroom and went down.

Francis, who was getting very hungry, was glad she'd come down at last. He looked up to greet her and his eyes widened slightly with surprise. He'd listened to the activity in the bathroom but it hadn't prepared him for her transformation. He'd noticed she was pretty when she first arrived, but now he saw she was like some medieval painting of a woman – burnished crinkly hair, long features, prominent eyes. The awkward moment passed.

'Did you find everything you needed?' he asked, to break the tension.

'Yes, thank you, sir.'

'Good, good. Now let's have our supper. I think we're both hungry.'

Guilt suffused Bridie's face again.

'Oh, I'm sorry, sir. I've kept you waiting. I didn't think.'

Francis saw the girl was beside herself with nerves.

'Look,' he said in his very kindest voice 'it's quite all right, and you must stop worrying. I'm very glad you've come to see me, and I'm hoping that over supper you'll tell me about my old friend Robert. I haven't seen him for several years, though we've kept in touch. You can tell me all about yourself, and what's brought you all this way. Now come and sit here. You'll feel better when you've had some of Mrs Goode's lamb stew. She's a wonderful cook.'

As he filled her plate and asked her one question after another about Father Robert and her journey, Bridie forgot her fright and began to chatter. She grew warm inside. Her skin glowed from cold water and scrubbing. Colour came back into her cheeks and her eyes sparkled. Much of the sparkle was the shine of exhaustion. Her eyes began to droop and, embarrassed, she struggled not to fall asleep.

'Right, Miss O'Neill, I think it's time to clear this away. I'll see to it. I want you to go up to bed.'

She began to protest that she'd see to the dishes, but there was no heart in it and Francis wouldn't hear of it. They bade each other good night and she once more climbed the stairs. The gaslamp burned at the side of her bed. She hung her clothes carefully over the back of a chair and dragged out her case to find her night-gown. Then, pulling back cold, stiff sheets that felt luxurious beyond belief, she turned off the gas and sank into bed.

Despite her weariness, sleep did not come. Her legs ached and stung. Behind closed eyes images began to unreel, a disjointed parade. She tossed and turned, half asleep, half awake, until she remembered Little May's woeful crying as Bridie pulled her arms from round her neck and walked away. Then tears came.

Francis heard the low sobbing go on into the night, until in the early hours the sound died away. He wondered what it was that made for such grief, but supposed it was a young, frightened girl's first, painful homesickness. He wondered again, though, how she got that discoloured swelling on her mouth.

Then finally the whole square slept. Vermin Ermin curled cosily in the warm hollow by Bridie's knees, until a blackbird woke him very early, and he crept secretly out of the open window into the summer dawn. Disturbed by his going, Bridie stretched in the space he had left, and slept on until the sun was high in the sky, and the grandfather clock in the hall downstairs gave out its sonorous chimes at midday.

Chapter Two

Earlier that sunny morning, Francis summoned his Mrs Goode to his study.

'I think we could do with the help,' he told her. 'Your arthritis isn't getting any better, I can see that for myself, and you could give her some of the heavy work that you shouldn't really be doing any more. She'll need showing, of course, but I think she'd learn quickly and be willing.'

Dora Goode, who had run his household for him, and his wife when she'd been alive, pursed her mouth thoughtfully. She stood nearly as tall as him, a wiry woman. Pernickety ways and a stern expression hid a kind heart full of fierce loyalty. Devoted to Francis, her upright and principled nature matched his. Her back was ramrod straight, and so was her sense of right and wrong.

Goode by name and Goode by nature, people said, sometimes admiringly but as often as not half afraid of her. If you were on the right side of the house-keeper, you had a friend indeed, but if she caught you out doing something that you oughtn't – 'Gawd 'elp yer,' as the coalman said, when she ran after his cart the time he'd not bothered to sweep up round the coalhole. Even Francis avoided her when he knew she'd taken badly to something. 'Do as you would be done by,' was one of her favourite sayings, delivered with a birdlike stare and a slight gathering of the lips. Now, this morning, considering the suggestion he'd put before her, she suggested giving Bridie a chance but no promises.

'I could give her a try and see how she comes along,' she offered. 'A lot of girls these days are lazy and don't know what work is. Out dancing and flapping or whatever they call it, and no good to anyone. I'd rather do the work myself than be chasing some idle good for nothing.'

Francis smiled. 'I have a feeling you'll get on well together,' he said. 'And it would be useful for me to have someone in the house when you go home. I've been thinking about it for some time, and since she's been sent by an old friend of mine, it seems an excellent time to put the idea to the test.'

Hearing the hint of a criticism, Dora took umbrage. 'If I don't work enough hours, sir, then I'm sure I think you might tell me so. I thought we had a satisfactory agreement on that matter.'

Oh dear, she would take offence. 'No, no, no.' He shook his head. 'It's not that at all. You do more than enough. It's a question of needing another pair of hands, and someone who can run errands for me, or be here when you cannot.'

He rubbed his hands together worriedly. 'Dear Dora, don't look so cross. Neither of us is getting any younger, and I think this girl could be a godsend.

You wait until you've seen her. She's been well brought up.'

He appealed to her sense of fairness. 'You wouldn't want to dismiss her before you've even met her. That's not like you at all, Dora.'

Mrs Goode was mollified. 'Well, so long as you're not saying you're dissatisfied,' she began.

Francis shook his head emphatically. 'You know me better than that. I'd have called you in and told you straight if that had been the case.'

She nodded. 'All right then, sir, I'll see how she does.' Her face lost its righteous air and broke into a surprisingly sweet smile.

Francis stifled a sigh of relief. Mrs Goode on her high horse was a trial that he bore with goodwill because most of the time she was one of the most sensible women you could ask for.

'Thank you,' he said. 'She arrived filthy and exhausted last evening. She spent a pretty long time in the bathroom, but she'll need showing one or two things about how we go on here. She comes from a poor family who will have had none of our modern luxuries.' He grinned at her, knowing that the bathroom upstairs was her pride and joy, scoured and scrubbed and polished until she could stand in the doorway and straighten her back in deep satisfaction that there was no cleaner bathroom, not even in Buckingham Palace, God bless them. She frowned suddenly, and Francis, who teased her sometimes about her perfectionism, knew what was passing through her mind.

'The bathroom'll be needing a going over and a half after her, I'll be bound.'

'Now then, Dora. The poor girl had travelled non-stop for more than two days. And she'll need clothes if she's to work here. Can I leave you to see to that in the next day or two?'

Mrs Goode brightened. It seemed she was to have the girl to mould properly.

'Yes, sir, I'll get her what she needs.'

'I think that's all then. When you hear she's woken, would you kindly give her some tea and breakfast and then send her here?'

'Yes, sir. Was there anything else, sir?'

'No.' He watched her black-clad figure march across the Indian carpet to the study door, closing it quietly behind her. He wondered why she always wore black. She had a wardrobe of pinafores and aprons, but the dress underneath, winter and summer, was black. He'd sometimes thought to ask her, but it seemed vaguely improper, so he never had.

Francis went behind his desk and sat down. Reaching down beside his chair, he lifted up a shabby leather briefcase and took out a pile of papers. Spreading them before him on the broad mahogany surface, he was soon absorbed in long columns of statistics that told a dismal story. Hidden in neutral numbers was a picture of misery, suffering and death that Francis painted in dry tones in Council offices all over London, and even to Westminster. (Rumour had it that the story had been told at the Palace, too, but that had never been confirmed.) Francis was a brilliant statistician and epidemiologist. An expert in the incidence of disease, he had come to devote his life to pleading, persuading and convincing those who had power, that the streets and sewers and water supplies of East London bred disease and should be cleaned up. He described conditions of filth, disorder, carelessness and indifference; poverty, overcrowding and dirt. He preached a gospel of cleanliness and possessed the immense patience to keep on with such a crusade. The politicians must in the end take note. Bent over his papers, he sighed. It showed no sign of happening yet. There was a knock at his door. Lifting his head he called, 'Come.'

Bridie stood in the doorway. As she crossed the room to stand in front of him, he saw that the long sleep had done her good. The bruised lip was less swollen, and although she looked serious and slightly apprehensive, her grey eyes met his directly and there was colour in her cheeks.

'Good morning, Miss O'Neill. You slept well?'

'Oh yes, sir.'

'Has Mrs Goode given you breakfast?'

'Yes, sir.'

'She and I have a suggestion that you might like. Would you care to stay and go into service here; help Mrs Goode and take charge when she cannot be here? She is agreeable, and I've been thinking for some time that I need someone to live in, as well as my housekeeper. She lives not far away, but she has her family and a good many other calls on her time. What do you think? She'll show you what to do.'

He smiled at Bridie. 'She can be a bit of a Tartar at times, but she's kind and you couldn't find a more careful housekeeper. You would have an excellent training if you work with her.'

A slow smile crinkled Bridie's freckled nose and her eyes widened with delight. 'Oh yes, please, sir. I'd like that. I'll do my best, sir.'

'I'm sure you will. Good. That's settled then. Your wages will be thirty pounds a year and all found, which is quite generous, I believe. You can stay in the room you are in now. Will that suit you?'

Bridie was overjoyed. She'd woken in the little blue room and, pulling back the curtains, looked around in the midday light. It was even prettier in the bright sunlight than it had been under the gaslamp. She wondered what to do about the smelly rags stuffed under the bed. They were horribly out of place, an embarrassing reminder of the state she'd arrived in.

Down in the kitchen she'd met Mrs Goode, who'd looked her over and noted the bare feet and creased dress, but said nothing. The girl needed taking in hand all right. Dora started happily planning a shopping expedition for sober cotton skirts and crossover overalls. Boots, stockings and a good stout shawl were added to the mental list. It was May so she wouldn't need a coat. Something had to be done about that hair, too. She'd show Bridie how to make a neat bun. Hairpins and ribbon went on the list.

Mrs Goode laid a plate of bread and jam and a pot of tea in front of her, and asked her about her travels. Bridie told her about the high wind that tossed and buffeted the old grey steam packet across the water, and how everyone had been sick. She said how friendly and helpful the copper had been in Euston station, how the cleaning woman in the City had shown her the way, and she told the housekeeper about the kindness of Daisy Davids, who'd shown her the square.

'Oh, so you bumped into Daisy, did you? Well, you want to stay well away from the likes of her.' Mrs Goode sniffed disapprovingly.

Bridie looked up in surprise, her mouth full. She swallowed and said curiously, 'Why? She seemed very kind. I'd have got much more lost without her.'

'Never mind now. Just mark my words, and you'll come to no harm.'

Bridie was puzzled, but the housekeeper clearly wasn't going to explain. For some reason she remembered the laughter that had burst from the open public house doors as Daisy had come out. She gave a little shrug and forgot about it as Mrs Goode told her that if she'd finished she was to go down the hall and knock on Mr Holmes' door. He wanted to see her.

Having settled matters with his domestic help, early that afternoon Francis took his briefcase and went off to the Town Hall in Stratford, where he had an office. Mrs Goode lent Bridie a pair of boots that were too big, but had to do, and together they walked down to the market in Roman Road. It wasn't far and Bridie could hear the hoarse voices of market traders shouting their wares soon after they'd left the house. They made their way slowly through the throng of shoppers, idlers, stall keepers and darting children. Dogs scavenged underfoot and snarled over titbits pulled from piles of waste mounting, as the day went by, at the sides of the street. Slimy puddles shone evilly in the sunlight and a stench caught at the back of Bridie's throat. Mrs Goode noticed.

'Foul, isn't it?' she agreed. 'It's worst in summer, when it's hot and the flies are bad.'

But Bridie was enchanted by the colourful stalls and the variety of goods on sale. Pallets heaped with vegetables stood cheek by jowl with carts piled high with bright fabrics, cheap imitation jewellery and racks of skirts, dresses and blouses. There was strange fruit, filling the air with ripe, exotic fragrance, as well as homely apples, pears and plums.

'We're near the Docks and Covent Garden here,' explained Mrs Goode, 'so we're lucky. There's always a lot of choice, and things you can't get so easy elsewhere.'

She stopped at a stall and bought a single orange. 'Here, you can eat it while we go,' she said, handing it to Bridie. The sweet juice ran over her fingers and she sucked them with enjoyment, following the house-keeper's narrow back until they came to the stall she had in mind.

Bridie stood patiently while Mrs Goode held one dress and skirt after another up against her, considering. Between them they picked out two dresses, two skirts and four blouses. Mrs Goode and the woman in charge of the stall knew each other well. They haggled briefly over the price until Mrs Goode nodded in agreement and a deal was struck. Bridie carried her new wardrobe over her arms, longing to get back and try it all on.

'Cardigan next,' announced the housekeeper, and dragged Bridie further down the market. Suddenly, behind them, there was a spate of shouting and then an uproar of protesting voices. Two children raced past, pushing their way violently through the shoppers. Twisting and ducking round crowded stalls, they vanished in opposite directions into side streets.

'Bloody varmints!' roared the man who'd lost a fur jacket to the thieves. 'If I get my hands on those . . . those . . .' He choked with rage and frustration. The crowd moved on. Children thieving was common enough. The luckless stallholder complained bitterly and colourfully, to anyone who would listen, for the rest of the day. Bridie meanwhile became the owner of three cardigans in plain dark colours that buttoned from the neck right down to her hips.

'It's expensive, buying them like this,' grumbled Mrs Goode.' You'll have to learn to knit your own.'

'I can knit. Mam taught me. We all could,' cried Bridie indignantly.

Mrs Goode looked taken aback. 'You can knit?' Her prejudices betrayed her.

' 'course I can. I'm good at it. You should have asked and I'd have told you.'

'Oh, well,' muttered the Englishwoman. 'Another time we'll get the wool.'

She felt uncomfortable. She would have to explain the expenses to Francis, and didn't relish the prospect of admitting that she'd taken for granted that Bridie, being Irish, was stupid. It was a bit of mean spiritedness that shamed her. Her black brows drew themselves together in a frown and she looked sideways at the ground while she digested the unpalatable fact. She'd not really given the girl a chance, she admitted to herself, not in her heart. After all, what did either of them know about each other? That soft, musical Irish voice was really quite lovely, and the girl had been so eager to please.

'Dora, do as you would be done by,' she admonished herself sternly, and decided that in a day or two, when Bridie had settled down, she'd buy her some needles and wool, and see what she could get her doing by way of making things for the three of them.

With a quieter conscience, she led the way to the boot and shoe stall where she always went for her own family. 'One boots, one indoor shoes, and one slippers. For this girl here,' she reeled off.

Florence, a small, thin woman with a nose that gathered dewdrops in slow, unstoppable progression, until they were absent-mindedly wiped off on the edge of her sleeve, ducked under the back of her stall and came up with several newspaper packets. She put her rough hand on Mrs Goode's sleeve.

' 'ere, Dora, 'ave a look at these.' She parked the bundles on the edge of the stall, and unwrapped the first. A small pair of sheepskin slippers lay fluffy and creamy in the sun. 'What yer think of them?' said Flo proudly. 'I reckin they'd fit your Sammy a treat.'

Dora's eldest grandson was seven years old, and the apple of her eye.

'Where'd you get them?' she asked suspiciously. They were real quality goods.

'I were given them,' cried Flo triumphantly. 'Down Bethnal Green. You know back of Northiam Street, nearly down in Cambridge Heath? Old Czopor the shoemaker? His place. He were throwing them out. 'e'd had an order from some place up the West End for the best quality, and the 'prentice did the stitching wrong, so he wanted shot of them. So he give them to me, seeing as I looked after 'is missus when she were took bad last winter.'

Flo stroked the sheepskin. 'Thruppence to you, Dora,' she offered.

Mrs Goode picked up one of the little slippers. 'You'll have them back if they won't fit?'

' 'course I will.'

'And what's in the other packets?'

'Two more slippers and two boots. But the boots don't match proper. The lad got the leathers mixed up. Silly sod.'

She unrolled the newspaper. The boots were for a woman, and were of fine leather. They'd small heels, and buttons all up the front, with a tiny leather bow stitched on the back. They would have been perfect, but the shoemaker had been dozing, and had stitched dark blue in with the black, so that they didn't look right at all.

'Someone'll be glad of those, but we'll not take them, ta all the same,' said Mrs Goode.

She tipped her head at Bridie. 'Needs slippers, shoes and boots, like I said.'

They began to rummage among the heap on the stall, comparing, trying on and considering, their heads on one side, until Bridie was fitted. Money changed hands, and calling, 'T'ra, duck,' Mrs Goode shepherded her charge to the last two or three stalls, where they picked up underwear, stockings and hairnets, pins, brushes and ribbons.

'That'll do you for now, I think,' she said finally to Bridie, who had so many things piled in her arms her chin rested on the top, and she couldn't even nod. On the way back Mrs Goode filled a string bag with onions and potatoes and carrots and crisp spring greens whose leaves squeaked as the vegetable seller stuffed them into the top of the net.

'I'll pick up a bit of cheese from Mac at the far end,' she told Bridie, 'and then we'll go back for a cup of tea and get off our feet.' Bridie, weighed down by precariously balanced bundles of clothes, struggled after Dora, through the crowds, back to the square and home, where she dropped the whole pile on to the kitchen table. Mrs Goode went to put the kettle on and called to Bridie over her shoulder to start unpacking it all.

With a fat brown teapot steaming on the table, they became happily absorbed in looking over their purchases. Mrs Goode told Bridie to strip to her drawers and bodice, then she buttoned and smoothed and tugged as Bridie tried it all on.

'Good thing you're nice and slim,' she remarked.

'It's easy to fit a figure like yours.'

The skirts needed taking in round the waist, just a little, and two of the blouses were on the generous side across the shoulders, but Bridie was happy. After more than an hour she stood in front of the house-keeper, neatly brushed and combed and with every button and tuck in place. The wild red hair had been scraped back and stuffed into a net that held it on the nape of her neck. Tendrils were already pulling free and making ringlets by her ears but, as Mrs Goode remarked, in the end you can only do your best with what you're given. An apron with its strings tied in a bow finished the effect, and, transformed into the very picture of a demure housemaid, Bridie was sent upstairs where there was a mirror. She looked at her-self in delighted amazement until Mrs Goode's voice told her to stop primping and come down and do some work. Swishing her new skirts round her legs as she went down the stairs, Bridie obeyed, and went willingly to work in the kitchen under the scrutiny of Mrs Goode's sharp eyes.

When Francis came home in the early evening, he smiled to hear the steady chatter of voices in the back room. All was going to be well.

Chapter Three

Mrs Goode turned out to be a demanding teacher. 'You mind, now,' she said sharply one day to Bridie, who'd been delegated to iron the linen.

Bridie glowered. Mrs Goode shook out the bright white sheet and examined it critically.

'Look here. Like this. You fold it in half, and half again this lengthways, not like you've done it. Then turn it. Take that end and we'll do it properly.'

Bridie grabbed the proffered sheet and tugged crossly. She'd spent ages with the heavy irons, one in use, one on the range to heat, and her arms were tired of pushing them over the sheets that lay spread out on the big deal table in the back room. Folded blankets covered the table underneath and made sure the iron didn't burn marks into its well-scrubbed surface. She shook the sheet straight so hard the linen made a cracking sound. Mrs Goode frowned at her.

Bridie lowered her eyes and silently called her a silly old bat. Pernickety Goodie Two Shoes, complaining about the stupid folds being in the wrong place. Daft, daffy, dippy, dopey, dotty Dora. The song of abuse ran delightedly through Bridie's head as she folded the linen obediently.

'That'll do, young woman.' Mrs Goode stared suspiciously at the bowed head that somehow didn't look meek at all.

'Why does it have to be folded like that, anyway? It only gets crumpled again on the bed,' demanded Bridie sulkily.

'Because Mr Holmes is particular, and so am I. You've done well, Bridie, but you've a thing or two yet to learn about running a big house, and you'd do even better to change your attitude, my girl.'

Bridie heaved a sigh that was just exaggerated enough to bring a tight-lipped glare from the housekeeper. 'You be careful,' she warned icily.

Suddenly Bridie's face crumpled and she started to laugh. She leant on the table, creasing the sheet in both hands. Giggling helplessly until her cheeks were red, she put her hand over her mouth and tried to stifle her snorts of merriment. 'Oh, Mrs Goode, you are funny. You look so cross, and your mouth makes a little round, like this. . . .' And she imitated the housekeeper's *moue* of disapproval to perfection.

Dora found herself, as always when Bridie behaved this way, nonplussed. The girl was impossible. How did you discipline someone who laughed in your face, and made you feel slightly pompous, even a little ridiculous, even though two moments ago you'd been absolutely right? Eighteen months had made Mrs Goode very fond of Bridie, whom she found a hard worker and honest. But she still couldn't make her out, sometimes, and when she did this, well. . . . Mrs Goode felt a smile begin to work its way up her own face, and hastily straightened her lips; before you knew where you were, there'd be no discipline at all. Briskly she picked up the cooling iron and put it to heat.

'Here. Get on with it, do. That's enough of your nonsense. I don't know, I'm sure.'

Bridie rubbed her apron where her chest ached from laughter.

'Yes, Mrs Goode. Here we go again. All folded and correct.'

The iron rose and fell, making a swishing sound as it steamed over the damp linen for the second time. Five minutes later Bridie held out a folded white oblong with mock solemnity.

'Madam's folds, neatly presented in a sheet for Madam's inspection.'

Mrs Goode slapped the newly pressed linen on top of the pile on the sideboard without comment. That verged on cheek, but she wanted to avoid a repeat of the giggles, so ignored it. She glanced at the wooden clockface on the wall.

'Time for a pot of tea. How much longer are you going to take?'

Bridie became serious, and looked at the linen basket with a practised eye.

'Ah, well now, about twenty minutes? Half an hour at the most, if you count clearing all the ironing stuff away.'

'All right, I'll put the kettle on and we'll sit down for five minutes when you're done. Then I have to go down to the market, and I want you to do the scullery floor. And sort out the cupboard under the sink, will you? It could do with a scrub inside and out.'

'Yes, Mrs Goode,' sighed Bridie. You'd think floors were for eating off, the way she carried on with the scrubbing brush. Born with one in her hand, Bridie reckoned.

'Jaysus save us,' she'd remark to the young women she met in the church porch after Mass on a Sunday morning. 'She's never satisfied, that Mrs Goode. You can scrub your fingers to the bone, and she'll find a fault somewhere.' Her grey eyes would widen to make her point, and they'd all move off down the path to the church gate, a shrill, gossiping little crowd, bright and sharp like East End sparrows.

Bridie's best friend, Lizzie Symonds, was learning to be a nurse at the London Hospital, about a mile away towards the City. Lizzie was clever and had been to the grammar school. After months of seeing each other at church, and then sometimes meeting for tea and a bagel in old Mrs Wisniewski's eel pie and mash shop just off the Roman Road, they'd become best friends. One day Bridie had diffidently asked Lizzie to help her take up reading and writing again, which had been so neglected while she was kept from school to help her Mam. 'Only if you've got time, though,' she said anxiously, 'because I know you've got your studies and everything.'

Lizzie, who was a free thinker and an independent spirit but still turned up at Mass most weeks, was delighted. She told Bridie that she had a duty to learn, and brought her some paper books with simple stories, used in schools. They pored over them together, sitting in the window of old Widow Wisniewski's. The wizened little Jewess watched them over the shiny grey metal top of her counter, where tin trays of steaming pies lay next to a bigger tray of live eels. Bridie and Lizzie would hang over the counter and watch them squirm malignantly, coiling and uncoiling in shallow water. 'Ugh, look at them!' they'd shrieked to each other the first time they'd ventured into the shop together, drawn by the fragrant smell of fresh bagels just brought round from the Jewish bakers in the next road.

'You want I should kill one for you, eh?' asked the old woman. She came along the counter to peer at the eels, and prodded them with one fat wrinkled finger. The eels suddenly came to life and Bridie drew back, revolted.

'Do people really eat them?' she asked the woman, who nodded.

'Eel pie. Very nourishing,' she said, in a heavy Austrian accent. 'You eat it one day, maybe.'

By the time her first Christmas in London had come and gone, Bridie was reading Lizzie's books faster and faster and going on to more interesting things. She took to reading bits of *The Times* when she was supposed to be rolling it up for firelighters. She didn't tell Mrs Goode what she was doing, but the house-keeper's observant eyes didn't miss much that went on in her kitchen, and she noticed Bridie's finger travelling slowly along the smudged print. She had made steady progress, and now, not long before her second Christmas, could read quite well, and write to a very passable standard.

'Why don't you go to evening classes?' suggested Lizzie. 'You're getting too good just to go on like this. And I've got exams coming up, so I'll be too busy to come over.'

'Oh, I don't know. I'm not too sure what they'd say.'

'Who? Why should anyone say anything?' asked Lizzie, puzzled.

Bridie shrugged. 'Dunno,' she said truthfully. 'They just might.'

In fact, the idea of classes frightened her. Having spent so little time inside one, Bridie had hazy and alarming notions of schools, and of nuns and teachers. Lizzie was different, being a friend. Mrs Goode could read and write well, but then she'd had schooling. Most people did in the East End, because most children, however poor they might be, went to school. Mr Holmes had been heard demanding wryly what was the good of money spent on children's minds if their bodies went and died before they could make any use of it. But then, Mr Holmes was known to feel strongly about such matters, and not to mince his words. Bridie had once seen him raise his fist in anger and say something about a long word that sounded like 'philanthropists'. He was angry with them for some reason to do with consumption. The rest was lost on Bridie, who'd been sent to fetch his new packet of cigars from the drawer underneath the coatstand in the hall.

My word, she thought to herself, to be sure he can get worked up about things.

Bridie was thinking about that as she dragged the tin bucket out from under the sink. Blink. A peculiar swimmy feeling went through her arms and legs. Memory of another bucket rose, ghostly, in the back of her mind and she shook her head, frightened. Her skin crawled all of a sudden as though her body wanted to remind her of a cruel, cold scrubbing inflicted in the midst of some distant nightmare. Bridie picked up the heavy wooden scrubbing brush and lifted the bucket to fill it with hot water from the range.

She swallowed hard and the sense of another time began to fade. She rubbed sweat from her brow with the back of her arm, and concentrated on swishing the bar of coarse soap around in the water to make suds. Then she carried the heavy pail to the cupboard beneath the sink, which she'd already cleared out, stacking the cleaning stuff on top of the copper. She crouched down on her knees, tucking her skirt and apron well under her, out of the way, and taking a brushful of suds, began to scrub.

She felt the cold air on her back as the front door opened and let in a draught that blew straight through the house. She half turned her head in the small space in the cupboard, expecting to see Mrs Goode's feet appear.

'Hullo,' she called, 'you forgotten something?'

'Hullo, Bridie.' Her employer's voice came from the hallway, where he stood taking off his muffler and

71

overcoat. Blowing on his hands, he came into the kitchen and looked into the scullery.

'You look busy,' he remarked, 'but I wonder if you could bring me some tea into the study. It's cold out. In fact I believe we could have snow later on; the sky looks heavy with it. I'd be glad of a cup of tea, if you please.'

' 'course, sir. I'll be along with it as soon as the water boils.' Bridie's voice was muffled by the cupboard and he watched her back moving as she mopped the soapy water from a corner of the floor. She drew her head out to wring the cloth into the pail and looked up at him.

'I won't be a moment, sir.'

He smiled at her, and her head disappeared back into the cupboard.

'I'll put the water on myself,' he said to her back. He picked up the kettle and leant across her to fill it at the tap above her head. As he turned the water off, his leg brushed against her side, and for a moment his eyes closed and, unseen, he swallowed and looked down at her. His eyes were full of longing, but he put the kettle to heat on the range and went to his study. Pulling his armchair up before the fire that Bridie had lit that morning, he passed a thin hand over his face.

His mouth turned down in a self-deprecating expression and he shook his head slowly. The long straight nose and kindly, quirky mouth were overshadowed by piercing grey eyes that looked out under fair, bushy brows. The whole face was thin and lined and rather sharp. He stretched his legs out to the fender and staightened his waistcoat. He found himself slightly ridiculous, mooning over an Irish servant who was the age his daughters would have been, had he and Emma had any.

The object of his attention wrung her rag out and slopped it over the edge of the pail. Done. The kettle was singing on the fire, so she made tea quickly and put a dish of Mr Holmes's favourite biscuits next to the cup. Then, taking off her thick apron, she exchanged it for the white pinafore Mrs Goode had taught her to wear whenever she served her employer. Balancing the tray, she opened the morning room door and took it along to the study.

'Come in,' called Francis, when he heard her knock.

'Here you are, sir,' she said. 'Where would you like me to put it?'

'On here, please, Bridie,' He patted the footstool that stood to one side of his outstretched legs. He bent forward and half took the tray, to help her set it down, and his hands covered hers. They placed the teatray on the stool between them, but he did not take his hands away. Bridie, bending right down over the tray, face averted, froze. Francis's hands moved up her arms and tightened.

'Dear Bridie,' he murmured.

He lifted her hands away from the tray and pulled her gently upright until he could see her scarlet face, eyes lowered in profound embarrassment.

He dropped her hands as though he'd been struck. She looked terrified. 'Oh, my dear,' he said in distress,

'I didn't mean to harm you. I mean, I . . . oh, Bridie, don't look like that.'

'No, sir,' she whispered.

She raised her eyes. Francis was dismayed to see tears in them.

'Oh please, Bridie, I didn't mean to upset you so.' He didn't know what to say; the situation seemed to have turned to disaster.

'Upset me, sir?'

'Yes, clearly I've embarrassed and frightened you, and I wouldn't have done that for the world.'

Her deepening blush told him that not all was lost.

'No, you've not really frightened me, sir. Surprised me, more like.' Bridie was not entirely astonished at what he'd done. She'd seen the way he looked at her when he thought himself unnoticed, and had often felt his eyes on her. She'd almost known his mind before he did, but the moment itself came out of the blue. She put out a hand to him and held it there, with all its suggestions and implications and future unknowns, until very slowly, unable to stop himself, he took it in his and drew her to him. He gently wiped away the tear that spilled and ran down her cheek.

'Don't cry, dear Bridie.'

She sniffed and wiped her nose on the back of her hand.

'Here.' He pulled a crisp white handkerchief from his pocket.

Bridie blew her nose and stuffed it into her apron. They lapsed into an awkward silence. Then, as the strain began to tell, they simultaneously turned, as if with one mind, to pick up the teapot.

'Shall I pour . . .?' they chorused, and both began to laugh.

'Come here,' said Francis. He put one arm around her waist and pulled her close to the armchair, and then, before either of them had a moment to think about it, she was sitting in his lap with her head resting tenderly just beneath his chin. Francis held her very carefully, and they stayed quite still, each looking into the fire while they longed to look at each other.

Then, with a deep sigh, Francis slipped one hand up her back and began to stroke her hair. Gradually the pins came out and were placed on the teatray. At last the glorious hair tumbled free, and, as in a thousand dreams, he ran his fingers luxuriously through the soft, glossy curls. Breathing more heavily, he gently turned Bridie's face towards his and kissed her. Her mouth was sweet and warm and soft, and she turned against him, reaching her arms around his neck and pulling him close. She made no move to stop him as his hands moved over her neck, down to her breast, and brushed over the soft fabric of her dress. He took his mouth from hers and murmured, half smiling, 'I can't be doing with the buttons, Bridie. Can you help me?'

She blushed richly and began to fumble with the long row of tiny buttons that did up the bodice of the dress. Their hands tangled together in mounting haste and excitement. Francis almost tore the last stubborn buttons open, and the dress at last fell half off her shoulders. He pushed the teatray and stool impatiently to one side, and they slid in a laughing heap on to the rug that lay, as if in readiness just for them, in front of the blazing coals in the fireplace. Bridie felt the flames warm on her face as she lay gazing up into his intense grey eyes.

'Bridie, I want you. I've wanted you for so long.' He kissed her long and hard so that she felt he'd bruise her lip. Blink. With a cry she drew away and turned her head wildly. He misunderstood, and instantly pulled away.

'No? Have I mistaken . . .? Do you mean you don't want me?' His voice was hoarse and filled with dismay.

She shook her head against his chest and her voice sounded like a little girl's. 'No, no. It's not that. I thought. . . . Oh, sir, you've been so kind, so very, very kind.'

She turned a flushed and eager face to his, and reassured he put his lips to hers once more. They drew closer and closer until, with her help, he drew the long skirt up round her waist and was in her, holding his breath to prolong the delicious moment. The flames leaped and cast a red glow over their delight. Bridie gave little sobs of pleasure and then at last he let go with a groan of release and joy.

They lay in each other's arms, eyes half closed and mouths part open with rapid breathing. Lulled by the warmth and the cosy sound of shifting coals and occasional popping of the flames, they dozed, Bridie held close in Francis's arms. After a while he stirred and kissed her neck. Thin, ink-stained fingers lay on her damp breast, and she looked down at them and saw how the light from the fire caught the fair hairs on the backs of his hands, making them glint a reddish gold. Light grey eyes gazed into dark grey, so close they had to draw their heads back to see each other.

'Oh, Bridie. Oh, Bridie O'Neill, who would have thought . . .?' Francis shook his head in wonder, quite captivated.

Bridie smiled up at him. His face, softened by pleasure, didn't look so old after all. He bent to kiss her but she turned her face away.

'Mrs Goode will be back, sir.'

'Ah, indeed she will. What a shame.'

He stroked her hair, which clung to her temples and tangled on the floor.

'Yes,' he sighed. 'You must go before she's back.'

He sat up and began to pull his clothes straight. Bridie felt languid, and got slowly to her feet. When she was dressed and had smoothed most of the crumples out of her skirt as best she could, she stood before him. Demurely she cast her eyes down, and with every appearance of innocence asked, 'Will you be wanting anything else, sir? Your tea, maybe?'

Francis laughed out loud.

'Bridie, you're a wonder. Go and brush your hair. Look, all your hairpins are here. Take the tray, and yes, I'll take my tea now, if you'll be good enough to bring me a fresh pot.'

They shared the gentle teasing with soft looks and shy glances. As the door closed on Bridie's departure with the tray, he leant back in his armchair and pure contentment stole over him.

'Emma,' he said after a while, to the portrait of his wife that hung above the mantelpiece, 'she reminds me so much of you. Will you forgive me, Emma?'

The dark eyes in the portrait seemed to look into his with a question in them. Francis felt his conscience stir uneasily and glanced back at his wife's painted face. 'I'll care for her, Emma,' he said defensively.

The painting simply gazed at him. Bridie came in with the tea.

By the time Mrs Goode came in from the market, bringing a great gust of icy air with her, Bridie had only half finished the scullery. The housekeeper dumped her load of string bags on the deal table and looked round in outrage.

'What on earth have you been doing, girl?' she cried. 'I've been gone an age, and you've done nothing.'

Bridie bent over her work and stifled a grin.

'You bin up to something, Miss?' Mrs Goode's voice was heavy with suspicion.

Bridie sat back on her haunches and looked up at the angry housekeeper. 'I've been helping Mr Holmes move some books in his study. He come home early, so's he could work in his study, and he called me in to lend him a hand.'

Mrs Goode looked doubtful. 'He never said nothing to me about moving books. I s'pose if that's what he wanted you to do, then it's your job to get on with it. But look at this mess.' She surveyed the wet scullery floor, arms akimbo. 'Hurry up and get it done. Then put the vegetables away in the larder. We'll be late starting cooking because of you.'

She grumbled her way round the morning room, banging cupboard doors irritably as she tidied away the groceries that were stocked in the tall shelves either side of the fireplace. Vermin ambled round the door in search of food, and mewed hopefully. Mrs Goode pushed him away irritably with her foot.

'Take yourself off, you mangy animal,' she said crossly. Vermin, sensing the atmosphere, scarpered hurriedly.

'Dratted cat!' muttered the housekeeper. When only the things that went in the cold larder, and the vegetables, were left, she poked her head round the scullery door and let the rest of her annoyance vent itself in the direction of Bridie's back.

'And another thing, my girl. If you haven't got them coal scuttles filled in double quick time, before we end up with all the fires going out, I'm going to ask Mr Holmes to have a word with you. He don't like to employ lazy workers, no more than I do, so you watch out, young woman.'

Bridie raised her eyes to the ceiling and stuck her tongue out in a gesture that Mrs Goode felt rather than saw. 'All right, you go and ask Mr Holmes for a word. Let him say I wasn't doing errands for him. You go right along and ask him.'

Bridie's thoughts made her shoulders twitch with laughter. The housekeeper, outraged, flounced through the morning room and along to the study.

Francis saw her tight-lipped expression and raised an eyebrow enquiringly.

'Trouble, Mrs Goode?'

Her lips tightened further. 'It's that girl. She's cheeky and now she's turning lazy. I've warned her, sir, but she don't listen.'

'I thought you were very satisfied with her,' Francis said mildly. 'Whenever I see her, she seems to be busy.' He turned the page of his book. Mrs Goode stood and waited.

'Is there something in particular that has brought you to complain?' Francis asked her after a pause.

'Yes, sir. I left her to do the scullery and cupboards while I was out, and when I reprimanded her for having done almost nothing, she was insolent.'

'Insolent, eh. That's not to be borne, Mrs Goode. But, you see, I wanted her to help me in here, so it was me who took her away from her work. You must blame me, not her.'

Mrs Goode felt flustered. 'Oh, well, if that's the case, we'll say no more, sir. But she can be insolent, and I've been quite firm with her that if it continues, you'll be wanting to have a word with her.'

'My word, Dora, she has upset you.' Francis glanced at her under his brows.

Mrs Goode stared back, mortified. He wasn't taking her seriously. She sniffed. 'Very well, sir. If that's all, I'll be back to the kitchen.'

'Very well, Dora.' He didn't even look up as she marched out of the study, and for the rest of the day she carped at poor Bridie resentfully, sensing that in some way she couldn't fathom, she was being made a fool of. Bridie did her best to soothe her ruffled feathers, and by the time Mrs Goode pulled on her shawl to hurry home, head bent against the bitter wind that was already gusting little flurries of snow, they had almost made it up. She answered the housekeeper's grudging 'Goodnight' with a cheerful 'Cheerio, Mrs Goode,' and the older woman was gone.

Bridie hummed carols to herself as she tidied away for the night. She pulled aside the curtains to look outside and see if it was snowing. It was. Fat white flakes whirled past on the wind and splashed on the warm windowpane. She closed the curtains with a small shiver and put the guard in front of the dying fire. Then she went upstairs to her cosy blue room. The velvet curtains were tight closed and the fire glowed in the darkness. She reached up and put a match to the gas. Night-dress and books on the counterpane, all ready, Bridie hurried to the icy bathroom to splash in freezing water. Running back on feet numb with cold, she huddled in her night-dress in front of the fire. Warm again, she read until the fire died down, then climbed into bed.

Much, much later, as she drowsed in the delicious warmth of a feather mattress and piles of thick woollen blankets, there was a hesitant tap at her door. Turning her head on the pillow, she could just make out in the dark the spare figure standing in the doorway. Neither moved until Bridie slid one warm hand from under the sheet and pushed the covers back a few inches. Francis closed the door and came towards her. She opened the covers wider and, wordlessly, they turned to each other in the narrow bed.

In the small hours of the morning, Francis went silently across the wide, square landing to his room. He fell asleep instantly and Bridie listened from the edge of sleep to the howling of the wind as it hurled snow in drifts and banks across the mean streets of London.

The grandfather clock in the hall ticked the hours away, its solemn sound falling into the icy air and beating like a steady heart against the wild shriek of the gale. In the morning, dawn came early, because of the brilliant glare of snow. The gale died away. Bridie, drawing back her curtains, gave a cry of delight and ran to dress and go downstairs, to open the door and throw crusts into the pure, perfect white blanket, pockmarked near the windowsill by the impatient red robin waiting for his breakfast.

He flew at the crusts and grabbed, wary of Vermin. Bridie clapped her hands with wonder and excitement, and, startled, the robin shot into the safety of a climbing rose-bush, bringing down a shower of glittering ice all around. It was a perfect winter's day!

Chapter Four

Outside in the square, snow had drifted deeply at one end, while the fierce wind had left the other nearly bare. The ground looked scoured by ice and air. Birds squabbled over crumbs and bits of bacon rind thrown by one of the women from halfway down the other side of the square. A flock of starlings, sharp-eyed, had wheeled in mid flight and landed gracelessly on top of the scattered crumbs. A sparrow landed, but the starlings screamed angrily and ran it off in a flash of blue-green wings. Standing legs astraddle on the back of the bench, Bridie's robin turned one beady eye on the marauders. He watched unblinking, with his head on one side.

Nearby, a front door opened, and two children, whooping and shouting with excitement, ran through the powdery snow, knocking it in glittering showers off the bushes as they went. The starlings screeched and flew up to a chimneystack above, pushing and shoving. The robin hopped down. Snatching a crust, he took it into the cover of some evergreen, away from running feet. One child slipped, fell, and got up laughing, white from head to foot. Their faces glowed in the bitter air and the harsh white light of sun on snow.

Bridie paused in her dusting and watched them from the window in the front parlour. Harsh-smelling whitish smoke curled up the back of the chimney as the coals spat and were slow to catch. She ran the duster round the fender in a desultory manner, and then did it again. If Mrs Goode saw dust there'd be trouble and Bridie was anxious to stay on the right side of the housekeeper, and be friends. When she'd done, she picked up the empty coal scuttle to take it down and fill it from the bunker in the cellar. Holding it in one hand, she looked out of the window again. Mrs Cotteslow from number three was rounding the corner on her way to the shops, a shawl clutched warmly over her coat and a bundle of bags under one arm. The children had started to build a snowman. It was half done when several others arrived, so wrapped up in woollies and coats and hats and boots and shawls and mittens that all you could see of them were red noses, and bright, excited eyes. A dark figure entered the square at the far end and stood watching. The copper slapped his arms round himself to warm up and got moving again.

'Bleedin' weather,' he muttered to himself as he followed his beat down the side street that led through to the Roman. Above him, in the window of the house on the corner, Bridie caught a movement across the way. The maid in number eleven was watching too. Bridie grinned and waved. The other girl lifted her hand and then disappeared, called by someone within the room. Behind Bridie the fire began to crackle and flames to lick round the damp coal. It would warm up soon. There was still a thin film of ice at the bottom of the window, on the inside. She listened to make sure no-one was coming, then scratched a little heart shape with her fingernail. The ice melted on her hand, and she hastily rubbed the heart away with her warm palm. Guiltily she grabbed her duster and ran downstairs to do the coal. She wasn't exactly frightened of the cellar, but she didn't like it either.

Wooden steps led down into a gloomy space that led off into smaller, earth-floored rooms with entrances that were no more than holes in brick walls. It was kept tidy and the earth smooth, but little was stored down there expect for the coal, which arrived through a coalhole in the path outside. Sack after sack, the coalman would tip, until the pile below reached right up, against the wall, to the coalhole itself. Bridie would stand on the pavement, counting the sacks and stroking the patient brown horse that pulled the cart.

She pulled a face as the strong smell of coal met her on the cellar stairs. Lizzie had once described the symptoms of consumption to her, with grisly relish, and for some reason the smell always reminded her of that. Hastily she shovelled the scuttle full and hauled it out of the cellar. The parlour was only one flight of stairs, if you didn't count the cellar, but the bedrooms meant a real long climb that nearly had Bridie's arms out of their sockets.

She was just putting the scuttle beside the fireplace

in the parlour, when Francis came into the room. 'Good morning, Bridie,' he said cheerfully.

Her cheeks, rosy from cold air, darkened to a deep blush. 'Good morning, sir.'

He stood looking out of the window. 'Snow, eh. The children make a pretty sight down there. Do you like cold weather, Bridie?'

She felt astonished. Everything had changed, and nothing. He was just as usual. Then, in confusion, she wondered just what sort of change she'd expected, and felt foolish.

'Tell Mrs Goode when she comes in that I'm out until about nine o'clock. There's a meeting. Please have my supper ready then.'

'Yes, sir.'

He seemed to notice her properly for the first time, and smiled. 'How are you this morning?'

She flushed again. 'Very well, sir, thank you.'

'So am I,' he said heartily. 'So am I.' He pulled on his gloves and picked up the briefcase that stood ready. 'Don't forget, supper will be late.'

He opened the front door and cold air stung their faces. Francis's feet spoiled the pillows of snow still lying on the steps. He looked back up at Bridie.

'These need clearing, please. First thing, before they become dangerous.'

'I'll do it right away, sir.' Mrs Goode's arthritis was worse in the cold weather, and she could no longer manage things like steps. Bridie stood and watched Francis walk round the square, raising a hand in greeting to the neighbours. He spoke to the milkman briefly, who was delivering frozen bottles in hands so cold he couldn't feel anything. Bridie wondered how it was that heat, in summer, made things smell stronger, like flowers, or dust, but in winter you could smell the cold itself.

Francis enjoyed cold weather. He felt alive and cheerful this morning, striding briskly along, dodging round piles of snow thrown to the edge of the pavement by householders clearing their paths. Outside the grey stone façade of Stratford Town Hall he met up with Angus Hamilton, the District Doctor, his good friend. They saw eye to eye on many public health issues.

' 'morning, Angus.'

His light voice was answered by the Scotsman's deep rumbling tones. 'Cold enough for you?'

Francis put a friendly hand on Angus's back as they went through the door together.

'I like it. I think it agrees with me.'

'Something agrees with you,' said the doctor, 'you look very chipper this morning.'

Francis picked up a *Times* from a pile on a table in the entrance lobby, and grinned.

'Let's have a look.' He shook out the paper. 'What's His Majesty's Government up to just now?'

Angus tucked his own copy under his elbow and looked over Francis's shoulder.

'Aha! Tories planning to field five women candidates at the next election. Oh my, what is the world coming to? Women in Parliament, whatever next?

Shall we see a woman Prime Minister in our time, do you think?'

Francis laughed. 'We may yet. And who's to say it would be a bad thing? What with our ludicrous wars and nonsensical policies, they could hardly do worse, now could they, Angus?'

The Scot decided to take the bait. 'That's practically Pankhurst talk. Are you really that converted to feminist views?' He looked at his friend curiously.

Francis shook his head. 'No, of course not. Not really. But sometimes I look round, and I see so much foolishness and greed and downright wickedness that it makes my heart go cold. And that's the truth, Angus. Have you seen any of the rehabilitation wards recently, where they've got the gas chaps? Every one of the poor blighters blind. But the worst are those who just stare, or talk to themselves. Do you know the chaps I mean? Out of their minds with shock, or some kind of thing. Some medical men, and even some of the Brass put it down to bombardment, shell bursts and what have you. We've given ourselves some terrible problems for the future.'

They turned a corner and climbed a flight of wide grey stairs. 'Of course I've seen them. But cheer up, old chap. You were looking bright when we came in, and now you're doing a grand job of depressing yourself.'

Angus turned bright blue eyes on his friend. 'You can't take on the world, you know. Sometimes I think you want to fight everyone's battles.'

They arrived outside Francis's office. 'Come on

in; I want to show you something. No, you're right. But this isn't the world – it's the problem of isolation at our local level.'

He sorted through two piles of paper and grunted with satisfaction when he found what he was looking for. 'See these?' he said, pushing them across the desk to Angus. 'Figures for beds occupied in isolation hospitals by scarlet fever patients. We're chock-a-block, Angus. They've beds in the corridors and the whole thing makes a nonsense of nursing procedures.'

He pushed across two more sheets of paper. 'Now look at the figures for admissions with diphtheria and typhus.'

Angus looked at the statistics and his brows drew together in a heavy frown.

'Quite,' said Francis.

There was silence for a while. 'So scarlet fever is at epidemic proportions, and we're admitting very few other cases.'

'And the result,' Francis finished for him, 'is that we're inviting an explosion of typhus and diphtheria, because without hospitalisation, the cross-infection in the community will go unchecked. We're on course for typhus and diphtheria epidemics in the new year, Angus.'

He nodded, eyes still on the papers.

'And the government is claiming there's no epidemic,' Francis went on remorselessly. 'They say the hospitals are coping. And if that weren't enough, we are desperately short of nurses because they're sent to the casualty wards to nurse soldiers. No-one wants to know about Mrs So-and-So's kiddies, dying at home because there's nowhere else for them to go. We're going to be at our wits' end, and damned Westminster sits on its hands and looks the other way.'

Angus looked up, his deep-set eyes sad and angry. 'A quick dose of typhus in the Commons drinking water would do the trick,' he remarked acidly. 'An epidemic in the West End would work marvels, I've no doubt.'

'I'm due in Limehouse this afternoon,' said Francis. 'I'll talk to Clem Atlee while I'm there, and see if I can persuade him to make a call or two in the Westminster direction. He has friends who may be of some use. I'll brief him before tonight's policy meeting, anyway.'

'Verra well,' the kindly doctor agreed. 'I'll back you all I can at the meeting, laddie, but expect no miracles.'

'Miracles!' Francis snorted.

Angus put on his thickest Scottish accent. 'D'ye often wonder whether presairrrving the human race is wurrrth it?' he asked.

Francis grinned. 'It's my crusade you're blaspheming, man. Don't mock the faithful.'

Angus heaved his long length out of the wooden chair. He rested his hands for a moment on the desktop. 'It's a fanatic ye are,' he said half seriously. 'They can be the worst.'

Francis indicated the door. 'I'm busy,' he said.

'See you later when I've talked to Clem.'

'Right you are,' the doctor answered amiably. He was so tall he had to duck his head under the door lintel as he vanished into the grimy passages that represented the East End corridors of power. Francis pushed his sleeves up a bit, and bent back to work.

Chapter Five

That winter dragged on into a late, drizzly spring. Mrs
Goode's fingers got a little more bent, and she complained sometimes of pain. In early May they were
still putting the gaslamps on early, because the dreary
weather brought dull grey evenings. Then, without
warning, the sun broke through, and it was summertime. Pretty frocks brightened the streets and by the
time the last blossom had dropped from the late
flowering of the magnolia tree, Bridie's face was pale
brown with being out in the sun. She and Mrs Goode
took their work outside and sat on the bench by the
kitchen wall. One day the previous year Francis had
come across Bridie stoning cherries, sitting on the seat
beneath the branches of the magnolia. A few weeks
later a stout bench was carried round through the
corner gate and placed on the paving stones outside
the kitchen window.

'There,' he said to the delighted girl. 'You can sit
here in privacy. There's no need for you to go out in
the square.'

So they took to sitting outside to peel the vegetables, exchanging gossip with the man who came to do
the garden several times a week. It reminded Bridie of

a convent garden she'd once seen as a young girl. Enclosed and quiet, high ivy-covered walls shutting out the world. Here, on warm days, she would sit with her face turned to the sun, day-dreaming. Intoxicated bees droned in the rose bushes, so laden with pollen they lurched clumsily from flowerhead to flowerhead. Bumble bees' deep hum could be heard right from the other end of the lawn. Cabbage whites fluttered over the walls.

'Pests, they are, even if they are pretty,' Mrs Goode said as Bridie tried to persuade one to crawl on to her finger. It flew away.

Lupins and foxgloves, hollyhocks and pinks, bloomed in the flowerbeds. The gardener knelt with the shears and cut the edges of the lawn in straight, sharp lines every week. Immaculate, it was, like a bit of Mrs Goode's ironing.

Summer drifted past. The three of them, Francis as well, went on an outing to Brighton, and Mrs Goode had a week's holiday, which she spent with her daughter and grandchildren. They went to Epping Forest for a picnic, and her face glowed as she told Bridie how the children ran and played in the trees and dropped icecreams down their best frocks. Bridie was given a week, too, but she stayed at home. Lizzie had asked for some off-duty at the hospital at the same time, and they went walking together out along the leafy banks of the River Lee. One weekday they walked the towpath that followed the canal down to the docks at Limehouse.

Bridie followed Lizzie reluctantly as she explored

the maze of streets that ran, narrow and sinister, between the high walls of warehouses. Chinese faces looked out at the girls and curiosity flickered deep in slanting sloe-black eyes. Bridie took Lizzie by the elbow and begged to turn round and go. The place had an unhealthy, creepy feel, and Lizzie, seeing that Bridie really was frightened, agreed to leave.

Long, summer walks brought them home tired and flushed with sun and laughter. Lizzie's homely round face caught the sun and tanned deeply, so that under her pale hair she looked almost pretty.

Some evenings they sat under the magnolia, reading. Lizzie was nearly qualified and had only one more set of exams. She'd started walking out seriously with one of the young doctors at St Bartholomew's. Bridie, seeing the stars in her friend's eyes when she described him, hoped that if she must get married, that she'd not move too far away. When Lizzie teased her, and asked when was she going to find a young man of her own so they could go out in a foursome, Bridie just smiled behind her hand and shrugged her shoulders.

Francis, whose desk was near the window, sometimes watched them, and had been touched and surprised the first time he'd realised that Lizzie was helping Bridie with reading. Afterwards, he'd offered Bridie his own books, and suggested that she might browse in the study to see if anything caught her eye.

'It's dull stuff, mostly, for you, I suppose, but there are some novels and travel books you may enjoy.'

She'd looked when he was out of the way, but

preferred the paper-covered romances Lizzie lent her, much passed round among the nurses and dog-eared from use.

Apples were ripening in mid-October, and the rosehips had turned a deep glossy red, when Bridie realised she was pregnant. She was more annoyed than dismayed. Francis tapped on her door once or twice a week, late in the evening, and they still loved with passion and tenderness. Sometimes he would kiss her hair in passing, if Mrs Goode was nowhere to be seen. But their unspoken agreement about discretion kept them circumspect, and even after ten months, no one but them knew their secret. A baby would soon change that. Unsure what to do, Bridie did nothing, until one day Mrs Goode caught her leaning against the kitchen table, clutching her stomach and white with nausea.

Pulling herself upright, with hands planted firmly on her hips, the housekeeper prepared to speak her mind.

'Not showin' yet.' She pursed her lips and looked Bridie up and down, by way of opening the topic.

Bridie screwed up her face and moaned.

'Gettin' what you've asked for, if you want my opinion,' said Mrs Goode sourly. 'Stupid girl! Fancy going and getting yourself in the family way. How long do you reckon you've been expectin'?'

Bridie shook her head, a sheen of perspiration on her forehead. 'Not long. Maybe two months.'

'You've bin out there throwing up in the morning several weeks. I've heard you, young woman, don't think I haven't.'

Bridie took a series of deep breaths and some colour began to come back into her face. 'Don't scold, Mrs Goode, I don't feel well.'

'Huh!' snorted the housekeeper. 'You're a fool to yourself.'

'My mother used to be sick, I remember, and it didn't last much after the first three months, she always said. So maybe I'll feel better by then.'

'You're getting no more than you deserve.'

Bridie ignored the jibe. 'Could you let me have a glass of water, please, Mrs Goode?'

The housekeeper couldn't help but feel sorry for her, she looked wretched. Running the tap until it was good and cold, she drew the water and gave the glass to Bridie.

'Here, this'll help. And you'd best sit down.'

'It won't last long, now. Thank you,' said Bridie.

'It's you'll not last long, the way you're going on,' retorted Mrs Goode piously.

Bridie ran her fingers through the front of her hair and said nothing.

'You said anything to anyone?' demanded Mrs Goode with no attempt at delicacy.

Bridie shook her head. 'No.'

'Well, what will you do?'

Bridie shrugged her shoulders. 'I've hardly had time to think. I've been so sick . . .' she tailed off vaguely.

Mrs Goode, frustrated by the girl's apparent indifference to her situation, clucked her tongue in concern and anger.

'You realise you could end up in the workhouse? You lost all reason? Don't you know what you've gone an' done?'

Bridie stared at her. Ah yes, the workhouse.

'You'll have to tell Mr Holmes, and my advice to you is to do it soon. If there's one thing he can't abide after stupidity, it's deceit. You wait for him to see for himself, and you'll be asking to go to the workhouse. He's bin so good to you, and this is how you repay him? I'm sure I don't know.'

Moral indignation fired Mrs Goode's eyes, and she flashed scorn at the top of Bridie's bent head. The girl was so worn out with sickness and the fright of being found out, that hysteria began to make her voice tremble.

'I'll tell him, I will. Just let me do it my way. After all,' and her voice began to shake dangerously close to desperate laughter, 'this is my business if ever anything was. If he wants to see me in the workhouse, that's between me and him.'

Mrs Goode had to admit the truth of that.

'And another thing,' she said, beside herself with curiosity, 'who is it?'

'Who's what?' asked Bridie obtusely.

Exasperated, Mrs Goode tried again.

'The baby. Whose baby is it?'

'Mine,' said Bridie, and looked her straight in the eye with such an expression that even Mrs Goode didn't dare go on. Then an even more scandalous thought hit her.

'Don't you know?' she gasped.

Bridie's fists clenched.

'How dare you?' she shouted. 'How dare you poke your nose in my business? I don't have to tell you anything, and I'd be obliged if you'd hold your tongue, Mrs Goode. I'll tell you, *if* I tell you, when I'm good and ready, and not before.'

Mrs Goode was speechless.

'That's a slander,' went on Bridie. 'How dare you suggest I wouldn't know who my baby's father is? That's a dirty, ugly, horrible thing to say.'

Bridie's fists clenched and unclenched and tears of rage and humiliation filled her eyes.

Mrs Goode, all prepared to shout back, suddenly felt ashamed. She couldn't help wanting to know. Unused to apologising, she fumbled for something to say that might begin to mend the situation.

'Shall I make us a pot of tea?' she offered finally, by way of an olive branch.

Bridie began to laugh weakly. 'You're a one, you really are,' she said to the housekeeper. 'Yes, please, a pot of tea.'

'How about a bit of toast?' suggested the house-keeper as she filled the kettle. 'I used to swear by that for morning sickness when I was expecting. You have it dry, and it seems to do the trick, somehow.'

'Yes please. I'll give anything a try if it'll stop me feeling so bad.'

They took the tray outside and sat at either end of the bench. It was a day when the gardener didn't come, and they had the place to themselves except for the pigeons calling softly from the roof.

'I owe you an apology,' said Mrs Goode eventually. 'There was no call for me to poke my nose in, as you say. I did it because I'm fond of you, Bridie, and I couldn't bear to see you end up in the workhouse, duckie, I really couldn't.'

'Do you think he'd really throw me out?' The question had been burning in Bridie's head ever since Mrs Goode had suggested it. Was Francis really a hard, cruel man like that?

'Well,' Mrs Goode considered, 'it would be very tricky, wouldn't it? Your place here is to work. How could you with a new baby? It's not his fault you've gone and got yourself in trouble.'

Bridie looked at the housekeeper solemnly. Indeed! She twisted her mouth in a wry gesture. Yes, it would be tricky, she had to agree.

They sipped their tea thoughtfully.

'I could pay a woman to look after it, out of my wages,' suggested Bridie.

'Maybe, but you'd have nothing left, and you'd still be lucky to find an employer who'd have a baby in the house what didn't belong.'

'I'd have nothing left in the workhouse, neither,' Bridie pointed out ruefully.

She could see that her position would be desperate if the baby hadn't been Francis's own, and apprehension was beginning to blossom on that score, too. She couldn't take it for granted that he'd look after her; she could see that now. He might throw her out and not think twice about it. Bridie took a gulp of cooling tea and tried to shrug off her mounting dread. She'd

100

coped before, and she'd cope again. You didn't have to go in the workhouse.

A vision of Daisy Davids in her pretty green dress rose before her. Daisy had got her face carved up in a drunken brawl between two impatient clients one evening, while cruising the labyrinth of horrible streets behind the Limehouse waterfront. Rumour had it one of them had been Chinese. Bridie shuddered. They'd stitched her features back together in the London Hospital, and Lizzie, who'd had a friend working on Women's Surgical at the time, said it gave you the shivers to look at her afterwards, when the scars began to heal. By all accounts she was practically what you'd call a freak now, and it was rumoured that when she went back to work they were queuing up for her. Things like that made you wonder, Lizzie'd said. It was ghoulish. Bridie got nervous just thinking about it; too many girls stayed out of the workhouse like Daisy had done.

'Oh, well,' she said in a more optimistic tone as she piled the dirty cups into each other, 'it's no use cryin' over spilt milk. Better get on.'

Indoors Mrs Goode covered the deal table with oilcloth and newspaper. Between them they carried the heavy trays of silver cutlery from the drawer in the morning-room sideboard, and settled down with silver polish and soft cloths to clean it. Mrs Goode impulsively leant across the table after a while, and put a stained hand on Bridie's.

'You'll be all right, my dear,' she said gruffly. 'And I'm here if you need me.'

Tears sprang to Bridie's eyes, and scraping back her chair, she ran to the housekeeper and threw her arms round her neck.

'There, there. Don't take on.' Mrs Goode patted her head. 'Here, come on, you start slacking and we'll be here all night.'

She pushed the girl away, and, smiling shakily, Bridie got on with her work.

In the event, it was Francis who raised the subject. He'd worked late, and Bridie was reading in front of the small fire in her room when he'd stopped at her door and knocked. Smiling, she opened the door wide for him to come in. He sank into the armchair by her little fender and looked at her through half-closed eyes.

'You look very tired,' Bridie told him.

'I am. I spend so much time trying to bring mountains to Mahomet that I sometimes think my back will break.'

Bridie leant her head on his knee.

'Did you enjoy going to the fine restaurant, anyway?'

The dinner had been mediocre and the company pompous, but he said yes to please her. He gazed into the fire and stroked her head, feeling the tension begin to seep away.

'May I stay?'

She smiled up at him. 'I'd like you to.'

She stood up and began to undress. It was late November and she was already wearing heavy winter clothes. As she drew her dress over her head, Francis saw her in outline against the blue curtains and was startled. He watched her thoughtfully as she slipped the long white night-gown over her shoulders and came to sit on the floor near him again.

'Bridie?' he asked after a long, companionable silence.

She looked up.

'You've gained weight.'

In the gaslight, her face went pale.

'Are you . . . er . . .?' He made a gesture with one hand, embarrassed at the suggestion he was making. She took a deep breath. At last.

'Yes,' she said simply. 'I'm going to have a baby.'

'Ah.' Francis was at a loss. He and Emma had had no children, and long ago he'd stopped thinking of fatherhood. He rubbed the bridge of his nose with two fingers, and realised he'd things to think through in his own mind.

That night, he lay smoothing Bridie's curls until she slept. Uncertainty lay between them like a bedfellow and they didn't make love, but lay quietly together. When he was sure she was asleep, he left her very carefully and lay awake for a long time in his own room, remembering the promise he'd made to Emma's portrait many months earlier, and staring into the dark.

Chapter Six

Two weeks later, as December brought preparations for Christmas and the market sprouted with holly, ivy and fir trees brought down by the cartload from the Norfolk forests, Francis made up his mind. There was tension in the atmosphere these days, and he was uncomfortable. He found himself evading Mrs Goode's eyes. It wouldn't do at all, he decided.

'Very well, Emma,' he said to the portrait. 'I know it's what you'd want of me.'

The following day was his fiftieth birthday. It seemed an appropriate time for new beginnings, so he asked Bridie to come to his study.

She stood with her hands clasped loosely over her thick skirt and apron. It was still hard to tell, thought Francis, as he tried to think of a good way to start. He realised that sitting behind his desk with her standing before him felt like an interview. He rose and went round to the fire.

'Come over here and sit down.'

They faced each other on the sofa, he well back with his legs crossed comfortably, she perched on the edge, afraid of what was to come. There was silence, and Bridie couldn't bear it any longer.

'Are you going to send me away?' she asked in a voice that was breathless with anxiety.

'Send you away?' Francis was astonished. 'Where to?'

Bridie's hands fluttered.

'I dunno. The workhouse?'

'Good God, no. Though I had wondered about your family. Would you be thinking of going home? To Dublin, that is.'

Bridie spoke with no consciousness of the irony.

'No, sir. Me Dad would beat the livin' daylights out of me if I went home now.'

'Your sisters could help you with the baby, though?' Francis pressed her.

'Sure, they would. They'd love a baby. But there's no work there, sir.'

Bridie knew that wild horses wouldn't get her back to Ireland, but she couldn't and wouldn't tell him that.

Francis stroked his chin thoughtfully.

'I'd been thinking that you might want to go, not of sending you away. That hasn't been my intention at all. Not at all,' he repeated.

Bridie felt her knees go quivery with relief. She smoothed her skirt anxiously with fingers that trembled.

'Do you mean I can stay here, sir?' she whispered.

'But of course,' said Francis, for the first time becoming aware of the depth of her fear. 'Do you think me a monster, Bridie? That's a poor opinion after all this time, I must say. Have I given you cause to believe so badly of me?'

Bridie looked down in shame. 'No, sir.'

'Well then.'

She chewed her lip. Francis waved a hand at the picture over the fireplace.

'Emma and I had no children, as you know,' he began, 'and I'm fifty today. That's a little late in life to begin a family, but I'm quite beginning to like the idea. However, I've no wish to have my son born with the stigma of illegitimacy, and I think we should be married.'

Bridie's heart shrank. When she finally spoke, it was with all the pride and defiance of a humiliated woman. 'No, thank you, sir.'

Francis was astounded. 'Pardon?' he said foolishly.

'I said, thank you, sir, but I'd rather not marry you.'

'Good God!' It had never crossed his mind that she might turn him down. 'What *do* you want, then?'

'I'd appreciate it if I could stay here, like we just said, and carry on the same as before. I'll go on working for you. Mrs Goode knows about the baby, but she don't know about you bein' its father. Do you want me to tell her?'

Francis was completely taken aback. 'Oh, well, I suppose she'll have to know sooner or later. Yes. But for Heaven's sake, Bridie, why won't you marry me? It seems to me the only sensible thing to do, in the circumstances.'

Bridie couldn't look at him. 'I don't know, sir. It doesn't seem so right to me, I suppose.'

'Well, think it over and we'll talk about it again,' he suggested. She was just surprised and unprepared, he told himself, and she'd be sensible when she'd had a bit of time.

'Did you want anything else, sir?' she asked after a lengthy silence.

'What?' He started out of his wandering thoughts. 'Oh, no, thank you. I wish you'd consider this matter carefully, Bridie. There's the child to think of, you must surely see that?'

'Yes, I do, sir. Can I go now?'

He nodded slowly, and watched her leave the room, hardly able to believe what had happened.

Mrs Goode couldn't believe it either. 'Have you taken leave of your senses?' she gasped, in utter astonishment.

'No,' said Bridie.

The housekeeper felt mortified and furious at the idea of all that carry on, all going on behind her back. She'd been made a complete fool of, and was beside herself with outrage. Only a fear in the back of her mind that it might anger Francis stopped her from boxing Bridie's ears.

'How could you?' she appealed for some kind of explanation. 'How could you behave so deceitfully?'

'I haven't. We was just . . . just discreet, that's all. You seem to think that everyone should tell you their business, but I don't want to go blabbing everything I do. You don't have no rights over what I do.'

'You're glad enough of my help, though, when your sinfulness comes home to roost.' Mrs Goode mixed her metaphors agitatedly. The barb shot home. Bridie was having trouble squaring her conscience about confession. She worried that she should be full of guilt and contrition, and since she wasn't, she couldn't really confess. So she'd avoided the parish priest, and wandered into old Mother Wisniewski's on Sunday mornings, instead of going to church. Sooner or later Father Eric was going to turn up to find out what was keeping her away, and she was dreading the visit.

'Anyway,' Bridie pointed out, 'we was both going behind your back, if you want to put it that way, not just me.'

Mrs Goode was scandalized by the direct reference to her employer's philandering.

' 'E 's a man,' she said loftily. 'It's different.'

Bridie had to admit that it was different for a man. That had become painfully clear earlier that morning. It was all right for him, sitting there cool as you please, wanting to get everything sorted so that his son wouldn't have that awful 'ILLEGITIMATE' stamped all over his birth certificate. Bridie didn't like the thought much, either, but it was no way to go and get married. Not to a man who only wanted to be married for a piece of paper. Bridie didn't reckon she could live with that. What about loving each other? What about all that tender sharing, and the loveliness? He hadn't said anything; he hadn't looked as though he'd thought, even, about that.

Under Mrs Goode's enraged eyes, she burst into tears, put her head in her arms and howled.

'Oh give over,' said the older woman angrily. 'Shut
the water works, Bridie, you'll get no sympathy that
way.'

Bridie looked up, scarlet-faced and streaming. She
wiped her nose miserably on her knuckles. 'He asked
me to marry him,' she admitted at last.

The housekeeper's expression changed from rage
to righteousness. 'Well I never! There, didn't I just
tell you he was a good man.'

Bridie quailed. 'And I said I wouldn't.'

Words failed Mrs Goode. She simply stood opening and shutting her mouth, like a fish. Bridie took a
bit of rag out of the cupboard behind her head and
blew her nose and wiped her eyes. The housekeeper
continued to stare at her as though she'd suddenly
sprouted a second head.

'What?' she squeaked finally.

Bridie, relieved that all her secrets were out, started
feeling a bit braver. 'Mr Holmes said he'd marry me,
on account of the baby, and I said I didn't want to,'
she repeated.

'You're mad. You must be. They ought to take you
away.'

'No, I'm not. I don't want to marry him for the
baby. If I hadn't fallen for the baby I don't think it
would have entered his head to marry me, nor me
him, I suppose. If he wanted to marry me because he
loved me an' wanted me, then I would and be glad.
But not this way. No, not this way.'

Indignation covered the wound in Bridie's heart,
and made her voice strong.

'Well, I never did,' said the housekeeper again. 'You're a wilful one, and no mistake. There's girls would give anything for the chance you've got, and you turn it down. You'll likely live to regret this, my girl.'

'Maybe I will, but I'll cross that bridge when I come to it.'

'What are you going to do, then?' Mrs Goode had calmed down enough for her natural inquisitiveness to re-assert itself.

'Carry on here the same as usual, at least until I have the baby. Then I'll see.'

'Mr Holmes agree with that?'

'Except for the marrying bit, yes.'

'Good gracious.'

Mrs Goode looked at the clock on the wall. 'Oh, my goodness, look at the time.' As she spoke they heard the front door open and bang shut. 'He's home already, and we've done nothing. It's your fault.' In a fine state of agitation, the housekeeper jumped as Francis put his head round the morning-room door.

'I'm in,' he said.

He looked from one embarrassed face to the other, and could well imagine that acrimonious words had been exchanged between the two of them. Something would have to be said to Dora, or she'd persecute Bridie out of mistaken good intentions. Francis felt his well-ordered life begin to slide towards confusion. What with the tension between his little household, Bridie's astonishing behaviour, and the fact that her pregnancy must soon be obvious to everyone, Francis wondered what his friends and neighbours would say.

'It's really none of their business,' he murmured to himself as he hung up his overcoat and propped his galoshes by the umbrella stand. It was raining cats and dogs outside; he'd got soaked coming home.

The following evening, after she'd finished the chores, Bridie lifted down her own coat, and taking a big black umbrella because it was still pouring down, walked up to Stratford High Street. Looking out from under the shelter of the brolly, she watched people hurry past, splashed and muddy and cold. Faces that were pinched and pallid on account of not enough to eat and horrible damp houses where people coughed all the time. Nits and lice and dirt. Smells you couldn't always put a name to, and others that had names as foul as the stench itself. Children with impetigo running over their faces. Sick children. Dead children. Mothers with tired, lined faces yelling at the bigger ones to look after the babies.

Bridie's feet slowed on the streaming path. Was this what she wanted for her baby? This ugliness, this awful, frightening world where girls like Daisy lost their souls and bodies in the back streets.

She'd arranged to meet Lizzie by the library, and because of the downpour they went in. They stood whispering in Adult Fiction, moving up and down the stacks pulling out books so that the librarian wouldn't catch them and tell them to be silent.

'So I said I couldn't,' she explained in a very low voice at the end of her story.

Lizzie had had her suspicions for a long time, but

had been much too tactful to say anything to Bridie until she saw fit to bring it up herself.

'I think you're right,' she whispered back, 'but how will you manage?'

Bridie shook her head at her friend.

'I'll take it one thing at a time. I don't know what will happen in the future. I've nothing to plan for, so what's the use of worrying about it. Take it as it comes.'

Lizzie turned a professional eye on Bridie's stomach. 'May, you said?'

Bridie nodded.

'D'you know Mrs MacDonald, down Stepney High Street, just by St Dunstan's? She's lovely, and she's the best person to go to if you need a midwife. I've heard she's really good. I've met a few women who've had her look after them, and they speak very well of her.'

'Oh, I'd not really thought that far ahead.'

'Well, you'd better,' whispered Lizzie sternly, 'because she's busy and you need to be sure she'll come when you need her.'

The librarian stopped on silent feet at the end of the shelves. 'This is a library, not a public meeting place. If you wish to stay, would you kindly not talk.' She pointed to the SILENCE notice at the end of the stack.

They burst into giggles as she stalked away.

'Come on, if it's stopped raining we'll walk back.' Lizzie grabbed her friend by the arm.

They loitered in the green-painted library entrance. Beyond the door the rain fell in sheets.

'Oh, bother!' Lizzie's fair hair was still stuck to her

head from the walk she had earlier. Hazel eyes
screwed up in thought, she wondered what to do on
such a horrid evening. It was pitch dark as well.
Behind them, the library was light and warm; someone coughed quietly and turned a page.

'Oh, come on. Can I share the brolly?'

They plunged into the miserable darkness, huddled
close together in the shelter of the umbrella, and
began to pick their way as best they could among the
rain-pocked puddles.

'Can't see a thing. We're going to get drenched,'
grumbled Lizzie.

'Never mind. We'll have cocoa and biscuits when
we get back, and you can give your hair a rub.'

Lizzie had been paid the honour of being invited
into Mrs Goode's kitchen some months earlier.
Satisfied that she was a nice young woman, with
decent manners, Mrs Goode had let it be known that
she was welcome any time. In winter it was cosy to sit
by the stoked-up range, toasting their feet and faces in
the red glow. Turning into the square, they gave up all
pretence of staying dry, and ran through the dripping
garden to the back gate. Bridie fumbled in the dark to
open the door into the scullery, and rain ran in cold
trickles all down her neck.

'There,' she gasped, and they pushed through the
door, making puddles on the scullery floor. The
brolly dripped rivulets that ran under the sink.

Bridie sucked her wet fingers. 'Perishin', isn't it?
Here.'

They spread their coats over the top of the copper

to dry off a bit, and Bridie lit the gas. She was just fetching milk from the larder for cocoa when Francis surprised them both.

'Good evening,' he said pleasantly to Lizzie. 'Bridie, do you know if there's any more brandy? The bottle in the parlour is finished.'

'Oh, yes, there's some in the sideboard.' Bridie went through and opened the cupboard. She took out two dark bottles. 'There's this kind, and this one. Which did you want, sir?'

'The French, please.' He smiled at her. 'It's Dr Hamilton. He's partial to this brand.' He disappeared with the bottle.

'He's ever so much older than you. Don't you mind?' Lizzie asked curiously.

'I never thought much about it,' Bridie answered honestly. 'He's so . . . interesting, I suppose. More than boys. Well, the ones I meet, anyway. Its different for you, Lizzie. You've got all those doctors and students and things to go round with. Me, I'm just a housemaid. You and me get on nicely, but I wouldn't know what to say to some of your lot.'

'Don't you say that.' Lizzie's voice was indignant. She shook an admonitory finger at Bridie. 'Don't you put yourself down like that, not to me, anyway. I won't listen. You're as just as good as anyone else, and don't you think otherwise. You're good fun, you are, and look how fast you learn things. I think you're cleverer by half than some of those doctors, and you've a mind of your own . . . a kind of truthfulness, and I don't mean just not telling fibs. Just look at the

way you won't be bullied into marrying. You've got
. . . what's the word? Integrity, that's it.'

Bridie looked at her friend's passionate little face.
'You're the best friend I ever had, except for my sisters.
I'm glad.'

'So am I,' said Lizzie, and they smiled at each
other over the cocoa mugs. 'Do you miss them – your
sisters?'

'Yes. 'course I do.'

'Wouldn't Mr Holmes let you go and visit?'

The open smile disappeared from Bridie's face. 'I've
not asked him.'

'And what about your Dad. Aren't you going to tell
him about the baby. It's his first grandchild, isn't it?'

'Yes,' said Bridie shortly.

Lizzie looked at her curiously and wisely decided to
say no more. She had a feeling there was more to the
O'Neills than met the eye. 'Can I come and help, when
the baby's born?' she asked, changing the subject.

'Of course you can. Why didn't I think of it myself?'

'You'll see Mrs MacDonald anyway, won't you?
She's got the experience. But I could lend a hand. Fetch
hot water or something.'

'Oh, yes,' cried Bridie, delightedly.

'Maytime. That's a good time of year for a baby.
Nice and warm.'

Bridie patted her stomach gently. 'I didn't exactly
ask this little one to come, but he seems to have
organised himself pretty well so far.'

'Might be a girl, you know.'

'He or she. Francis thinks it's bound to be a boy. To

hear him, you wouldn't know there's such things as girl babies.'

'What you goin' to call it?'

'I haven't thought yet. Maybe Lizzie – well, Elizabeth – if it's a girl. After you.'

Lizzie grinned. 'If it's like me, you'll be in for a handful. My mother still shakes her head when she talks about some of the wild things I did.'

'Get along. You? Wild? The pillar of the London Hospital.'

'I'm reformed,' said Lizzie virtuously. 'And with that baby, you'd best reform and get plenty of early nights. That's professional advice for free.'

She stood to go and collected her wet things from the scullery. 'Ugh! Sopping,' she said.

Bridie saw her to the garden gate. Lizzie kissed her cheek as she said goodnight.

'You take care walking back,' said Bridie.

'And you. See you next week.'

Lizzie walked quickly into the dark, and, turning back beneath a shower of raindrops from the overhanging bushes, Bridie looked up at the stars, shining in a sky washed clear of clouds, and thought that it might not be so bad, having a baby, after all.

Chapter Seven

Bridie's son was born on May Day, 1921. The pains started on the Tuesday afternoon. Bridie put on her shawl, took up the basket of baby clothes and the bundle of her own night-gowns, and walked slowly over to Mrs MacDonald's house in Stepney. Several times she stopped to lean on a wall, breathing deeply as the pain came and went.

'You all right, ducks?' asked a woman, passing by with two small children.

Bridie waited for the pain to pass. 'Yes, ta,' she said. Now the time had come, she was quite calm.

She arrived at Mrs MacDonald's small house at teatime. The midwife took the bundles from her, and showed her upstairs to the clean, whitewashed little room at the back where she'd offered to look after Bridie when the time came.

'I just don't,' was all she'd say in answer to Francis's questions as to why she didn't want to have the baby in her own room. Mrs MacDonald had asked no questions and had promised Bridie that she could stay with her as long as she liked.

By nightfall the pains were coming stronger and more often. Mrs MacDonald popped in and out and sat for a while with her knitting at Bridie's side. As she felt the baby sometime near midnight, with cool, firm hands, she told Bridie she thought it most probably would be morning before he arrived.

'You're as bad as Francis,' joked Bridie, between pains. 'He always says it's a he, never a she.'

Mrs MacDonald clucked her tongue. 'There's many as thinks it's better to be born a boy,' she said, smoothing her grey hair back after bending over Bridie. 'I'm afraid there's truth in it, too, my dear.' When Mrs MacDonald smiled you could tell from the way her eyes crinkled that she smiled a lot.

The night passed slowly. Soon after dawn Bridie began to groan and clutch the edge of the sheet with white fingers.

'I think I'm nearly there,' she called in a squeaky, breathless voice, hearing the midwife's footsteps coming up the stairs.

'Indeed you are.' Mrs MacDonald's thin, kind face disappeared behind Bridie's raised knees.

'Yes, my dear. You can push when you feel you want to.'

A fierce pain came and seemed to last forever.

'Lizzie,' she gasped. 'Has anyone told her?'

'Yes, our Jimmy was going by the hospital on the way to Spitalfields, first thing. If she can come, she will.'

Bridie's face screwed up and the pain tore a shriek out of her. The midwife spoke soothingly.

'There, there, my dear. That's it, push now. And again. Another one.'

The room was silent except for Bridie's panting breathing.

'One more, dear.'

And it was over.

Mrs MacDonald bundled the baby in a clean towel and handed him to Bridie.

'Here we are, lovie, a perfect little boy.'

Bridie scarcely noticed as the midwife busied herself with the final stages of the birth and began to clear up. Pulling herself half upright, she gazed at the baby. He didn't cry. Two bright, alert blue eyes stared unwaveringly back at her. The tiny red face was intense and serious, and the drooping little mouth opened and closed as if he were silently talking to her. Bridie was enchanted. She carefully stroked the little wrinkled cheek. The baby's head turned to grope for the finger, and he began to cry.

'You put him to the breast,' advised Mrs MacDonald. He suckled eagerly.

'Oh look, Mrs MacDonald. Look at his little ears. Did you ever see anything so sweet?'

'He's a lovely baby, my dear.' Mrs MacDonald nodded approvingly. The baby fell asleep on Bridie's breast, and when all else was done the midwife lifted him gently away.

'Let's freshen you up, too, my love,' she said, bringing a bowl of cool water to the bedside. Gently she washed and dried Bridie's face and arms, helping her into one of the fresh night-gowns she'd brought with her the day before.

'There we are.' She brushed the tangles out of the

red hair and stood back to survey her patient. 'How about a nice cup of tea?' she suggested, tucking the baby into Bridie's arms under the sheet.

Easing her baby so they were both comfortable, Bridie laid her head back on the pillow and nodded.

'Yes, please.'

The window stood open and a slight breeze billowed the pale green curtains lazily against the white wall. It moved deliciously over Bridie's face, and she closed her eyes in utter contentment. When Mrs MacDonald climbed the stairs a little later, she found mother and baby fast asleep. Smiling to herself, she took the tea back down again, and quietly got on with her work.

The afternoon turned to evening. Outside, shadows began to lengthen in the slanting sunlight. The street bustled with homecoming workers and women called from their doorsteps to children to come in for their tea. Bridie stirred and woke, and her movement woke the baby. He promptly started to cry. Mrs MacDonald hurried upstairs.

'He's hungry,' she said.

'So am I,' said Bridie, as the baby settled down to suckle. 'In fact, I'm starving.'

'Well, you would be, after all that hard work,' the midwife said briskly.

'Could I have some toast, Mrs MacDonald? And a huge pot of tea?'

' 'course you can.' Mrs MacDonald went off to make toast by the range, and Bridie looked down at her son. His eyes were half closed in contentment and even when he finished feeding, he made little sucking movements with his mouth.

'Oh, you are beautiful,' Bridie whispered to him. 'You're the most beautiful thing I ever saw. You're mine. It's just you and me, baby. And I'll love you forever and ever.'

The baby turned his head and snuffled.

'Here you are,' said Mrs MacDonald, as she put the tray of hot toast and steaming tea on the end of the bed.

She took the sleepy baby from Bridie.

'I'll see to him, and you get that down you.'

Bridie ate hungrily, and had nearly finished when there was knock at the front door downstairs. Lizzie burst in, half hidden behind a bunch of flowers, bought from the stall outside the hospital.

'Oh, my goodness! Did you ever see such a gorgeous baby?' she cried, as Mrs MacDonald stood holding him while Bridie pushed away the tray and Lizzie stooped to hug her. 'Was it all right?' she asked.

'She had an easy time,' answered the midwife. 'You was no trouble, was you?' she added, looking at the baby.

Lizzie put her finger into the tiny fist. 'Did you ever . . .' she marvelled.

Bridie lay on her pillows and watched. Lizzie turned to her. 'You got a name for him yet?'

Bridie nodded. 'David.'

Lizzie and Mrs MacDonald exchanged approving nods. 'That's nice,' they agreed.

Bridie held out her arms for her baby. 'David O'Neill, come here,' she said quietly.

Lizzie sat on the end of the bed. 'I couldn't come earlier,' she said. 'I was on duty, and Matron was in one of her moods, so I didn't dare ask for time off. But you're all right, and he's so lovely, and I'm here now.'

Mrs MacDonald left her chattering, and went to put the flowers in water. When she came up, Lizzie was standing preparing to go. 'I bet you're tired out,' she said to Bridie, who nodded, because she was.

'If this young man lets her get some sleep, she'll be as right as rain,' said the midwife.

And so it was. David woke Bridie several times, with mewling little cries. She fed him sleepily, and felt such joy that she held her breath in wonder. They were both wide awake at six o'clock and the midwife, shaking the night's ashes from the grate in the range, heard the soft murmur of Bridie's voice talking to her son. She smiled into the raked embers. Bridie was going to make a lovely mother.

Four days later the euphoria passed. Outside it had turned chilly and a thin drizzle misted the window. The weather seemed to echo Bridie's mood. She told Mrs MacDonald that she didn't want visitors, meaning Francis, but the midwife remarked bluntly that a father ought to see his baby if he wanted to, and never mind the circumstances.

'I don't approve,' she said, when Bridie pouted and

held the baby so tightly to her he began to cry.

So they agreed that Francis would come on the fourth day, and maybe Mrs Goode the day after. Saturday afternoon, and Francis was shown upstairs by Mrs MacDonald. He seemed to fill the room in his dark, damp overcoat.

'I'll be downstairs if you want me,' the midwife said, and, closing the door discreetly behind her, left the three of them together.

Francis found Bridie in a distracted mood. All her delight and joy at the baby's birth seemed to have vanished, leaving her fretful and edgy. She turned her cheek for him to kiss in an offhand sort of fashion. Francis's heart sank; it wasn't going to be easy. He bent over to look at the baby, almost hidden beneath the cover, held close in Bridie's arms.

'Can I see him?' he asked in a hushed voice.

'You don't have to whisper,' answered Bridie crossly. 'He's dead asleep and won't wake up until he's hungry again.'

She pulled the blanket back. The tiny boy was flushed with warmth and sleep and the fine, fair fuzz on his head was slightly streaked with sweat. He snuffled rhythmically and stirred as Bridie moved him a little, for his father to see him better. Francis was awe-struck. His mouth opened and closed several times, and Bridie was amazed to see tears gather in his eyes.

'Oh Bridie, oh dear. . . .' He couldn't find words. He fumbled in his coat pocket and tugged out a handkerchief, then brew his nose discreetly, so as not to wake the baby.

'Yes, well . . .' Bridie said uncomfortably, wishing he'd sit down and stop mithering.

'Mrs MacDonald tells me he's to be called David.' Francis scratched at his sidewhiskers as he spoke. 'I wish you had talked to me about his name first, before you decided, but David is a good name. There's been no Davids in my family as far as I know, but it'll do well.'

They sat in uneasy silence for a while, and then Bridie, with no warning at all, burst into tears. She wailed aloud and rocked to and fro, knuckles pressed against her mouth to check the sobs.

'Oh dear,' cried Francis distractedly, 'you mustn't carry on like this. Bridie, when are you and David going to come home?'

He rubbed his hands together anxiously, wishing she'd stop. Bridie wept harder. The baby woke at the uproar and his thin, shrill cries added to the sounds of distress reaching the midwife's ears below.

'This won't do at all,' said Francis agitatedly to the room in general. 'They've got to come home.'

Mrs MacDonald poked her head round the stair-corner to see what all the fuss was about. 'Ah, Mrs MacDonald.' Francis turned to her in relief and appealed for help. 'Can you do something for her?'

As Bridie's hysteria showed no sign of abating. Francis threw all caution to the winds. 'Tell her to come home,' he said loudly to the midwife. 'For God's sake, this can't go on. Bring my son home, Bridie.' His voice rose and cut across the din. He took the howling girl by the shoulders and gave her a shake. 'Do you hear me?'

Bridie opened her eyes and looked at him bleakly. Then she looked down at the baby, gave a sob that shook the bed, and said, 'Yes,' in such a small voice he hardly heard her.

'That's better,' said Francis, looking at Mrs MacDonald, who nodded. Bridie hiccoughed quietly for some while after, but the worst was over. The baby, amazed at the disturbance, settled down to suckle, and calm descended once more on the small white room. Downstairs, Francis arranged with the midwife that she'd see Bridie home at the soonest possible moment after her lying-in had safely passed. Upstairs, he was firm with Bridie, who was reduced to meek reasonableness.

'We'll be married as soon as you are able,' he told her. 'My son can and must be properly cared for, and you can only do that as my wife.'

If only you'd say you *want* me as your wife, thought Bridie, but she merely nodded at all his instructions, and kept her thoughts to herself. Many years later, when she was in a reflective mood and recalling the past, she'd complain he took advantage of her when she was weak.

'Everyone knows your nerves are low after a baby,' she'd remark, 'and he took advantage. Lots of things might have turned out different if he hadn't done that.'

Chapter Eight

Mrs Goode lifted the heavy grey silk dress over Bridie's head. Its smooth cold folds slid down her body and made her catch her breath. The bodice was boned and stretched glossily round her midriff. She tugged at it and wriggled to get comfortable.

'Stand straight,' instructed Mrs Goode, 'so's I can do the hooks up properly.'

'I'm too fat,' complained Bridie.

'Nonsense!' retorted the housekeeper. 'What do you expect, anyway, hardly five minutes after you've had a baby? You just wait and see. The work of him will have you trim in no time.'

'Hm.' Bridie sounded unconvinced.

'Hold your breath in a minute.' Mrs Goode pulled hard at the hooks in the small of Bridie's back. She did as she was told, and pulled her shoulders back as the housekeeper rapidly threaded hooks into eyes all the way up the back of the dress.

Bridie let out a sigh as the last one, at the base of her neck, snapped into place. She put down the thick shining plait of hair gathered into a knot with a white ribbon and stood back to look at herself in the long mirror they'd wheeled from Francis's room into hers that morning. She tilted her head on one side and considered. She saw a young girl, straight and square, with direct, grey eyes set in a rather tired, freckled face that was a little plumper than it used to be.

The high-necked dress of plain, pale grey silk fell in straight folds to the floor, the perfect complement to the bright hair and its ribbon.

'Oh, it's lovely.' Bridie half turned, and lifted her skirts to show the matching grey slippers that had delighted her more than anything.

She looked at Mrs Goode in the mirror and her face lit up with a slow smile. 'It really is lovely.'

Delighted, she turned and threw her arms round the beaming housekeeper's narrow shoulders. 'You've been ever so good to me. Me and David, we wouldn't have got along so well without you. Thank you for everything.'

Mrs Goode set her shoulders back and blinked with pleasure. 'Get along with you,' she said briskly, to cover her embarrassment.

She held Bridie away from her. 'The veil, now,' she said.

It lay in a box on Bridie's bed. The housekeeper took it out carefully and held it up. The bright June sunlight poured through the window and the plane tree threw shadows on the bright, white lace that draped between the housekeeper's hands. Bridie stared at it. For her, more than anything else, the veil told her that she was about to be wed. A sudden chill shivered through her.

*   *   *

'Have what you need,' Francis had said. They'd sat together in the parlour, that rainy day four weeks ago. Bridie, tired after getting up to feed David several times a night, had drowsily watched raindrops running down the glass, resting her cheek on the smooth velvet of the big armchair, curled up cosy enough to drop asleep only Francis insisted on making arrangements.

With eyes half closed she watched him take money from the strongbox that lay in front of him. Francis's long fingers counted out the big white bank notes. Bridie had never seen so much money all at once. She wondered if he was rich – really rich.

It was strange, she suddenly thought, that you could be so close to someone but not know something like that about them. She wished that Little May could come, she thought sadly. Lizzie and Mrs Goode were to be witnesses at the wedding, but it wasn't quite the same. She studied her future husband's face. The mouth that could be so loving was set in a stern, straight line as he counted banknotes. He looked austere, yet she knew how generous he could be. Bridie sighed. She'd never really make him out.

'There.' He finished folding bank notes. 'You must go with Mrs Goode to the West End and buy what you need. I have asked her to be sure that you have everything.'

'Yes,' said Bridie.

'I've spoken to Father Eric,' he went on remorselessly, 'and he says he can offer us the last Saturday in June. I said that it would suit us quite well.'

Bridie's mind went far back to her village church and the lined face of the priest who knew her well. She tried hard to hold back tears. An image formed slowly in her mind. She saw herself standing at a familiar altar, shimmering in white, with Little May behind her and flowers all around. A tall stranger stood beside her, in his good dark suit . . . a young man from a farm outside the village. . . .

'Bridie, you're not listening.'

Francis's voice broke in and dissolved the vision. Bridie let it go, sadly because it was strangely familiar, and made herself attend to what he was saying.

'He suggests two o'clock. We'll be back here at about half-past three. Mrs MacDonald has kindly said she'll come and take care of David, so you needn't worry about him. Lizzie will come back and have a glass of champagne with us, but I asked Mrs Goode to prepare supper for just you and me. We'll be very quiet.'

No, thought Bridie, you'd not want anyone else, seeing as you're marrying the servant.

'Yes,' she said again.

Francis frowned. 'Don't the arrangements please you, Bridie?' he asked. Her indifference puzzled and upset him.

She sat up straight in the armchair. 'Oh yes, yes of course they do.' She spoke more energetically. 'I'll love to go shopping in the West End. Just fancy, me going to the big shops for my wedding dress. It takes a bit of getting used to, all this does, sir. That's all.'

Francis rose from his seat at the table and wandered to the window. 'It's still pouring. You'd never think it was summer,' he remarked.

He pulled the dark brocade curtain aside and peered out. Beyond the railings at the front of the tall house, at the edge of a flower bed, a gardener stood, leaning on his fork, gazing at something he'd turned up in the soil. Rain drip-dripped off his sou'wester. An old man, he moved very slowly. Old men had plenty of work these days; there were few young men left. Feeling Francis's eyes on him, the fellow looked up and raised a hand in a gesture of salute. Francis nodded at him. He turned back to Bridie.

'Old Tom is getting soaked out there. I trust it won't rain for us like this,' he said more lightly. 'That would be a disappointment.'

'I can't wear a white dress,' said Bridie suddenly.

'Ah, no, I suppose not.' Francis was taken aback. He was not used to thinking of dresses, and this situation was proving trickier than he had foreseen. 'Does that matter very much?' he enquired cautiously.

Bridie spread her hands in a dismissive gesture. 'No, I suppose not. I just thought you'd best know that I wouldn't be buying white. I'll look to see what else might do. Mrs Goode agrees, because I've asked her about it, and she says, with David and all, that it wouldn't do at all to wear white.'

It was a kind of protest. Bridie had a feeling that this wedding was a kind of half-truth. There was something not quite right about it which made her uneasy.

'Getting wed for appearances isn't a real wedding, to my mind,' she'd said to Lizzie angrily, when the demands of the baby left her tired and low-spirited. Then she'd remembered how sweetly Francis cared for her, and felt badly. 'Oh blow it all,' Bridie muttered under her breath, dismissing all the doubts that went round and round in circles until her head ached. 'Just get on with it, do.'

She stood up and, crossing the room to where Francis stood with his back to the window, kissed him lightly on his cheek. 'I'll see Mrs Goode directly, about going to get the things in the West End. Maybe we can go the day after tomorrow, if Mrs MacDonald could look after David. I'll send and ask her.' She stroked his face very gently. 'You have been dear to me.'

Francis's expression softened. 'Will you be happy, Bridie?' he asked. 'Sometimes you are so distant, I wonder.'

Bridie kissed him again silently. She smiled at him. 'I'll find Mrs Goode now, and then go up to David.'

Francis watched her leave the room; a vague unease weighed on his heart. Something about her eluded him; she was open as a book, and yet . . . yet there was something secretive. It puzzled and bothered him. Often he sat alone in his study, urgent papers spread before him, and yet these days, he realised, he often caught himself gazing with unfocussed eyes, day-dreaming.

His heart ached sometimes, but he could not have
said why. He was well aware that theirs was an odd
affair, looked at askance by a good many people, but
for the elusive sadness between them, he could find
neither reason nor solace. The middle-aged man
sighed to himself and started to lock up his strongbox. He tried to picture Bridie in a wedding dress,
bought with the money he had just taken from it, but
for some reason the picture wavered and blurred until
the dress became a shroud. Horrified, he shook his
head until the evil image vanished.

Shaken, Francis busied himself with putting the
box away, and turned for comfort to his neglected
paperwork. He became absorbed in reports about the
incidence of infant death in East London, and didn't
lift his head again until Mrs Goode came in to see if he
wanted a fire lit in the early evening, as the rain was
still falling and the air was cool.

On this, her wedding day, the rain had gone, and the
sun shone for Bridie. Mrs Goode shook out the beautiful square of French lace and said admiringly, 'It's
just exactly right. You've a good eye for what suits
you, my duck, indeed you have. You'll take Mr
Holmes's breath away, I don't doubt.'

Bridie's mind lingered on that cool May evening
and the shopping expeditions that followed. They'd
walked themselves weary round the great shops,
Bridie wide-eyed at the smart dresses and haughty
shopgirls who brought out box upon box of lace, silk

and velvet. She'd picked the grey silk the moment she saw it. Their heads together, the grey and the red almost touching, she and Mrs Goode had fingered and stroked the fabric, excitedly nodding to each other that here was just the very thing.

'I fancy it quite plain,' Bridie had exclaimed. 'But with a long veil that should be lacy so as to set off the way the dress is simple.'

Mrs Goode said she could picture it well, and so they'd agreed the cut and style, and ordered the first fitting. Then they'd wandered around and around the displays of lace and trimmings, looking for ribbons and a length of lace that would be right for Bridie's wedding veil. They'd come away empty handed that first time, but when they made their third, last journey westwards for the final trying on of the completed dress, they'd passed the lace counter and there it was, lying in a small bolt on the counter, waiting to be put on display.

'Look!' Bridie had cried. 'Isn't that just lovely?'

Mrs Goode looked. The shopgirl, seeing their interest, had held up one end and unrolled a yard for Bridie to see.

'It's newly in from Lyons, France,' she said.

Bridie stroked it gently. 'It's for my wedding,' she confided. 'It's the prettiest I've seen.'

And so the veil was bought, followed by dainty grey slippers to match the dress. 'I shall look quite the lady,' Bridie exclaimed to Mrs Goode, laughing. 'Who'da thought it? Me, with a fancy wedding like this.'

'You'd best get used to it,' answered Mrs Goode acidly. 'Because you're wedding a gentleman, young woman, regardless.'

'Regardless? Regardless of what, I'd like to know.' Bridie's expression darkened.

Mrs Goode looked at her squarely. 'Don't you take that tone to me, young woman. You may be marrying that man, but it don't make you no better than you was before unless you become a lady by your own efforts. I'll speak my mind to you whether you like to listen or not. And I'll thank you to remember that you being wed won't make no difference to that. I speak my mind, and I ain't doing no different.'

Mrs Goode held up her head defiantly. The question of the change in their respective positions had been much on her mind of late, and she'd resolved to get it clear with Bridie before the wedding day.

Bridie looked astonished, then chastened. 'Oh, I never did think about that. I thought you meant David. Not being able to have a white dress, an' all.'

She giggled suddenly. 'My lady won't get above herself, I don't think.' She hugged the box with her dress in it to her. 'I'm just so excited. I never had nothing like this before.'

Mrs Goode softened. 'Just so long as we've got an understanding, then.'

'Oh, I 'spect I'll still scrub the kitchen and you'll still go on about the cupboards and tidying. He said we'd get some more help, anyway. He's talking of a nursemaid and another girl to come in for cleaning. We'll do nicely, you and me, Mrs Goode.'

'That's all right then. It won't really do for you to scrub, not now. I just wanted to be plain with you.'

They skirted round the milling crowds and headed for the tram stop, clutching their purchases. A newsboy shouted above the roar of trams and the hubbub of chatter from jostling shoppers. Bridie breathed deeply of the dusty air and hurried after Mrs Goode's black-shawled back, thrilled by the noise and excitement of the great city. She gave a little skip of pure joy and ran on ahead for the tram.

Now, after all the preparation, the moment had come to wear the veil. Bridie bowed her head as the housekeeper placed it carefully over her hair and fastened it with two tortoiseshell clips. Bridie turned back to the mirror and slowly drew it down over her face. Then she turned.

'I'm ready.'

Mrs Goode opened the door of the room with the plane tree at the window which had so often whispered to Bridie in the dark of the night. A last backward look at the bed where she and Francis had loved for so long, and, straightening her back, she marched across the familiar landing and down the stairs, head held high, to meet her future. He stood, frock-coated and grave-faced, at the foot of the stairs.

'Why, Bridie, you are beautiful,' he said as she came down towards him. 'You truly are beautiful.'

She tucked her hand under his arm, turned a smiling, half-hidden face towards him, and said, 'Let us go, then.'

They went, accompanied by Mrs Goode. Lizzie met

them at the door of the church. They made their vows almost in solitude before the young priest. As Bridie lifted the veil from her face and kissed her husband before the altar, she felt solemn, as though something was given to her alone, to have and to hold, from her innermost strength, from that day on. Unsmiling, she gave her flowers to Lizzie.

They left the church in a small, quiet group and, with her veil floating gently behind her in the warm air, Bridie in her dainty grey slippers walked slowly home with her husband.

Chapter Nine

The wind howled dismally round the streets and whipped at the long dark skirts of women trudging home from market, carrying string bags of vegetables in red, chilblained hands. In the warmth of the parlour at the front of the house in Tredegar Square Bridie paused, heavy red curtains half drawn to shut out the wintry scene. She looked up and down the road in the half light, but there was no sign of her husband. It was early for him yet, she thought.

She pulled the curtains together and looked round the room with satisfaction. It was warm and inviting. Flames flickered in the grate, blacked by the maid that morning until the metal shone. Number twelve had not changed much from the bachelor house it had been, but she'd re-covered some of the parlour furniture, and here and there her touch was beginning to turn a residence into a family home.

Kneeling to brush fallen ash back under the grate she stayed there, gazing into the coals. Through the half-open door she could just hear Mrs Goode chattering away to the baby as she fed him before taking him up to his nursery. Susan, the nursemaid, would put him into his little flannel night-gown and call Bridie to say goodnight when he was ready. Bridie put her arms round her knees and hugged herself in contentment. Sitting on the thick carpet she thought of the red and blue Indian rug in the study where she and Francis had made love for the first time, almost two years earlier.

She smiled at the memory, unconsciously turning the wedding ring around and around on her finger. Enjoying the warmth of the firelight on her face, she ran her hand over the slight swell of her belly. It wouldn't be long before everyone would be able to see they were expecting their second child. Francis wanted to announce it at once, but Bridie was enjoying her secret and had persuaded him to wait and say nothing. This time, they talked delightedly of sons and daughters, names and futures. Bridie sometimes looked at David, more like his father every day, and wondered if babies could possibly know if they started out not completely wanted. It would be a terrible thing, because you could never put the clock back, never start again, to take the feeling away.

Lizzie said that books and doctors didn't think babies knew much about anything, and that it didn't matter. But Lizzie hadn't had any babies, and Bridie privately doubted if what she said was true, even though she hoped that it was right.

Mrs Goode, a little greyer than when she and Bridie had shopped for wedding dresses, stuck her head round the door. 'David's going up. Will you be coming now?'

Bridie got to her feet and smoothed down her dress. 'I'll come up directly. Will you tell Susan to put another blanket on his cot, please? It's getting so cold.'

The housekeeper nodded and disappeared. Bridie heard her going upstairs, humming under her breath as she so often did. It was a habit she sometimes apologised for, only to walk away humming again, quite unaware.

She went to the window again, just to see if Francis was anywhere in view, hoping that he might be home in time to say prayers with David. The bleak street was quite dark, and as far as Bridie could see, deserted. She closed the curtains again and left the room. Outside, the hallway was cold after the warm parlour and she shivered.

Climbing the stairs, the smooth wood of the banister was chill to her touch; the thick walls of the house kept the heat inside the rooms while the hall and landing could be freezing. You had to be brave, sometimes, to go from one room to another, when the real wintry weather came, putting frost on the inside of windows and freezing the chamber pots under the beds. Bridie loved winter. It made her feel like an animal, curled up in a snug nest, half asleep, while the winds and snows roared outside and devoured the unwary and unprepared.

Upstairs, David's shrill little voice came babbling from the nursery. Susan, the fourteen-year-old nursemaid, chattered to him in her rough, Cockney voice. Every day the baby learned something new. Bridie said he was clever, like his father. Francis, pleased, would smile and shake his head. He sometimes looked in on his sleeping son, when he came home late, and wonderingly touched the fine, silvery hair. Francis didn't say anything to Bridie, for he knew he'd get the sharp end of her tongue for it, but he longed for a daughter. Each night he silently prayed that this second child would be a healthy girl. He pictured a small girl, another Bridie, as flame-headed as her mother, and felt that she would be the most perfect gift that life could give him.

When Bridie went into the nursery, David was sitting in his cot with Susan beside him. They both looked up. The baby face broke into beams of delight. His mother picked him up and, holding him under one arm, checked the blankets and sheets.

'I've put on an extra, like Mrs Goode said to,' said the girl.

Bridie felt the weight of the blankets with one hand. 'Even that may not be enough. It's very cold, and getting colder, I think, so maybe you'd best fetch another.'

Susan went to get the bedding and Bridie sat down with David on her knee. She put her cheek against the baby hair, then brushed her lips to and fro across the little head. He chuckled and clutched at her hair.

'Ouch!' said Bridie in mock pain. The child tugged harder until Bridie disentangled the small fingers because he began to hurt. Placing the little hands together between her own, she began to repeat the simple prayers her own mother had said with her in just such a fashion when she herself was tiny. Bridie remembered her mother each evening, as she, in her turn, began to repeat the lessons of her own babyhood. 'God bless Mama. God bless Papa. God bless Mrs Goode, and Susan . . . Keep Grandpa safe and watch over Maire, MaryEllen and May. God bless all the poor people. . . .'

The little boy watched her with serious eyes. Downstairs the front door banged.

'Papa,' cried Bridie. 'Here's Papa home. Papa to say goodnight to David.'

Francis, still in his overcoat, came round the door. 'Davey.' He held out his arms to the child and Bridie lifted him across. Her husband bent to kiss her and then turned to his boy. 'What have you done today?' he enquired.

'Mama,' said the small boy, wriggling because the touch of the coat was rough and icy.

'Mama indeed,' replied his father. 'Papa has been busy today. Papa has in fact been very busy,' he repeated, looking over the child's head at Bridie.

'It looks as though we are making progress on the sewerage extension problem,' he said, his face lit up with unusual excitement. 'Clem Attlee is to go to the Minister in a week's time, to see what might be done about making a special case for parts of the East End. If they'd agree to spend the money, we could have work start almost immediately. That's real progress, Bridie, to gain the ear of the Minister.'

'To be sure that's a thing to be proud of,' she answered. 'Will you be going with Clem to see this Minister?'

'No, he'll go and present the case, and if there are

more discussions to follow, then I may become involved in them. My main task has been to prepare the brief that he'll take with him.'

'Maybe you'll now stop working 'til past midnight,' suggested Bridie.

He shook his head. 'If this goes through, it'll be more work, not less.'

Bridie threw up her hands in pretend dismay. 'And where would you be without it?' she asked. 'You and your paperwork.'

'Why don't you do some?' he suggested. 'You could go much further with the studying, go to night classes up in Stratford. You've done so well at what you've taken up so far.'

'Lizzie suggested that, ages ago.'

'Well, why not, then?'

She was silent. She'd had the same thought herself, but had dismissed it, even though Mrs Goode had urged her on. She felt irritable and upset at the suggestion coming from Francis.

I was good enough the way I am before we was wed, and I count myself good enough now, so he can leave his lessons out of it. The thoughts came unwillingly and guiltily because she knew the suggestion was well-intentioned.

'I don't know,' she answered vaguely when the subject was brought up again, 'I'll perhaps think about it when the baby is born. Not before, though.'

'Very well, dear.' Francis knew better than to try to force the issue. Maybe one bookish person in the family was enough. He put his son in his cot and, pulling off his overcoat, went downstairs. Bridie kissed a sleepy David goodnight and left him, seeing Susan place the nightlight on the mantelpiece and tiptoe round clearing up the last little bits of baby clothing that lay discarded on the nursery table.

Bridie went into the morning room, where they took their meals, and began to lay out the silver cutlery that she and Mrs Goode polished together each week. The housemaid clattered pots in the scullery and the smell of boiling vegetables was strong. Bridie pulled a face and her hand went to her stomach. She wasn't tormented this time by the violent nausea she'd suffered with David, but strong smells brought back queasiness.

'Ellen,' she called to the girl in the scullery.

'Yes, Missis?'

'Can we do without cabbage and sprouts for the time being? I can't be doing with the smell of them just now.'

Ellen put down the pan of potatoes she'd been about to empty and came to the door.

'Them's the cheapest this time of year, Missis. That's why Mrs Goode said to get them. And there's plenty of fresh down the market, so she thought. . . .'

'Oh yes,' Bridie interrupted impatiently, 'usually they're what we have, but just for now, don't get any more. Choose something else.'

'Yes, Missis.' Ellen's head disappeared back into the steam.

I surely don't have to have cabbage if it makes me

147

sick, Bridie thought rebelliously. The poor ain't going to notice one way or the other for a bit of cabbage.

She had got to know all too well how quickly her husband's kindness could turn to cold disapproval if she failed in some way to match his inflexible standards. If criticised unjustly, she'd stand her ground, but inwardly she was sometimes afraid of him.

'Never mind, Ellen,' she called finally. 'I'll talk to Mrs Goode tomorrow.'

Over dinner they talked about Christmas. Francis enthusiastically raised his idea for the holiday.

'Bridie, why don't you arrange for your family to come and see us? It doesn't seem right that you've been away from them so long and never tried to visit them. You can hardly make the journey on your own now, but I've been thinking what a good idea it would be for them to come to stay with us. Not for Christmas this year, it's too late now, but what about in the spring? It'd be easier travelling then. I'd like to meet them, and after all David has a grandpa he doesn't know!'

It was not the first time the question had been brought up. 'Christmas is a time for families,' he'd said as autumn brought the first mild frosts and the end of the year seemed to be approaching fast. 'I've no one, but you shouldn't be so neglectful of yours.'

Bridie chewed her food and stayed silent. Her husband looked at her curiously. 'Why do you avoid it like this?'

'I don't avoid it. I just don't think anything about it now.'

'But you told me once how you miss your sisters, and the youngest one 'specially. Would you not like to see her?'

'No,' said Bridie flatly.

Francis was at a loss. He could hardly believe her; he was sure she wasn't telling the truth.

'Why do you never write to each other?'

Bridie shifted impatiently. Her lips clamped together, she shook her head and refused to discuss the subject any further. Baffled and mystified, Francis had the dishonest thought of writing to Robert himself, to enquire discreetly into the circumstances of Bridie's family. Her stubbornness only served to sharpen his curiosity. For the time being, he decided to let the matter rest.

'We'll fetch the tree from the greengrocer's next week,' said Bridie, by way of changing the subject on to safer ground.

'How many days is it now?' Francis smiled his acceptance of her change of tack.

'Only ten. David's first Christmas, just think. This year has flown by so fast.'

You're making talk, thought her husband suddenly. As if you're nervous.

Bridie saw his sharp look and became agitated. 'I don't feel so well, with the baby an' all. You'll excuse me.' She left the room hastily. In the cold air of the hall she felt she could breathe more easily. Blink. Oh dear. Please, not again. Don't let the panic come. Blink. Blink. No, please, I'll do anything if you'll just go away.

149

Rubbing her forehead with the back of her hand, she could feel the cold sweat that had broken out at the mention of going home. If only he'd realise that she couldn't even think of it – not even think. She sat down abruptly on the stairs. Trembling, she pressed her hands to her face.

'Stop it,' she whispered fiercely to herself. 'Just stop this, do you hear? Take no notice. Think only about what's right now. There's nothing, nothing else at all.' She clung to the polished banisters, leaning on their solidity. Peculiar feelings racked her limbs and for a moment she thought she'd fall into bits like a broken doll, but they passed.

A painful effort of will brought her laboured breathing back to normal. She stayed on the stairs, too weak to move, praying that Francis wouldn't leave the morning room and find her before she'd got herself in hand. After a little while she was able to pull herself on to her feet and make her way, still trembling, into the study. There the warm fire brought colour back into her cheeks. She rubbed her hands together; they'd gone numb. By the time Francis came in with his paper and a fresh packet of cigars, followed closely by Vermin, she was busy with her sewing. She looked up with a smile as he settled down opposite her.

'Are you unwell, Bridie?'

She shook her head. 'It's probably me being silly, because of the baby.'

The explanation didn't satisfy Francis; the same thing had happened before when there'd been no baby. But he said no more.

He began to open his cigar case. Outside, in the black December night, a bitter gale lashed at the windowpane. The thick, lined curtains swayed very slightly as the wind forced its way between every slender entrance it could find. A draught slid like a knife across the room and Bridie felt the cold touch her ankles. She drew them beneath the hem of her long skirt. An inner chill touched her heart and she sensed a darkness in the depths of her being that howled as desolately as the winter winds. An invisible shudder ran through her. Picking up her sewing, she pricked her fingers clumsily as she struggled to banish the sense that some unnameable threat hung over her, a darkness that lurked just at the edge of consciousness, waiting to engulf her.

Vermin Ermin raised his big head sleepily and looked at her with knowing yellow eyes. He stared at her, unblinking, for a very long time.

Chapter Ten

Christmas Day in the year 1921 was nearly over. The small wax candles in their holders had gone out one by one against the dark green needles of the fir tree standing in the corner of the parlour. Thin trails of smoke hung on the air and spiralled lazily in and out of the twinkling, shining decorations that Bridie had hung three days earlier. The little family had enjoyed the last carol service of the year on the wireless, Bridie humming along cheerfully with her favourite hymns.

She sat on the floor with David. She held his fat wrists and rocked him back and forth, clapping his hands together and shaking her head at him. The baby laughed so hard his eyes disappeared behind his plump, pink cheeks.

'Clap hands!' cried Bridie and the baby chuckled all over.

Francis watched them over the top of his book, smiling. 'Gently, dear,' he advised.

Bridie sat back on her heels and raised a flushed face to her husband. 'He loves it,' she replied. 'He likes rough and tumble.' 'Don't you, then?' she asked the baby. 'Aren't you a proper little fellow?'

David rolled over and began to crawl rapidly over the carpet. Bridie reached to catch his feet and pull him back, but he was too quick for her.

She caught her breath, coughed, then coughed again, quite painfully.

'I've got a bit of a sore throat,' she remarked. 'I hope it's no more than too much singing. I don't want a cold, not at Christmas.'

She beckoned the baby. 'Come on back, Davey. Look at you, Mischief.'

'Honey and lemon might do some good,' suggested her husband.

'Oh, it's probably nothing. A catch in the throat.'

'You'd be well advised to take care anyway,' replied Francis. 'It's a bad time of year to take chances. There's so much sickness, it's in the air everywhere.'

'Very well,' she said, to please him. 'I'll take some before I go to bed.'

She caught David's bare foot in her hand and played idly with his small toes. Then, for a moment, she was quite still. 'Francis?'

He looked up.

'I felt it move, the baby. I'm sure I did.'

Francis gazed at her. These were mysteries. For want of knowing what to say, he nodded.

'It's a fluttering, like a trapped moth.' She faltered as she saw his blank look.

Moths. Francis was bemused by the idea and picked up his book from where it lay beside his chair. 'Remember to take the honey and lemon,' he remarked as he turned his page.

Bridie grimaced behind the book. He was hopeless sometimes. She picked up David and cuddled him close. The warm little body wriggled away from her and reached to be put down. All he wanted to do these days was crawl and get into everything. Bridie watched him set off for the far end of the room where a small pile of bright wrapping paper waited to be put away and kept for next year. David seized it with interest and began experimentally stuffing some into his mouth.

'No.' Bridie got to her feet and took the paper away. 'Come on, if you're that hungry you'd best go to Susan for your tea.'

Susan had shared their Christmas and would go to visit her mother for a couple of days when Mrs Goode was back. 'I'd stay,' the housekeeper had apologised, 'but I promised my married daughter that I'd go to her this year, and I can't let her down.'

'Her daughter has four children including a son who is a cripple,' Francis had explained to Bridie. 'Mr Goode seldom says anything about it, but I know she feels an obligation, and goes and helps her daughter quite a lot when she's not here.'

The story saddened Bridie, who regarded Mrs Goode with renewed respect after what she'd heard.

'You never know what people keep to themselves like that,' she'd remarked thoughtfully to Susan, who, being born and brought up not a stone's throw from Mrs Goode's daughter's household, knew far more about it than Francis.

'She's a close one, that's certain,' Susan had

agreed. 'But the little un's got a head that's too big for his body and they take him around in a pushcart. Give's you the creeps to see it, it does. I 'spect that's why she don't like to say much.'

The tale reminded Bridie of the stillborn lambs her father used to bring home, sometimes, to burn. It upset and unsettled her.

'Sure and it's horrible to see such things,' she said, frowning, 'I don't know how a person would be able to bear a burden like that. I'm sure I couldn't.'

'What else can you do?' asked Susan. 'No one's going to take the babby for you, and you can't just leave it. Anyway,' she added matter-of-factly, 'that kind of babby don't live long, usually.'

'No, I suppose not, though it would depend, wouldn't it?' Bridie answered after a pause.

'Well, David's fine and bonny so you don't need to go fretting about it.' Susan was unaware of the new baby, or she'd have spoken more carefully.

Bridie gave her young nursemaid's blunt, round face a sideways look as she folded David's small clothes into a tidy pile.

'Hm,' she said, half to herself, 'but I still don't know how they can bear it, though if it's your own, perhaps it might be different.'

She'd intended to ask Lizzie about it, but it had been driven from her mind the next time they met when her friend, shyly radiant, had shown her the small diamond ring on her finger. Jonathan, her long, lanky doctor, whose good-natured, intelligent face was as homely as her own, had asked her to marry him. Overcome with excitement and delight, Bridie threw her arms round Lizzie's neck and hugged her tight. Francis and Bridie invited them both to tea the following Thursday, when Lizzie had a day off. They'd sat close together on the settee, delighted with each other, and finding it so hard not to hold hands that Bridie's face ached from the big smile she could feel just refusing to fade.

Lizzie held her cup and saucer so that the little ring sparkled in the bright light from the window. She tried not to look at it too often, but her eyes kept lingering on it until she'd catch herself with embarrassment, and turn her finger away again. Bridie was so joyful for them that all mention of crippled babies flew out of her head. The conversation came back to her, for some reason, as she bent to pick up David and take him to the kitchen.

'You're getting heavy, young fellow,' she told him. As she put him into his baby chair her arms felt tired. He really was getting to be a weight for her now. Leaving Susan to feed him, she went back to the parlour. Sitting in the armchair opposite Francis, she turned her thoughts to the following day. They'd agreed that Christmas Day would be quiet but on Boxing Day they were to entertain several of Francis's colleagues, and Bridie was anxious that the afternoon should go smoothly. She knew very well that some of Francis's friends looked with real disapproval at what they regarded as an ill-advised marriage. She'd been frightened, at first. The intrusion into her home of possibly hostile observers had made her quail, but she had given herself a talking to.

'Stupid girl,' she said aloud to herself. 'It's them that's ignorant. I'll show them whose an Irish peasant.' She'd cracked eggs into the cake she was baking and stirred the mixture energetically; they'd find no fault with her baking, that was sure. She'd planned carefully for the tea she'd offer them, and had rolled up her sleeves and ironed the table linen herself until she was satisfied that even Mrs Goode at her most picky wouldn't be able to fault it. The silver spoons were polished to brilliance, and the glass cake dishes buffed with a soft tea towel until there was no trace of a smear however much you held them up to the light and looked. The afternoon was to be Bridie's declaration of respectability, and she had determined to match the best of them. The tiredness was probably all that hard work, along with Christmas.

'I think I'll go to bed early, even though it is Christmas night,' she murmured in the direction of Francis's book.

He looked up. 'You've a busy day tomorrow,' he agreed. 'Leave Susan to see to David, and ask her to bring you up a hot drink. A good sleep will see you right in the morning.'

Bridie rose with an effort and kissed the top of his head as he bent back to his reading. She hesitantly put out her hand and touched the back of his neck.

'It's been a lovely day. Our first real Christmas. Thank you.' She spoke quietly. If Francis had looked up, he'd have seen the unshed tears in her eyes.

But he just put his book face down on his lap and took her hand from where it lay on his shoulder. 'I have you to thank, my dear.' He fumbled for words. 'I'd not expected so much. I have been fortunate, dear, you make me so happy. . . .' He patted her hand awkwardly.

The stilted words came from his heart, Bridie knew, and she bent and kissed him again.

'You go up, my dear, and have an early night.'

She determined more than ever to make him proud of her the next day, and, bidding him goodnight, left the room to climb the two flights of stairs to their bedroom above.

An hour later Bridie lay propped against her feather pillows, sipping the last of the honey and lemon that Susan had brought up from the kitchen. An unaccountable lethargy crept over her, and yet she found herself fidgeting, unable to get comfortable.

I must have caught a chill, she thought with frustration. Fancy getting it now, today of all days. Oh, bother it!

She lay back and closed her eyes. Her head swam slightly and she sat up again. She pressed her forearm against her brow and wondered what to do. A cold cloth. She'd put one on her forehead and that would ease the dizziness. Pushing the covers back, she swung her legs out of bed. Her knees buckled under her and she slid to the carpet in an ungainly heap.

Astonished and frightened, she lay there, all tangled up in her long white night-gown. Moments passed and she began to get cold. Little by little, she dragged herself up again and determinedly crawled back into bed. She lay still, exhausted. She opened her mouth to call for Susan, but realised that she'd gone to her room, out of earshot, after bringing up the lemon toddy. She considered calling as loudly as she could for Francis, but all that came out when she tried was a hoarse whisper. She daren't call again. She dreaded disappointing him with her illness, for she knew that tomorrow was important to him as well as to her. So she lay alone and afraid, in the big mahogany bed, watching as the glow of the fire in the grate opposite slowly died away until all that was left was pale grey ash.

Long past midnight, Francis put down his book. He sat contemplating what he had been reading until the great grandfather clock chimed one o'clock.

'Time to go up,' he murmured to himself. The room was deathly silent save for the occasional shifting of a coal in the grate. He stretched out and pulled the fireguard into place then stood and began to turn off the gaslamps. Closing the parlour door quietly behind him, he silently climbed the stairs. The house was still as the grave except for the sound of the clock.

Francis opened the door of the bedroom, trying not to make a sound. Emerging ten minutes later from his dressing room, he bent over Bridie and looked at her sleeping face in the soft gaslight that spilled from the half-open door behind him.

He smoothed the damp curls from her brow and frowned. She felt hot. He bent lower to kiss her half-open lips and stiffened from head to foot. He sniffed cautiously at her breath and his heart went cold as stone.

He shook her by the shoulder. 'Bridie. Bridie, wake up,' he whispered urgently. 'Wake up, Bridie, will you?'

She stirred and opened her eyes. They were shiny with sleep. Blinking, she lifted her arms to put them round his neck as he bent over her, but they sank slowly back to the counterpane.

'Francis? I feel so strange.' Her voice was hoarse.

'Dear God, Bridie, you're sick! I shall call the doctor directly. You are to stay quite still. I'll wake Susan. She can stay with you until I get hold of Dr Hamilton. Do you understand me?' Fear made his voice sharp and Bridie shrank back.

'No, no, my dear. Don't be afraid. I'll call Susan now.'

Trying to calm the dread that made a vice around his heart, he ran upstairs and banged on Susan's door. Her sleepy, good-natured face eventually appeared, topped by a crown of curlers in her straight brown hair.

'Susan, you are to put a gown over your nightdress and come down at once. My wife is sick, and I want you to stay with her while I telephone Dr Hamilton. Pray God he's in tonight. Take a bowl of lukewarm water and sponge her face and arms. Keep doing that even if she tells you to stop.'

Susan's dark eyes grew round. 'What is it, sir?'

'Never mind that now.' The startled girl went back into her dark room to fetch her gown, and Francis hurried downstairs to the telephone. He fumbled with the gas tap in agitation, and when it flared at last, turned with relief to the black telephone standing on the hall table.

Angus, for Heaven's sake be in, he prayed silently.

The bell at the other end rang for what seemed a long, long time. Francis tapped the cold, polished surface of the table impatiently. 'Come on,' he said to the sound of the ringing.

At last the phone at the other end was taken off the hook. 'Hello? Yes?' said the unmistakable deep voice of the Scottish doctor.

'Angus, thank God you're there! This is Frank Holmes. Bridie is taken ill. Would you come? I'd not wish to disturb you tonight, but I believe I must.'

'I'm here to be disturbed,' said the doctor shortly. 'What's wrong?'

'Bridie has a fever if the touch of her is anything to go by, and she's complained of tiredness. Angus, I think it's diphtheria,' Francis blurted in his anxiety.

'Hold your horses a moment, Frank,' the doctor protested. 'She may have nothing but a chill. What makes you think it's something more?'

'Smell of it,' said Francis succinctly.

'Ah.' The doctor's voice became grave. 'I'll come as fast as I can. If she's quite feverish you could help by sponging her with tepid water. Try starting that at once.'

As he put the earpiece back on its hook, Angus reflected that Francis was unlikely to be mistaken. He and diphtheria were old acquaintances. Angus knew he'd know that smell, the unmistakable musty stench that gave sinister warning of the fast-spreading membrane on the back of the throat. The killer web that could choke its victims – and if it didn't, thought the doctor wryly, was liable to kill them weeks later from heart failure and paralysis. Angus took the stairs back to his bedroom two at a time.

'Must you go out?' his wife asked sleepily.

'It's Frank. Bridie's unwell.'

Elsie Hamilton digested the information and raised her head. 'Nothing serious, is it?' she called through the door to where her husband was pulling on his boots.

'Well, Frank says he thinks it may be diphtheria, but he may be mistaken. Let us hope he is.'

'Oh dear,' said Elsie. 'That's bad.'

Angus came out with his black bag in his hand. He kissed his wife quickly and hurried out of the room.

The doctor slammed his front door behind him and began to walk rapidly through the streets towards the house in Tredegar Square. The Christmas festivities were almost over. Here and there a lighted window still shone in the early morning darkness, and distant voices called from somewhere eastwards, towards the river. The sky was sprinkled with stars and frost crunched underfoot.

It had been an unseasonably cold snap, thought

the doctor, which made his work all the harder. His breath streamed white as he walked faster, to warm himself up. A quarter of a mile and, turning a corner, he was in the square. The lovely façade of the terrace of tall houses loomed blackly to his right, and he could make out a slight glow on the third floor of the end one. He knew that behind that window Bridie could be beginning to fight for her life. He bounded up the steps to the front door and lifted the heavy knocker. Its dull clang echoed loudly in the silence. A shadow moved on the edge of his vision. Narrowing his eyes he could just make out the stealthy shape of Vermin. The cat slunk up the steps and mewed round his knees.

'Too cold for you, out here, is it?' Angus said amiably. 'Wait a minute and you'll get yourself let in.' He knocked once more, waiting on the steps until the door opened. Francis stood there, as he had three years and more earlier when Bridie had first crossed his threshold, and gestured the doctor inside. Vermin shot indoors before anyone could grab him and throw him out again. Francis dodged him and swore.

'Blasted cat. Come on in,' he said, now as then, and took the other man's overcoat. 'I'm glad you're here. Come straight up.'

The doctor followed his friend upstairs, silently offering a brief prayer that he would not have to confirm Francis's diagnosis of the deadly disease.

Susan stood up as the doctor approached the bed. She removed the bowl in which she'd been wringing

164

out a piece of rag. Standing to one side, she watched the doctor feel for Bridie's pulse. Bridie opened her eyes again and laid her hand on the doctor's arm.

'My throat,' she rasped. The doctor nodded at her.

'I know,' he said very gently. 'I'll look in a moment. I know it is hurting you.'

He slipped his watch back into his pocket and took a little flashlight from his big bag. 'Can you open your mouth, Bridie, so that I can see?'

She pushed her head back into the pillow and raised her chin. The doctor peered into her open mouth and saw what he had hoped would not be there. A greyish mass covered her tonsils and spread down the back of her throat. He clicked off the little light and looked up with a sombre face. Francis did not need to ask; the doctor's expression told all.

'We have a chance,' said Angus. 'We've caught it very early. Come now, let's fight this thing with everything we've got. I've the serum here and she can have that immediately. Susan, will you get fresh water and several cloths? The fever is quite high and I want you to continue to sponge Mrs Holmes to try and bring it down. It will make her more comfortable.'

He busied himself with a large ampoule of clear fluid and a syringe then looked over at Francis, who stood gazing at Bridie as if transfixed.

'Man, you'll be no help to her unless you put your fears aside, and do as I tell you. You know that. You know the nature of this thing, and you know it can be beaten. Go downstairs and give yourself a stiff brandy, then come back up and we'll get to work.'

Francis turned a dazed look on him.

'I'm ordering you to do it, as your doctor.'

Francis nodded. He went with a heavy step out of the room while the doctor prepared Bridie's arm with alcohol, ready for the injection.

Angus heard him speak to Susan, who was hastily bringing to life the banked fire in the kitchen range for all the warm water she'd be needing. The big doctor turned back to his patient. His face was very grave and he talked to her as he gave the injection.

'This is excellent. You've had the serum early enough to make a real difference to how ill you may get. Tonight, Susan will keep trying to lower your fever. You won't get much sleep, I fear, but that can't be helped. Tomorrow is Boxing Day. It'll be the devil of a job to get you into hospital on that day of all days, but I'll try to send an ambulance as soon after breakfast as I can get someone moving. There's no point in even trying to move you tonight.'

Bridie's eyes glittered as she listened.

'What about David?' she whispered.

'Once you've gone, he should be in no danger.'

Bridie tried to nod, and winced.

'Stay still,' ordered the doctor. 'Don't try to do anything. If you want anything, ask someone else to do it.'

Francis came back, looking more himself. Angus repeated what he'd told Bridie.

'I'll contact St Leonard's first thing and let you know,' he said.

Francis agreed that he and Susan could manage between them until the morning. Angus put a reassuring arm round Francis's shoulders.

'Chin up, old chap,' he said gruffly. 'She's young and strong.'

Francis ran a hand over his face and made no response. He was grateful to the doctor for his kindness, but each man knew as well as the other that in truth Bridie's life was in danger, and for all her youth and health, they were all about to engage in a battle that no one could promise they would win.

Chapter Eleven

Boxing Day dawned cold and bright, with a pale, wintry sun low in the blue sky. Angus rubbed his eyes and stretched. He'd returned at half-past five, and had been sitting at Bridie's bedside for nearly three hours. He pulled out his watch and felt for her pulse. Then he checked her breathing, and noted that the colour of her lips was as usual. Satisfied, he rose and left the room.

Francis met him at the foot of the stairs. 'Susan will bring us some tea in a moment. Come on into the study.'

The curtains were pulled back, and Angus walked to the window, enjoying the cheerful winter's scene outside. A group of children played with skipping ropes in the corner just by the garden wall. Shouts and shrill laughter alternated with chanted rhymes as they turned the ropes for each other. Heavy rope thwacked at the paving stones. One little girl tripped and fell. The others gleefully pushed in her place, and she stood to one side, thumb in mouth and face solemn with the effort not to cry. A clock chimed the half hour somewhere in the distance, the sound carrying clear on the chill air. Angus's breath condensed on the windowpane as he leant to watch the children. He rubbed it off with his hand, then turned to Francis.

'The hospital lab will be working normally again tomorrow; there's no point in trying to send in a swab until then, but I think the diagnosis is certain from the clinical signs.'

Francis nodded agreement. 'Faucial?' he asked.

'By the look of it, yes.'

It was the commonest, and most virulent, form of diphtheria.

'I'm a little puzzled by the fever,' the doctor continued. 'It's higher than I'd expect. Occasionally there is an unusual fever, but Bridie is very hot. Has she been unwell apart from the last twenty-four hours?'

'She's complained of being tired, and of having a sore throat, but those were presumably the onset of diphtheria.'

'Hm,' said the doctor thoughtfully. 'She's maybe hiding tonsillitis behind the diphtheria. She's very sick, Frank.'

Francis sank into his armchair and ran his fingers through his untidy hair. 'I know. When can you get her to hospital, Angus?'

'I'll send her in as soon as I can.' The doctor tried to sound reassuring. 'For now, though,' he continued, 'you must keep on with the sponging. I'm hoping the serum will prove effective; it should, as we caught it so early on.'

Angus looked at his friend pityingly. He was well aware that Francis already knew every word that he was saying. Angus and his wife had shaken their heads disapprovingly over the Bridie affair; Angus had even considered approaching Francis, unasked, and advising him that the general feeling was that he was making a fool of himself. Now, he was glad he'd done no such thing. The peculiar marriage was obviously working.

The door opened and Susan, rings under her eyes from having been up all night but with her curlers out, brought in a steaming pot of tea and a pile of toast.

' 'ere you are,' she said as she put the tray down. 'What do you want me to do about David, sir?'

'Do?' Francis looked at her blankly.

'I've bin working all night, sir, and I'm very tired.'

'Of course.' He thought for a minute. 'Can you first run down to Mrs MacDonald and ask her if she would do me the greatest of favours and take David while you come back and get some sleep? Can you manage that?'

'Oh yes, sir. I'll do it as soon as I can. Is Mrs MacDonald to come 'ere, or is she to take David to 'er 'ouse?'

'Not here, with infection in the house. Ask her if she can just do me the kindness of having him for today.'

'I 'spect she'll 'ave 'im, sir, she's ever so fond of 'im.'

'Yes, Susan, she is. When you've done that, you may go and sleep for as long as you need.'

'Ta,' said the girl, and went humming back to the kitchen to finish giving the little boy his breakfast.

Then she wrapped him up very warm, put him in his carriage, and prepared to push him over to the mid-wife's house, where she knew he'd be welcomed like one of the family and spoiled all Boxing Day long.

Pouring tea, the two men discovered that they were hungry. The toast disappeared in no time, and over their tea they agreed on what was to be done for the rest of the day.

'My word, that's better,' said the doctor as he pushed his cup aside. 'I'll go up and see Bridie again, and then I'll be off to see to all the necessary. I'll do my best to get her into hospital by midday.'

He stood to go upstairs again, then paused and looked at Francis. 'Frank,' he said, 'Bridie needs you to take care of yourself. You can't look after her or David if you're exhausted yourself, so my advice to you is to take yourself to another room and go to sleep as soon as Bridie leaves. Let me and the ambulance crew take over; it's our job and what they're trained to do. David will need you, for Bridie won't be up and about for several weeks at best, and even then she'll face quite a convalescence. Susan's good with him, but you'll still need to keep an eye on things.'

'Mrs Goode will be back in a day's time.' Francis clutched at straws.

'Well, you have my advice. I suggest you take it.'

Francis turned a haggard face up to the doctor. 'I hear you, my friend,' he said. 'I merely meant that Mrs Goode's return will make what you say easier to do.'

'Fine,' the doctor said in a mollified tone.

'You speak of convalescence. Do you believe that Bridie can recover?'

Angus began to feel angry. 'Look here,' he said very sharply, 'if you sit around feeling sorry for yourself you'll do no one any good. Your young wife is a strong, healthy woman, and she's got every chance of recovery, if we help her. Pull yourself together and remember you've a family to be responsible for.'

Francis did not respond, and the doctor thought he'd gone too far. After a pause, though, the older man sat forward in his chair and heaved a great sigh.

'You are right, of course. I thank you for your bluntness, Angus, and I will do what I can. Now we'll go up to Bridie.'

Once more they climbed the stairs. Bridie was awake and turned her neck painfully towards the door as they came into the room. She tried to smile at her husband, but the movement made her wince.

'You'll have a very painful neck for a little while,' Angus told her.

She made a tiny face.

'Yes, I know,' he replied, 'but I tell you now so you won't be too frightened if it gets worse. You might get some swelling, too, which is one of this disease's horrid symptoms. It's not nice, I'm afraid, Bridie. You are going to be very poorly for a while, but I believe you'll get better quite fast.'

Her eyes were very serious as she followed what he was saying. She swallowed, and it was an obvious effort.

'Doctor,' she whispered, 'what about the baby? Will the baby be all right?'

Angus had been prepared for this question, and scratched his ear as he considered it. 'Are you brave, Bridie?' he asked.

She shut her eyes for a moment, then opened them and said hoarsely: 'Yes. I'd rather know.'

'There's a chance the baby will come through. It really depends on whether the diphtheria leads to any complications. If it does, we can help you, but it's not so easy to help the baby. I can't promise. You're fine and strong, and there will be other babies later, I'm sure.'

Bridie stared past him at the ceiling. That's what she'd thought, lying there alone with time to remember what she'd heard about this illness. She knew a lot of children died of it, but she hadn't heard of any adults who'd had it. Under the covers her hands strayed to her stomach. Poor baby. She felt helpless sadness creep over her; she couldn't do anything to protect it, only love it and hope for it, and for herself. Tears spilled out of the corners of her eyes and ran down past her ears. Angus pulled out his handkerchief and gently wiped them away.

'We'll just have to wait and see, Bridie, my dear. There's no other way.'

'Yes,' she murmured in that harsh whisper.

He took her hand and held it firmly. 'It's you who matters most. The better we look after you, the better chance your baby has. While you are in hospital, Susan and Mrs Goode between them will take care of

David. All you have to do is try to get well again.'

He squeezed her hand in encouragement and smiled at her. Downstairs he took his leave at the door.

'Try to keep her spirits up,' he told Francis, and ran down the steps. Back in his surgery he began to make telephone calls. Call after call. His face grew grimmer each time he hung up the earpiece to dial again. There was no bed for Bridie.

In Clayhill Isolation Hospital an overworked nurse answered the ringing telephone.

'Yes?' she said, and listened for a moment or two.

'We've not a bed to spare. We've got patients practically two to a bed – well, not literally, but it's so crowded they might just as well be.'

A heavily accented voice roared down the earpiece. The nurse held the instrument away from her ear.

'No, I don't think I caught the name,' she answered cautiously.

'Mrs Holmes. Wife of Mr Frank Holmes. And you say you've no bed?'

The nurse began to get nervous. Mrs Holmes was someone. 'I'll see if I can find the physician superintendent,' she said. 'Can you hold the line, sir?'

'Certainly.' This, at least, was progress.

Angus waited, rearranging his pens in their ebony holder.

'Dr Hamilton?' A new voice came down the telephone.

'Yes.'

'We can offer Mrs Holmes a bed, but I'm afraid that, as my nurse has explained to you, we are well over capacity already. Mr Holmes is, I've no doubt, one of the few people who is actually aware of the kind of pressure we're under. It's most unfortunate that his wife should be needing us. I can't offer you the best, I fear, but I have one room. But I have to say, sir, that it may not suit. . . .'

'Thank you,' Angus's voice cut in. 'Mrs Holmes will be arriving as soon as I can arrange the ambulance.'

He put the black telephone back on his desk, tired and irritated. Clayhill was way out in Essex, miles from anywhere. But then they all were, the isolation places. He picked up the telephone again and arranged for an ambulance. Then, taking his overcoat and case, he left his consulting room and made the ten-minute walk to Tredegar Square once more.

The ambulance attracted a small crowd from around the square. Women stood, arms folded, shivering with cold and nervous excitement.

' 'oo's took bad?' demanded Mrs Cottesloe of her next-door neighbour.

'Number twelve.'

They gazed in fascination at the ambulance. The back doors stood open, and the two drivers had taken a stretcher and three red blankets into the house, but no one had been seen to come out as yet.

'Ooh, there's Dr 'amilton. My Sid says 'e's bin in an' out all night.'

'And what would your Sid be doin', watchin' out the winders at night?' asked Mrs Cottesloe's neighbour ˊsuspiciously. 'Nosey Parkerin', if you ask me.'

'Huh, you can talk, Alice Higgins. Look at you, eyes out like organ stops.'

Alice sniffed.

Milly Savage from the other end stopped at their gate. 'Trouble, then,' she remarked.

The three women moved in a little group to stand next to the empty ambulance. A housemaid from Number four was chattering to three or four other women, still holding her broom.

'Do we know who's ill?' asked Milly.

The housemaid gestured with her broomhandle. 'Bridie, I think. I'm sure I heard one of the men say Mrs.'

Mrs Cottesloe's little black eyes lit up.

'There you are,' she cried triumphantly. 'Didn't I say she'd come to no good, the madam! Pride goes before a fall, I always say.'

Opinion was deeply divided among the inhabitants of the square as to the goings on in the Holmes household. The older women clucked their tongues and muttered about his being old enough to be her grandfather. Well, almost. The younger women, in a world that had buried their brothers and fiancés, were more charitable. If they weren't, it was more out of envy that Bridie had her man at all. Bitter words had been said on occasion by both camps.

'You always say too bloody much,' retorted Milly

Savage. 'You want to wash your mouth, talking like that. It's a disgrace.'

'*She's* a disgrace, carrying on like she done,' cried Mrs Cottesloe.

Milly grabbed the broom off the housemaid and waved it threateningly two inches from Mrs Cottesloe's outraged face.

'Don't you dare!' yelled Milly. 'Another word about Bridie outta you and I'll see your nose broke.'

Alice Higgins decided to put in her ha'porth. 'Look who's talkin', any road. What about your girl's Maisie, then? I 'eard she's in the family way an' all. What does your girl think about that? Yer own granddaughter.'

'Yes,' shrilled Milly. 'You old hypocrite! You shut your mouth.'

Mrs Cottesloe's eyes narrowed. 'You'll not speak to me like that, Milly Savage.'

'Oh no?' Milly shook the brushhandle. The women drew back to give the antagonists space to swing the broom. Then a sigh went up, and all their heads turned. The dour-faced ambulance crew had come through the front door, and were easing the stretcher down the front steps. Vermin appeared from the end of the garden wall and jumped down. He ambled over to the group of legs and began to purr round Milly's ankles. She kicked him hard. He squawked and, tail held high, wandered off in dudgeon and sat down to wash on the pavement, a bit further up.

'It's Bridie,' they murmured as her face appeared, just visible above the red blankets. Each woman's right hand crept up to touch her collar in superstitious dread. To ward off the plague. Please God, take her, not me.

'Come on, ain't yer got no 'omes ter go to?' a crewman said sourly to the gawping women.

Bridie's eyes were closed. She could hear the murmuring voices of the women and longed to be safely away, out of sight. She felt the men slot the stretcher into its rack, and the vehicle tipped as Angus climbed in.

'All ready?' he said to the crew. 'You both go in front, and I'll stay here.'

They nodded, and the group of watchers moved back as the ambulance men swung themselves into their seats.

'Where're you taking her?' called Alice.

'Clayhill, if it's any business of yours,' said the driver.

The women exchanged glances. Clayhill was for isolation cases. Collars were furtively touched again. She must be bad.

The driver's mate climbed out again with the starting handle. He puffed, red in the face, as the engine turned and turned, then finally caught. He climbed back in and slammed the door. Angus braced himself with his long legs as they turned in a circle and chugged smartly out of the square, into Bow Road, where they turned east, and began the long drive to Clayhill.

* * *

The Essex countryside was flat and barren. Bare trees made lacy patterns against the horizon. A grey river crawled between muddy banks and gulls swooped, screaming, over a rubbish tip nearby. The steely sky turned from blue to white in the distance. Angus peered out of the windows in the doors and thought how dreary the English landscape could be when it tried. He pressed Bridie's hand, where it lay curled in his big palm.

'It's not far, now, lassie. We'll have you tucked up in no time.'

She tried to smile 'My head aches so,' she whispered.

'Aye, it would,' said the doctor.

The driver swung the wheel hard left and they passed through some high iron gates. The ambulance went slowly up a drive that was bordered on one side by bushes and on the other by a wide, sweeping expanse of grass. The hospital was the only sign of human habitation in sight.

It's a bit like a leper colony, thought Angus. Tuck 'em away, miles from anywhere. It makes medical sense, but it's unpleasant all the same.

They came to a stop in front of a long, low building with wide green doors.

'Here we are, mate,' said the driver.

Angus got out of their way, and waited while they carried the stretcher out and up the steps to the green door. Inside, a porter sat in a little cubicle, drinking a mug of tea. Angus had to bend down to speak to him.

'Could you call the physician superintendent for me. He's expecting us.'

'What name?' enquired the man.

'Holmes. That's the patient's name.'

The man got slowly off his stool and opened his cubicle door. 'Right you are. Wait here.' He disappeared through a pair of swing doors that led to some stairs.

The arrivals waited in silence. Eventually the swing doors opened again. The physician superintendent was remarkable for nothing so much as his resemblance to a toad. He waddled forward on short squat legs as he stretched out a hand to shake Angus's. He was completely round; a spade-shaped head with no neck and bulbous eyes.

'Dr Hamilton. How d'you do.'

'Sir.' Angus ducked his head at him. He was fascinated; man or reptile?

The superintendent looked over at Bridie. 'If you'd care to bring Mrs Holmes this way,' he said to the crew. He waddled off along a corridor, and Angus watched that amazing shape lead the way past long yellow walls with windows inset every few feet. Beyond the glass they could see beds, crowded so close together they almost touched. Children – forty-odd in a ward intended for twenty-five. The acutely ill lay listlessly in bed, or tossed and turned feverishly.

Convalescents played in groups, and a few ran up and down in a game of tag, banging carelessly in and out of beds where the sick ones lay. A hubbub of voices penetrated the glass. Angus stared, shocked. A child sat in a bed in the far corner, rocking fast, to and fro, to and fro, to and fro. No-one took any notice. Another cried steadily, with its thumb in its mouth and a dirty bit of rag pressed against its face by way of comforter. Many of the children had peeling skin on their faces and bodies, with the raw flesh underneath exposed, unprotected and untreated. Peeling was an unavoidable symptom of scarlet fever, but to leave it like this, on children who could end up disfigured. . . . The Toad saw his expression of horror. 'Oh yes, it's bad all right. I can show you wards worse than this. Would you like me to take you round?'

Angus nodded reluctantly. 'While I'm here,' he said, with no enthusiasm at the prospect.

The Toad stopped outside a green door. All the doors in this place were green, noticed Angus. 'Dr Hamilton,' he began, 'I tried to warn you on the telephone that I had nothing suitable for this patient, but would offer her all I had, which is this.'

He swung the door back on what Angus saw was little more than a broom cupboard. It was windowless, and contained a single, high hospital bed which had had a pile of linen dumped on it, presumably by way of preparation for Bridie's arrival. A single gaslight stood out of the peeling yellow walls. It smelt stuffy and dusty. As Angus stared, a nurse hurried down the corridor towards them. Her wide starched cap made wings on either side of her anxious face. They flapped as she walked.

'I'm sorry, sir,' she said to Toad, 'but Matron called me away before I had time to finish making the bed.'

The spade-shaped head swivelled towards her. 'I want it done immediately.' The oily voice was cold.

Angus came to life. 'No, nurse. Don't bother.'

The Toad looked at him without surprise. 'I warned you,' he repeated, with a shrug of the massive shoulders.

'She can't stay here,' said Angus. 'It's impossible.'

The ambulance crew shifted their hold on the stretcher. It was starting to get heavy. Angus looked up and down the ugly corridor. 'What about one of the wards?' he asked. 'Do you not have an Adult Diphtheria at all?'

He knew the hospital was overcrowded, but surely . . .

'No. We're not getting diphtheria. It's all this.' He gestured at the scarlet fever patients behind yet another row of windows just a few feet further up the passage.

'I can't put diphtheria in with a ward full of scarlet fever.' The Toad was adamant. 'We'd have the lot of them catching it from each other. It's here or nothing. It's all I've got.'

'Yes, yes. I realise that, doctor.' Angus began to accept the unavoidable.

Bridie lay looking from one to the other. She wished they'd just let her get into bed, and go away. Angus thrust his hands into his coat pocket and looked at his feet, considering. One of the crew coughed meaningfully.

'Back home.' Angus spoke to no one in particular. Toad opened his mouth. 'I'm sorry to have taken your time for no purpose,' Angus said before the other man could speak. 'It was good of you to take the trouble. You are indeed overwhelmed with patients, I can see. Thank you for your kind offer, but I really don't think Mrs Holmes can stay here.'

Toad's face went a purplish colour. 'I warned you,' he said again. 'I told you.'

'Yes, yes. The fault is entirely mine.' Angus didn't want the odious creature upset. 'I owe you a full apology. You shall have it in writing. Tomorrow.'

Toad glared at him. 'So long as it's understood. We can't do the impossible, Doctor.'

'No, of course. One might say you already do the impossible, Doctor. Working in such conditions . . .'

Damn Toad, he was making him grovel! Angus nodded at the crew, who were watching his discomfort with amusement.

'Back down, please.'

The little party trailed back the way it had come. Inside the ambulance, Angus took Bridie's hand again. 'Oh, my dear, I'm so sorry. I had an idea it would be dreadful, but I have an obligation to try to take you to hospital. I have to make my best efforts, or there'd be real trouble. I think now that I have pulled every rabbit out of the bag that I could hope to find, and all we can do is take you home.'

They jolted as the engine puttered into life again. 'Here we go,' murmured Angus. 'It'll be getting dark before we're back.'

He sat, head bent, weighed down by a feeling of hopeless anger. Such conditions were unthinkable, yet they were happening in every hospital within reach of London. Not a bed to be had. The very crisis that he and Francis had foreseen eighteen months earlier was now well and truly and intractably upon them. Diphtheria had a firm hold in the slums of East London, and there was nowhere to send their patients. Those children weren't being properly nursed. It was a scandal.

Angus leant uncomfortably against the side of the ambulance, and his head bumped back and forth as they made their way back towards London. Eventually he dozed, and Bridie, watching his head droop slowly forward until he was doubled up, with his head resting on the red blanket not far from hers, put out one hot hand and held him carefully so that he slept the rest of the way back and didn't fall.

The ambulance lights disappeared out of Tredegar Square several hours later. Angus ran a hand over the stubble on his cheeks and said to Francis, 'I'll arrange for nursing. She'll have to stay here until there's a bed free, and God knows when that'll be. I'll get on to the agency at once. Then you'll just have to leave her in the nurses' hands, and I'll take the case myself for as long as is necessary.'

He shook his head at Francis's offer of a whisky. 'I'll go and get it arranged, then I'm going to ask Dr Patton to take my calls, and sleep like a dead man,' he said cheerfully. 'Elsie can take messages if you need anyone. I'll see Bridie again tomorrow.'

He shrugged on his coat and opened the front door. 'Just give the nurse a free hand. She'll know what to do,' he repeated, then went briskly off into the frosty evening. Francis closed the door and the square fell silent once more.

'Come on, Vermin Ermin.' Francis picked up the cat, and went upstairs to wait with Bridie for the nurse's knock at the door.

Chapter Twelve

Angus did his work well. Two hours later Francis hurried down to answer a knock at the door. On the steps, bag in hand, stood a young woman.

'Good evening,' she said cheerfully. 'I'm the nurse, Emmy Dobson. Dr Hamilton sent me. You must be Mr Holmes.'

'I'm so glad you've come,' Francis told her as she hung up her long blue cloak in the hall. 'My wife is upstairs.' He looked over his shoulder at her as they went up. 'Has Dr Hamilton told you what has to be done?'

'Oh, yes,' she answered. 'Your wife is sick with faucial diphtheria. He's explained it all to me.'

They stood outside the bedroom door. 'Have you experience of nursing diphtheria patients at all?' Francis was too anxious to be tactful.

'Oh yes, sir. I did my training at Bart's and I've been doing private nursing for two years. I've looked after seven cases of diphtheria on my own, and I've worked for Dr Hamilton before.'

Francis heaved a sigh of relief. He should have trusted Angus more. The little nurse put her hand gently on his arm. Her eyes were steady and intelligent and she spoke in an unhurried voice.

'It's very worrying, sir, I know. I've seen others go through it, but I do know what I'm doing.'

Francis hesitated. Then, 'Tell me something,' he said in a low voice, 'did any of the other seven survive?'

She looked him straight in the eye. 'Yes, sir, one. The other six were small children, and they all died.'

'Thank you,' he said, and led the way into the bedroom.

At lunchtime the following day Angus arrived to find the bedroom rearranged into a sick-room. He put the two shiny metal bedpans he'd brought on the top of the bureau and looked round with approval. The little nurse was rubbing Bridie's ankles briskly.

'Bedsores,' she'd said to Bridie. 'They're horrid, and we don't want you getting them, so several times a day I'll rub you and turn you, so you don't lie in one position all the time. You just stay still and let me do everything.'

Bridie, who felt lightheaded and in dreadful pain, wasn't inclined to argue. She simply watched the nurse through glazed eyes, passively letting her lift and turn and sponge. Sometimes the nurse seemed to float before her. The pain became agony.

'Hm,' said Angus when he examined her.

To the nurse he expressed concern. 'She's too hot,' he said worriedly. 'She shouldn't have such a fever.'

'I'm worried about that, too,' said the girl in her calm manner. 'It's not usual, though I have seen patients who've been quite feverish with diphtheria.'

Angus asked Bridie to open her mouth so that he could look at her throat again. Crying openly, she did her best. He peered at the grey mass he'd seen the night before.

'I could try to remove it,' he said to the nurse,' but I don't think it would come away easily, and might make things worse. I'm concerned that there's an additional infection there.'

The nurse nodded. Her reddish hair caught the light and the doctor's eye. 'I've been wondering about that.'

Angus stood up and paced to the window. 'No,' he said decisively, 'we won't touch it. We'll proceed by constant observation, try to lower the fever as we've been doing, and pray there are no complications.'

He took Bridie's pulse once more. 'Slightly fast. Not significantly,' he said to the nurse. 'That's a very good sign,' he added to Bridie. 'You carry on the way you are, and you'll be just splendid.'

Francis had been immensely relieved to hand the sick-room over to the capable hands of the nurse. He'd spent a good deal of time on the telephone, letting people know that Boxing Day tea had been overtaken by illness. Their sympathy and anxiety came as a surprise. The withdrawn, self-absorbed man had cocooned his little family and his private life inside the walls of his tall house. The telephone calls left him feeling vaguely betrayed. His child bride had become a woman, and he'd scarcely noticed. Other people had.

Late that afternoon, Francis heard his name being called from outside the study door. He found the nurse standing in the hall, looking for him.

'Did you want me?'

'Yes, sir. I'd like to use your telephone.'

'Help yourself. Use it when you wish. There's no need to ask each time.'

'Thank you.' She hesitated 'I'm going to ask Dr Hamilton to visit.'

'Why?' Francis looked at her, suddenly anxious. 'Is something wrong?'

'There's a change, really, and I wondered. . . . Mrs Holmes has come out in a rash, and I'd like Dr Hamilton to look at her. To my mind, she's got the scarlet fever, but of course it's not really for me to diagnose.'

Francis's face brightened unexpectedly. 'The fever. It would explain it, wouldn't it?'

The nurse nodded her head. 'It would, sir.'

Francis counted on his fingers. 'Let's see. Two, going on three, really. It's the right number of days. Let's go up and see her.'

He took a mask from the pile outside Bridie's door and pulled a face at the overpowering smell of carbolic inside. A sheet that was wrung out in the stuff every two hours hung, sodden, across the doorway. Feeling that any germ that could survive the stink deserved to live, Francis pushed it to one side with a finger and ducked into the room. His eyes watered with the fumes. Blinking the tears away, he peered at his wife. Pulling the sheet away from her body he saw that she was covered in a bright red rash. Her face was flushed, except for around her mouth, which was ringed with a bluish tinge.

'That's scarlet fever, all right,' said Francis. 'As clear a case as ever I saw.'

'That's what I thought,' agreed the nurse.

He stood, his breath damp inside the thick mask, and considered. For a patient as ill as Bridie, anything like this was bad news. But – and here Francis felt more cheerful – it was a diagnosis. They now knew the fever would go quite quickly.

'Yes I'm sure of it, but you'd better ring Angus anyway.'

The doctor confirmed their diagnosis. 'The lassie has hit the jackpot,' he said sardonically. 'Two in one. No wonder she's hot. I wonder if she didn't pick it up from that hell-hole at Clayhill.'

'She couldn't have,' Francis said.

'I know, I know. But if you'd seen it there, Frank, you'd believe anything was possible in this worst of all worlds.'

They edged round the horrible curtain again and pulled off their masks.

'Well, it's a case of carry on as before,' continued Angus. 'At least now we know we're doing all the right things for both diseases. That's some comfort.'

Bridie lay in a fog of carbolic, windows carefully

closed against draughts. The air in the sick-room grew fetid – bedpans, carbolic and vomit. Unable to do anything for herself, she simply lay, sometimes barely conscious and at others wandering in and out of delirious dreams. If she so much as tried to turn in bed, the nurse tut-tutted a warning and lifted her skilfully into another position. Bridie got thinner, easier to lift. Her face began to look gaunt. The fever still persisted.

'Three days,' noted Dr Hamilton that evening. 'I'd hope to see it go down soon.'

He eyed her uneasily, though the signs were still good. On the fourth day the swelling on her neck became grotesque.

'It gets in the way,' Emmy complained as she tried to tidy Bridie's long thick hair out of the way. 'I'd like to cut it.'

Bridie listened. It might ease the pain if the nurse had to turn her less. 'Cut it off,' she croaked.

The young nurse raised her pale eyebrows. 'It would be a help, but would you mind dreadfully?'

'Yes, but just do it.' She spoke with a terrible effort. 'Please cut it.'

Emmy fetched a pair of sharp surgical scissors. 'It's such beautiful hair, it's a shame, but it'll grow again, and I do think you'll be more comfortable with it shorter.'

Bridie tried to move her head to one side so that the nurse could get at it with the shears. The pain raged. A thin trickle of bloodstained pus ran out of Bridie's ear and down her neck. The nurse wiped it away with a piece of wet cottonwool.

'It must be agony,' she said in a low voice to Bridie. 'But if the boils in your ears burst, it'll relieve the pain wonderfully.'

She placed a hot towel, from in front of the fire that burned night and day, under Bridie's other ear. 'There. Let's encourage the other one to burst. You'll be so much better when they've started to clear.'

Carefully, the girl started to cut off the long, curling tresses of bright hair. 'There we are,' she said as she finished. 'It's not the best haircut you ever saw, but short hair suits you, I think, and just now it's ever so fashionable. You never know, you might want to keep it that way when you're better.'

She put the hair into a twist of paper, in case Bridie wanted to keep it. Half an hour later Francis put his head round the sheeted doorway. He looked taken aback when he saw Bridie's shorn head.

'I look horrible,' Bridie whispered.

Francis couldn't say anything. She did indeed look frightful; the loss of her hair accentuated her swollen neck, the horrible 'bull-neck' of diphtheria. A yellowish mess was running down her cheek. His throat went tight and and he tried push away his shame at his sudden revulsion. He sat down by her bedside and looked at Emmy.

'Is she still as feverish?'

The nurse nodded.

Gently, he touched Bridie's cheek. It was burning.

'She's as hot as ever,' he said.

'I know.'

'Horrible,' cackled Bridie again.

Shocked, the others turned their heads to stare at her. She lay, swollen and hideous, with great shining eyes. Blood ran from the same ear. The nurse hurried to fetch the bowl of water she kept for sponging Bridie, and began to lay a wet cloth on the poor disfigured face.

'I think you'd better telephone for the doctor,' she said quietly to Francis.

He almost ran from the room, swearing furiously as in his haste he caught his face on the cold sodden sheet over the door. He swore again in frustration when he could not trace the doctor directly, but had to be satisfied with leaving messages for him to come with the utmost urgency. Entering the room again, he found Bridie with wet towels on her body. After lying still and passive for several days, she was now twitching from head to foot.

'Dear God, what's happening?' asked Francis helplessly.

'Fever,' said the nurse. 'She's delirious.'

'It's horrible.' The voice was dry as bone.

'No, Bridie!' cried Francis in distress.

'No? No, Bridie? No? No!' Bridie's painful croaking got louder and her hands beat at the air in front of her. Her body began to rock from side to side.

'Help me hold her,' said the nurse. 'It's dangerous for her to carry on like this.'

They pulled the sheets tighter round the thin, thrashing body. Francis tried to restrain her by putting his arms round her. Bridie let out a hideous shriek and fought him like an animal. Horrified, and frightened of her astonishing strength, he pulled away from her.

'No,' she hissed. 'Get away, Dad. You hear, Dad? Get off, get away from me.' Broken screams began to tear out of her agonised throat.

'No Dad, no Dad. No no no.' Her hands plucked in a frenzy at her stomach and legs and her whole body arched off the bed, in a shocking gesture of desperate refusal. One hand suddenly flew to her mouth and she began to cry with horrible, hoarse tearing sobs as she sank back into the mattress and shrank into herself like a creature mortally wounded. Above the desolate mouth that stretched in an awful silent scream, her eyes stared at something only she could see, but which was dawning with the most appalling clarity on the watching pair.

The little nurse had her hands to her mouth in horror, her eyes quite round. As the ghastly cries faded and Bridie collapsed, breathing raggedly, she came towards the bed almost unwillingly.

'I'm sorry, sir,' she whispered to Francis, 'but I've never seen the like. It's awful, sir.'

He stood as though turned to stone. The nurse looked at him and realised she'd get no support there.

'He's in shock. We're both in shock,' she muttered to herself. She wiped a trembling hand over her brow and began to wring out the sheets that now lay in tepid disorder around Bridie's still form. She worked frantically to get her patient back in some kind of order. Clean linen replaced the sweat-sodden mess, and, fetching a bowl of warm water from downstairs, she forced herself to stop shaking and bath Bridie in a blanket. It took her twice as long as usual, but eventually Bridie lay fresh and cool in an immaculate bed. The nurse was clearing up the great pile of discarded bedlinen when Francis finally came to himself, and stirred. A pair of tired, dazed eyes sought out the little nurse and registered what she had done.

'Oh, thank you. That's better now.'

She looked at him, and young though she was, she drew away from him, afraid of what he might say. 'I think she'll sleep for a while, sir,' she said, to break the silence.

'Unspeakable,' said Francis to himself.

'Yes, sir, it was.'

He raised his head; she averted her eyes from his, overcome with embarrassment at the knowledge they had unwittingly shared. 'You must never speak of this,' he said to her.

She remained silent. She was duty bound to report her patient's crisis to Dr Hamilton, but she wasn't sure it was necessary to give the details of the nightmare.

Francis looked back at his wife and with a long groan laid his head on the side of her bed and wept. The nurse crept out of the room. She went downstairs into the parlour and found the brandy in its decanter in the cabinet Bridie had so recently polished for her guests. Pouring two glasses with hands that still shook, she took them back to the bedroom.

'Here, take this, sir,' she said. She steadied his hand for him as he raised the glass. He tasted his own tears on the rim as he drank.

Emmy sipped at her own, pulling a face at the strong taste. 'There we are, sir,' she said as she put the glasses on the bureau, ready to take away. 'You'll feel a bit stronger in a minute.'

They stood together like conspirators, uneasily wondering what might come next. Downstairs there was a loud banging on the front door. Mrs Goode, who had returned from her daughter's to find her employer's house upside down and Bridie half dying, hurried to open it. She'd been calming the indignation of Ellen, the scullery maid.

'What do they think I am?' she shouted. 'A bleedin' washerwoman? If I've lit that copper once this week, I've lit it every day.'

Francis had heard the shrill voices from upstairs. Mrs Goode's voice had been raised in reply.

'You'll do what's needed, my girl. There's poor Bridie so sick upstairs and you complaining about the washing. You should be ashamed.'

Ellen poked sullenly at the huge pile of sodden bedlinen. 'It's so bleedin' 'eavy,' she whined.

Mrs Goode could see her point. 'Come on now, I'll lend you a hand.' She was just putting on her apron when the doorbell sounded and she opened it to an anxious Dr Hamilton.

'Hello, Mrs Goode,' he said as she stood aside to let him in. 'I believe I'm needed.'

'There was some commotion upstairs, sir,' she answered. She'd heard Bridie shriek and had stopped her work to stand with one ear tilted in the direction from which the sound came. She registered the turmoil coming faintly from the bedroom, but had not heard the words clearly enough to understand what had happened. Even if she had, wild horses could not have dragged out of the housekeeper anything of a private matter between members of the household. Irrepressibly inquisitive herself, she was discretion itself when it came to outsiders knowing their business, and she held the doctor as being no exception.

'She's real bad, isn't she, sir?' she asked as she hung up his coat.

'Let me go up and see her first,' he answered.

The two already up there turned almost guiltily when he came into the bedroom.

'Thank God you've come!' said Francis. He gestured at the sleeping form on the bed. 'She's had some kind of turn, a crisis.'

The doctor looked enquiringly at his nurse. She felt Francis's silent gaze on her and it seemed to her, in her heart, that there were things that could not be put into words, and sometimes a person shouldn't even try.

'Yes,' she told the doctor, 'there's been a crisis. Mrs Holmes went into delirium and it was as though she had a nightmare. Delirious ravings. But she's quiet now, as you can see. Her pulse is good and respiration's rather fast – but I'd expect that after what happened.'

She looked at Francis. 'Mr Holmes was here to help me cope, fortunately, and between us we managed.'

Angus went over to Bridie and gently pulled back the cover. Her face was grey and sunken, but her breathing was indeed reassuring. He felt for the hundredth time the vital regularity of her heartbeat.

'She's incredibly resilient,' he observed. 'No recent vomiting, either. She'll pull through yet.'

'I think the fever is going down, too,' said the nurse, looking at the thermometer that she'd taken from her patient's mouth.

'Yes, that as well,' agreed the doctor. He smiled at Francis and remarked lightly that Bridie would be fashionable with her cropped hair. Francis smiled back weakly and rocked on his heels, for once at a loss for words.

'Should she not be taking more fluid?' he asked, more to break the silence than to interfere with the doctor's handling of his patient.

Angus glanced at him from under heavy brows. 'We'll see how she is when she wakes. If she can take glucose by mouth, we'll let her. Otherwise I may put in a tube, but I prefer to do that as a bit of a last resort since it only adds to the poor lassie's discomfort.' He replaced the covers over Bridie's arms. 'I think we have good cause to be optimistic.'

He repeated his cheerful prognosis as he left. Mrs Goode hovered in the background, and her face went all crooked with relief as she heard him say: 'I'll look in on her tomorrow, Frank, but I believe we'll win this one. I can't be pessimistic about a patient who puts up the kind of fight Bridie has. She's got an extraordinary will to live, and that kind of patient often pulls through against the longest odds. So cheer up, man, your wife is doing splendidly.'

Yes indeed, thought Francis as he closed the door

on his departing friend. Bridie is a survivor, that is certain. But, dear Lord, what is it that she has survived that I did not know? I hardly dare understand things that made no sense before. Her refusal to see her family, to go back to Ireland. . . .

Reluctantly he began to consider what he and the little nurse had witnessed. Nausea crept over him as he let his mind touch cautiously on the edges of understanding. He went into his study, closed and locked the door, and, sitting in solitude, stared fixedly into space while his mind filled with images that could drive a mad mad.

Chapter Thirteen

New Year had come and gone. The clear, cold weather of the last days of the old year had given way to a dismal shroud of grey rain that fell ceaselessly beyond Bridie's window. Night seemed to run into brief, dull days, and then long before teatime the faint light faded into night again. The gaslights were on all the time in the sick-room, and Emmy was glad to draw the curtains on the dreary scene outside when Mrs Goode brought up her pot of afternoon tea.

'There's some seed cake, fresh from the oven,' she remarked as she put the tray down on top of a chest of drawers.

Emmy pulled a chair out at Bridie's bedside for Mrs Goode and smoothed the cover with a sweep of her hand as she came to get the teatray.

'I expect Mrs Holmes could do with some of that,' she said conversationally to the housekeeper. 'I imagine she's sick of glucose and pap by now, poor thing.'

They both looked at Bridie, who lay with closed eyes, half asleep. The ugly swelling that had so upset Francis several weeks earlier had disappeared, and beneath the cropped hair Bridie's white, freckled skin stretched taut over bones that were almost visible, so skeletal had she become. The nineteen-year-old girl had become like a wizened old woman on the verge of death.

And yet, Bridie had not died. By some extraordinary effort of will she had survived an illness the ferocity of which had had no parallel in Angus's experience. The double infection she'd suffered had taken her so close to death that Francis had called the priest.

She'd lain, so weakened that she was barely conscious, as the young Father from the presbytery intoned the last rites over her motionless body. Unable to hear confession from the dying woman, he'd prayed for forgiveness for sins which, he said, God would know about whether Bridie was able to tell them or not. Francis had turned away, unable to endure the words. Emmy Dobson had watched him, the only one of the group around the bed who knew what was passing through his mind. She lowered her head and prayed silently and passionately for her patient, and her awful secret.

Angus had stayed behind after the priest and the rest of the little household had gone. He'd taken Bridie's pulse, frowned, then dropping her hand back on to the covers he walked to the window, whistling tunelessly through his teeth. He waited with his hands in his pockets for several minutes then, still whistling, went back to the bed and took her pulse again. Twice more he did the same, then heaved a sigh and shook his head. Bridie's heartbeat, which had remained miraculously steady throughout the long weeks of sickness, was soft and slightly irregular.

'It's the end,' murmured Angus to himself. 'She's so weak that heart failure will kill her almost immediately.'

He sat at the side of the bed, and held her hand in both of his. He could feel the bones limp in his fingers. Francis, his back to the window, made a dark figure against the light, watching.

'Bridie,' said the doctor softly. He bent his head so close that his mouth was only an inch from her ear. 'Bridie,' he said again. 'Do you hear me? Can you hold on, Bridie? You've fought so hard, and so well, don't give up now. For me, for David, for Francis, can you cling on? Live, Bridie. A little more effort, and you can live. I know you can. Bridie, live.'

He stroked the transparent hand so gently. 'Come on, lassie, you're a true fighter. Don't give up now.'

Bridie, who was sliding further and further away into a blessed light that was so peaceful, heard the plea with some part of herself that stopped and half turned at the sound of Angus's words.

There was a pause. With terrible reluctance, her soul turned from the beckoning peace of death and looked backwards. To come back again? Her exhausted body protested that it could not be, that enough had been done. But she was alert now, and the decision made despite herself. Bridie began to struggle back to consciousness, to life and all the pain that still remained for her. Watching, Angus saw her eyelids twitch and a small sigh escape her. His heart leaped with excitement and hope; he was sure that she could will herself back if she could be helped to make this one final effort.

'Good girl,' he said quietly. 'You are hearing me, Bridie. I'll stay here with you, lassie, and we'll bring you back together.'

Francis came from his post at the window. He pulled up another chair at the opposite side of the bed, and took Bridie's other hand. The doctor continued to talk to the girl in a deep, slow voice. Sending the night nurse away to busy herself in the kitchen as best she could, the three of them fought for Bridie's life long into the night, refusing by sheer willpower to let her die. Her heart remained irregular, but no worse. Towards the dawn Bridie's eyelids slowly opened and she looked at Angus as though she'd drowned and then risen from some depths that lay beyond his living experience. He smiled at her and ran his finger along her thin cheek.

'We're here, lassie.'

Bridie gave a look of assent and her eyes closed once more, but this time she slept in the land of the living.

Since that long night she had steadily gained strength. She still slept a great deal, and Angus knew that she was by no means out of the woods, for some of the complications of the illness did not usually appear for many weeks after the patient began to feel better. But he was hopeful that the damage to her heart was minimal, and that she would come through without permanent disabilities.

As Emmy poured out her tea, Bridie's voice came from the bed. 'Sure and I would love some tea, if I may.'

The nurse put down the teapot and turned a beaming smile on her patient.

' 'course you can.'

Mrs Goode bustled downstairs to fetch another cup. The housekeeper helped Emmy prop Bridie up against her pillows and held the cup to her lips when the tea had cooled a little.

'There, my duck,' she said happily 'Oh, it's a real pleasure to see you asking for tea again. You'll be wanting cake next! It's a real sign you're getting properly well again.'

'That's nice,' said Bridie, as she pushed away the half-empty cup, 'but it's enough for now, thank you.'

The nurse helped herself to a second slice of seed cake. 'Your cooking's delicious,' she said to Mrs Goode.

The housekeeper was pleased by the compliment. 'That's one of Mrs Beaton's,' she explained, 'and I don't reckon you can do better for cake recipes than hers.'

'Where's David today?' asked Bridie.

'Mrs MacDonald's,' said Mrs Goode.

'It is good of her,' said Bridie, 'to have him for all this time.'

'It was the best thing for him,' said Emmy. 'We didn't want him catching anything off you. She's so nice, that Mrs MacDonald, to have a child from a house with diphtheria. It's very good of her, to my way of thinking.' Her small, capable hands crumbled seedcake onto the plate in her lap.

'She's always had a soft spot for Davey,' replied

Bridie, in a voice already weak from the effort of conversation. 'She saw him born, and she took to him almost as strong as I did. I wonder if he's missed me. Between Susan and Mrs MacDonald, he's probably been spoiled so he won't want to come home.'

It was seven weeks before Angus pronounced Bridie well enough for a visit from David. The carbolic curtain had long since been discarded, and Emmy said no-one coming in need wear masks any more. Three weeks earlier, Bridie had been carried out of the bedroom, and tucked up on the settee downstairs in front of a roaring fire. Emmy stayed with her, while upstairs Mrs Goode and Ellen went to work. Lizzie turned up on the second day, and rolling up her sleeves, borrowed an apron and mucked in with a will. The bedroom was stripped. Linen taken out to the end of the garden and burned. Books, too. The windows were thrown wide and at last fresh air streamed in, banishing the stink of sickness. Rugs were taken up and beaten outside 'til dust flew everywhere and made Ellen cough badly. The long green curtains that had shrouded them from the outside world for so long were unthreaded from their poles and thrown on the bonfire after the linen. Bridie said she fancied a warmer colour to replace them, and Mrs Goode brought home samples for her to finger. They chose a very beautiful textured velvet in deep crimson. Francis agreed that it was expensive, but told Mrs Goode to go ahead and have it made up anyway.

It took the three of them as many days before the room, scrubbed and fumigated and aired in every nook and cranny, was ready for redecoration. Workmen arrived at seven in the morning and the scraping and painting and papering and varnishing went on for almost a week. Then the women took over again, and everything was put in its proper place. Furniture shone with polish and reflected the gorgeous heavy folds of the new curtains. The impedimenta of the sick-room had shrunk to two bedpans and a neatly folded pile of blankets used at bathtime. Flames flickered cheerily in the grate, and Bridie settled back between fresh, starched sheets.

She was so light that Francis, carrying her upstairs, felt he could break her just by tightening his arms. All her night-clothes had had to be replaced. Mrs Goode, grieving over the skeletal little body, had been extravagant. Lace and fine cambric lay soft on Bridie's skin. It had taken a long time to heal from the peeling of the scarlet fever, but amazingly there were no scars. No scars on her body at all. Extreme weakness. A porcelain, doll-like fragility. But no visible scars.

'You're a miracle, d'ye know?' Angus told her. 'No room at the inn, two deadly sicknesses, and all you have to show for it is a wee bit of weight loss. Mind you, from what I saw at the hospital, it's probably just as well they'd nowhere for you. They'd take one look at a case like you, and. . . .' He jerked his thumb down.

Mrs Goode popped her head round the door. 'Can I come in?' she asked.

'Come on, Dora,' Angus said heartily.

She placed a paper bag on the side of Bridie's bed. 'Here, I brought you something. It's to help give you something to do. Sitting there all this time, you'll soon be well enough to be bored, I thought. Have a look.' She pushed the bag towards Bridie.

With hands that were weakened by the effort, Bridie slowly pulled out the contents. Several bright hanks of lambswool tumbled out, and Bridie drew out two pairs of bone knitting needles. A pattern book was discovered, folded at the bottom.

'Oh, Mrs Goode, you are such a dear. Thank you.'

'You won't get much done to start with, 'cos I expect you'll get tired easily, but I remembered when you said your Mum taught you to knit, and I thought that that would be the very thing.'

'It's lovely.' Bridie chuckled. 'And I remember you thinking I was too stupid.'

Mrs Goode patted her hand as if to say, 'We won't say no more about that.'

Bridie raised a face that was all eyes, to ask Angus: 'Is that all right. Can I do some knitting?'

'Certainly,' said the doctor. 'From now on, you'll get a little stronger each day, and may do what you feel like doing. And eat – little and often – as much as you can.'

Bridie's eyes met the doctor's. She must eat for two. Despite her illness, she had not lost the baby. It had preyed constantly on her attendants' minds that she might do so. Angus had briefed the nurse on what she should do if Bridie started to haemorrhage.

'The aim is to save her, not the baby,' he spelled out very clearly.

Throughout her sickness, Angus had worked for Bridie's life first. It was true to form, he thought when he examined her, that she'd hang on to her baby, just as she'd hung on to life. Eventually, as she began to recover, she'd asked the inevitable question.

'Can it possibly be all right, Dr Hamilton? I've got so thin, I don't see how it can be. Are you sure it's still alive? I haven't felt anything.'

Angus re-examined her. 'Your baby is without a doubt alive and growing. I can hear the heartbeat. Its growth may well have been slowed down, though.'

Bridie voiced her real fear. 'What if it's been harmed. Might I have a baby with something wrong with it?'

Angus was equivocal. 'That's a risk in any pregnancy. There's no knowing at this stage whether your illness has increased that risk, or by how much. It's one of those situations where I have no answers, I'm afraid, Bridie. We have to wait and see.'

Emmy found she didn't have to coax much for Bridie to eat. The baby needed food, so Bridie ate. The baby needed her to get strong, so Bridie sat up one day, got up the next, and was soon hobbling weakly round the room on legs as thin as matchsticks. Determined to be back on her feet as soon as she could, she was the most willing and helpful patient Angus ever had. Lizzie, who was staff nurse on a surgical ward at the time, suggested some exercises that she'd seen the physiotherapists do with patients after they'd lain in bed a long time on account of operations. Bridie co-operatively wiggled her feet and legs and did cautious sit-ups and arm swings. It all helped and at last they told her that David could come to see her, and if all continued to go so well, could come home for good a day or two later.

Bridie sat in the chair by the bedroom fire, tense with expectation. She'd decided to ask Lizzie to bob her hair properly. It was too curly to go into a fashion-able sleek line, but the result was pretty nonetheless. With her thin cheeks and short hair, she wondered if David would recognise her. Doors banged downstairs, and there was the sound of voices on the stairs. The bedroom door opened and Mrs MacDonald's excited face peeped round.

'Look who's here,' she exclaimed, and opened the door wide. David stood, shyly holding on to her skirt, one finger in his mouth. Bridie's mouth fell open in astonishment. He was walking! She held out her arms.

'Davey! Oh David, darling. Come and see me.'

He shrank closer to Mrs MacDonald.

'Come on,' begged Bridie.

Mrs MacDonald took his hand and began to urge him into the room. He turned to grab her skirt in both fists and started to cry. The midwife picked him up and brought him over.

'Don't let it upset you,' she said, seeing Bridie look as if she wanted to cry as well. 'It's only 'cos he's been away for a long time. He'll be as right as ninepence in no time, you'll see.'

She plonked the child firmly in Bridie's lap. 'Now

you be a good boy and say 'ullo to your mum,' she ordered.

David kicked angrily and reached for the midwife, who backed away. 'No,' she said sternly. 'You're to stay with your mum, and give her a nice kiss.'

David scowled and hid his head from Bridie.

'My word, we're cross,' observed Mrs MacDonald.

David scowled harder. Bridie stroked the little boy's head.

'Are you angry that I've been ill so long?' she asked him in a low voice. 'I'm sorry. I've missed you terribly, Davey.'

David's lip stuck out and he wriggled.

'If you won't give me a kiss, then I'll just give you one.' Bridie put her lips to his round, red little cheek, and he swung a fat arm up and knocked her right on the nose. She gasped with shock and pain.

Mrs MacDonald took a hold on the two small waving arms and said loudly: 'David O'Neill, don't you dare. You wicked boy.'

David, surrounded, looked up at his mother. She rubbed her nose. 'This is a fine welcome, I'm sure,' she said to her son. 'What a temper.'

He suddenly got to his knees on her lap, and pulling himself up willy nilly by her clothes and hair, put his baby arms round her neck and hugged her so tight she could hardly breathe.

'There,' said Mrs MacDonald. 'What did I tell you?'

Bridie ached, she loved the little boy so. Keeping him close, she looked at the midwife.

'I don't know how we'll ever thank you, Mrs MacDonald. There's no way to repay kindness like yours, except to say . . . well, I can't find words. We owe you such a debt.'

'Nonsense,' said the midwife brusquely. 'It's just nice to see you lookin' better, is all.'

David started to slide off Bridie's lap. Lizzie caught him as he set off on two quite steady legs to explore the room. She let him go again when he struggled. 'He's strong, isn't he?' she remarked.

'Oh my, yes. A real little lad, that one. A mind of 'is own, like 'is mum.'

Mrs Goode arrived with a tray of teacups.

'Stay and have yours with us,' Bridie told her.

Perching the tray on the top of the bureau, the housekeeper poured milk into a glass for David and tea for the rest of them. The child, a half-eaten biscuit going soggy in his hand, leant against his mother's knee and patted her gown with one fat fist. He crammed biscuit into his mouth and held up his arms to be lifted. Lizzie hastily leant over and helped Bridie pick him up. She watched their faces, each so different, and each so loved, over the top of her son's small head. Resting her chin gently on it, she thought how strange it was that being so close to death somehow brought you closer to life. As if you discovered in some odd way that life and death were but one.

She bent her head to hide tears. Maybe the price of her life would be the death of her baby. Only time would tell.

Chapter Fourteen

Bridie's baby didn't die, though the few people who ever saw her agreed that it would have been better if she had. Bridie had known immediately. The labour had been very long and difficult. Angus and Mrs MacDonald had been with her for hours before the baby was finally born. Looking at their faces over the mound of her stomach, Bridie saw them go white. They glanced at each other and then at her.

'What is it?' she cried anxiously. 'Something's wrong, isn't it?'

She struggled to sit up and look. Mrs MacDonald pulled herself together hastily and ran round the bed. She went to push Bridie back down, and leant across to block her view. Bridie, weak after almost two days of labour, sank back under the midwife's hand.

'Tell me what's wrong. It's the baby. What's wrong with my baby?'

Between Bridie's raised legs, Angus forced himself to stay calm, and helped the tiny body into the world. His deep voice came from behind Mrs MacDonald.

'Ye've a wee girl, my dear.'

'Why won't you let me see her?'

The doctor didn't answer. He was staring at the

baby. Such a one shouldn't live – wouldn't surely
live? But even as he watched, the baby's skin began to
turn a healthy pink and she gave tiny, mewling cries.
Angus cut the cord and very gently wrapped the baby
in a soft white towel that had been warming by the
fire.

Mrs MacDonald stroked Bridie's hair off her face.
'Now don't take on. There, there,' she soothed. The
midwife's worn, kindly face creased with concern.
She looked enquiringly at Angus, who reluctantly
picked up the baby and nodded. All Bridie could see
was a white bundle. The baby cried louder. Mrs
MacDonald pulled away from Bridie, her face was
grim. Angus stood, holding the baby, not giving her
to Bridie.

'My dear,' he began painfully, 'do you remember
that we talked a long time ago, when you'd been so ill,
about whether your sickness might have affected the
baby?'

Terror filled Bridie's heart. 'It has, hasn't it. She's
not right, is she.'

Angus slowly shook his head. 'No, my dear. She's
not at all right. I don't know how to say this without
giving you the most dreadful shock, Bridie, but. . . .'
He sat down on the edge of the bed and bent forward. 'Look,' he said in a voice that trembled
slightly, and pulled back the edge of the towel.

The blood drained from Bridie's face. Mrs
MacDonald got a bowl to her lips just before she was
sick.

The tiny girl was beautiful. Fuzzy red hair promised

that she would fulfil Francis's dream, and be just like
her mother. The little mouth was the image of Bridie's
and as she stopped crying, with Angus's movement,
her baby blue eyes met Bridie's, which, glassy with
horror, wandered from the angelic little face to the
baby's featureless second head.

No one could say a word.

After a bit, Angus laid the baby on the side of the
bed, and got on with clearing up. He moved stiffly, as
if he had to force himself. When he and the midwife
had completed their work, they discreetly left Bridie
alone with her child.

'I can't believe it's alive,' the doctor muttered. 'By
all that's holy, it should die quickly. It's unthinkable
it should live.'

'Whatever will she do?' asked Mrs MacDonald.

'I've no idea. I can't imagine.' The doctor shook
his head. 'And there's Frank, as well. Someone's got
to tell him.'

He looked hopefully at Mrs MacDonald. 'That
would be best coming from you,' she said. 'You'll be
able to help him through it. . . .'

'Oh, aye. Help him through.' The doctor's voice
was sardonic. 'How d'ye help a man come to terms
with, with . . . that?' He raised his hands and let them
fall hopelessly. 'As if they haven't had enough. Poor
wee bairn.'

Mrs MacDonald wasn't sure whether he meant
Bridie or the baby. Probably both.

* * *

The baby cried harder. The little white bundle kicked and began to unroll itself. The tiny face screwed itself up and yelled. Bridie stared, transfixed, but didn't touch the baby. She felt numb, dead, frozen. The baby yelled louder. She worked herself into a rhythmic screaming. Bridie watched. Then, suddenly, the noise stopped. The small mouth gave a pathetic sob and the baby lay quiet, her eyes beginning to close. As if in a trance, through no will of her own, Bridie's cold hands reached out and picked up the bundle. Startled, the baby's eyes flew open and gazed at her mother. They looked at each other with that peculiar kind of intimacy which can bind executioner and victim.

The baby's gaze questioned Bridie, who finally nodded, as if they'd reached some sort of truce. After a bit, Bridie began to unbutton her night-gown.

When Angus told Francis, he fainted.

Bridie didn't leave the house while her baby lived. She hardly left the room where the child had been born. She asked Francis, through the door, to get the priest to come, and she alone was present when the infant was christened. She called her Rosa, for Dolorosa – sadness. Francis saw his daughter once. He emerged from the room ten minutes later, his face a frozen mask, and never went up there again. He took to spending much of his time in his study, with the door locked. Even David found himself locked out, out of his parents' presence and it seemed his parents' hearts.

Rosa lived four months. Angus, who alone was

allowed to see her, was relieved when he signed the death certificate. The small coffin stood in the room for two days, and then Bridie and Francis went silently together to the graveyard and watched the priest bury the child. As the gravedigger began to throw the first shovels of earth into the hole, Bridie turned away.

'It's over,' she said dully.

They walked, unable to speak any comfort to each other, back to the square.

Outwardly life returned to normality of a sort. Bridie tidied away every trace of little Rosa's brief life, then closed the door on the room and never entered it again. She didn't cry. Angus wished she would, but she seemed bent on burying the memory of the child as silently as she'd buried the sad little body. Francis said not a word about the child. It was as if Rosa had never existed.

Bridie took up her household duties again, and Francis spent less time in his study, but more time at work. He took to leaving early in the morning, returning late to solitary suppers in the morning room, while Bridie sat alone in the parlour. David, growing fast, loved to be out of doors, so Bridie walked for hours in streets and open spaces, pushing his carriage when he tired of all his running and climbing, and was ready to go to sleep.

The exercise did her good. Four months shut up indoors had left her wan and thin. Walking and walking in the open air brought colour back to her cheeks. She began to feel hungry and her gaunt look softened as her face rounded out once more. She was still lovely, but no longer a young girl. Experience had aged her. Lines round her eyes and mouth were the indelible effects of what she had suffered.

Lizzie felt her heart ache as she looked at her friend. Bridie had sent a message of congratulations on her wedding day, but had said through the closed door that she could not attend. Lizzie had first begged, then suggested putting the wedding off, Bridie's absence upset her so much, but Jonathan pointed out that no one knew how long this would go on, and it wasn't fair on either of them to wait indefinitely. So they'd married, both conscious of the empty space where Bridie should have been. Francis sent his apologies.

One evening, weeks after, he came home at midnight. Bridie heard the front door close and looked at the clock. He got later and later. She hesitated, then slipped out of bed and put on her robe. She found Francis standing in the hall, head bent, rubbing his eyes wearily as he undid his coat.

'Dear? You're home very late? Is everything all right?'

Francis didn't meet her eyes. 'Oh yes,' he said vaguely, 'there's a lot to do at work.'

'Have you had anything to eat?'

'Yes. Thank you.'

She followed him down the passage to the morning room. 'Can I get you anything?'

'No, thank you. I don't want to keep you up, Bridie.'

'It's worry about you that's keeping me up,' she said after a pause. 'I worry because I hardly see you, and because we never seem to talk to each other.'

Francis gave a humourless smile. 'It's difficult to talk to someone who locks themselves up,' he agreed.

Bridie stared at him in disbelief. His eyes on hers were hurt and cold. 'What else would you have had me do?'

'You could've sent it away. Angus offered.'

'It? Is that how you think of her? Never!' Bridie's voice was hard and flat. 'I couldn't. I tried, and I did talk to Dr Hamilton about it, but in the end he saw how it was. He understood that I couldn't ever have sent her away. Not if she'd lived four years. He understood, even if you can't.'

'I understand that she took everything. I didn't matter. Nor David. How much time did you have for him?'

'Please, Francis. Please try to understand. I didn't mean to shut you and David out, but I didn't know what else to do. I did the only thing that seemed right. I thought and thought about it, but there wasn't any other way.'

'You kept that . . . that . . . monster. You didn't have to.'

'Don't you dare,' hissed Bridie. 'Don't you ever call her that again. Do you hear? Ever.'

'You pretend it wasn't?' asked Francis icily.

'I'm not pretending anything. I'm telling you never

to call her that wicked word again. Her name was Rosa. She was yours and mine and I looked after her. I'm glad she's dead, poor mite, but I could never have done one single thing to make her life shorter, or not to make it as happy as it possibly could be.'

'I didn't mean that,' said Francis defensively.

'I think I know what you mean. I couldn't do it. And it sounds strange, hearing this kind of thing from you. You come home at midnight because you are too busy working for them, out there,' she waved a hand that shook with anger, 'to want to see your own family. We need you more than they do. It's been an awful time for all of us. I'd never want to have to go through a time like this again. But you're making it push us apart.'

'No.'

'Yes.' Her voice dropped. 'Look at us. We've never quarrelled before.'

Francis's eyes looked hunted. Bridie put her hand on his arm.

'Please let's love each other again. I do love you.' She went to put her arms around his neck, and he stepped backwards.

'Please? I want to be close again, try to put this terrible thing behind us.' She put her hands out to him in appeal.

'No. I can't.'

She shook her head, not believing the words. 'But why? What do you mean? Darling?'

The rare endearment made him look painfully at her. 'No, Bridie,' he repeated. 'I can't.'

'Can't what?'

'Anything. Touch you.'

She recoiled. 'What do you mean?' she whispered, shocked.

'Bridie, you are forcing me to say things we may both regret. I'd rather go up now, and we can talk in the morning if you wish.'

'No.' She spat the word at him. 'You can't do this. I have a right to know what you mean when you say you can't touch me.' She barred his way to the door. 'Tell me.'

'You may wish I hadn't,' he warned.

'You've no choice. I won't give you one. Not now.'

Francis spoke in a level, cold voice about what had happened in her sick-room, many months earlier. He might have been reading statistics.

'The nurse saw you, too. It was only too clear what had happened. You were raped, weren't you? After all this time, to discover that my wife was raped by her own father! Now do you see, Bridie? Every time I even think of touching you, that memory comes back, so clear and so – so –' he groped for words – 'filthy. I can't bear it.'

Bridie was white as a sheet. Blink. Blink. Then like the slow sharpening of a photograph on paper that was already full of pictures while seeming blank, it came back. She felt her head spin wildly and then come to a sudden stop. It all came back.

'Yes,' she whispered.

Francis looked at her with pity. 'You see?'

'Yes.'

'That's why you came to London, isn't it?'

'Yes.'

'Lies! All this time.'

She shook her head despairingly. 'No, not lies. I forgot, I truly did.'

'More lies?'

Mrs Goode's voice rang hollowly in her ears. 'If there's one thing he can't abide more than stupidity, it's deceit.'

'No,' she said in a dreary voice, 'it wasn't lies. I did forget. It was like a dream. You know you've been dreaming, but you can't remember what. Sometimes there are flashes, funny feelings, and then it's gone again. I did forget, and I never told no lies. If you'd asked me outright, I don't think I could have told you, not until now. There were things I didn't understand myself. Now I will.'

Francis didn't believe her. Out of the blue, after all these years, the anger finally came as she saw bitter rejection in his face.

'It was not my fault,' she cried fiercely. 'I was young, and I knew nothing. He was drunk out of his head because Mam had just died. He thought I was her, and I fought him, but I couldn't stop him.'

She shook with fury and distress. 'I never lied to you, but dear Lord, how I've paid! I've paid and paid and paid. Rosa – she was part of the paying, too. I don't owe nothing, no more. I knew when I didn't die after the fever, there'd be paying, and there has been. A death for a life.'

Her grey eyes blazed at Francis. 'Well, I'm done

paying, now. No more. Not to you, nor no-one else.'

Francis listened silently.

'I'm goin' up now, Francis,' she spoke more calmly, 'and in the morning I'll take what's mine, and go. I wouldn't stay another day in the same house as you, not if you begged on your bended knees.'

He looked at her bleakly. 'Very well, if that's what you want.'

'It is.' The coldness of her tone matched his.

The door closed behind her. Francis suddenly looked haggard and old. He fumbled in the cupboard until he found an unopened bottle of brandy. Sitting by the cold grate, he quietly set about blotting out the pain that threatened to knife his heart in two. He was fast asleep in the chair, an almost empty bottle on the floor beside him, when Bridie, after a sleepless night, came down early the next morning. She propped a cushion under his head, put a blanket over the rest of him, and cautioned Mrs Goode to leave him alone. He still slept when, some hours later, she picked up her case, and, taking David firmly by his small hand, left the house for the last time.

Chapter Fifteen

Three women sat toasting their toes by the fire. They were considering Bridie's future.

'I could go back into service. Mrs MacDonald might agree to have David for me.' Bridie's voice wasn't very sure. It didn't sound a practical idea.

'Anyroad,' said Ethel DuCane, Susan's mum, 'who round here would give you a job? No offence, ducks, but everyone knows your husband, and I don't think any of 'em would want to put 'im out, if you see what I mean.'

Bridie saw very well what she meant. 'It's David. I've got to find some way of looking after him, at least until he's much bigger.'

Susan's mum nodded sympathetically. 'Everything's trickier when there's kiddies, no mistake.'

'Well, I'm without work, now, ain't I?' said Susan. 'If David's here, Mr Holmes won't be wanting me no more. Until I find meself another position, I'll 'ave David, as usual, while you sort yourself out.'

Her round young face broke into a generous grin.

'Yes, how about that?' cried Ethel. 'See how you go, anyroad.'

Bridie began to brighten up. 'You sure?' she asked.

'Go on with yer. 'course.'

'Oh, Ethel, you're kind. And David will be happier with Susan than with anyone else.'

Bridie's face fell again. 'We've still got to think what I can do, though. It's not much use Susan looking after David, if I'm not doing anything to earn some money to pay her.'

There was silence while they all considered the problem.

'You never worked before you come to London?' enquired Ethel.

'Only at home. I never had a job. And I'd help Dad about the place, but nothing that's any use here.'

'Could you work in a shop?'

'They wouldn't have me, with a child and all. The big ones, you have to live in and not be married. They wouldn't look at me.'

Ethel pursed her lips and nodded. 'Buggers, they are. Minute a girl gets married – out. It's wicked.'

'Well, it's no help to me.'

'What can you do? Let's look at it that way.'

Bridie turned to her and ticked things off on her fingers. 'Cook, clean, look after babies, run a house, bake, do accounts.' She hesitated, then added, 'I can read and write, and I'm quite good with figures. Dora Goode an' me, we always did the accounts, and I liked it. I used to enjoy it.'

Susan said, 'Well, most of them things aren't no use, but the reading and figures might be. What can you do with them? It could be shop work again, only we know that's out.'

There was silence again. Ethel broke it.

'It's probably not the kind of thing you'd think of, but what about something like behind the counter in a betting shop? That's money and accounts and things. Or Old Finkelstein has women in the office to keep his books.' She slapped her knees and laughed at the idea.

Susan chuckled. 'I can just see you and that skinflint getting along. Evil old beggar, 'e is.'

An idea dawned at the back of Bridie's mind. She shook her head, it was too bold. But having arrived, it wouldn't go away again.

It sat there, beckoning for attention, while they prepared their supper and ate when Ted DuCane, Ethel's old man, got in from Billingsgate, where he worked as a porter.

' 'e stinks but the money's good, so you can't complain,' said Ethel to Bridie over the washing up. 'An' talking of money, it's been on my mind to ask you summat.'

Bridie looked round from the soapsuds. 'Go on, then.'

'Well,' said Ethel slowly, 'I know if it were my Susan in your position, I'd want her home here, where she belongs, regardless. I might think she'd made a fool of herself, or I might not, depending. But here's where she'd come. Now, I can't help wondering why you aren't goin' to your family. Blood's thicker than water, I always think, and if you can't rely on your own family, who can you?'

Bridie sighed inwardly. It seemed that this question

was going to haunt her wherever she went. She fished in the suds for knives and forks, and made up her mind.

'I know Ted's asleep in there, but would you mind shutting the door? Being more private.'

Full of curiosity, Ethel closed the door on her husband, his bald head just visible over the top of the chair where he dozed by the fire.

Bridie told her tale, briefly and without emotion. 'So that's what finished Francis and me, and now I 'spect you can see why I can't go back to him, not to me Dad neither. I've got to manage on my own this time.'

'Oh, you poor girl,' said Ethel quietly. 'I'd never have guessed. Oh my word, what you've been through. Oh my lor'.'

She put two beefy arms round Bridie, soapsuds and all, and hugged her tight against her big, none too scented, bosom. The sharp smell of sweat stung Bridie's nose, as she returned the hug warmly.

'Now don't you fret, ducks, you can stay 'ere and welcome until you've got going,' soothed Ethel, still overcome by the story she'd just heard.

Bridie decided to let the idea loose and see what happened. 'You know you mentioned Old Finkelstein, and his loanshark office?'

Ethel nodded. 'Goin' to ask him?' she asked.

Bridie shook her head. 'No, but it gave me another idea. I don't know whether it would work or not, but it might be exciting to give it a try. I've got a bit of savings from the last two years. Not a huge lot, but a little bit put by out of housekeeping with Mrs Goode. We were so careful, there was often some left over so I saved it. What if I put it into a business? I could lend out myself. Small amounts. A personal sort of business, for small borrowers.' The idea sounded more and more exciting. 'What d'yer think, Ethel?'

She mused on this novel suggestion, pleating and unpleating the drying-up cloth in her big rough hands.

'Well,' she said finally, 'it's not exactly what you'd call a woman's job, is it? Anyroad, I never heard of no woman moneylender. It's usually them Jews, an' all the ones I know of are men.'

Bridie drew a pound sign in the suds. 'That's not to say a woman couldn't do it,' she answered.

Ethel dried a bundle of knives and spoons. 'No, p'raps not. You thought how you'd start, then? How do you get going in a thing like that?'

Bridie shrugged. 'I only thought about it at all this afternoon. But it's the first thing that's come into my mind that I really think I could do. And it's independent. I wouldn't be asking no man to help me out. I don't want to do that. I've had enough of that carry on.'

'Well, if you feel that way, you should give it a try, I reckon,' said Ethel. ' 'ave you thought, though, that you might put their noses out? Old Finkelstein, an' Sam Saul – them lot. They ain't nice people to offend, Bridie. You'd need to be real careful.'

'The way I see it is, they're big. They deal in a lot of money. What I'm thinking of is small amounts – stuff they wouldn't be interested in.'

'Well, p'raps,' said Ethel doubtfully. 'You'd have to be ever so careful, though, not to get on the wrong side of 'em.'

Bridie pulled the plug in the sink. 'All done,' she said.

Ethel had another thought. 'And there's another thing,' she said. 'You look at Sam Saul's place, for instance, and you'll see it's all over barbed wire. You noticed? Windows blocked off, and all that. It's not a safe thing to be, a shark. You get yourself hated without even trying. And all that money. It's asking for trouble. What would you do about that?'

'I wouldn't be a shark,' said Bridie. 'I'd help people out.'

'I don't doubt that's what Old Finkelstein would say he does,' said Ethel sourly, 'but there's not a soul does business with him, and still has a good word for him.'

'You don't sound like you think it's a good idea.'

'I never said that. I'm wondering if you know what you'd be taking on, is all.'

'Well, beggars can't be choosers, can they? And I've no intention of going begging, so I have to find something that'll keep me and David going. I've a feeling I could do it if I tried, and I could be different from that other lot.'

'All right then, dearie,' said Ethel comfortably, 'you give it a try, and count us behind you. You're welcome to the room upstairs as long as you want it. Six shillin' a week and all found. That fair by you?'

'That'll be very fair. Me and David will do nicely, thank you, Ethel.'

Ethel's back-to-back was in one of the many long sooty rows of squalid houses in Plaistow. A sour, sunless back garden led to the privy at the end.

Bridie cupped her face in her hand and leant on the windowsill of the back room she and David would share. Outside in the November halflight, she saw windows lighting up, and the smell of a hundred cooking pots temporarily drowned the odours from the end of the gardens. It was a far cry from Tredegar Square. One small room held a bed she'd share with David, a chair, and a cupboard built into the corner took her clothes. She had a washstand and basin, but water had to be carried from downstairs. If she wanted a bath, Ethel had said, she was welcome to take down the tin tub, and have a washdown in front of the fire, provided no one was about.

'You'll find the clothes horses out the back, and if you put towels over them, it keeps the draughts out,' Ethel advised her, 'but if you don't want a public bath, do it when Ted's at work.' She grinned. 'Not as he'd mind, but you might not want 'im walking in on you.' Meals, offered Ethel, could be taken with them downstairs. All in at six shillings, plus extra for coal in winter.

Bridie knew she was lucky. They were a decent, friendly family, and the rent was more than fair. Ethel was a happy-go-lucky housekeeper, though, and the place was none too clean. Bridie felt a pang of guilt. She was comparing this with Mrs Goode's impeccable standards, and if she went about doing that, they'd feel she was looking down her nose, and that was the quickest way to end up out on the street.

'Anyway,' she said to herself, 'who are you to talk? Back home, you shared a bed and washed under the tap. You've left the grand living behind, my girl, and don't you forget it. It's up to you to make the best of it, now. Ain't no one going to bale you out.'

There was a set of small flags pinned on one wall. They made a colourful splash against the drabness. Bridie could pick out the Union Jack, but the others were all foreign.

She decided to ask Ethel about them after she'd put David to bed. He took a long time to settle, and was grizzly and bad-tempered about his new surroundings.

'Where Papa?' he cried at bedtime. 'Where Papa?'

'Papa's at home,' answered Bridie, 'but we are going to live here now, you and me, David.'

The little boy looked around him with big, bewildered eyes. Bridie took him in her arms and rocked him to and fro, smoothing his hair and whispering in his ear until his eyelids drooped shut. She laid him carefully in the middle of the double bed, and pulled the shawl he'd had from a tiny baby, round his shoulders. Then she put the rough blanket over him. As she turned away to tiptoe out, there was a series of bangs from next door, and through the thin walls she heard a man and woman start shouting at each other. Someone else slammed a door and ran down the street, steel-tipped boots ringing noisily on the cobbles. Ethel's voice said something audibly downstairs. David started awake and looked round, frightened, for his mother. She turned in the doorway at his cry. He was sitting up, looking at the wall, where more bangs resounded, his small face bluish with weariness and fear.

'Bumps, Mama, bumps,' he quavered, pointing at the wall.

'Yes, bumps,' agreed Bridie, sitting back down on the bed. 'I'm afraid I think we're going to have to get used to them, Davey. They won't do you any harm. Lie back down again, or you'll get cold.'

The child obediently sank back. 'Stay here, Mama,' he begged.

It was more than half an hour, after the racket had subsided, before David went to sleep again, holding tight to Bridie's hand. In the dark room, feeling the warm little fingers hanging so fearfully on to hers, her shoulders slumped. She felt tired and lonely.

'Oh, David,' she whispered to the sleeping child, 'I'm sorry. What are we to do, you and me?'

She pushed off her shoes with her toes, and curling up under the blankets, put her face against his soft little head. Fully dressed, she let weariness and sadness carry her into sleep. She dreamed of great fish swimming after her in a small pool. She went round and round and round, but they got nearer and nearer. She woke, sweating with panic, her chest aching from holding her breath. David slept on his back a little way away from her, and the night was pitch dark.

She'd fallen asleep, and now everyone in the house had gone to bed. She lay wakeful in the strange place, turning plans over in her head, trying to find ways round the multitude of problems she could solve only by using her wits. Time dragged. Nearby a clock chimed and she counted. Three o'clock. David would wake her by seven at the latest. She seemed more wakeful than ever, but when the clock chimed the half hour she was dozing fitfully, and by four o'clock was once more fast asleep.

'Oh, them flags, yes,' said Ethel the next morning. 'They're Edward's.'

'Of course,' cried Bridie. 'I forgot. How stupid of me.'

'Edward's me eldest,' said Ethel proudly.

'I know, Susan often talked about him. It's his room I've got.'

'Yes, but it don't matter,' Ethel answered. 'I'd have let it any road, seeing as he's away such a lot. We need the money, and he can always kip down somewhere else when he's at home.'

'He's in the Navy, isn't he?' said Bridie.

'Yes. Joined two years ago. Engineer, 'e wants to be. He were clever at school, and the Navy gives a first-rate training, so 'e reckons. If he stops long enough, and does well, he might make officer. So he says, anyroad.' Her plain features crumpled in a broad smile.

'I'm real proud of him. His dad is, an' all. He

comes home on leave, all togged up in his sailor uniform, an' he's so handsome you wouldn't believe. All the girls run after him, but he's too busy getting on, he says, to tie hisself down to anyone. You'll see, next time he comes home.'

'Is that often?' asked Bridie.

'Well, depends where his ship is. If it's in dock fer repairs or summat, he stays a while. But they're at sea for long stretches, and then we don't see him for months on end. The first year he joined, well, it was seven months he stayed away, then he had a month at home. It was grand to hear him talking about all the places he'd been. The things he sees!'

It was plain that Edward was the apple of his Mum's eye. That's lovely, thought Bridie. I hope I talk like that about Davey when he's a man. I hope he's as good a son as Edward.

'Susan's a good 'un, as well,' said her mum. 'I'm real lucky with my kiddies. They're both a credit, I reckon.'

Bridie smiled and nodded. 'They are, they really are,' she agreed.

A real credit.

Which was more than David was over those first few weeks. He missed his old life sorely, and let everyone know it.

'David, for goodness' sake, shut up!' hissed Bridie, near the end of her patience one afternoon. 'You get us thrown out, and you'll really have something to moan about.'

He whined and stamped and yelled and rolled on the

floor, until the palm of Bridie's hand itched to smack him.

'Why don't yer?' asked Ethel affably, when Bridie confessed to feeling like hitting him. 'Spare the rod an' spoil the child, I reckon. You let him get the upper hand, an' you've made a rod to beat your own back. You'll regret it, mark my words if you don't.'

Bridie thought back to the black eyes she'd had from Dad, and doubted whether hitting did much good, but when David continued to play up so much that she feared he'd try Ted and Ethel's patience too far, she smacked him. Shocked, David turned frantic eyes on his mother. He began to cry, a thin, lost wretched sound that tore Bridie's heart in pieces. She held him to her, and rocked him.

'I'm sorry. Oh, I'm sorry. I didn't mean it.' Anxiety about smacking the child was added to her anxiety about keeping the room.

'He'll get over it. You fret too much,' observed Ethel.

'But he's making such a nuisance of himself. I can't think you'll want us to stay if he carries on,' cried Bridie in despair.

'Oh, you goose! He's only little. What do you expect?' exclaimed Ethel, half exasperated. 'Give him a chance and he'll settle. I wouldn't want you out of the room just for that.'

Bridie felt overcome with relief that Ethel had said it at last.

'But just the same,' she said, 'the sooner I can get rooms of my own, the better. It's good of you, Ethel, but it gets on my nerves, and I feel I ought to keep him quiet, and he just won't.'

'P'raps if you was to get out and working, and let Susan have 'im, he might settle quicker than with you fussing around him. No offence, dearie, but you do.'

Bridie thought over what had been said that night, lying awake only ten days before Christmas. Ethel was right. She was too cooped up with David, and too worried to take a balanced view of things. And Susan would get another job before she knew it, and her chance would be gone.

'Yes,' said Bridie to herself into the blackness, 'it's time I got going. Tomorrow I'll start. Bridie O'Neill is going into business – tomorrow. It's a promise.'

She reached over and drew David's warm little body close. 'It's a promise,' she whispered. 'For us both.'

Chapter Sixteen

Halfway down Vallance Road Bridie knocked on her hundredth door. There was no response. She banged again, and was about to turn away when it opened a crack and a suspicious eye looked her up and down.

'Whatcher want?' a short-tempered voice demanded.

'I'm Mrs O'Neill,' began Bridie once more, 'and I make loans. Small to medium, but nothing over ten pounds, and that only with security. Up to five pounds, no security. Decent interest. No loan too small.'

The eye sharpened with interest. The door opened a bit wider. 'Never seen you before,' said the voice truculently. 'You new round 'ere?'

'In business, yes,' said Bridie truthfully.

'What interest you charge?'

'Four per cent. Nothing compared to some.'

'That's right.' The voice had become thoughtful. The door swung wide. The voice's owner was a bent little woman whose face was lined and tired. Hair still unmarked with grey was wound tight round curlers and hidden under a scarf. Her eyes were young.

'Me 'usband's bin off with the fever. The doctor's bin, and said he's through the worst, but 'e won't be back at work a whiles yet. We're skint fer Christmas. You ready to lend us money?' The voice was flat with disbelief.

'How much do you need, and again, how much can you repay when he's back to work?'

The voice rose incredulously. 'You'll lend us?'

'What's he do, your old man?'

'Not a bad job, when 'e's fit. He's a baker, down Commercial Road way.'

'All right. How much?'

'Fer coal, and food, 'is fags and summat fer Christmas dinner.' The woman began to do rapid calculations on her fingers. 'Would three pound— no, make it four pound – be all right?'

'Yes,' said Bridie. 'To repay plus interest the end of his first week back. Interest only, and it goes up to ten per cent.'

The woman's eyes narrowed. 'Steep, innit?'

'Not really. Sharks can charge fifty.' Bridie shrugged. 'Even a hundred per cent if you get unlucky. I do small loans, and the interest is low if you repay it all. It's fair and reasonable.'

The woman grunted. Bridie took out a notebook from under her thick shawl.

'Name?'

'Grundy.'

Bridie looked at the door.

'Number Fifty-two. Mrs Grundy. Four pound.'

The woman signed her name. Bridie unclipped the

heavy moneybelt that was tied round her waist, and counted out four pound notes into the woman's outstretched hand.

'There you are.'

The woman, unable to believe her luck, grabbed it. 'Ta, Missus, you've saved us.'

She folded the precious notes into her bodice. 'Week after he goes back. Guaranteed.'

'Right you are.' Bridie stepped away from the door and went to move on to the next.

'Missus?'

Bridie turned back.

'You doin' this regular?'

'If there's enough custom, yes.'

'T'ra then.'

Bridie nodded her head, unsmiling, at the bent woman. 'T'ra.'

She banged on the next door. Business was better than she had dreamed possible. And her fears had been vivid. Closed doors and angry, hostile faces. Jeers and menaces. Instead, she met suspicion, then caution, then a reticent, concealed relief at the small sums she'd loan, and the unheard-of low interest rates.

'It bein' Christmas, we're real pushed,' they said, one after another. The moneybelt was getting lighter and lighter as coins changed hands, and the notebook's pages were filling fast. As early winter night set in, Bridie made a note of the next address, for tomorrow, and turned to retrace her footsteps back to Ethel's house. She felt tired, shaky after all that bottled-up apprehension and tension, which had gradually seeped away as the day wore on and she'd begun to realise that she'd fallen, by sheer good chance, into something for which there was a great need. She could hardly believe her success, and, tightening the moneybelt, loosened from good business, hurried home to count up the profits that should start making her a living of sorts from the start of the following week.

When she let herself in through Ethel's front door, she heard Lizzie's voice out the back, where Ethel was getting supper. Hanging her heavy shawl up on the nail by the door, she slowly untied the moneybelt and walked through to the scullery.

'Hello, Lizzie.'

Her friend spun round from peeling potatoes over a colander in the sink. 'Bridie!' She dropped the peeler and ran, wet hands and all, to hug her.

'How long have you been here?' asked Bridie, still holding the moneybelt.

'A couple of hours. Ethel kindly said I could wait. I wanted to see you, and I've been trying to find you everywhere. Bridie, what on earth has happened? Why are you here? What's going on? Why haven't you told me?'

Bridie put out her hands to stem the flood of questions. 'Wait a minute.' She raised her eyebrows 'Have you seen anyone back at the square?'

'Yes, Mrs Goode. She said Francis wasn't seeing anyone, and that you'd gone but she didn't know where, and that so far as she knew you wouldn't be back. Oh, Bridie, she'd been crying, I could tell, and I've been so worried.'

'How'd you find me, then?'

'I bumped into Susan over in the High Street, and she told me.'

'What else did she say?'

'Nothing. Please, Bridie, what has happened?'

'Ethel, is David with Susan?'

'Yes,' said Ethel. 'She took him over the Roman to do a bit o' shoppin'.'

'Come on up with me, then,' said Bridie to Lizzie, 'and I'll tell you.'

The two women climbed the stairs, Bridie groaning softly that her feet ached fit to kill. She sat on the edge of her chair and began to unbutton her boots, while Lizzie perched on the side of the bed and watched her, agog with curiosity.

'Well?' she demanded, when Bridie showed no sign of saying anything.

'Oh, Lizzie, I don't know what to say, or where to start. It's a pickle an' I'm doing my best to get out of it. Francis and me, we fell out over something that happened a long time ago. He's an unforgiving man, Lizzie. He sees things good or bad, black or white, but not much in between. And there was something between us that he couldn't ever let go, that's what he said, and I knew it was true, so I came away for good. It wasn't any use stopping there. Even for David. It would just have been a misery for everyone.'

She looked at Lizzie for the first time. 'So here we are. Ethel's being very kind, and giving me a chance to pull myself together. Her and Susan, they've been such a help. I don't know what I'd do without them. Even Ted's good to us.'

Lizzie looked upset. 'Why didn't you tell me? Why do all this in secret?'

'I haven't. It all happened too quickly, and I've had so little time, and so much on my mind. I was going to come and see you, of course I was.'

'Whatever it was happened suddenly? It wasn't Rosa, was it?'

'Well,' said Bridie hesitantly, 'Rosa didn't make things easy, and the way Francis spoke of her, it did upset me. But by itself that wouldn't have driven us apart. It was this other old thing, and it's done and gone as far as I'm concerned, but it never will be for him.'

Lizzie was desperately curious, but didn't like to ask any more questions. 'Oh,' was all she said.

'Any road, as Ethel says. . . .' Bridie smiled. 'How's things with you?'

Lizzie beamed. 'The house is lovely. I walk round it when no one else is there, and hug myself. It's like having a doll's house to play with, only it's real. Jonathan walks to Bart's every morning, and it only takes him ten minutes.'

They'd rented a house in a small turning by St Bartholomew's, their first real home.

'But I do feel badly. It seems all wrong that you've lost your lovely home at the very time when I'm nesting away like mad. Why don't you and David come and stay with us?'

Bridie had a moment of sore temptation. Then she shook her head. 'Thank you, Lizzie, but no. I'm going to stay here. Here, Susan will look after David for me, and today I started work. I can manage here, although it's not luxurious, without imposing on anyone. And I would be imposing on you and Jonathan, even if you were kind enough to pretend I wasn't.'

They sat quietly while Lizzie thought that over.

'You can understand if anyone can,' said Bridie into the silence. 'You're independent. You always have been. You've got a real job, a real training, and if anything happened to you and Jonathan, you can look after yourself. That's what I want—independence. I want to live . . . how can I say what I mean? . . . for myself.'

Lizzie nodded. 'I think I understand,' she said slowly, 'but you're making it hard on yourself, doing it this way.'

'Well, it is hard. That's a fact. and I won't pretend it ain't. But I'm doing it the way I want to.'

'Ethel said you're going out moneylending. Isn't that dangerous?'

Bridie drew her nail over her skirt thoughtfully. 'Yes, I 'spect it could be. But I haven't got what you've got by way of schooling and things, so I have to use what I can do, and I decided to try going into business. I don't know yet whether it'll work, but what matters is that I decided to try, and I am.'

Lizzie eyed her with respect. ' 'course, you could try applying for something like nurse training?' she suggested.

Bridie shook her head stubbornly. 'Lizzie, shut up. I've said what I'm doing, and that's it.'

Lizzie laughed out loud. 'And you say Francis is stubborn! There's nothing to choose between the two of you. Stubborn as mules, the both of you.'

Bridie grinned. 'Come on, let's go and give Ethel a hand. You stopping for supper?'

'If I may. I'd like to see David.'

When Susan arrived, pink-cheeked with cold, the three women were busy setting and serving stew and vegetables, edging round each other in the cramped space. Susan and David added to the crowd, and David was put to sit at the table, out of the way. They were just ready when Ted came in, stamping frozen feet and his big ears all red with cold, saying he was hungry as a horse. Steam rose in mouthwatering clouds from the pan on the table, and the chatter of women's voices became subdued as they all picked up knives and forks, eagerly attacking their piled plates. The clatter of cutlery stopped conversation altogether for a while, as they sat elbow to elbow round the table. One by one, they pushed their chairs back a bit and wiped their mouths. David wanted a drink of water, and Bridie squeezed between chairs and the wall to get to the scullery. On the way she put her hands on Lizzie's shoulders. As she got behind the chair, she bent and planted a kiss on her friend's cheek.

'Thanks for coming tonight.'

Lizzie smiled up at her.

'She'll do all right, ducks, you see if she doesn't,' said Ethel from across the table.

Looking round the steamy little room at the circle of good-natured faces, Lizzie's heart was warmed for her friend. She would be all right here, indeed she would.

Three days before Christmas business had been so good that Bridie's moneybelt was empty by early afternoon. She was glad to turn homewards. An unexpected warm spell had brought fog, which had been getting denser as the day went on. Passers-by coughed and cursed. The streets were hazardous enough when you could see what you were walking in, but horrible when you were fumbling blindly along in what promised to be a real pea-souper. She was almost at Ethel's front door, when she heard a voice calling her cautiously from above. Looking up, the fog stinging her eyes and nostrils, she could just make out Ethel's round anxious face, hanging out of the upstairs window.

'Oi, Bridie?' she called.

'What you got the window open for, in this?' Bridie called back.

'I bin watching out fer yer. You got a visitor. In the front room.'

Bridie peered up through the murk. 'Who?'

'Mr 'olmes. Yer 'usband, ducks.'

'Oh.' Bridie paused, then asked: 'Is David there, too?'

'Yes. It's too foggy for 'im to go out. Anyroad, I didn't want fer you to get a shock. So I come up 'ere to see if I could spot you comin'.'

'Thank you, Ethel,' said Bridie, coughing into mittened hands. 'I'll go in and see him.'

She found Francis sitting in the parlour, looking ill at ease, with David on his knee. They avoided one another's eyes. Bridie hung her shawl on its nail.

'Hullo, Francis,' she said, with her back to him.

'Bridie.' Unseen, Francis ducked his head in greeting.

She sat down on a chair opposite him and smoothed her skirt over her knees. Damp clung to the fabric. It smelled of fog.

'Did you want something, comin' here?' she asked after a bit.

Francis made a thing of transferring David to his other knee. The child wriggled and slid off, running to Bridie. Sitting on his mother's lap, he stuck his fingers in his mouth and solemnly stared at his father.

'I came to see my son,' started Francis, 'and to try to talk to you.' He folded his hands round one knee and leant forward earnestly. 'I believe we are making a mistake, Bridie. I don't think you should go on like this.'

'Why not?'

He gestured round the room. 'It's not right for you and David.'

'What *is* right for me an' David?'

'I think you should come back to the house, and we'll work something out.'

'No,' said Bridie flatly.

Francis took a deep breath. 'Look, my dear, please try to be reasonable. We must think of David. Bridie?'

A dull flush reddened her cheeks. 'You got a nerve,'

she said in a quiet voice. 'You come 'ere, telling me
what's right and wrong. "Should this, and should
that"—just like when we got married. It's all "my
son" and what everyone else oughter do. I don't want
to come back and be worked out. You hear?' Her
voice was rising.

Francis was shocked. Bridie had always been
respectful. He dismissed the memory of the last time
she'd shouted. She'd been under strain. Upset. That
baby had been a terrible thing for them both.

'You don't mean this,' he began. 'I'm sure if you
consider. . . .'

Bridie's temper erupted. 'Who do you think you
are to tell me what I mean? I mean what I say. No,
Francis, David an' me are stopping here. Is that
simple enough for you to understand? We're stopping
'ere.'

Her rudeness shook him. 'I don't recognise you,'
he muttered.

They sat, each shaking from the anger that hung
round their heads, thick as the fog outside. Francis
rubbed his eyes with finger and thumb, then sat, head
bowed, pinching the bridge of his nose.

'I cannot believe that this is what you want.'

'Since when did you ever ask me what I wanted?'

'Weren't you happy, then? Was that all a sham?'

'It was you that talked about sham!' she cried.
'You! I couldn't stay after what you said to me, and I
ain't never comin' back. So you might as well go now,
because nothing you can say is goin' to make any
difference.'

Francis got up stiffly. 'I shall make some financial arrangements for my son,' he said coldly, 'and will inform you of them.'

'He's not legally yours. You can arrange what you like, but he's mine when it comes to it.'

White-faced, Francis faced her. 'His illegitimacy,' the word was cruelly stressed, 'is on your head. You refused to listen to reason, then as now. I shall not try to talk to you again.' He slammed the front door behind his departing figure, and vanished immediately into the fog.

Ethel stuck her head round the door. 'You all right, ducks?' she asked.

Bridie began to laugh and half cry at the same time. 'Oh, Ethel! If you could have seen it. He's so . . . so . . . what is it? Pompous. I don't know how I stood it. He wants me to go back, and he's no idea how to ask. I couldn't.'

'Well,' said Ethel, 'I can understand after what you told me, but it do seem an awful lot to give up.'

Bridie sobered down. 'It is,' she agreed, 'but I'd be miserable, however much comfort money would give us. It'd never be worth it, Ethel. You've got a lovely man in Ted. You don't know what it's like to have a man speak to you like Francis does to me. I ain't desperate enough to put up with that.'

'Well, least said, soonest mended. There's enough bin said already, I reckon,' said Ethel briskly. 'Let's make a pot of tea, and I'll be quiet while you go over your books. If all that writin' in your little book is anythin' to go by, you're thrivin'.'

Bridie, carrying David, who had watched the whole episode in silence, went down the dark little hall to the back room, and setting the child to play with an old pan and some wooden bricks, spread her elbows on the kitchen table. She was soon absorbed in rows of figures, and simple interest sums. Ethel sat sipping hot, sweet tea, and threaded cotton reels on to string to make a pullalong toy for David. The room was cosily busy.

I feel that comfortable with them two, it's like 'avin' another daughter, thought Ethel, looking at Bridie's bent head. I'm sorry on account of the little un, but fer meself, I'm glad she ain't going.

Chapter Seventeen

They were shelling peas in Ethel's kitchen when Susan made her announcement.

'I'm ever so sorry, Bridie,' she said, 'but I 'ad a message to go see that Mrs Anderson that lives over near St Dunstan's. They've got a big house near the vicarage, if you know the one I mean. Her husband's a businessman in the City, she told me. Anyway, she's expecting next month, and wants a nursery maid. She's offered it to me, and it's live-in and ever such good wages. So I said I would.'

Susan didn't say that it had been Angus Hamilton who'd recommended her, unaware of Bridie's dependence. After all, she said to herself when the question first came up, you have to take your chances in life, however they come up. And Mrs Anderson spoke to her so nice, she couldn't turn down an offer like that. All the same, she'd dreaded telling Bridie.

She needn't have worried. Bridie had noticed that Susan had been restless of late, and sympathised with her wanting to move away from home and Ethel once more.

'It's all right, Susan,' she said. 'Don't take on. I

expected it. It's been real kind of you to take David as long as you have. I don't take no offence.'

Susan broke into a happy smile. 'You really don't mind? I was worried to death about it.'

'Of course I mind,' said Bridie, 'but only because there's no one as good as you with David. He's known you since he was a new baby, and he'll miss you.'

'What'll you do?' asked Ethel.

'Look after him myself. Not much else I can do, is there?'

Angus would have been more than upset if he'd known.

The morning Bridie left him, Francis slept so long that in the end Mrs Goode panicked and asked Dr Hamilton if he'd step round to have a look at him. Angus had taken in the scene at a glance.

'What's happened?' he asked the housekeeper. 'He's drunk as a lord. That's not like Frank.'

Dora hesitated.

'Come now,' said Angus, 'you've called me in, so you'd better spill the beans as to why this house feels like a funeral parlour this afternoon.'

He folded his arms across his chest, and waited for an explanation.

'She's gone and left,' Dora said.

'Who's left? Bridie?' Angus sounded astonished. 'What do you mean?'

Dora's hauteur collapsed suddenly, and she sat down abruptly on a kitchen chair. 'Have a seat,

Doctor.' She waved at the chair at the end of the table.

'All right. From the beginning,' said Angus.

'I don't rightly know what's brought it to a head,' explained the housekeeper, 'but they've been very standoffish and silent with each other ever since Rosa was born.'

Angus nodded. 'I know that caused a great strain. But I hoped they'd come to terms with it and, not get over it, exactly, but at least put some of the bitterness behind them.'

'They wasn't very forgiving, either of 'em, if you ask me,' said Mrs Goode. 'Then this morning I come in, and there's Bridie packing her bag and putting David's coat on. She just said not to disturb Mr Holmes, and never said where she was going, just that she'd be off, and not to expect her back. She didn't look as if she'd slept a wink. I thought they must have had a to-do, and that she'd be back, but she never. I ain't seen her since. I feel all cut up about it, Doctor, I can tell you. And I'm worried about him.' She jerked her head at Francis.

Angus pulled one of Francis's eyelids up. 'Nothing there that aspirin and black coffee won't cure,' he said.

Francis, disturbed by the cursory examination, stirred and groaned.

'Hello, old chap,' said Angus heartily, as Francis painfully opened the same eye. Then the other one. He winced at the loud voice.

Angus grinned maliciously. 'Head hurt, does it?'

Francis raised a hand and cautiously touched his forehead. 'Oh my,' he muttered, 'it's agony.'

'You've indulged yourself rather freely, by the look of you,' said Angus. He saw the brandy bottle rolled under the chair and bent to pick it up. 'Aha! The best stuff. Seventy per cent proof. You'll be having a splendid hangover for a while yet.'

'Shhh,' begged Francis.

'Medication, please, Mrs Goode,' ordered Angus, ignoring the plea. While Dora went into the scullery to fill the kettle, Angus looked sternly at his wretched patient. 'What on earth brought this about?' he asked.

Francis started to shake his head, and his eyes glassed over.

'I'd keep rather still, if I were you,' said his medical adviser.

'She's left me,' Francis admitted in a low voice.

'Good Lord, has she really? Do you want to tell me what's happened?'

'No.' The one word had a bleak and final sound about it.

'Verra well,' conceded the doctor. 'It's not my business. But for her to take off, it must have been bad. She's a loyal little lassie, one of the best. You've lost a treasure, there, Frank.' He shook his head at his friend. 'And it's no good carrying on like this. If ye can't make it up, then at least accept it with a bit of dignity.'

'Make up?' asked Francis, holding his head. 'She said she was going for good.'

'Where?'

'She didn't say.'

'Well, man, ye've to find her, and maybe, if you ask her, she'll come back again.'

'Thank you for your advice,' said Francis as Mrs Goode came through the door, preceded by the fragrance of boiling coffee. Francis pulled a face as she clattered cups and saucers on to the table.

'And the doctor says these as well,' she said, putting two aspirin into Francis's shaky hand. He sipped cautiously at the scalding drink.

'That's getting better, though my head still goes round.'

'Aye, it will for a while. Fresh air and some exercise when you feel fit enough. That's the best cure.'

Angus stood up to leave. 'I'd try to find her, and talk to her,' he repeated his counsel as he left the room.

So Francis asked Mrs Goode to make enquiries, and it was only a matter of hours before the news came down the prolific East End grapevine that Bridie was staying at Ethel's. The outcome of the advice was that Francis eventually found her that foggy, clammy afternoon, and returned, still alone, sourly reflecting that Angus didn't know as much about women as he liked to think.

Now Angus had put a spoke in her wheel for sure. Bridie gave the matter some thought, then asked Susan a favour.

'Could you nip over and get David's carriage?' she asked the nurserymaid. 'Mrs Goode will let you in, I'm sure. And they've no use for it. There's not much space for it here, but we'll just have to manage.'

She obliged, and was eagerly offered tea by the housekeeper, all agog for news. 'She sends her regards,' Susan said on her return, 'and says to tell you she misses you an' David.'

'I miss her, too,' said Bridie absently. She was examining the inside of the carriage. 'It's a little dusty, but it'll do the trick nicely. With some blankets and a cushion, he'll be able to sleep even though it'll be a bit small.'

She turned to Susan. 'I'll look after him meself. We'll go round together. It's good quality, not hard to push, and it won't likely do him no harm to be out in the air. Not so good when it's foggy or pourin' with rain, but we'll cross them bridges when we come to them.'

And so Susan went off the following week to Mrs Anderson, and, bundling an excited David into the baby carriage, Bridie left Ethel's house at seven in the morning, moneybelt full and paperwork tucked down at the end of the carriage, by the child's feet.

'Off we go to work,' chirruped Bridie cheerily as she began to push. David clapped his hands, and looked over the side at the uneven cobbled street.

'Off we go, off we go,' the high little voice sang back.

Bridie's back ached after an hour or two, but having David with her gave an unexpected turn to her doorstep negotiations.

'That your son?' asked one housewife after another.

Bridie said he was her son.

'Well, I never!' was the general response. Her regular customers smiled benignly at the carriage, and seemed rather pleased that the moneylender had a child. The slums of Plaistow, which made up Bridie's business territory for the most part, were sufficiently removed from Tredegar Square, in every respect, for Bridie to go unremarked as anything other than the Irish woman what lent out at decent rates.

She took to hiding her hair, and so to some extent her youth, under a headscarf which she tied tightly under her chin and round the back of her neck. Men looked speculatively after her sometimes, but she had a no-nonsense way, and a ready tongue for them as got cheeky, so that for the most part they merely looked and gave her a wide berth. Women found her honest and straight. Not generous. She was never generous. If you couldn't pay, you was in trouble, and the interest promptly mounted up something alarming. But if she treated her clients with unsentimental manners, she treated 'em fair. They agreed on that.

So she became a familiar figure, pushing her carriage, trudging from door to door in a pair of black men's boots and long skirts in drab colours. Always the headscarf to disguise the glorious hair underneath, and deepening frown lines on her forehead as she wore down stub after stub of pencil, noting, lending, collecting, calculating. Weary, footsore, often soaked and chilled to the bone, Bridie went her rounds, month after month after month, until the months began to turn into years. Business flourished and David grew.

One spring morning, just after David's fourth birthday, Bridie was on her way to collect a debt that had been outstanding for too long. She was in a determined mood. The woman who owed the money made excuses. Bridie occasionally encountered bad debts, but her personal appearance on the doorstep, regular as clockwork, and the fact that she didn't lend more than she reckoned the borrower could afford, meant that usually her accounts balanced pretty well. David dawdled behind her. He'd found a bit of stick in the gutter, and was dragging it in the dirt to make patterns.

'Come along,' called his mother, leaning on the well-worn carriage. She hitched up her moneybelt which was so full, it sagged. Fridays were usually busy, with people needing more of everything because the men were at home all day of a Sunday.

David ignored her.

'Oh, come on, do,' she repeated. Leaving the carriage, she went back to get him. 'Come on, get in. I haven't got all day.' She picked up the child and popped him inside. As she pushed him, protesting, round the next corner, she came face to face with two men.

'Hello darlin',' said the bigger of the two. 'We bin waitin' fer you.'

Bridie looked from one to the other. 'What d'you want?' she demanded brusquely.

'That,' said the big man, pointing to the moneybelt.

Bridie glanced up and down the street. A few front doors stood open, and a dog rooted hopefully in a heap of rubbish fifty yards away. Otherwise it was empty.

'There's no one about,' sneered the smaller one, a fat creature with tattoos on the back of his pudgy hands.

'Let's be having it quick,' said the first one. He started to move towards her.

'Shove off! I'll have the law on you,' shouted Bridie, standing her ground.

'Aw, give it 'ere,' called Podge, following his partner nearer. He raised a clenched fist. 'Don't want yer nose broke, do yer, love?'

The taller, bearded thief glanced up and down the street. 'Cut the cackle,' he ordered. 'Take it off.'

'No,' said Bridie.

They moved in. One fist landed on her cheek, and the shaggy man's rough hands scrabbled at her clothes, trying to find the fastening to undo the belt. Bridie screamed with shock and fury. She lashed out ferociously with clawed fingers, and drew two long red scratches down Podge's face. He roared and stepped back, shaking his head. The tall man had an arm round her neck, trying to hold her still, while with his other hand he pulled clumsily at the belt.

'Give me an 'and,' he shouted at Podge, who was wiping blood off his cheek.

Bridie fought and twisted away from his grasp, and, feeling Podge coming at her a second time, made a last desperate effort. She jabbed the tall man viciously in the midriff with her elbow.

261

'Ouff!' he gasped. His face darkened with pain and rage as he let her go. 'You've asked for it, now, you bloody cow!' he snarled. He raised a huge fist. Bridie swung at him and her skirt swirled up round her knees with the force of the movement. The beard split open into a howl of agony as the steel toe of her man's boot dislodged his kneecap.

An incoherent string of obscenities rolled frantically off his tongue as he hopped, staggered and finally fell, rolling into the gutter.

Podge stood with his mouth open. 'Gawd!' he said finally.

The commotion brought people to their doorsteps. A row of faces up and down the street watched the progress of the fight with detached interest. No one would have dreamed of interfering.

' 'ere, you all right?' Podge asked his partner, voice querulous with fright. 'I'm off, or we'll 'ave the Law turnin' up.'

Bridie glared at him. 'I'll break *your* knees an' all, if I ever set eyes on you again. Push off, yer fat bastard.'

Podge fled.

Bridie went over to where the injured man sat holding his leg, tears running down into his whiskers. She drew back her foot. He let out a howl of terror.

'You bloody hellcat! Gerroff,' he yelled, shrinking from her in panic.

Bridie put her foot down again, slowly. 'You come near me again, an' I'll cripple you. You hear?'

He nodded, too agonised to speak.

She swung on her heel and, grabbing the carriage, wheeled a frightened and fascinated David in a defiant march straight up the middle of the street. On either side, people watched her.

'Be a while afore anyone tangles with her again,' they murmured to each other.

When Bridie had long disappeared in the direction of Stepney and her defaulting customer, Podge crept back to his cursing would-be partner in crime.

'You want an' 'and down the London?' he enquired.

'Took you bleedin' long enough to come an' ask, dinnit?' replied his friend ungraciously. He allowed Podge to haul him to his feet, and leaning heavily against the little man, he hobbled and scraped off down the street, cursing women at every excruciating step. He emerged some hours later from the Accident Department, knee in plaster and propped on a pair of wooden crutches.

Word soon got round that Bridie had put a bloke in plaster, and the fight was described in ever more dramatic and spectacular terms in public houses from the far end of Stratford to the other side of the Commercial Road.

Bridie herself had had to sit down when she got out of sight. Her legs simply gave way. David clamoured to be let out of the carriage, so she let him out, stick and all, to play in the gutter while she sat, head on her arms, and waited for the trembling and sick feeling to pass.

'It was strange,' she said, when peacable Ted,

intrigued, asked her if the rumours were true, 'I never even hit anyone before, but when they threatened me, I was so scared, and so furious, that I'd have done anything to stop them. They might have hurt David an' all. It was like I was another person, I was that mad.'

It was several days later that another man stopped her in the street and said he had a message for her.

'Sam Saul told me to tell you he wants to see you.'

'What for?' asked Bridie.

'I dunno. Business between you an' him, I suppose.'

'I don't have business with Sam Saul,' she said.

'If you've any sense, you'll not ignore him,' said the man. 'I'd not cross Sam if I was you.'

'Ta, anyway,' said Bridie. It wasn't wholly unexpected. Her business was doing well, and she guessed she must be having some effect on the loansharks whose territory she worked.

'Tell Sam Friday afternoon, I'll stop by and see him then.'

'Righto,' said the messenger agreeably. 'Friday. I'll tell him.'

Friday came. It was nearly midsummer. Bridie asked Ethel if she'd mind her taking down the tin bath early and having a good scrub. Ethel helped heat the water, then stood guard in case of anyone dropping in. Bridie washed and dried and brushed her hair until it shone. Working out of doors had turned her naturally pale complexion a dusky, glowing rose. She presented herself to Ethel and said, 'What d'you think?'

Ethel turned her round and said, 'Very nice. You'll bowl 'im over.'

Bridie laughed. 'That's just what I mean to do.'

She'd exchanged her steel-tipped boots for fashion-ably heeled leather shoes. Her bare ankles were slen-der and her hips in the low-waisted yellow dress were slim. Constant exercise had fined her down, and from the chrysalis of the dowdy workaday drudge emerged an elegant, confident woman. Only her hands betrayed her. Surveying her broken nails and the stains from ceaseless handling of coins, she sighed. Rubbing glycerine in, to soften them, she had to concede that they were no lady's hands.

'Ah, well,' she remarked to Ethel. 'Sam will prob-ably see them as signs of success. All that money they've handled!' she gave a mock leer and rubbed her fingers together greedily.

'You be careful with that Sam Saul,' cautioned Ethel.

Bridie grinned in reply. 'Got a reputation, ain't he?'

'Yes. And not just for meanness, neither. You watch your step there.'

Bridie twirled an ankle, kissed David goodbye and said, 'Be good for Ethel, now.'

Out on the street, men stared. She walked carefully in the unaccustomed heels, head down against the appraising looks. It took her almost an hour to walk across to Stepney, to the corner shop above which she saw the familiar boarded and wired windows of the loanshark's offices. She sniffed derisively. They were hated, the big boys, and went in fear of their lives, avoiding ever setting foot in the back streets where there wasn't a soul what wouldn't look the other way if one of them them was to be found in the gutter. They'd be left there for dead. She found the door round the back, barred and bolted, with a small steel grille in the top. She pushed the bell and waited. The grille squeaked as it was pulled back, and a woman peered out.

'Yes?'

'I've got an appointment,' said Bridie. 'Mrs O'Neill.'

The grille squeaked shut and moments later the door was pulled half open. The woman gestured her in. 'Hurry up.' she said, anxious to throw the bolts again, just in case.

Bridie climbed the narrow stairs behind the woman's fat, tired legs. A small anteroom held several filing cabinets and a desk with a huge diary open on top. It was covered in tiny, regular handwriting, and down each page, at the edge, ran columns of figures. The woman saw Bridie glance at it, and hurried round the desk to close the book.

'Ain't your business,' she said, rheumy eyes staring up at Bridie. A door behind her swung open.

'Mrs Holmes? Come in.'

The man who stood smiling in the doorway was so tall his head brushed the door jamb. He had beautifully groomed glossy black hair, and a neatly trimmed beard. Elegant eyebrows rose as his black eyes took in every detail of the woman standing before him. They widened appreciatively. Handsome, rich and suave, he was used to drawing attention from women, but this one was unusual. An expensive education had removed all but a trace of his Yiddish accent.

'Come in, Mrs Holmes,' he repeated.

Bridie walked round the desk under the hostile stare of the receptionist and followed Sam Saul's gesture to the chair beneath the window, to the side of his desk. There were more filing cabinets, tops were piled high with ledgers. Gaslamps burned at each end of the narrow room, as the windows let in only a suggestion of light. Bridie felt it was a place where it might get hard to breathe.

'You asked for me to come and see you,' she opened the conversation. 'Why did you do that?'

Sam Saul spread his hands. 'We are in the same business, and it has come to my attention that you are proving remarkably successful. I like success, and I wanted to meet you.'

'I get by,' acknowledged Bridie.

'You more than get by, I think,' replied Sam. 'According to my accounts you are doing much better than that.'

'I make a small profit.'

'Mrs Holmes, let us not beat about the bush. You are proving a little expensive to my own operations. You have encroached on the small loans market, and you have done it so successfully that you are affecting my profits. I have asked you here to discuss what we might do to remedy the situation.'

Bridie smiled sweetly. 'You run a real big empire. How can someone like me affect you?'

'I have just told you. You are taking my customers.'

'We all have to earn a living, Mr Saul.'

'Sam.'

'We all have to work, Sam.'

'I work for profit, Mrs Holmes, and you are taking some that rightly belongs to me.'

'Well, what do you want, then?'

Sam Saul hesitated. When he'd sent for her, he'd seen her in the distance a couple of times, and had remembered with indifference a drab figure in large men's boots. Now she was in front of him, he felt far from indifferent. He admired the combination of beauty, toughness and high spirits. It appealed to a man who was himself ruthlessly greedy under the smooth, urbane manner. He contemplated her through half-closed eyes, wondering how much she'd give.

'Is it true you broke a man's knee?' he asked at last.

'He attacked me. I kicked him. I never meant to hurt him bad.'

He looked at the slim figure, and shook his head wonderingly. 'You are a very determined lady, Mrs Holmes. Or may I call you Bridie?'

'You've been checking up on me, haven't you?' she asked calmly.

'Well, I was curious,' he admitted.

'Then you know I've got what you might call connections.'

'That is true,' he agreed. 'One might say you are not entirely what you seem.'

Bridie crossed her legs, and Sam's eyes followed the movement. 'How about a partnership?' she suggested bluntly.

Sam felt the interview beginning to slip away from him. *He* was supposed to be doing the bargaining. *He'd* called *her*. He was the aggrieved party. He gazed at her, surprised and discomfited.

Bridie crossed her legs again, and her skirt slipped accidentally over her knees. She straightened it. Sam, mesmerised, cleared his throat.

'A partnership? What sort?'

The grey eyes looked straight into his. 'You'll fund me for larger deals. Not often, because I don't get much call for that kind of money. But I'd like to be able to if I want. And at a quarter the rates you charge. In return I'll pay you a percentage on my everyday business of one quarter of one per cent.'

Sam threw back his head and roared with laughter. Bridie folded her hands in her lap demurely. 'You mean it?' Sam stopped laughing.

'Yes.'

'Many deals like that, and I'd be out of business.'

'A deal like that, and we can both stay in business and help each other.' Bridie's voice was amiable.

'Whatever makes you think I need help?' Sam spoke in astonishment.

'You can't just run me off the streets,' said Bridie composedly, 'because if you tried I'd have the law on you. I ain't ignorant. I listen to a lot of people in a lot of places, and I hear things, Sam Saul, that could put you in prison.'

His mouth went grim. 'You trying to blackmail me?'

'Isn't that what you called me here to do?' retorted

Bridie. She rose from her chair and, walking elegantly across the room, perched herself on the edge of his desk. He found he couldn't think straight.

'So I thought a deal that made it easier for both of us?' she suggested.

His black eyes stared unwaveringly back at her. This close, he could see all the tiny freckles on her nose.

For the first time in his life, Sam Saul gave in. 'You got a deal,' he agreed. What he wouldn't do to have this woman! Reading his mind precisely, Bridie slipped off the desk.

'That's that, then,' she said briskly.

'I'll have to see you again, go over details. Paperwork,' he said quickly.

She nodded. 'You know where I live. You're welcome to stop by and we can go over it.'

She watched him struggle with his feelings. He lost.

'Very well.' He pushed himself out of his chair, hands on his desk.

'I'll see myself out,' she said, opening the door to the tiny outer office. 'If this lady will kindly unlock the front door.'

Sam waved a hand at the receptionist, defeated. 'Go ahead,' he said. 'Whatever you like.'

It was a meeting he never forgot. Bridie giggled herself almost into hysterics, so that she tottered in her heels and had to take them off, walking barefoot on the baked earth at the road's edge, laughing out loud to the amazement of passers by.

Chapter Eighteen

Ethel gave a cry of delight and waved a sheet of notepaper at Bridie.

'He's comin' home,' she declared happily. 'Our Edward's got leave.'

'When?' asked Bridie.

Ethel consulted the letter again. 'He says he'll be docked at Portsmouth from the first week in September. Ooh, that's not long, is it? It's only another ten days. And they're stopping for six weeks. Ooh, ain't it lovely.'

Bridie agreed it was, but it gave her something to think about. She'd paid Ethel extra and had Susan's room for David, except for when Susan came home for a rare night away from the Anderson nursery. Edward would no doubt want his room back, and it would make for a very squashed household, especially if Ethel's son was built on the same scale as his mum.

Pushing the carriage round dried-up pot-holes, while David chased pigeons, Bridie decided that she'd have to move. Sam Saul had been right. She was doing well, and the profits in the heavy steel box under her bed were mounting. She could, if she was careful, afford a place of her own. But it meant moving out of Ethel's friendly, homely house, and she loved it there. She'd been in two minds about it for a long time, but now, with Edward coming back, it seemed she would have to get on with it and take a decision.

That Saturday she hung up her working clothes and put on the same silky yellow frock she'd worn to go and see Sam Saul. The sun was warm on her bare arms as she went down the High Street in Plaistow, studying the advertisements in agents' windows. Reaching the end of the parade of shops, she turned back and resolutely opened the first one's door. The woman inside was kind, and went through her property list for Bridie, but there was nothing in the right place, at the right rent.

'Sorry, dearie,' she said affably. 'You could come and try again next week.'

Bridie smiled and nodded and went out of the gloom into the brilliant sunshine. She screwed her eyes up against the glare, and saw the next agents a little further up. The man in there was helpful, too.

'I tell you what,' he suggested, when he'd listened to what she wanted, 'there's something a bit different that might interest you. Depends how you feel about graves.' He grinned.

Bridie raised her eyebrows.

'Corner of Hermit and Grange Roads. On the corner by the entrance to the Cemetery. There's an end of terrace house. It's standard – two up, two down, privy outside. It's goin' a bit cheap on account of being so close to the graveyard. Lot of funerals, you see. Some people mind.'

'How much?' asked Bridie.

'Well,' drawled the young man, 'round there you'd expect to pay ten shillin' a week, but for you, this one's nine and six.'

Bridie was silent. A house of her own. Alone for the first time in her life. What a wonderful idea!

'Can I go and see it?' she asked.

' 'course,' nodded the agent. He fetched his hat and together they walked the length of Upper Street, and down to the huge graveyard gates.

'Get a good view of all the best buryin's,' joked the agent, as they turned into the weedy little front garden. Two upstairs windows and one by the front door, all peeling brown paint. Bridie could smell the soot on the bricks. The agent went round the side and unlocked the back door. Inside was as unprepossessing as outside. Peeling green and brown walls flanked a range thick with cold, dirt-encrusted grease. Nothing had been cleaned, ever. Bridie went into the front room. Dark, as well as filthy, because the windows let in only smeary grey light.

'You expecting nine and six for this?' she demanded sarcastically. 'Pigs might fly! It's gloomy as the grave in here, never mind over the way.'

She didn't say anything about the view out of the back bedroom, straight into the leafy branches of a great old apple tree standing in waist-deep grass.

'Well,' said the agent hopefully, 'an adjustment might be possible. It does need a bit of paint. Not,' he added hastily, 'as there's anything wrong with the structure. Sound as a bell.'

Bridie stared at him derisively until his eyes dropped.

'Six shillin'?' she offered.

'Not a chance. You'll lose me my job,' retorted the young man.

Bridie wandered to the grimy window and looked round. She had a vision. Fresh brown paint on the walls, the range scoured and blackleaded 'til it shone, reflecting its own cosy glow of an evening. Cotton curtains at windows polished bright, two big armchairs, a box of knitting by the hearth. . . .

'You interested or what?' demanded the agent, getting impatient.

'Seven and six.' Bridie spoke in her take-it-or-leave-it voice.

'Oh, all right. Good thing I don't get many of you.' He hid his relief. The place had been on the books ages.

'I'll come back with you and pay the rent in advance now,' said Bridie, making up her mind on the spot.

'Won't your old man want to see it first?' enquired the agent cautiously.

'It's for me,' said Bridie. 'And my son.'

'Oh.' The man was taken aback. 'We don't usually rent to ladies, it's generally their husbands.'

'Rent's rent, and if it's paid regular what's it matter to you?' asked Bridie defiantly.

The man shrugged. He'd noted the wedding ring. War widow? He eyed her doubtfully.

'Don't be daft. Take the rent, and be glad you've let this stinking place.'

He saw her half-smile, and knew he was beaten. 'Go on, then, we'll say no more. Rent's two weeks in advance, Tuesdays,' he grumbled.

He chatted amiably all the way back, but Bridie listened with less than half an ear. She was planning her decorating campaign.

Bridie broke the news to Ethel when she came in from shopping. Ethel dumped her string bag crossly on the table and said: 'What for? Why do you want to move out?'

'It's not that,' Bridie explained, 'but with Edward home, you and Ted need the room. Don't take offence, Ethel love. Living here, it's been like having a second mum, and I'll miss you. It's time for a change, that's all.'

Ethel was upset, though, there was no pretending she wasn't.

'All right ducks,' she said at last, 'it's not far anyway if it's this end of the cemetery.'

'Ten minutes if you dawdle, five if you hurry,' said Bridie. That didn't sound so bad. 'It's in an 'orrible state, Eth. It needs cleaning and painting before it's fit for man or beast to move into.'

'I'll be glad to lend a hand,' cried Ethel, as Bridie had hoped she would, 'and Ted'll come an' all. He's handy and willing when he's not dozy.' She laughed and pinched Bridie's cheek.

That weekend, a small crocodile made its way to Hermit Road. Bridie led the way, followed by Ethel,

Ted, Lizzie and Jonathan – like Snow White and her Dwarves. They carried buckets and pails, brushes and brooms, rags and scouring powder, polish, paint and blacklead for the range. Jonathan had borrowed a pair of stepladders from the porters at Bart's, swearing to have them back in their cupboard by Monday morning. David carried the picnic. Food, Lizzie said, for the workers. Herself expecting, she said she wouldn't do the strenuous stuff, but would look after David.

Bridie stood aside to let Lizzie go in first. She stood looking round with the practised eye of a housewife.

'It's pretty,' she cried. 'Underneath all that muck, it's lovely. What a find. You have been lucky.'

Ethel, still smarting from Bridie's desertion, conceded that it would be a dear little house, looked after proper.

Jonathan and Ted exchanged meaningful looks. Women! They rolled up their sleeves, wrapped themselves in old aprons it wouldn't matter if they ruined, and settled down to stripping old paint and paper. Bridie drew a bucket of cold water and started on the horrid job of cleaning the range. Ethel began on the windows. Seeing everyone busy, Lizzie took David out into the garden at the back.

He gave a whoop of joy and raced into the jungle that flourished between the back wall of the house and the broken wooden fence some eighty yards away. Brambles, thistles and columbine grew densely among the tall grasses. A prickly thicket of gooseberry bushes made an impenetrable wall down one side. The apple tree was covered in tiny green fruit that would ripen and fall in the autumn. David found a stick and sent thistle fairies spinning in the air. Lizzie sneezed and brushed seeds from her skirt. A movement under the gooseberries caught her eye.

'What's this, David?' she called to the little boy.

He stopped decapitating plants and came to look. Hidden in the undergrowth was a nest. Safe beneath the prickles a mother cat bared her teeth uneasily at them. Curled by her side were two very tiny, new kittens. David put out his hand and the cat snarled.

'Careful! Don't touch her, she's quite wild,' warned Lizzie. 'She's worried you might touch her kittens, and so she might bite if you went too near.'

David looked solemnly at the mother cat, who stared back with unblinking green eyes. One of the babies stretched and David saw the tiniest red mouth yawn wide with contentment, then close with a little snap.

'Ooh, babies,' he said, awed. He sat on his haunches, keeping quite still, and watched.

'Would you like to give her some milk?' asked Lizzie. 'The mother might like some, and we can put it in a saucer just a little way away, so she doesn't get frightened.'

'Yes, let's,' said David, jumping up eagerly. They fetched a bottle of milk from the picnic basket, and one of Ethel's saucers.

'Do you want to pour it?' asked Lizzie. 'Carefully, now.'

Carefully, the tip of his tongue sticking out as he

concentrated, David poured milk into the saucer and pushed it towards the cat. She stiffened and nudged at her kittens to get behind her, then the smell of milk tempted her. She crept forward until she could lap at the edge of the saucer, and the milk disappeared in no time.

'Shall I get her some more?' asked David.

'Later on,' said Lizzie. 'Wait until she gets thirsty again or the milk will go off in the sun.'

'Babies like milk,' remarked David.

'They get their milk from their mother, like you did when you were a baby,' said Lizzie.

David put his hand carefully on Lizzie's big belly. 'This one too?' he asked.

Lizzie smiled down at his serious little face. 'Yes, my baby, too. Let's go and see how they're getting on indoors.'

The house was a hive of activity. Damp, mouldy paper lay in drifts on the floors. Ted was scrubbing down paintwork. He paused and looked over at Jonathan. 'Fancy a beer, mate?'

Jonathan grinned and nodded. 'Lizzie, love, what about taking David down to the pub, and fetching us a jug of ale?'

Lizzie took a shilling from Jonathan's shirt and she and David walked hand-in-hand to the nearest public house. She told the landlord they were just moving in, so he lent her a jug with a lid on it, to carry the ale.

'Hungry?' she called, unpacking the picnic basket. One by one they put down their tools, rinsed their hands under the tap and sat down, leaning against the walls, munching bread, cheese and Ethel's home-made mustard pickle.

'There's kittens in the garden,' announced David with his mouth full. 'Me and Lizzie saw them.'

'How many?' asked Ted.

'Two,' said David. 'And mother cat.'

'We gave her some milk. If you feed her regularly, she might tame,' said Lizzie.

David jumped up. 'I'll show you.' He pulled at Bridie's hand.

Outside, he pointed. 'There,' Bridie squatted down and peered into the prickles. The mother had retreated a little further back, but the two little ones were there to be seen.

'Oh, tabbies,' said Bridie. 'They'll be pretty later on.' She pulled herself upright. 'Come on, we've lots more work to do. Will you help Lizzie put the food away?' David nodded and trotted back inside.

Ted and Jonathan made heavy footsteps overhead. They'd made a start on the bedrooms. Every window was thrown wide. Loose plaster and dust hung in the air. Lizzie took a broom and began to tidy damp wall-paper into heaps. She and Ethel carried armfuls down to the end of the garden, where it could be burned later.

'She's got a job and a half on her hands,' observed Ethel, looking round.

'She'll do all right,' replied Lizzie. 'I bet you don't recognise this place in a few months' time.'

They kept going until the light faded so that indoors

you couldn't see your own hand. Ted reported the bedrooms ready for painting, and they all exclaimed over the miracle cold water and determination had wrought on the range.

'It's not that bad, actually,' said Jonathan to Bridie. 'I must say that at first I wondered what you'd got yourself into, but really it's just dirt and neglect. The house itself seems sound. I've kept an eye open for rot and what have you, but I haven't found any.'

Lizzie heaved a sigh of relief. It really was all right. Bridie grinned from ear to ear. She'd never doubted.

The tired little crocodile wound its way back to Ethel's house, where all the tools were laid ready for the next day. Lizzie and Jonathan called goodbye and goodnight from the darkness as they went home.

At first light, Bridie was up and ready, chivvying the others as they grumbled and groaned. Back in Hermit Road by six, the other two joined them at nine o'clock and the small house resounded once more to the banging and scraping and sweeping.

Late that evening six very tired people and one sleepy child looked round in triumph. Fresh flowered paper hung on walls, paint glistened in the gloom as it began to dry and the smell was thick on the air. Windows shone, letting moonlight fall on bare, scrubbed boards and gleam dully on the blackleaded range in the kitchen. Bridie's home was ready. Ethel stood, arms akimbo, surveying the scene in the dark.

'Ready when you are,' she announced to Bridie. 'We done a good job here. We should be proud of ourselves.'

Bridie hugged her, wet apron and all. 'I couldn't have done any of it without you.' She kept her arms tight around Ethel. 'Thank you,' she said, to everyone.

On Monday morning, Bridie was out first thing, round the second-hand furniture shops. A lot came from the pawnbroker, too. When she added sheets and blankets to her great heap of goods, he blessed this as his lucky day and offered her a cup of tea. Young lads came and went up the weedy front path, humping chairs and beds and carpets, cooking things and curtains, while the neighbours stared and Next Door offered tea and a piece of cake in the afternoon. The coal merchant arrived to fill the bunker at the back, and Bridie was just putting a match to the range for the first time when Ethel turned up with David in tow. She dumped a suitcase by the front door.

'That's the last of your things,' she told Bridie, who was blowing on her fire to help it catch. She wandered into the front room and saw how homely it looked. Bridie had filled a milk bottle with wildflowers from her garden and it stood before the still-drying front window, on the newly delivered oak table.

'It's lovely,' she said to Bridie, who was still trying to get the range to go. Bridie stood up at last and said she thought she'd got it going and could make tea later. The two women stood together, listening to David run around upstairs.

'It'll be good for him, you having a place of your own,' remarked Ethel generously.

'Yes,' said Bridie. 'I think it will.'

'I'd best be going along then. Let you get on.'

Bridie smiled at her. 'I'll see you every day,' she said. 'You'll hardly notice the difference.'

Ethel nodded. Then she was gone.

Late that night, as David slept in his own bed and Bridie leaned on her bedroom windowsill, she gazed at the dark shape of the apple tree, so close she could almost reach out and touch the tips of its branches. Below, in her tangled territory of gooseberries, two golden eyes stared up at the head in the window. The cat's nose snuffled and twitched at new scents on the cooling night air. People had come to stay.

Chapter Nineteen

Ethel's broad face beamed with joy as she threw her arms round Edward's broad shoulders and gave him a great big smacker, right on the mouth.

' 'ere,' she cried, holding him away from her, 'let's be lookin' at you.'

She surveyed her bearlike son from top to toe. He stood still tolerantly while she exclaimed that she thought he might, just might have got even taller since last time. He nodded good-naturedly, both of them knowing that at twenty-six he wasn't going to change much in either direction. They were so alike, mother and son. Both were tall, broad, with big, kindly features. Edward's nose was blunt and wide, just like Ethel's. But where she had brown eyes, Edward had inherited Ted's, bright blue and humorous. They lifted his features from being plain to almost handsome. The mouth, so ready to smile, grinned now at his mother.

'Come on, Mum, it's only me.'

'Only, indeed,' protested Ethel. 'You hear that, Ted? After all this time away, he says only me!'

Ted gazed at his son affectionately. He was proud

283

of him, standing so straight, in his blue and white uniform, on the dockside at Portsmouth.

'Come on, Eth, put him down, 'e's a big lad now,' he advised mildly.

The three of them walked slowly across the cobbles, under the shadow of the great ship that towered above them. Around them, groups of young seamen loitered, canvas bags at their feet. Mothers and fathers, sisters and brothers, gave little shrieks of delight, and everywhere there was a hugging and a kissing and a few tears wiped away on the edges of sleeves. Young wives handed bemused children into their father's stranger's arms, and older children stood aside and stared. Officers in white and gold watched from the rail high above. Two policemen sauntered past, nodding affably at the sailors.

Edward pushed his mother gently away and picked up his bag. 'Come on Mum, Dad. I've been looking forward to being home for weeks, an' all you can do is stand and stare.' He put a beefy arm round Ted's shoulders, and hoisted his bag over his own shoulder. 'Let's go.'

During the train journey back to Waterloo they chattered eagerly about his months at sea, about Susan, about Ted's promotion to foreman at Billingsgate, about this and that, and how they'd had a lodger who they'd been ever so fond of, but she'd moved out to a place of her own near the Cemetery, just in nice time for him to come home.

Edward listened to their excited voices, and the wonderful warmth of them flowed over him. His rolling stride began to quicken as they got off the tram. Within a few yards of their door, it flew open and Susan came running down the road to throw herself at Edward, who dropped his bag and caught her, swinging her round so her dress flew up and her shoes were two feet off the ground.

'Mrs Anderson said I could have the afternoon off,' she gasped, answering her mother's unspoken question. 'So here I am. Welcome home.'

She tucked her arm into her brother's, asking teasingly what he'd brought back for her this time as she led him into the house. Ethel went to put on the kettle, and there was a hubbub of voices in the small back room as they all talked at once. Edward, trying to answer a dozen questions, fished at the same time in the top of his bag for the presents that always came out to 'Oohs' and 'Aahs' of excitement and curiosity. Susan unwrapped a tiny twist of paper and found in the palm of her hand a small, pale heap of gold – a delicately engraved head of a sun god with crooked rays depicting sunlight instead of hair. There was a fine gold chain from which to hang the figure. 'I got that in Thailand,' said Edward. 'I thought it would look pretty on you.'

She held it up against her neck. 'Oh, it's beautiful. Put it on for me.' His huge hands opened and closed the tiny clasp with delicate care. 'I'll wear it always, it's so lovely,' she said, bright-eyed with delight.

For Ethel there was a shawl of Indian cotton, brilliant colours for a summer day. Ted fingered a pair of Turkish slippers, intrigued but doubtful that he'd ever quite put them on his feet. They were of soft leather, sewn with fine thread and embroidered with layers of intricate stitching.

Edward, seeing his face, laughed. 'They actually wear those in Turkey, Dad. And fezzes with tassels, and great baggy trousers. The women are veiled, and all in black robes. You can only see their eyes. It's all another world.' He shook his head. 'Things you see out there, you wouldn't believe.' There was a knock at the front door.

'See who that is, Ted,' Ethel called, busying herself with the teapot in the scullery.

They heard Ted's voice say, 'Come on in, love.' Footsteps across the front room, and Bridie appeared in the backroom doorway with David in front of her. Edward looked up from delving in his bag for more goodies, and stopped.

The girl in the doorway was the one in his dream. It came repeatedly when he was far away at the other end of the world. When he turned restlessly, hot and sweaty in tropical nights, as the ship rolled under him and cramped, sleeping men muttered and grunted around him, Edward would have a dream. It was always the same. A lovely, fiery-haired girl called him from across a river but as he waded in to go to her, the riverbed sloped steeply. Water rose over his head and turned to ice. It froze him, trapping and cutting with cruel spikes and shards, until pain woke him and he'd lie still until, as always, he dreamed again.

This time, his soul floated high above a frozen river, looking down at his body, trapped in ice. Light filled the air. A hand in his pulled up and up and up, until the earth was left far beneath them. In every dream, he turned to find the glowing face of the girl by the river, who led him ever higher. The dream ended as the earth became a pin-point in the infinite blackness of space. Gripped by panic he strove to keep the earth in sight, to make it out from all the myriad stars that filled his vision, and he'd wake again, trembling, afraid of something nameless in the darkness. The nights he dreamed those dreams, he always slept like the dead afterwards, no matter what the rolling of the ship, nor the human sounds around him.

He realised that everyone was staring at him as he sat, wide-eyed, gazing at Bridie. He lowered his head and fumbled in his bag, shaking off the peculiar sensation of something seen before.

'Meet Bridie,' said Ethel, drying her hands on her apron as she came from the scullery. 'She's bin renting your room while you was away, like we told you.'

Edward stood up and held out a hand. 'Pleased to meet you.'

He wondered if she felt like him, that this was not the first time they'd met. Her hand felt long familiar, as a mother's hand to a child. He looked at her face, curious to see if she gave any sign. Then Ted started pulling out the table, and gave Edward the knives to lay, and Ethel brought in a steaming teapot followed by plate after plate of sandwiches, biscuits and cakes until they laughingly protested that they'd never be able to eat another bite after this.

The homecoming lengthened into drowsiness. Edward told stories of far-off people and places, funny tales about his shipmates until, tired by excitement and laughter, the pauses became longer and longer and Ethel began to brush crumbs into a pile on the table-cloth.

'I'll be clearing away,' she announced. 'No, you've got David,' she added to Bridie's offer of doing the washing up.

The little party began to break up. Bridie and David kissed Ethel goodbye in the scullery, and calling goodnights to all, made their way home. Bridie put David to bed and, taking a shiny new pair of shears she'd got down at the ironmonger's, went out in the garden. Kneeling on an old mat, she began to cut the long grass in tall swathes. The cat watched indignantly while her protective wall of grass and weeds fell away. Bridie put the shears down and fetched a drop of milk to soothe her.

By the time her arms began to ache, more than half the garden was just rough stubble. Ruefully inspecting the red patches on her hands that would be blisters tomorrow, Bridie started to plan her garden: phlox and hollyhocks, roses and marigolds. At the bottom a small vegetable patch. String beans fresh from the poles in early summer. Transplant the raspberry canes, and prune the gooseberries. Here was something that Ireland had taught her, gardening and growing things. The ironmonger had racks of seeds outside.

She wiped the green stains off the blades of the

shears and stored them up on a nail in the scullery, where David couldn't reach them. And all the time, at the very back of her mind, she wondered about Edward.

He took to popping round to see Bridie of an evening. Ethel noticed, and was pleased. In fact a good deal of his time he was over in Bridie's direction on one pretext or another. When David was tucked up in bed, they'd work in the garden together, sometimes talking, sometimes not. He found Bridie cutting the undergrowth at the far end of her patch one evening, and offered to help. It had become a delightful habit, to plan and potter together. He brought over Ted's spade and fork, and began on the vegetable patch.

'It needs leaving, turned over, all winter. Then the frost breaks the clay and it gets the air to it, and it's easier to break up fine in the spring,' explained Bridie, when they were wondering which jobs to do first.

Sometimes Ethel and Ted strolled over, after Ted had had his supper. He brought her a wooden box of wallflowers.

'Put them in now, and you'll have blooms next year, love,' he told her.

Bridie collected windfall apples, and they ate sour applecake, sitting on a rug on the shorn grass. September passed, fine and dry. October began golden, but went rapidly downhill into autumnal damp. The day came for Edward to rejoin his ship.

The morning he was to leave was soft and drizzly. Tiny droplets of mist clung to the thick serge of his uniform and shone on his hair as they all stood to bid him farewell on the station platform. Ethel pretended she wasn't crying. David hung round his knees, begging to go too. Edward, tall enough to look over his mother's head at Bridie, smiled. Susan clung on his other arm and blew her nose loudly.

'Would you mind if I wrote to you sometimes?' he asked Bridie across the tearful women. She smiled back.

'No, I'd like that.'

He grinned broadly. 'I will, then. You'll hear from me. And you, nipper,' he said to David, ruffling his hair.

Bridie watched him kiss his family one last time, then, saluting her solemnly with his blue eyes steady on hers, he turned and hefted his bag across his shoulders and climbed into the waiting train. For a while he disappeared, then they saw him, one face in a long line, all pressed against windows and hanging out above closed doors. A forest of hands waved and waved. The train rounded the far end of the platform and drew slowly out of sight. The disconsolate crowd of relatives and friends took one last look and trailed off the platform with lagging feet. Edward was gone.

Life returned to normal. Bridie continued to push the carriage, by now decrepit with bumping and humping round pot-holes and puddles and the onslaughts of bad weather. It really only served as a shelter these days. If David whined he could sit in it and doze with his head propped on a blanket against the side. Bridie was looking forward to the spring. David would be five years old then and she could enrol him in school. She was determined that he should have all the schooling she'd missed.

'I'm not having 'im do it the way I had to,' she told Lizzie firmly.

Lizzie felt her own baby turn in her belly, and agreed. She asked Bridie if she'd heard from Edward.

'No, not yet. Maybe he's changed his mind. When you get that far away, I expect your mind gets filled with other things.'

Bridie was busy, what with traipsing the streets and keeping up her accounts, but each day the absence of a letter was a small disappointment. Which made it all the more exciting when the postman knocked at the front door early one morning and delivered a small packet, all covered with brightly coloured foreign stamps. Bridie's name and address were printed in bold black ink on the brown cover.

'That looks interesting. Got a boyfriend?' remarked Bert the postman.

Bridie took the little parcel and turned it over. On the other side it had Edward's name, and the name of his ship, printed in much smaller letters.

'It's from a friend,' she said sharply, shutting the door on the postman's nosey look.

All day she kept the packet, unopened, in her skirt pocket. She could feel it as she did her rounds. Her doorstep transactions were not usually sociable. Often children would spot her coming, and run to call their mothers. They came to the doorstep, pennies in hand, and the exchange of money was brief. Occasionally someone would query the interest, or ask Bridie for more time to pay. She was invited to step inside the doorway only in the worst of weather, when the women themselves didn't want to shiver. She made no attempt to make friends. But this morning, her step was light and she had a pleasant word for her borrowers. When David fell in a puddle, despite being warned a dozen times, she merely picked him up and said, 'Silly child,' instead of pulling him up to his feet with a jerk and an angry smack on the bottom.

That evening she cooked their dinner of Irish stew, thick with mutton and potatoes and leeks, humming happily around the warmth of the range. When she'd set David to play on the floor with a box of picture books and some plywood puzzles, she pulled out her packet and opened it. Half a dozen letters fell out. Each had been carefully dated on the outside fold, so that she could sort them into order. She unfolded the first. Edward had written the week he left England. He started by explaining that he could only post letters when they went into port, so he'd write regularly, and post each voyage's letters together.

That explains it, thought Bridie, delighted that he should be thinking so much of her.

His letters were just like Edward. Full of lively descriptions of life on board, his fellow crew members, his success in his engineering training, and how he hoped to get promotion if all went well. Then there was a colourful account of a stop in Hong Kong before going due south into Malaya and then on into Indonesia.

Bridie sat with dreams in her eyes, seeing it all, the hustle and bustle, the queer smells and sights. She tasted salt spray on her lips, felt the glare in her eyes as the early morning sun rose red over the horizon, dazzling straight into the wheelhouse, making the skin prickle with sweat.

At the end of the last letter there was a box number and address for Bridie to write to, care of the Port of Singapore.

'We go south, through the South China Sea, calling at Brunei in Borneo, and then on to Malaya and Singapore,' he had written. 'Please do write, because I would so much like to hear from you. How is the nipper? Truly yours, Edward.'

Writing back was a business. Bridie went up to the High Street and came back with two packets each of pink envelopes and paper. She bought a fresh supply of black ink, like Edward's, and called on Lizzie, whose baby was due any moment. She came to open the door and, when she saw them, pulled a face.

'Come on in, if you don't mind me moaning and groaning. I feel so enormous I wish this baby would come, before my tum sags to my knees. I'm turning into a human elephant.'

She ruffled David's hair and kissed the top of his head. 'D'you want a biscuit?' she asked. 'If you do, they're in the tin on the dresser.'

While David ate fig rolls, Bridie and Lizzie talked

babies. When the topic was not exactly exhausted but thoroughly explored, Bridie said she wanted some help.

'What with?' asked Lizzie. 'I'll be upstairs with my legs in the air, having a baby any minute now, so it'd better be quick help.'

Bridie took a book out of her basket. 'I need to know how to use this,' she said. It was the Oxford English Dictionary.

'Righto. Come here and I'll show you.'

Together the two women pored over the blue bound volume, Lizzie turning pages, running her finger down the columns and columns of words. Long words, short words, a whole language that Bridie had never heard before.

'It's all a matter of the alphabet,' explained Lizzie. 'First letter, second letter, and so on. Look.'

She looked up several words, then asked Bridie to try for herself. After a false start and some embarrassment, Bridie got the hang of it. 'That's marvellous,' she cried. 'I can write proper now.'

Lizzie raised an inquisitive eyebrow.

'Oh, Edward's written me such lovely letters. They all came the other day, together in a bunch. I'm going to write back, but I wanted to do it right. So I got this.' She stroked the cover of the dictionary.

Lizzie clutched her swollen stomach and groaned. 'They keep coming, but I don't think I've really started yet. It's just those practice ones, you know?'

Bridie nodded. She certainly did.

'So the great Edward has written? That's nice. He's

one of this world's truly decent people, Bridie. You're lucky.'

Bridie shook her head. 'We're only friends,' she demurred.

'So?' demanded Lizzie. 'To have a friend like that is lucky, is what I meant. Why, you got something else in mind?'

Bridie flushed. 'No, not really. It's just that the letters were so . . . like they was to an old friend, like we'd known each other a long time.' She broke off, confused. 'Don't you start teasing, Lizzie Norris.'

Lizzie shifted uncomfortably and groaned again.

'Here!' cried Bridie. 'You sure you aren't on your way? Them pains seem pretty regular to me.' Lizzie's face stayed screwed up at least a minute, then she let her breath out again.

'You think this might be it?'

'Lizzie Norris, here's you supposed to be all educated and expert at people's bodies, and you don't even know if you're in labour! You get upstairs quick and into bed, and I'll run over for Mrs MacDonald. Where's Jonathan?'

'He's on duty. He might be home at five o'clock, he said, but he often doesn't get off when he's supposed to.'

'David, you stay there like a good boy. I'll be back in a tick,' said Bridie.

As Lizzie lumbered upstairs, stopping halfway to hold tight on to the banisters as another pain came and went, Bridie picked up her skirts and ran for the midwife. Mrs MacDonald took one look at her hot, panting face and reached for her shawl and bag. They hurried back, Bridie holding her hand to the stitch in her side while she explained that she reckoned Lizzie was well advanced in labour. They ran into the house, and before they were in the front door could hear Lizzie crying out upstairs. Mrs MacDonald ran up, while Bridie hastily put pans of water on the hob and opened the vent to make the fire roar in the range. She told David to stay in the back room and play, while she popped upstairs to see if she could help.

Lizzie, propped on pillows, was panting hard while Mrs MacDonald's voice called, 'Don't push, dearie, don't push.'

Lizzie turned despairing eyes on Bridie and moaned, 'I have to.'

'Go on then.'

Two minutes later Mrs MacDonald held up a very tiny baby boy for Lizzie's inspection.

'He's a small one, but he's fine. A grand little boy.' Mrs MacDonald asked Bridie to fetch up some water while she wrapped the new infant in a clean white shawl.

'He'll make a mess of the shawl, I'm afraid, but if you will leave everything until the last possible moment, young woman, you have to make do. I'll give him a little washover when Bridie fetches the warm water.'

Lizzie held out her arms eagerly for her baby, and let out another great groan.

'Goodness me,' observed the midwife, 'the afterbirth doesn't usually hurt much.'

'I want to push again,' gasped Lizzie, her face straining.

'Oh, my word.' cried Mrs MacDonald. She hastily put the baby boy into the crib standing ready by the bed, and ran back to Lizzie. A tiny head appeared. The midwife pushed Lizzie's legs apart, and said, 'There's another one. Push!'

In no time at all Lizzie's and Jonathan's daughter was born, yelling thinly and thrashing her arms.

'My word, she's goin' to be a madam, if she's started like she's going to go on,' remarked Mrs MacDonald. Both babies cried, and Lizzie too with joy and shock.

'Twins! Oh my word,' she said feebly to the midwife.

'And both fine babies,' said Mrs MacDonald reassuringly.

Bridie helped bathe the twins and their stunned mother, and into all the commotion walked Jonathan, who sat down very suddenly on the linen chest at the far side of the room when he looked at the two women, each busy with a different baby.

'Good God,' he said in a faint voice. 'It's twins.'

'No wonder you felt like an elephant,' remarked Bridie.

Lizzie laughed, hysteria not far away. 'Oh my word, yes,' she said.

A small hand pushed the bedroom door open, and David peeped round.

'Let him come in,' said Mrs MacDonald fondly. 'We're nearly done here.'

'I wondered where you were,' said David timidly. 'You didn't come back.'

'No, because I was helping Lizzie. Look, David, Lizzie's babies. She's got two new babies. Twins. Isn't that wonderful?'

David eyed the crumpled red faces dubiously. 'They'll cry,' he announced.

Lizzie laughed hollowly. 'I'm sure they will,' she murmured.

Tall Jonathan bent over the crib, with its two little bundles, who were defying David's prediction for the moment and not crying at all. 'Amazing,' he muttered to himself, and drew back the shawls slightly, to examine their faces and hands. 'Lizzie, you must look as soon as you can sit up. They're amazing. Like nothing you ever saw. You're so clever!'

Mrs MacDonald was bathing his wife's face and combing her hair. 'She'll be right as ninepence in a moment, Dr Norris, but she's ever so tired, and if you don't mind, I think she should sleep a while.'

As if in agreement, the twins' faces too relaxed into sleep and their father carefully put the shawls down. Bridie fetched another cover and laid it over the sleeping pair. 'Have to keep them warm, they're small,' she said to Jonathan.

'Yes.' He still gazed at them, unable to believe his eyes.

'Come on,' ordered Mrs MacDonald, 'downstairs, all of you.' She turned to Lizzie, pale and exhausted. 'You get your sleep now, my duck,' she said, 'and we'll be up again as soon as they wake.'

Downstairs Jonathan poured glasses of wine for all of them with a none too steady hand. 'Twins! Wait 'til my colleagues hear. There'll be no end of ribbing.'

'You don't sound like you mind,' said Bridie.

He shook his head in wonder. 'I'd never have guessed. Never entered my mind, nor Lizzie's as far as I know.'

Bridie drank down her wine, and rose to go.

'Bless you for your help,' said Jonathan, having been assured by the midwife that if she had arrived a moment later, things might have gone decidedly less well.

Bridie grinned. 'Congratulations,' she said, and kissed his cheek. 'You've got two lovely babies, though I've no doubt you've got some hard work ahead of you. I'll go and leave you in peace now.'

Mrs MacDonald gave David a resounding series of kisses and a mint humbug from her pocket. 'Come and see me soon,' she ordered. 'I don't see you half often enough.'

'We've been ever so busy, Mrs MacDonald. But we'll call round soon. Tell Lizzie from me to take care.'

As Bridie and David hurried round the end of the road, they could hear in the distance the shrill, demanding wailing of Lizzie's two tiny, hungry babies. Bridie shook her head and laughed into her hand.

'Oh, my,' she said to David,' 'what a turn-up for the books. Twins, indeed. Did you ever!'

It made the perfect first letter to Edward, first

written in pencil and checked with the dictionary. Then neatly copied in ink onto the pink paper. It ran to eight pages, the most Bridie had ever written in her life. She'd set it down so eagerly, and with such a sense of talking to Edward and hearing his deep chuckling voice answer, that it hadn't even seemed like hard work. She folded it in three, like he'd folded his, and tucked it into its envelope. Then she wrote the date on the outside. The 14th January 1926. The first letter.

Chapter Twenty

The time had come round for one of Sam Saul and Bridie's impromptu business meetings. Sam parked his elegant legs on Bridie's brass fender and considered the proposition she'd just put to him.

'How about a broader partnership?' he suggested, a wicked glint in his gleaming black eyes.

'Broader? With the likes of you? I wouldn't get mixed up with you,' Bridie retorted.

'My dear, you *are* one of the likes of me, you just have a different – ah – style. Why do you think I enjoy doing business with you if we are not, as you put it so delightfully . . . mixed up?'

'You know very well what I mean,' she said crossly.

'I know I'd heartily enjoy a partner such as yourself.' He flickered a glance at her to see how she responded. If only, he thought, he could dismiss her as common. But she was one of the most uncommon women he'd ever met, damn it! He looked at her again hopefully, hiding the expression under his eyebrows.

Bridie was getting nervous. This was the most direct proposition he'd made, although there had been plenty of hints and jokes.

'You hold your tongue,' she snapped at him. 'I'm a married woman, remember?'

He spread his hands apologetically.

'Forgive me. Your husband's presence being notable by its absence, I took liberties,' he pronounced pompously. Then he laughed aloud. 'Come on, Bridie, we're two of a kind, you and me. I know you. We could have a wonderful time together.'

'I 'spect your wife would like that,' she replied acidly.

'My wife is my business, and your husband is yours.'

'You're rotten right through, you know, Sam Saul? A real bastard.'

'So they say, my dear,' he said comfortably, 'but you see, it doesn't worry me in the least.'

'Well, it would worry me,' said Bridie firmly. 'I know we could have fun, but it would be the sort of fun that hurts other people, and would get us in the end, too. I don't care much for that kind of fun, Sam.'

He shrugged, disappointed.

'I'll do business with you, provided it's honest, but I'll not have the other, if you don't mind. I couldn't start anything like that.'

'Very well,' he said irritably. 'But don't you ever look round you and think "killjoy" to yourself? Don't you fancy any men after that aged husband of yours?'

His malice went too far. Bridie rose from her chair behind the table and her stack of papers and slapped his face hard. 'You talk like that again, and you won't set foot in this house again, ever.'

He rubbed his stinging cheek and glared back. 'All right, all right, keep your hair on,' he muttered resentfully. No other woman on earth would get away with it but her, and the more she turned him down, the stronger the fascination got. He swung his feet off the fender and reached over for a bit of paper.

'Let's get on with it,' he said with abrupt bad temper.

They discussed and agreed figures, and then returned to the proposition that had led to the argument in the first place.

'Why here? That's the obvious question. It's a crummy area, to be candid. You could do better somewhere else, say up towards Mile End, or even over in Hackney.'

' 'cos I don't fancy moving. An' this is where I work. An' there's Ethel easy to walk to. An' I live here already, an' I like it.' She ticked the reasons off on her fingers.

He shrugged again. Once she made her mind up about something, he was blowed if he could ever change it. He studied the calculations on the scrap of paper again.

'Next question. Why not go to the bank or a Friendly Society?'

'Don't be stupid, Sam. They wouldn't deal with me except I take Francis along, and I won't do that.'

Sam glanced at her in agreement. Banks wouldn't lend to a woman on her own. She was right.

'And because you'll charge me two per cent and the

bank will be nearer four. So will the Society charge me four, only they won't lend me, neither.'

He suddenly lost his cool manner. 'What?' he shouted, unable to believe his ears. 'Two per cent! Are you mad?'

Bridie looked at the ceiling and waited.

'All right, how can you explain a deal that is on the face of it daylight robbery?'

'It's part of our original agreement,' she said calmly, 'that if I wanted larger sums, I'd come to you and you'd take a quarter your usual percentage in return for some of my regular earnings. Well, you've bin gettin' your part of the deal ever so nice and regular. Now I want to borrow off of you to buy this house. You'll have it as security.'

Sam swallowed hard. 'You expect me to lend you one hundred and forty pounds.'

Bridie smiled sweetly. 'No, I don't expect you to, I know you're goin' to.'

'At two per cent?'

'That's it.'

'And I don't get anything by way of recognition that it's criminal generosity? Ludicrous? Extortion?'

Bridie giggled. 'You sure know all about them things, Sam Saul,' she agreed.

Sam felt his blood pressure near boiling point. 'No recognition?' he said with emphasis.

'Yes, I'll give you a nice cup of tea afore you leave,' she said cheerily, and went to put the kettle on. Sam groaned and banged his fist on the chair arm.

'You're the hardest woman I know. God preserve

me from any more like you,' he called.

'Yes,' came back the light answer, 'but you see, my dear, I don't mind.'

He laughed ruefully.

Bridie came to the doorway. 'We'll draw the papers up tomorrow, then. I've got a lawyer who will do it.'

Sam groaned again. 'It's legal, yet. Oi yoi yoi.' Distress brought the Yiddish lilt back to his voice.

'Don't be a fool,' said Bridie. ' 'course it's got to be legal and proper. It's property.'

Drinking hot sweet tea gave them both a few moments of companionable silence. 'Well,' she said, putting down her cup, 'you'd best be getting home to that patient wife of yours. How she puts up with you, I don't know.'

'She's nothing like you, that's for sure,' said Sam dourly. He gave a little snort of laughter. 'Just as well, isn't it? I'd soon be bankrupt.'

Bridie just grinned. He bent down and kissed her cheek. 'You're my *bête noire*,' he whispered in her ear. 'You know it, don't you?'

Bridie had never heard of a *bête noire*, but she got the drift. She gave him a little push.

'Go on, get along home where you should be,' she said, and leaned on her front door to watch his tall figure stride off down the road. She hugged herself with nervous delight. She was really going to buy her house. The lawyer had seen no problems, the agent had said the landlord would be willing to sell and Sam Saul, against all his better judgement, was going to lend her the balance of the money.

Bridie pressed her hands against hot cheeks, and said, 'Oh my word, it's really going to happen.'

She went inside and sat down to consider the other matter that was pressing for a decision. She pulled out the letter in its stiff white envelope and slowly made her way through the complicated, verbose sentences again. She understood the main part of it, but was uncertain about all the fancy language that might be hiding things she ought to know. Francis wanted David, or at least to see him. At first, when it became clear what the letter meant, Bridie had been outraged. What a thing to do, to make some fat-assed lawyer ask to see her son! If Francis had come round and asked nicely, Bridie would have been agreeable enough, but to do it this way made her so angry she felt like saying no.

The letter acknowledged that since she and Francis had got married after David was born, he was still illegitimate, and that in law he was hers. But, it pointed out, Francis had in every respect been a father to his son, until the separation, and had a moral right to see him, or even to have him live in his house. Bridie shivered when she got to that bit.

Never. Over my dead body, she thought furiously. All this time, an' all he does is pay money into the bank. He hasn't been to see us, an' he hasn't sent any presents on birthdays, not nothing. An' now he comes marching in with 'is lawyers and his long words. Oh damn!

A tear trickled down her cheek, a tear of fear and loss and being alone with only David. No one could take him away. She'd given up Rosa without complaint, had stoically accepted what had to be. But David . . . she'd fight tooth and nail anyone who tried to take him from her. She wiped her eyes. Just the threat of it threw her into turmoil. She didn't sleep well that night, and was troubled by dreams and nightmares. The following day she called in at her lawyer's office and told him to go ahead with the purchase of her house, she'd got the money.

Then she said, 'There's another thing. My husband has written me this.' She handed over the letter.

The lawyer read it carefully, then looked at her over his glasses. 'Do you want my advice as a lawyer, or as an old man who has seen a lot of life?'

'What do you think, yourself?' asked Bridie.

'My dear Mrs Holmes, you are a remarkable and resourceful woman, but I do not have the impression that you have a taste for malice or unpleasantness. Am I right?'

Bridie nodded.

'Then my advice to you is, avoid the law at all costs because it only ever serves to make things like this worse. Take your little boy, in his best clothes, to see his father. Swallow your understandable feeling that the thing is offensive, and be as charming as I'm sure you know very well how. That way, you son will not suffer, your husband won't have a leg to stand on in any argument, and you will have merely the passing inconvenience of a little hurt pride. That is my advice. It is what I would endeavour to do myself if it were my child.'

Bridie sat with head bowed. Hurt pride, she thought, *hurt*. But he was right.

'Thank you,' she said, raising her head. 'That's not the advice I thought I wanted, but it's what me and David needed. I'll do it.'

The old lawyer smiled compassionately. 'That's the brave way, you know,' he said. 'The other – the fighting and the arguing – that's the real coward's way, for those who cannot endure their own feelings and have no respect for the feelings of others. A lifetime in the law, and I have been more sure of that with every passing day.'

Bridie stood up and shook his hand warmly. 'Thank you,' she said again. 'I'll wait to hear from you about the next step on the house.'

'Yes,' replied the old man, smiling at her. 'It's an excellent thing, this house buying. Property is the best investment, always has been.'

Bridie went down the dark, narrow stairs to the butcher's shop below the lawyer's office. The smell of meat hung round the entrance, and sawdust from the butcher's floor lay in little drifts in the lawyer's doorway. She bought two chops for their dinner, and then made a decision. There was a tobacconist's three shops down. Waiting to be served, Bridie sniffed the fragrance coming from the rows and rows of packets and tins, all neatly stacked on shelves the length of the shop. A mahogany pipe holder stood on the glass counter, with pipes of every size, colour and wood sitting in glossy rows. She bought a packet of Francis's favourite cigars. She'd go one better than her lawyer's advice, and take David to see his father carrying a gift.

Collecting him from a long looked forward to afternoon with Mrs MacDonald, she confided in the midwife what she had done.

'He's right, in my view,' said Mrs MacDonald. 'Do you recall, when David was born? You didn't want his father in then, and I disagreed with you at the time. Well, I'd say the same today. You heed what you was told.'

'I am,' said Bridie meekly.

It took two weeks to make satisfactory arrangements for David to visit Francis, who had been taken aback by the friendly answer his letter had received. The first week in June, Bridie's letter to Edward was all about the visit, and how it had gone. It hadn't started too well.

It had been unseasonably chilly that week, so Bridie had put a woolly over David's grey cut-downs. He looked every inch the East End kid, though better turned out than many. Bridie wiped his nose and gave him the handkerchief to put in his pocket. She put a knitted shawl over her own light dress, and wore a fashionable new pair of brown leather shoes with a strap across the front. A spot of powder on her nose, and they were ready.

They went up to Manor Road, and caught a tram that took them into Abbey Lane, past the school in Three Mills and up on to Stratford High Street. Bridie gazed around at the familiar places as it took them down into Bow Road and they jumped off at Maplin Street, just opposite the Tredegar Square turning. The square gardens were in the full bloom of spring, the magnolia

309

tree just beginning to shed its waxy pink blossoms and open its leaves.

Bridie bravely led David up the front steps of number twelve and banged on the door. Mrs Goode answered. Bridie impulsively went to hug her, as in days of old, but the housekeeper drew back.

'Good afternoon,' said Dora formally. 'Hello, David.'

'Hello, Mrs Goode.' Hearing David's high voice, Francis could wait no longer, and emerged from his study into the hall. He nodded stiffly to Bridie, and squatted down in front of his son. 'Hello, young man,' he said. 'Would you like to come in?'

David looked up at his mother questioningly. She nodded. 'Yes, go on.'

Francis took the child's hand to draw him in. His eyes met Bridie's. 'Do you wish to stay?' he asked.

Bridie had thought about what she would feel, and say, at this moment, but now it was upon her, it was easier than she had expected. She shook her head.

'No. You and him, you'll get on better if I'm not there watching. You and Mrs Goode have him for a while, and I'll take myself down the Roman and do some shopping. I'll fetch him again after tea.'

Relief flooded Francis's lined face. 'Yes. That will do us very well. Thank you, Bridie.'

David ran forward anxiously. 'Don't go, Mum.' He plucked at her hand.

Bridie picked him up and put him firmly on the hall floor. 'I'll be back after tea,' she said calmly, 'and you'll be a good boy and stay with your dad. I bet Mrs

Goode's got a big biscuit tin in her kitchen. I remember it. If you go along and ask her, she might let you have something out of it.'

In the background, Dora nodded. 'There might even be chocolate,' she remarked, as if to no one in particular.

David's head turned. The housekeeper beckoned. He turned back and allowed his mother to kiss him, then followed the housekeeper down the passage, to be fed biscuits and milk until he felt sick. Afterwards he and Francis sat outside on the weathered wooden bench by the kitchen door, and Francis asked so many questions that David chattered nineteen to the dozen and climbed excitedly on and off the bench, until he ventured further and further away, to explore the whole garden. It was much bigger than his own, but had the same slugs and snails and spiders.

Francis wandered after him, hands folded behind his back. He was pleased with the child's bright interest, found him clean if shabby, and his speech not completely uncivilised. With a pang, Francis looked into the small face and saw himself. But here, at least, whatever the regrettable past, was a child whose mind could be educated. Francis resolved to ask Bridie what she had in mind in the way of schools. David was ready to start after the summer. That was how they ran into trouble.

Francis invited her in, when she came to get David, and she sat once more in the same old chair opposite his desk. David sat on her knee, sucking his thumb.

'I wanted to ask you about schooling,' began Francis.

'He's going to Falcon Street. It's Catholic, and near to where we live,' said Bridie.

'He'll be taught by nuns?'

'Yes. Any objection?'

Francis decided not to make an issue of it. 'No. They provide a good education. What did you have in mind for when he's eight?'

'Oh my,' said Bridie, 'he's barely five. I'll worry about when he's eight when the time comes.'

Francis sighed in a way familiar to Bridie, and disturbing. It was a critical, dismissive sort of sigh. 'If he's to go to preparatory school, his name must go down immediately. It should have gone down at birth.'

Bridie stiffened. Francis had been plotting. 'What's that? Preparatory school?'

'It prepares boys for public school. They go as boarders when they are eight, then to public school at eleven. If they get in, that is. It's all been left very late for David. I shall have to get in touch and pull a string or two.'

Bridie passed a hand across her brow. This was the very thing from which she had fled. Here it was again, unchanged, ruthless.

'No,' she said, feeling her knees begin to tremble. 'David is going to an ordinary school – The Falcon. Then I hope he'll go to the grammar school, if he passes the examinations. I've talked to Mother Superior at The Falcon, and she's explained it all to me. Me not having been to school as much as I should have, I made a point of finding out. And I wouldn't send him away on no account.'

'You would deny him a decent start in life?' asked Francis.

'He'll get as good a start as I can give, and it'll have to do, because he's not going away to some fancy place with posh accents. He belongs here, and he ain't going nowhere else.'

Francis winced. 'You'd have him illiterate? Crippled in life by poverty and a coarse environment?'

Bridie felt rage beginning to boil, then abruptly it vanished, leaving pity for this lined old man whose life, devoted to others, was a sham.

'I'm sorry, Francis. You haven't ever been to see us, so you don't know that we don't live in no slum. I have a nice house of my own. We're not grand, it's true, but we get by, and David don't go without. And we got lots of friends who love him, and I couldn't think of sending him away, ever.'

'Then if you are intransigent, you leave me powerless. All I can do is place money in his bank account, and hope that it will be used wisely later on. I shall ensure that there is enough for him to stay on at school after thirteen if he wishes, and for university later. I hope you take this with the seriousness it is due, Bridie.'

'As one who had no learning, I respect it more'n you, probably,' she cried, stung by the implication.

'I doubt it, somehow,' replied Francis, 'but let us not argue. Money there will be.'

'That's David's. I don't touch it,' she said. 'That's for him to decide when he gets old enough.'

'And . . .' Francis started again. Bridie closed her eyes. She'd had enough. 'I wondered if we could repeat this visit?' Francis thawed for the first time. 'It's been such a joy to see him, Bridie. Could you bring him again, please?'

At last they were on safe ground.

'Yes, I'll gladly bring him. I'd be pleased. Or you can come and see us. You'd be welcome. How often?'

Francis, anticipating resistance, hadn't thought that far. 'Oh, er . . . would twice a month be possible? Every other Saturday, maybe?'

Bridie smiled at him. 'Yes, if he wants to. 'course, I wouldn't make him come if he didn't like to. I'll bring him in the morning, and you can have him for the day, if you like?'

They looked at each other with a faint trace of the old affection.

'Thank you,' said Francis gently, 'you really are being very generous.'

'I'll be off then.' Bridie spoke briskly and put David down, brushing crumbs off his woolly.

'You'll bring him a fortnight today?' asked Francis anxiously.

She nodded. 'Don't worry, I will. And if there's anything goes wrong, like he gets took bad or something, I'll send you a note.'

They parted, not touching, at the doorstep. David, tired but excited, fidgeted and sucked his thumb in the tram until Bridie felt exasperatedly that if visits were going to end like this, then maybe they weren't a good thing after all. Shortly before they got to their stop he fell heavily asleep, and she had to carry him all the way home.

Chapter Twenty-One

Ethel and Ted were talking about going hop picking in Kent in the early autumn. They'd done it several years running. Ethel, who went for a full three weeks, always came back brown as a berry and with hands torn and stained. She loved it. Bridie thought about having a week down with them, then had another idea. It was Francis going on about education that put it in her mind. She asked him what he thought when she delivered David to him one hot Saturday in July.

'I'd like to take him to the seaside,' she explained. 'For a week. It would be good for his health, and set him up before he starts school after the summer. And it would teach him things. He's never seen countryside and sea. He could go in the water and try swimming. It would be so good for him.'

'It would,' Francis agreed. 'So what do you want?'

'For you to pay his way, if I pay mine? Since I took on buying my house I'm pushed. I can run to it for one of us, but not for two. I've never asked you for money before, but it's for David, not me.'

Francis thought it was a splendid idea. Of course he'd help out. 'Where will you go?' he asked.

'There's a place in Kent called Romney. Romney

Marsh. It has wonderful beaches, by all accounts. It's safe, and there are plenty of guest houses that put you up comfortable, and don't charge the earth.'

She wasn't going to let on to Francis that the source of all this information was Sam Saul. He'd been round one evening to collect her house loan repayment, and to spend time sitting in her back garden under the apple tree, trying, half joking, half seriously, to suggest that she needed a holiday – with him. He'd painted a lewd and vivid picture of their elopement to the seaside, while his wife went to stay with her elderly parents in Golder's Green. His black eyes flashed with suggestive good humour, and he gave an exaggerated gesture of despondency when she giggled and said, 'Give over, Sam Saul. You're a caution!'

'You won't make me a happy man, then?'

'Yes, I'll bring you out a glass of lemonade. I made it fresh this evening.'

'If at a loss, feed the beast,' groaned Sam, and rolled on his back in the crushed grass. He came eye to eye with one of the kittens, now grown into a graceful tabby cat. She mewed, showing small, perfectly white teeth.

'What do you do with women?' he asked her. She hitched up a hind leg and started to wash, turning her back indifferently. 'Yeah,' said Sam to her busy head, 'you're just like the rest.'

He raised himself on his elbow, and watched Bridie and David carry out a plate of cakes and a big brown jug of lemonade.

'Aren't you going to bed, young man?' he asked David.

'The nights are so light, there's no point. He only plays, so he stays up later for the moment. When he goes to school he'll need his sleep.'

'He ought to have a holiday, too,' remarked Sam idly. He had no children, a fact which was the cause of much wailing and throwing up of hands in his wife's parents' home, but didn't bother Sam himself in the slightest.

It was a whole new thought. Hop picking was hop picking, but a real holiday was something few East Enders would have entertained. A day out, yes, but to stop away . . . out of the question.

'Bridie . . .' Sam implored.

'Shut up,' she said. 'I'm thinking.'

Miffed, Sam popped a cake in his mouth and turned his back on her. 'You get some cards, and I'll teach you some games,' he said to David with his mouth full.

'You leave him be,' said Bridie, 'I don't want him learning gambling games off of you.'

Sam looked hurt. 'I only meant snap, or things like that. Can't you give me any credit, you harsh woman?'

'Only the sort that comes as bank notes,' snapped Bridie. 'Listen, where's a good place to go? On holiday?'

'You've changed your mind!' cried Sam.

'You are getting dull, Sam. I mean for me an' David.'

'Ah. . . . Well, now, I'd say down in Romney, on the Kent coast. Big flat beaches. Can be windy, though.'

Open spaces, the fresh sweet air in your face, a horizon that stretches the eyes. Bridie suddenly felt a rare pang of homesickness for the uncrowded, lazy Irish countryside. The little garden she loved so much felt cramped and seedy all of a sudden. She'd made up her mind at that moment, and now Francis was agreeing. A wide smile of delight lit her face. Francis, despite all that had gone wrong between them, still found himself gazing at that face with an ache in his heart. The passing years had brought depth, an inner strength, to her expression. She was apparently quite unaware of it, but, he thought sadly, she had become beautiful since Rosa's death.

'Would you do something for me, as well?' he asked.

Bridie looked up at him enquiringly. 'You remember the small room at the back, that you had when you were here?'

Puzzled, she nodded.

'It's being redecorated throughout, and I'd very much like David to feel that it's his. Would you let him stay overnight sometimes?'

'Yes,' she said promptly. 'It's the same as always – if David wants to, he can.'

It had actually come in quite handy to have David stay a whole weekend with Francis. Sam Saul had done some telephoning for Bridie, and had booked a room for her in a small guest house next to the beach. It was Tuesday to Tuesday, so she spent her weekend without David washing and ironing and bathing. It was, she discovered, a luxurious feeling, time on her own. She didn't even feel inclined to rush round to Lizzie, who was so overcome by babies that she hardly came out of the house these days. She was looking tired and drawn, and Bridie, remembering Rosa, felt sorry for her. But it wasn't enough to make Bridie give up her newfound freedom, and by the time she fetched David home on Sunday afternoon, their clothes lay in two carefully folded piles, ready to go in the case. Sam came over on the Monday, and took away with him, on the passenger seat of his shiny new motor car, Bridie's strongbox. It had proved a good time to persuade her to do something he'd been urging for a long time.

'You're asking to get done over,' he'd cried in exasperation, time and again. 'I know you've got a reputation round here for standing no nonsense, but if a couple of really determined men came after you, you could get badly hurt.'

It was clearly out of the question to leave the house for a week with money inside, so at last Sam had his way. The box was safely stored inside his own safe that evening. Bridie had given him a very old-fashioned look when he'd first brought up the idea of her money in his safe.

'How do I know I can trust you?' she'd demanded bluntly.

Sam looked pained. 'Would I cheat on a friend?' he asked plaintively.

'Probably. Given the chance.'

He was genuinely hurt. 'I'll make money any way I can. I love money, and the more I have the more I love it. But I love you, too.' The words were out before he realised they were on his tongue. They were both equally astonished. Sam hastily tried to put things right.

'That is,' he said, in his best, urbane manner, 'I esteem you highly as a friend and colleague. I wouldn't want to harm you, Bridie, and I swear I'm straight with you,' he finished lamely.

'You're a strange man,' said Bridie softly. 'And I'm fond of you in a funny kind of way, but it can't be any more than that.'

'I know.' Sam looked cast down, then brightened up. 'But I can still try, can't I?' He gave an irrepressible grin and pretended to leer.

Since that time, Bridie had accepted Sam's gestures of friendship, and even protectiveness. She let him arrange the holiday for her, and was overcome to be offered a ride to the station in his new motor car. The Tuesday morning of the journey dawned fine and clear. Bridie and David were up ridiculously early, and ready to go long before Sam puttered up to their front gate and hooted. Neighbours came to their doorsteps and watched as the three of them settled on to the high polished leather seats. Several small boys sidled over to gasp at the wonderful sight. One put out a hand to touch the elegant trim of the high back, and his mother called him sharply away. Bridie was accepted. Sam Saul was a different matter. He had a bad reputation and people drew aside from him. Gossip wondered at the strange relationship between him and Bridie, who had an equally strong reputation for honesty.

Ted and Ethel at first looked askance when Bridie mentioned Sam's name in a friendly sort of way, but, having met him at Bridie's on occasion, when he'd put himself out to charm and entertain, they had to admit that he was an appealing rogue.

'But you watch that man,' Ethel had advised. 'He's dangerous.'

'I know,' said Bridie. 'And I do take care.'

Looking at his dark, handsome face close to hers as he solicitously tucked a rug around her knees, she sat up very straight and let excitement wash through her. Oh, to be off to the seaside, and in such a fine car! David knelt on the back seat and waved to his friends as they set off down the road. Bridie imagined herself resplendent in furs, veiled hat, and tiny satin shoes. Oh, she felt grand. They chugged smoothly along, Sam hooting and waving at drivers in passing vehicles and mockingly doffing his hat at pedestrians. Utterly enchanted, Bridie looked here, there and everywhere, storing away all she saw for a letter to Edward.

They bowled along through the City and across the river. A light breeze ruffled their hair and they sniffed at the river air. It was in full tide, long strings of barges up and down. A river police boat idled in the middle and watched a cruiser coming down fast from its mooring further up at Hampton Court. Gulls swooped and screamed harshly. London Bridge station came into view all too soon. Sam drew up smoothly outside, leapt out and hurried round to open

321

her door and hand her down. Bridie chuckled.

'I'm quite the lady today, ain't I?'

He raised her hand to his lips and kissed it.

'For me, always,' he said gallantly, and lifted out their case, then David, who said he felt sick.

'Don't you dare, it's just excitement,' warned Bridie.

In the station, Sam went off to buy the tickets, leaving the other two to sit on a bench with their luggage. It reminded Bridie of that afternoon, seven years ago, when she arrived in Euston with no knowledge of what would become of her. Sam came back, and, handing the tickets to Bridie, escorted them on to the platform. He settled them into seats with their backs to the engine, and stowed the case underneath the seat so that she wouldn't have to lift it down. With a flourish, he produced a bag of assorted sweeties, several comic books, and two magazines. David grabbed the sweets and immediately began sorting them through. Whistles blew, the sound of the steam from the engine turned to a straining chuff, chuff, chuff, and Sam leapt for the carriage door. It was already moving as his feet touched the platform. Bridie pulled down the window and hung out. He walked, then ran alongside, waving first to her, then to David, then her again, and all the time calling orders.

'Take care. Have a wonderful time. Teach the nipper to swim. Don't get sunburn. Look after yourselves now. . . .'

The words were torn from his mouth as the train picked up speed and he fell back, almost at the end of the long platform. Bridie gave one last wave, and turned to David, who was counting green and red and yellow fruit drops.

'Can I have a purple one? They're my favourites,' she asked.

David nodded and picked one out of his little bag. Her cheek bulging with the tart-tasting sweet, Bridie settled down and picked up her magazines. Through the slightly open window steam and smuts flew in on the wind, and this time the singing rails told her, 'Sunshine and sea, sunshine and sea, sunshine and sea,' as they tore through the quiet Kent countryside. Oast houses built of warm red brick raised their odd circular roofs among fields of high-strung young hops. Sheep grazed peacefully on green slopes that were formed as deliciously as the curve of a child's cheek. David knelt up on the seat and pressed his nose to the window, his eyes quite round. He kept turning to his mother and plucking at her, crying, 'Look, Mum, look. . . .' The sweeties and comics were forgotten.

In a little over an hour, they slowed for the umpteenth time and drew into their destination.

'Folkestone. This is Folkestone,' shouted the guard up and down the train.

'Come on,' ordered Bridie, helping David down the high step to the platform. She told him to put his sweets in his pocket and carry the unread comics for later. They had their tickets clipped, and Bridie asked the inspector the way to the bus station.

'Where are you going?' he asked.

'Dymchurch,' answered Bridie.

'That's easy, then,' he said. 'There's a stop just across from the station. It's frequent. You shouldn't have to wait long.'

They found it at once, and within fifteen minutes were sitting on top of an omnibus, trying to see the sea as they whizzed along the coast road, through the tolls to Hythe. David stared and stared.

Bridie soon found herself in a village with a wide main street leading directly down to golden sands at the end. While David tugged at her skirt and begged to go and play right now, Bridie asked directions. Their guest house, as Sam had promised, overlooked the beach itself. A stout little woman welcomed them in and said she was Mabel, the owner.

Two flights of stairs up she showed them to a room with cool green walls. There was a big bed for Bridie and a truckle bed to one side, for David. Mabel offered Bridie a cup of tea and a bite of lunch, but David clung and begged to go out, so she shook her head and said she'd like some tea later on, if Mabel didn't mind. Wise in the ways of children, Mabel didn't mind at all, and offered to make up a sandwich for when they came back. Leaving their case on the floor between the beds, they hurried outside. David went to run off, but Bridie pulled him back.

'Here. Take off your shoes and socks.' Then she gave him a little shove, and the child ran delightedly down the beach. It was wide and flat. When he finally reached the edge of the sea, he stopped and looked. It went on forever and ever. Small waves hissed at his toes and made bubbles in the sand, ridged and sculpted by the eddying water. David jumped and shrieked. A crab the size of his thumbnail emerged from the sand and hurried into the sea. David fled back to Bridie, overcome by it all. She had taken off her own sandals and was nearly at the water's edge.

'What?' she asked, laughing, to his jabber of explanation. 'Crabs won't hurt you. They're more scared of you than you are of them. Was it a big one? I once saw a huge one the time I went to Dublin Bay.'

'Yes,' said David, 'like this.' And he made a circle of his finger and thumb. His mother laughed again.

'Huge,' she agreed. 'Would you be wanting to go and find a bucket and spade?'

They set off, hand in hand, along the waterline to where they could see a shack at the top of the beach, displaying buckets, spades, balls, and windbreaks. They reached it just as its owner was shutting up for lunch.

'All right, dearie, I'll serve you,' she said, seeing Bridie's look of disappointment. 'What colour did you fancy?' They chose matching red buckets and spades, a windbreak and a white beachball. David ran off, joyously banging his bucket with his spade, and settled down by the water's edge. Bridie, rolling his cut-downs up as far as they would go, planted the windbreak, although there was no wind, and lay on her side on the warm sand, watching him.

The small blond head was bent in concentration, filling and emptying his bucket more times than Bridie could count. She got up, and taking her own, showed him how to pat the wet sand down, turn the bucket over and bang the top before lifting it off a perfect sandpie. Soon there was a line of wobbly sandpies between her and the sea. The quiet plash of the waves made her drowsy, so she got up and paddled, not wanting to fall asleep with David near the water. The sun reddened their faces and beat on their arms.

Eventually, hunger drove them indoors again. Mabel took their sandy things into a lobby already full of beach items, and in the dining room served a brown pot of boiling tea, and two platefuls of sardine, cheese and pickle, and cucumber sandwiches. A jug of milk for David, and fruit cake for afters.

'Now you just call out if you want anything. I'm out back getting ready for dinner.' She fussed and bustled around them, her rosy, motherly face eager to see them pleased. 'It's any time between seven o'clock and nine this evening. So you finish up as much as you can, and you can have a good hot meal inside you tonight.'

Bridie felt like she'd ended up inside Buckingham Palace by mistake, but she didn't want to let on so she just nodded her head and thanked Mabel for her kindness. David grabbed at the food. Bridie caught his hand and held it.

'Manners,' she said sternly. 'Here, you use manners. You don't reach and grab. You say excuse me, and I'll give you what you want.'

David, starving, opened his mouth to argue, but seeing how determined his mother looked, desisted. He knew that look. It meant she was serious and he'd better watch out.

'I want a sandwich.'

'No. Can I have a sandwich, please.'

David sighed. She was being difficult and he was oh so hungry.

'Can I have it, please.'

Bridie handed him the plate.

'Here, take two. An' I want you behaving yourself like a gent, you hear? Please, and thank you, and sit still at table.'

'Yes.' Too hungry to argue, David accepted the conditions.

They wolfed down the meal in silence. Afterwards Bridie sat back and stretched. She felt like going for a walk. They piled up the plates for Mabel, and went back down to the beach. Strolling along, watching holiday-makers basking in the sunshine, Bridie felt contentment steal over her like a soft shawl warms on a cool day. Heads bobbed far out in the cold sea as the braver ones went shrieking and gasping, knitted swim-suits water-logged and sagging, in and out of the blue expanse. Showers of droplets caught the sunlight as a fast swimmer back-stroked dramatically out to a yellow buoy that floated lazily on the incoming tide. Bridie decided to buy swimming costumes for them both, tomorrow. She couldn't swim, but she felt that here, in this magical place, she might do anything.

By seven o'clock the sun was fading. They dragged the windbreak through the sand back to Mabel's guest house. The dining room was full of chattering children and parents. A mouthwatering smell of roast chicken caught at their noses, and suddenly the pile of sandwiches might never have been.

There was a big bathroom upstairs. Bridie sighed with pleasure, and occupied it for the next half an hour. She and David emerged scrubbed from top to toe and smelling of coal tar soap. Wearing their best clothes, they sat down to platters of chicken, mashed potatoes, cabbage and carrots, placed before them by Mabel's two daughters.

Bridie caught the eye of a woman at a table opposite. She nodded amiably and lit a cigarette with a lighter. It was a Trench. Bridie's gaze turned to her husband. He must have fought in the War. Later, when the family rose to leave the dining room, Bridie saw the man had a pronounced limp as he made his way to the door among the cluster of tables. He moved awkwardly, as if his wounds had left him disjointed in some strange fashion. His wife turned to ask him something but he shook his head, and she offered him her arm in such a loving gesture that for the first time Bridie felt a pang of loneliness. But it didn't spoil the moment.

She and David sat together, gazing out of the wide window at the view over the sea as the sun began its slow descent to the horizon. Long before dark, David was curled up, rosy with sun and fresh air, fast asleep. Bridie lay on her bed, reading Sam's magazines, until dusk passed into dark and the whole house slept.

That was the pattern for seven idyllic days. They rose early, eager not to miss a moment. They made a habit of sandwiches in the early afternoon, and avoided the crowded dining room at lunchtime. Evenings, they had 'their' table, a very small one under the window, because there was only Bridie and a child. In the evenings, they feasted on the view, until David made friends with the soldier's three children. Then they all ran off to play hopscotch and grandmother's footsteps in Mabel's backyard until it was time for bed, and the two mothers reluctantly called their children in.

'Seems a shame to bring them in,' admitted the soldier's wife, 'but if I let them stay up 'til all hours they get fretful in the day, and I get no peace then.'

She lit a Players and leaned on the doorjamb, watching a skipping game. 'Been here before?' she asked.

'No. It's lovely, isn't it?'

The soldier's wife blew out a thin stream of smoke. 'Mabel's a dear. We've been coming for four years. My husband was wounded in the Somme, and at first he found it really hard to get about, but Mabel never minded. She gave us a room on the ground floor, 'specially, and fetched and carried for us like a mother. She's a darling.'

'A friend recommended her to me,' said Bridie. 'I think she's lovely. She's been ever so kind with David.'

'You lost your old man in the War?' asked the other woman. 'I noticed you're on your own.'

Bridie gazed at the children in the yard. 'Yes, I'm on my own,' she said.

The soldier's wife squashed out her cigarette with

her heel. 'There's ever such a lot of women having to manage like you. I've been real lucky, myself. Come on in!' she shouted to the children. Like a troop of chickens they followed her obediently upstairs and Bridie heard the chirruping of their voices quickly fade into silence as they were put into bed.

It would be wonderful to live here always, she thought as she and David climbed the stairs to their room. If only this could go on and on and on, and never end.

But later, as she sat downstairs in the sitting room, absently turning the pages of a magazine and listening to soft music on the wireless on a dresser at the far end of the room, she remembered Edward, and the letter she'd written on the beach while David built an elaborate sandcastle, and she smiled, shaking her head to herself. No, she didn't really want it to go on forever for then she'd lose Edward, Sam Saul, Ted and Ethel and Susan, Lizzie, Jonathan, twins Oliver and Bridget, and dear Mrs MacDonald. All the people she loved. It would soon be time to go back to them, to where she belonged.

'Well, my dears, you've had the best week of the summer, it looks like,' said Mabel cheerfully as they licked the last vestiges of marmalade off their fingers. Breakfast was over. Their case lay waiting in the hall, buckets and spades washed free of sand and salt, ready to take back to London. Outside a warm drizzle fell on the beach, empty except for a few hardy souls, walking dogs up towards the dunes.

'It's been a wonderful week. Look at him, a picture

of health,' said Bridie, nodding at her son. 'He's even started to learn to swim. Well, we both did. It wasn't very warm, but at least we both got wet all over!'

They'd ventured bravely out in bathing costumes, and had sat in the shallows, shrieking as the waves broke over them. David had danced like a dervish, throwing up swirling, whirling waterfalls of spray with flailing arms and feet. He'd make a good swimmer, thought Bridie, showing no fear of the water at all.

'Perhaps we'll see you again next year,' went on Mabel. 'You'd be welcome any time, my dear.'

Bridie smiled at the friendly little woman who'd made them so welcome. 'If we can, we will,' she said.

Then it was time to go. Their bill was paid, farewells said to the soldier's family, who were staying a second week, and a kiss from Mabel sent them on their way.

Walking over London Bridge to find a 'bus to take them home, Bridie breathed in a great gulp of sooty air. It smelled lovely – like home.

It was early evening before they were properly back in their little house again. The range had to be lit and fresh food bought from the corner shop up the road. Bridie grumbled at the expense compared to the market, but for now it had to do. David gobbled his tea and ran up the road to play with the gang of five, six and seven year olds who roamed the street, kicking an old football and swapping boasts. Swimming in the waves – David really had something to boast about, and was bursting to tell stories.

Bridie cleared the table, and sat down to open the packet from Edward that had been waiting. It had been one of the things to look forward to, that had made the end of the holiday happy. She was just sorting the letters when there was a bang on her front door. Sam stood on the doorstep.

'Hello,' she said, resigned to the fact that she'd have to wait for her letters now.

'I wanted to assure myself that you were both back safely.'

'We are, and we had the best week you could imagine. Come on in, and I'll show you the picture postcards I bought.'

Sam installed himself at the table and eyed the pile of letters jealously. Bridie swept them up without a word and stuffed them into the dresser drawer. She pulled out a handful of cards instead. They sat side by side, Sam nodding in a familiar kind of way as she explained and described the walks they'd taken along country lanes behind the beach. She told him about swimming and sun-bathing and eating so much they thought they'd burst.

'Nipper behave himself?' asked Sam.

'It did him good. He had to behave, and the other children there had ever such nice manners, so it was a good example to him.'

'Good. I've missed you. It's been a long week. But my wife came home today.' He pulled a face. 'So life returns to normal. I'm glad you enjoyed yourself, and the nipper. But I'm glad you're back, as well.'

He leant forward and kissed her cheek. 'Welcome home.'

Abruptly he got up and pushed his chair away. 'I'll leave you to read your letters from loverboy,' he said, then regretted his tone. 'Didn't mean to sound spiteful. I just sometimes wish his ship would sink.'

Bridie knew it was useless to protest.

'I'll need my strongbox tomorrow,' she said instead. 'Can I come by and get it?'

'You could, but why take it away? You can leave it, if you want, like I keep telling you. There's nearly always someone in the office so you can treat it as your own. I've told Miriam to give you access to the safe. You see,' he said pointedly, 'I trust you.'

'All right,' decided Bridie, 'it does make sense. I'll come over first thing and take out what I need.' She eyed the moneybelt, hanging empty over the back of a chair. Work as usual tomorrow.

Sam got up to go. 'I'll be in the office early, so I'll see you.'

He'd make sure he was there whether he needed to be or not. Bridie stifled a sigh. He got worse and worse. She just hoped he'd get tired of the frustration of unrequited love and start behaving normally again. Sam hopped into his motor car, singing under his breath. They were back again, and that was all that really mattered.

Bridie got out her letters and smoothed the creases out. She was absorbed in the fifth of the pile when David ran in.

'Mum, can I go down with Cissie and get chips?'

Bridie fished in her pocket for two ha'pennies. 'Here, get us some as well, will you?'

David took the money and nodded. The fish and chip shop at the far end of Hermit Road sold delicious crisp, vinegar-soaked chips. A big twist of newspaperful for a ha'penny. A lot of kids didn't eat much else. Bridie returned to the letters. Edward wrote that they'd had yellow fever on board and that several of the men had been taken off. He himself was well, though. In letter eight, he had splendid news.

The Captain had asked to see him, to say that his application for officer training would be favourably considered at the end of this voyage. And letter number eleven, the last, gave the news Bridie had been looking forward to. They were returning to base in August, and would once again have six weeks of shore leave.

Bridie gave a little jump for joy. Ethel would have had her letters, too, and now they could plot all manner of treats for when Edward came home. The back door banged and a strong smell of malt vinegar wafted into the house.

'Here's yours,' called David, his own mouth bulging. He ran off back to Cissie's backyard, where seven or eight small boys were squabbling over extra vinegar out of a brown bottle. Popping the hot, fat chips into her mouth, Bridie sat and imagined Edward's homecoming. She could hardly wait.

Chapter Twenty-Two

There was the most awful noise from downstairs. Bridie struggled awake and raised her head. Someone was banging and banging on her front door. She had no idea of the time, just that it was the early hours, and the banging on her door sounded urgent and insistent.

David's frightened voice came from the next room. 'Mum? What's that, Mum?'

'Someone at the door. I'm going to see, don't worry,' his mother called back, and hurried into her dressing gown. Still pulling it round her she ran downstairs and called, 'All right, all right, I'm coming.'

The banging stopped. Bridie fumbled with the lock and opened the door a crack, on the chain. She peered into darkness, then realised that she was looking at the policeman who patrolled her part of the streets. He was a familiar sight, sometimes on foot, sometimes on a pushbike. Tonight, Bridie saw out of the corner of her eye, he had his bicycle propped against her wall while he made enough noise to waken the dead. She shut the door and released the chain, then opened it wide and said: 'What on earth . . .?'

'Mrs Holmes, I've got some bad news for you. Can I come in?'

Bridie clutched her dressing gown tighter to her neck and a thin tendril of fear worked its way coldly round her heart.

'What? What's happened?'

She showed him in with one hand. Oh please God, don't let it be Edward!

'Your husband has been took very bad. Heart attack, the doctor said. He wants to see you and the boy, if you please.'

Bridie shook her head, at a loss. 'How? At this time of night . . .? Oh yes, of course we must go.'

She began to turn to go to the stairs when the copper's voice went on: 'Seein' as it's three o'clock in the mornin' I took the liberty, and I hope you won't mind, of asking that gentleman friend of yours to take you over in his motor car. He was very obliging and will be round directly.'

Bridie stared at him. 'Sam Saul?' she asked finally.

'Mr Saul, yes.'

'Well, I never! What else don't you know about me?' she said, angry and suddenly afraid of him.

'It's a small patch, round here. We know pretty much who knows who. I said it was a liberty, but in the circumstances . . . Only Mrs Saul seemed at all put out.' The policeman spoke stolidly, without a trace of irony.

'It certainly was a liberty. But thank you, anyway.'

They turned their heads as the putt putt putt of Sam's car came round the corner and down the sleeping street.

'There he is now,' said the copper unnecessarily.

Outside in the ghostly light filtering through the high wrought iron gates of the cemetery, Sam clambered out of his motor and ran to Bridie's door. He and the policeman met with a bump. Apologising to each other, they drew back and the copper said, 'I'm glad you're here, sir. Mrs Holmes is upstairs getting dressed. She'll not be long.'

'Is she all right?' asked Sam anxiously.

'Oh, I think so, sir. She's quite calm.'

The copper was right. Outwardly Bridie was calm. Inwardly she was in turmoil. Pulling a woolly over David's protesting head, she wondered what was about to happen. A heart attack. That sounded so serious. Was Francis going to die? Her confused and frightened mind tried to turn over this new and shocking idea, to get to grips with it, but it was too sudden. David was pale with sleep and fright underneath the seaside tan.

'Come on, lovey,' she whispered, scooping him out of his warm bed. 'We are going to see Dad. In Sam's car, I think.'

'In the night?' asked David in bewilderment.

'Dad is not well. He wants us to go to see him. Now, in the night.'

The little boy, so like his dad, surveyed her face anxiously. 'Sam's coming too?' This was unheard of.

'To take us. In the car. Come on, now.'

She carried him downstairs. The policeman and Sam waited in silence. 'Here, take him for me,' ordered Bridie, giving David into Sam's arms, 'while I brush my hair. I can't go looking like this.'

She fumbled agitatedly in the dresser and brought out a brush and comb. Going into the scullery, she brushed her long hair and quickly twisted it into a knot. Speaking through hairpins, she said, 'Do you know how bad he is?'

The policeman looked warningly at Sam and shook his head slightly. 'No,' he called back, 'just that the doctor is with him, and he's expressed a wish to see you.'

'Is that Dr Hamilton?' asked Bridie, coming in looking wider awake and more composed.

'Yes, that's him,' said the copper.

Sam shifted David to his other arm and put his free arm round Bridie's shoulders. He gave her an encouraging squeeze.

'Come on, I'll take you there now,' he told her very gently, seeing with a lover's eyes the real depth of her shock and fear.

They shivered in the early morning chill. Dew had fallen on the seats of the car, and Sam wiped Bridie's front seat with his handkerchief before allowing her to climb in. 'Here, you take him,' he said, lifting David on to her lap. He shook out the blanket and tucked it well round them both.

'Thanks, chum,' he said to the policeman, who stood watching.

'Hope he's all right, Mr Holmes,' said the copper sombrely. 'They need the likes o' him around here.' He looked at Bridie, wondering once again what had brought her, the wife of such a man, to these mean streets. He shrugged. None of his business, but he hoped the old gent pulled through. He pushed his bike slowly down the pavement as the red lamps at the rear of Sam's car disappeared round the corner, heading for the High Street and Tredegar Square.

Bridie half saw the streets go by through unfocussed eyes. She saw the years of her married life pass disjointedly through her thoughts. David put his thumb in his mouth. He hadn't sucked it for months, now, Bridie thought distractedly. Then, before she had realised quite where she was, Sam turned the corner into the square and parked a few houses from number twelve.

'Listen,' he whispered to Bridie, 'I can see the doctor's motor here, and with that many lights on, there's a lot happening. You go on in, and I'll tuck myself up here and wait. Don't worry about me, I'll wait as long as needs be.'

He slid down his side of the motor and helped Bridie out, with David clinging round her neck. He kissed her briefly.

'Hope he's all right,' he said gruffly, then gave her a tiny push towards the house. He saw Mrs Goode open the door to her, and they all went inside. The door closed behind them. Sam got back into his motor and putting the rug round his long body, settled down to wait.

Upstairs Angus heard the motor car draw up, and the door open and close. He looked at the figure on the bed and murmured, 'Thank God, they're here,' under his breath. Francis's breathing was heavy and loud and laboured. Angus, checking the rapid, thready pulse, was surprised he was holding on as long as this. It was almost as though he refused to die until Bridie and David had come. He crossed the room with long strides and met them coming upstairs. He opened the door of another bedroom, and said, 'Please come in here first, my dear. I want to talk to you.'

Bridie looked from Angus to Mrs Goode's serious face and back again. 'He's really bad?' she asked in a low voice.

'He's been asking for you constantly, my dear,' replied the doctor. 'He had a major heart attack early this evening. My colleague Dr Potter was here earlier, and we agreed that we'd not move the poor man to hospital, but make him comfortable here. I don't think he has long to go, Bridie, but he seems to be holding on until he sees you. I'm desperately sorry to have to give you such news, my dear, but you'll see for yourself in a moment. You can take the wee boy in, as well. Come.'

He led her gently by the arm into the room where Francis lay dying. Mrs Goode had placed an oil lamp at the foot of the bed, with its wick turned low so as not to glare in the sick man's eyes. Bridie approached the bed slowly, leading David by the hand. She knelt down until her head was on a level with her husband's and said very quietly, 'Francis? We are here.'

She leant forward and kissed him very gently. The lined face, stony in semi coma, softened. Francis opened his eyes and looked at her. It was a long, long look, as of a man going on a far journey, who longs to imprint a memory of a beloved thing he cannot take with him.

'David?' he asked at last. The normally sharp, incisive voice was blurred by pain and approaching death.

'Here,' whispered Bridie, and lifted the little boy up on to his father's bed. Francis made a tremendous effort of will and put up his hand to touch his son's fair hair. 'Take care of your mother,' he murmured.

He turned his eyes back to Bridie. 'I have tried to take care of you. I was at fault. I'm sorry, Bridie.' There were long pauses between each word, as he struggled to stay with her. 'Will you forgive me? I can die at peace then. Rosa. Everything. Forgive me.' He moved his head in a gesture of humility.

A movement disturbed Bridie and David. They had not noticed the priest standing in the shadows of the room. The black figure moved silently towards the bed.

'He refused confession and the last rites until you had been here,' he murmured to Bridie. 'I would like, now . . .' He gestured.

Bridie nodded slightly and turned back to the sick man. She put her face against his and her arms crept round to hold the thin shoulders. 'Of course I do. You always had that, although I never said. 'course I do. I never blamed you. Oh, don't think that.'

The priest's voice began to murmur in the background.

Francis's eyes opened again, painfully. 'God bless

you,' he whispered to her. 'Now I shall have peace. I have provided . . . for David.'

His eyes closed once more, and as the priest repeated the words of the last rites, the final farewell, Francis sighed and the awful breathing stopped.

Bridie lay with her head buried in his shoulder while the onlookers prayed for the soul of the man who had been Francis.

'Mum?' David looked at his father, lying so quietly after making that horrible noise, and saw that his mother was crying silently. He was frightened, and shook her arm.

'Mum, why are you crying?'

Angus stepped forward and lifted the boy out of her reach. He wriggled and tried to get down.

'Listen,' said the doctor gravely, 'your mummy is crying because your daddy has died, and has gone to Heaven.'

Round-eyed, David looked back at the still figure on the bed. He knew what death meant. The mother cat had been found stiff under the raspberry canes one day, and while they buried her at the very end of the garden, Bridie had explained that the cat had been very old, and that when you died you went away to Heaven. She wasn't sure whether cats went to Heaven, but she thought they probably did. Now his dad was dead, like the mother cat.

David, suddenly terribly frightened, burst into noisy tears. He struggled free of Angus's grip and slid to the floor. Running to Bridie, he threw himself against her. Automatically, she turned and held him

342

close against her. They sobbed, the three of them together for the last time in this world.

When the first storm lessened, Angus gently helped her to her feet. He took the white sheet and carefully ensuring that Francis's eyes were fully closed, pulled it up, and led Bridie and David from the room. The priest stood with bowed head at the foot of the bed, praying silently.

Mrs Goode stood in the doorway. 'He's gone?' she whispered to Angus.

'Aye, the poor man's gone.' She put a handkerchief to her eyes and sniffed loudly.

In the bedroom, the priest gathered up his book and beads and with a last nod of respect to the corpse, emerged blinking on to the brightly lit landing.

Bridie, white with hectic cheeks, looked at him. 'Thank you, Father,' she said automatically.

'Shall we all go downstairs?' the man suggested.

Bridie brushed a hand across her brow. 'Oh, yes,' she said, and led the way down. David was already in the parlour with Mrs Goode, still with her handkerchief dabbing at her eyes.

The curtains had not been drawn, and the sky was tinged with the dawn light. Birds chirped intermittently in the trees and the dawn chorus would soon be in full swing. Bridie seeing the world unchanged, felt bleakly disorientated. Nothing was different, yet she and her life had been changed irrevocably. Her head swam, and she staggered. Angus caught her and helped her into an armchair. He poured a glass of brandy and gave it to her.

'It's shock,' he said kindly. 'Drink this.'

The strong fumes made her cough and cleared her head. She rubbed her eyes and heard the birds singing with all their might and main outside. Was Sam still there? What was she to do with him? And David? She had somehow to go on with all these people, all these . . . things, situations. She handed the glass back to Angus.

'There'll have to be a funeral. What do I have to do?'

He shook his head kindly. 'Nothing much, unless you want to. Mrs Goode knows which funeral parlour to call, and will do that now. Usually they do all the organising, at least until you feel stronger. I shall sign the death certificate and do that side of things. Then there's Frank's Will. That will have to be read. But there's no necessity for you to be much involved, unless of course you want to,' he repeated.

'I'll go to the funeral, of course. And David,' she said.

'Naturally.'

She gave an unnatural, high-pitched laugh. ' 'course, it's funny, because I live right next to the cemetery. I see lots of funerals. We're quite used to them, in fact.'

'I know you do, my dear.' Angus looked with concern at her feverish excitement. 'Look,' he said, making up his mind, and taking a small bottle from his bag, 'I'd like you to go home, now, and go to bed, and take two of these. I think you are very shocked, and it might be the best thing to help your poor mind accept what has happened. Would you do that?'

Bridie closed her eyes. 'I don't know,' she said in a small voice. 'I'll take the bottle and see, if you don't mind.'

She did feel exhausted, it was true. But there was David. He sat, pale and quiet on a chair by the window. Bridie suddenly wanted to go home more than anything else in the world. She nodded at Angus.

'All right.'

'Would you mind if I called round to see you this evening?' he asked as he fetched her shawl. 'I'd like to make sure you are all right.'

She smiled wanly. 'You'll be welcome. You know where the house is?'

He nodded. 'Yes.'

It seemed everyone knew everything about her, from the police to Angus. It was somehow disquieting, but Bridie pushed the thought from her head. From the top of the front door steps she could see Sam Saul, muffled in his rug, fast asleep at the steering wheel of his lovely motor car. Suddenly she wanted nothing more than to lean on his arm and have him take care of her, with his funny, sardonic poses and his fierce, sarcastic love.

She took David's hand and turned to Angus. 'I'll be seeing you tonight. Thank you for all you've done. I can't seem to think properly just now, but I know I have to thank you for making Francis's death right for him.'

Tears spilled again. She hurried down the steps, avoiding looking up in case neighbours were already peering from surrounding windows. She felt like an animal must when it flees for its burrow. At the car, she shook Sam's arm gently.

'Sam,' she said.

His head flew up out of his arms. 'Ah! Just forty winks,' he explained, taking in immediately what her face told him.

He leant down and put an arm round her shoulders. 'It's over, then?' he said gently. She nodded and her lip trembled. He got out of the car and lifted David into the back. Then he stopped and lifted Bridie like a baby, and placed her tenderly in the passenger seat. Out came the rug once more. He put her unresisting arms inside his own jacket, and in shirtsleeves and braces, he drove her back home, taking every corner with unusual care, so that she wasn't swayed or jolted.

Disregarding the stares of both passers-by and neighbours, he carried Bridie into her house, David tagging behind. Up the stairs he took her, and laying her on her bed, he began to loosen her clothes and take off her shoes. The covers were pulled up, the curtains drawn on the waving tips of the apple tree. He told David to stay with his mum, and went down to brew a pot of tea. With a hot, very sweet cup in one hand, and Angus's bottle in the other, he went back up. Propping Bridie up against his strong chest, he let her sip the tea until it was cool enough to swallow two of the pills. Her eyelids began to droop.

'David and me will spend the day together,' he reassured her. 'We'll not be far away, so if you wake and need us, we'll be near.'

A dizzy feeling started to fill Bridie's head, then a worry pushed its way forward. 'Your wife,' she said, in a slightly slurred voice. 'What will she say?'

'My wife will take care of herself. She's a kind woman, for all I'm cruel about her. She wouldn't like it, but she'd understand if she knew what's just happened.'

Bridie nodded drowsily. 'You stay, then. I want you to, please.' She was already half dreaming.

Sam sat beside the bed, watching her slide deep into drugged sleep. David came and leaned on his knee, his own eyes drooping. Sam felt that if he lived for ever and a day, he would never love anyone like he loved this woman. He took her sleepy son into his own room, and tucked him into his bed. Then he went downstairs, and, taking the garden tools that Bridie stored in the scullery, he rolled up his sleeves and started to dig a new flower bed along the fence that separated her garden from next door's. He'd plant flowers in abundance for Bridie, some for every month of the year, living, beautiful things, like the love that lived in his heart.

When Angus kept his word and arrived to see Bridie at six o'clock that evening, he found Sam and David busily digging flowerbeds. The chatter of voices had led him round the back. He stopped to watch them, unseen. The tall Jew who cared nothing for children was listening seriously as David explained in a breathless voice that you shouldn't chop worms in half because they were good for the garden, and grew new heads like magic.

'My dad told me that,' said the small boy proudly.

They carefully removed the worm that was clinging to Sam's forkful of earth.

'You keep the edge straight when you start that bit,' ordered Sam, and the two of them squatted down and began to mark out the next section.

Angus shook his head in wonder. He knew of Sam Saul by reputation, and could hardly believe with his own eyes the gentle patience he was showing with David. Yet. . . . He coughed and both heads turned.

'Dr Hamilton, come on in,' said Sam, rising from his knees and brushing loose soil from his grey trousers.

Angus held out a hand and, Sam glancing apologetically at his dirty fingers, the two men shook hands.

'How is Mrs Holmes?' enquired Angus, smiling at David.

'She's slept all day,' said Sam. 'So's the young man here. He only got up a couple of hours ago, and came to help me here.' He gestured at the new flowerbed.

'I'll pop upstairs, if I may, and have a look in on her.'

'By all means. I'll show you.'

The two tall men had to duck their heads through the back doorway, then Sam showed Angus upstairs. Bridie stirred and their entrance woke her. For a moment she was confused, then it all came back. Francis – he was dead. She sat up and pulled the covers up under her chin.

'Hello, Dr Hamilton,' she greeted him. 'It's kind of

you to call. I'm afraid I'm still half asleep.'

'Good. It was the best thing.' He turned to Sam. 'May I have a wee word with Mrs Holmes, if you please.'

'Of course.' Sam obligingly started back down the stairs. 'I'll look in the larder to see what I can do about something to eat.' His black head disappeared from view.

Angus perched himself on the end of the bed. 'Do you feel able to talk?' he asked.

'Oh, yes.'

'Mrs Goode has asked the funeral director to make the arrangements that are necessary. They would like to arrange for Frank's funeral to be held next Tuesday. Would that be all right with you?'

'Yes,' said Bridie in a whisper.

'Are there any special wishes you'd like me to tell them to observe?'

'No, I don't think so. I shall be there with David, of course.'

The doctor nodded. 'I'll have a motor car sent to fetch you to the house, and the funeral will go from there. You must let me know if there is anything you want, Bridie.'

She shook her head, puzzled. 'I haven't got used to the idea of it. My head feels funny.'

'It will take time. Like Rosa.'

'No,' said Bridie, 'this isn't like Rosa at all. We have been apart a long time, Dr Hamilton. I feel strange that Francis isn't there any more, but it isn't like Rosa. Nor Mam. We wasn't close at all, not for a long time. Not since I got used to what had happened, and made my own way.'

Angus wondered once again what had happened. 'And there's another thing,' he said, into the pause that followed. 'Frank asked me to be his executor, and there is of course his Will to be read. I imagine it will be a matter of me, you and Mrs Goode getting together. Would you care to do that after the funeral? Do it all in one day, as it were?'

Bridie nodded. 'Funny. I never thought about Wills,' she remarked. 'He did say he'd provided for David. So maybe it'll be mostly him in the Will.'

'One never knows,' cautioned Angus. 'Though as far as I know Frank had no other family.' He stood up. 'No point in speculating, anyway,' he observed. 'We'll read it on Tuesday.'

'What did he want?' Sam enquired nosily, when Angus had gone.

'To see how I am. And to talk about the funeral and the Will,' said Bridie.

Sam suddenly looked thoughtful. 'That's a point. You may come into a lot of money.'

'I don't know that he had a lot of money. He was always very careful. It was odd, it was one of those things I never got to know, whether Francis was rich or not. It never seemed to matter.'

Sam gave an evil grin. 'That's why you'll never make a real fortune in business. You do good business, but underneath you don't really love money. Not enough.'

Bridie glanced at him. 'You're probably right,' she

said indifferently. 'So long as I have what I need, it's enough. What's David doing?'

'Digging.'

'Where?'

'Come and see.'

He took her arm and led her into the garden. They'd dug about ten feet along the edge of the fence, and the border was three feet deep. It was untidy, but a start had been made.

Bridie looked up at Sam. 'Whatever is it for?'

'A border of flowers. You've got vegetables, and apples and fruit bushes, but not many flowers. So I thought we'd make a bed along here, and plant a variety of things that would always have something blooming, even in winter, like Christmas roses.'

Bridie squeezed his arm. 'What a kind thought. That's you all over, Sam, a horror one minute and a real romantic the next.'

He looked at the face turned up to his and considered kissing it, but decided against it.

'You get us dinner, and me and David'll get this cleared up.' He bent down and started to gather handfuls of grass lumps and weeds. 'This lot can go on the compost heap,' he directed David to help.

Bridie rubbed the last traces of sleep from her eyes, and, still smiling at the idea of the year-round flower-bed, went indoors to cook dinner.

Sam eventually went home late that evening. His long-suffering wife wailed as soon as he walked in.

'Where have you been? Oy yoi yoi, I sit and I wait, and I wait, and I think – he's come to no good, he's done something and been caught. And still there's no word. You want I should suffer?'

'Woman,' roared Sam, 'be quiet. I have a friend in trouble, so I stayed. A good Jew should help a friend, no?'

'Friend?' shrilled his wife suspiciously. 'You got no friend. Money you got plenty. Friend, you got none.'

'That's all you know,' said Sam angrily. 'I got a friend. Now hold your tongue.'

Muttering under her breath, and with swift suspicious glances, Mrs Saul subsided and did as she was bid. But she wondered about it for a long time, even though Sam, being disinclined for trouble at home, was diplomatically present and charming for the rest of the week.

Bridie and David went alone to the funeral. Sam had offered to accompany them, but Bridie thought it best he did not. They arrived first at Tredegar Square, and then at the church, in the promised motor car, driven by a chauffeur. It was a slow and dreary ride. Back they came the way they'd gone, to the cemetery gates. Down long wide avenues to a corner where the newly dug grave lay waiting.

There had been a large congregation of mourners, many of whom had followed the coffin to its resting place. Bridie, dry-eyed, accepted condolences and curious stares indiscriminately. Angus hovered. The priest's voice came to an end. Out of respect for the widow, people stood back and waited for Bridie and David to leave first. Glad it was over, Bridie, David and Angus, with a silent, red-eyed Dora, were driven back to the house. Dora opened a bottle of sherry and fetched three glasses, while Angus sat down behind Francis's desk and prepared to read the Will. It was very brief and to the point.

Francis left Mrs Goode an annuity of one hundred pounds, at which Dora gasped and burst into suppressed tears. He left his books to his old friend Angus Hamilton. The rest of his estate in its entirety was left to Bridie, with the proviso that she look after his son with every possible care and there was a request that David should receive the estate in his turn if Bridie herself so willed. Angus continued to read the details of her inheritance. The freehold property in Tredegar Square and all its contents, Francis's pension and the holding in the bank after Dora's annuity had been deducted. Stocks and shares and investments amounting, according to their value at the time of writing, to about twenty-five thousand pounds.

Bridie went very pale. Her head swam for the second time in this room. Francis had been wealthy. Now she was wealthy. She was stunned by the size of it all. Dora and Angus watched her, waiting for her to say something.

'Oh,' was all that came out.

'Well,' said Angus finally, 'ye're a woman of means now, Bridie.'

She nodded slightly. 'I . . . I had no idea,' she stumbled. 'I never thought . . .'

'I think ye'd better go and have a wee talk with Frank's solicitor. And soon,' suggested Angus. 'Ye'll be needing to make some decisions about where you are going to live, and how to manage the house and so on.'

'Yes, I will. I'll have to think. Would you arrange for me to see him tomorrow, please?'

Angus smiled. 'The telephone downstairs is yours now,' he pointed out. 'You'll be able to do such things for yourself.'

Bridie put her hand to her mouth in astonishment. So it was! She looked round the familiar room. To live here again? A little shiver ran down her back. She didn't know if she could. There were memories here that might be best left to rest in peace. It would need thinking about. Meanwhile she wanted to get away, see what had happened from a bit of distance.

'Dr Hamilton, thank you for everything you've done. Mrs Goode, thank you, too. If you wouldn't mind asking the driver to bring the motor, I'd like to take David home.'

Angus gathered up the pages of the Will that lay on Francis's desk. 'I'll go and see the lawyer tomorrow, I promise.' She nodded at Mrs Goode reassuringly as well. Angus took one of her hands in his big fists and gave her an encouraging squeeze.

'I'm glad Frank has done this. It seems quite right to me,' he told her.

Bridie half smiled. 'I can talk to you on the telephone when I have talked to the lawyer.'

'Aye, that you can,' answered Angus. 'I'll look to hear from you tomorrow, then.' Bridie nodded agreement.

The three of them went to the front door, where the driver waited patiently. He drove her in silence back to Plaistow, his stiff back betraying distaste for the narrow streets and huddled houses. People turned to stare after the woman, dressed all in black, who rode next to the child in his black suit and cap.

Bridie was relieved beyond words to shut her front door on the rest of the world. She took off her black bonnet with its heavy veil, and sat down by her unlit fire.

'My goodness gracious me,' she said to David, stroking his head as he leant on her knee, 'what are we going to do with it all?' She looked tenderly at the fair hair. His future was assured. She could give him the world now, if she wanted to. The thought lightened her heart, and she picked the child up. Putting him in her lap, she kissed his soft cheek and sat rocking him quietly, imagining . . . dreaming . . . wondering . . . what in the world they would do.

Chapter Twenty-Three

Ten days later a very tall, very broad figure dressed in white strode round the corner of Hermit Road, and, quickening its pace, turned into the little front path that led to Bridie's door. It knocked several times. The door opened, and there was a moment's stillness before Bridie put out her hands, to be swept up into a great bear hug that left her breathless and laughing.

'Oh, Edward! I didn't expect you 'til tomorrow. In your letter, you said tomorrow.'

'I got discharged early so I thought I'd surprise you. I haven't even seen Mum yet.'

'Oh, what a surprise! And you look so grand. My word. Just look, all starch and braid. How do you keep clean!'

Edward laughed. 'We don't. It's overalls most of the time.' He grinned at her. 'I've been looking forward so much to seeing you. How's the nipper?'

'At school!'

' 'course. Time's gone so fast.'

He placed his cap on the kitchen table. 'Not fast enough, though, for me. To get back, I mean.'

Bridie smiled shyly. 'Yes. I've been longing for you to come home. So many things have happened since I last wrote, I hardly know whether I'm coming or going. Oh, Edward, Francis died a couple of weeks ago. It was so sudden and it's changed everything. One minute I knew where I was, but now – oh, it's all of a heap.'

'Whoa, slow down,' cried Edward. 'Francis dead?'

Bridie nodded. 'Of a heart attack. It was all over in a few hours. I saw him, an' he said goodbye. Then he was gone.'

Edward digested the news in silence. 'Two weeks ago?'

'Yes.'

'So the funeral and everything's all over.' He might have been speaking to himself. Bridie watched him. He raised his head thoughtfully. 'How's he left you?'

Bridie knew exactly what he meant, and had been dreading the effect of the answer. 'There's the house in Tredegar Square, and some money.'

There was a long silence between them. Finally Edward spoke calmly.

'It's not too bad, a junior officer's pay, though of course I'd be away for long spells. I was thinking that we could manage on my wages, once I'd been made an officer. This puts a different light on it, though.'

Bridie shook her head. 'A different light on what?' she asked, her heart tight.

'You and me. I was going to ask you to marry me, one day in the future. When you were free. I'd have waited and waited for you, Bridie. But now you're a rich woman, by the sound of it. . . .'

Bridie sprang to her feet and stopped him by

putting a hand over his bearded mouth.

'No, don't say that,' she begged.

Edward's bright blue eyes looked into hers very seriously.

'I was waiting, too, Edward,' she promised him. She took her hand away. 'I've waited for you, too,' she said again, a blush rising from the neck of her dress and travelling all the way up to her hair.

Edward held the hand that she'd taken from his mouth. 'Do you really mean that?' he asked, trying to stop the overwhelming flood of joy that threatened to burst out in a roar of delight.

'Yes. I've meant it, I think, since the first time I saw you, in Ethel's back room. I think I knew then.'

With a great whoop of happiness he swept her on to his knee and held her tightly. He gazed at her for what seemed like a long time, then, lifting her as easily as a doll, set her on her feet. Standing up so that he towered over her, he took her hand in both his.

'Will you marry me, Bridie?' he asked formally. 'And please say yes, or something terrible will happen to my heart that won't be very repairable.'

'Oh, yes, I will, dear Edward. Oh, yes, of course I will, as soon as some time has gone past. That's only decent.'

Understanding, Edward nodded. She could smell the salt tang of the sea on his face as he kissed her, the thick brown beard soft on her mouth. They clung to each other, holding each other and not wanting ever, ever, to let go. Bridie felt as though, after an endless wandering, she had at last truly come home.

When the clock ticking away on the mantelpiece chimed softly, Edward lifted his mouth from hers and said, 'Nipper?'

She nodded.

'Let's go and get him together.' He kissed her again because he couldn't bear not to.

'What about Ethel? She'll be ever so put out if anyone sees you before she does. Even seeing me first might upset her.'

Edward smiled, the most loving smile she ever saw. 'Not when I take my future wife home to see her. She thinks the world of you, Bridie. She's always thought of you as a daughter, just like our Susan. She'll be over the moon.'

Tucking her hand in the crook of his arm, he walked with her round to the convent school where David went every day. 'House and money, eh?' he remarked as they went. 'Do you know what you're going to do with it all?'

Bridie smiled up at him. 'That depended on you,' she confessed. 'I'd thought ever such a lot about it. I don't want to go and live in Tredegar Square. It wouldn't feel right. So I think I'll sell the house and sell this one, too, and buy another one somewhere else. There's enough money to start up a proper business, though I'm not sure what just yet. But if you hadn't asked me, and if we weren't going to be married, I'd have just sold Tredegar Square, and stayed where I am. But I'd love to go somewhere new with you, to start afresh in a home that's only been ours. That's why it depended on you.'

Edward put up a hand. 'I don't fancy living on my wife's earnings or property,' he said, with a serious look at her. 'You keep what's yours, and it'll see the nipper right later on, but I wouldn't like to live way above my own means because it would make me uncomfortable, Bridie. I wanted to look after you myself.'

'We could maybe look after each other, instead?' she offered. 'I've been on my own a long while, Edward, and I'm used to seeing to myself. And you'll still be away so much, I'll need something to keep me busy. What about a house we put equal money into, and the rest held for David through a business? The lawyers are clever at working out how to invest money, and how to keep it in trust for someone.'

Edward thought it over as they strolled along. Just before they got to the school gates, he nodded, satisfied.

'So long as its fifty-fifty on our house, and you have the rest for your business. We'll use what you earn, and what I earn, but keep the capital. How would that be?'

To the fascination of several mothers waiting for their children outside the gates, Bridie put her arms round Edward's neck and hugged him close.

'That would be just splendid,' she whispered.

He bent down to murmur in her ear. 'I love you so much, Bridie. I don't know how to say it.'

She drew back and smiled. 'You do already. And I know, because I love you too.'

The whispered conversation was interrupted by the

shrieking of children let out of school. David came bounding down the school steps, swinging his bag and jumping the last three steps. He looked round for his mother, and, seeing her standing with a familiar figure, gave a cry of excitement and rushed through the jostling crowd of children to hurl himself at Edward. The big man caught him and swung him high in the air.

' 'lo, nipper!' he shouted, swinging the boy round in a hug.

' 'lo,' answered David, all out of breath. He planted a kiss on Edward's ear and slid down to the ground again.

Bridie took one hand, Edward the other, and, by unspoken consent, the three of them walked slowly round to Ethel's house, to break the good news to all and sundry.

Chapter Twenty-Four

Things didn't go altogether as they'd expected. Ethel had reservations which, in their delight with each other, they had not foreseen. She didn't beat around the bush.

'You're Catholic, love,' she pointed out to Bridie, 'an' he's bin brought up Church of England.'

'Oh, Mum,' protested Edward. 'I go to the service on board sometimes, and if the men have problems there's always the ship's chaplain to talk to, but I wouldn't say I minded very much one way or the other. And you and Dad aren't exactly regulars, are you?'

'That ain't the point,' said Ethel firmly.

'Then what is?'

'It's things like . . . the kiddies. You'd have Catholic kiddies. Wouldn't you?' she appealed to Bridie for confirmation.

'Well, me being a Catholic, my priest would say I should bring the children to church. But does it matter so much? David goes to a Catholic school, an' I go to church some Sundays, but it never seemed to make no problems either way. I don't see as it matters.'

'And what about the wedding?' Ethel went on to

her next worry. 'You'd have to be wed in your place, wouldn't you?'

Bridie took Edward's hand in the shelter of the hanging table-cloth. She was starting to feel anxious. Ethel's broad features had lost their usual beaming good nature and were creased up with doubt and uncertainty.

'Well,' began Bridie, 'there might be ways round it. I'd have to go and ask. Perhaps we could go to the register office, and then have a blessing or something.'

'Blessing!' squawked Ethel. 'Me only son get wed in the register office, and then 'ave a blessing. I never heard the like.'

'We're looking for a way round it, Mum. Don't get all upset.'

Ethel turned her gaze from Bridie to him. Love and hurt fought a battle over her plain features.

'I am upset,' she told him, 'and I ain't pretending otherwise. It's not you, ducks,' she explained to Bridie's unhappy face, 'goodness knows I couldn't ask for a better daughter-in-law. I'd be real pleased. But there is a problem, and I can't make out there ain't.'

Edward turned to Bridie. 'What about getting married in the register office, and leaving it at that?'

'I'd be livin' in sin,' said Bridie miserably.

'Here's your father, at last,' Ethel said, hearing the door bang.

'Sorry I'm late. There was overtime going so I took it,' explained Ted as he came through the door.

'Hullo Dad,' said Edward.

BRIDIE

Ted stopped unbuttoning his coat, surprised. 'Thought you was coming tomorrow,' he said.

'I got off earlier than I thought.'

'It's good to see you, lad,' said Ted, clapping him on the shoulder. Then he looked round the circle of serious faces. 'What's 'appened?' he asked.

Ethel put him in the picture. 'Our Edward wants to marry Bridie.'

A huge grin spread over Ted's face. His long, kind face lit with delight. 'But that's wonderful news. What you lot looking so glum for?'

'She's Catholic,' said Ethel, outlining the problem succinctly.

'Ah.'

Ted knew his Ethel, and he instantly appreciated the glumness. He fell silent and scratched his chin, wondering how to steer around this one. Eth was a good soul, but when it came to Family and Sticking Together, she could be stubborn as a mule. Ted realised that Ethel would find this very hard to bear.

'Can you imagine our Dan and Dot, or Bert and 'is stuck-up wife Clara, grinnin' all over their faces at me in a Catholic church? Ooh, it don't bear thinkin' about.'

'Why should they mind?' asked Ted mildly.

'Yes, Mum,' Edward broke in, 'why should they? If I'm marrying the woman I love, why should anyone give tuppence about where I do it? And if they are going to feel offended – well, why invite them?'

Ted nodded, but he knew it wouldn't work.

'What?' Ethel was scandalized. 'Not invite them?

My only son, and not invite the family to 'is wedding. What an idea! 'course I'd have to invite them. I'd be a laughing stock, else.'

There was silence. Bridie picked at the edge of the table-cloth, wishing she was anywhere but here.

Ted spoke first. 'It seems to me, we have a choice. They can get married in the register office, and the relations can be invited there, and then go an' do whatever has to be done in church afterwards. Or they can be wed in church, with only a few family, who wouldn't make you feel badly.'

'What about the kiddies?' persisted Ethel.

'That's for them to decide, Ethel love. It ain't our business, and that's a fact.'

For a moment Ted thought his wife was going to cry.

'Mum, what's really more important? Me and Bridie doing what is right for us, or a bunch of aunts and cousins who probably don't care much anyway?'

'Don't you say that, son,' said Ted reproachfully. 'There's not one in the family who wouldn't put theirselves out for you if you was in trouble.'

'I didn't mean it that way,' said Edward. 'I meant they are fond of us, what we are, regardless. I bet if you asked them, they'd mostly say it didn't really matter, so long as we're happy with each other.'

'Ooh, the shame of it,' whimpered Ethel again.

'No, Mum. You're wrong. You just see.' He put his arm round Bridie. 'Look at us, Mum. Do you see anything to be ashamed of?'

Ethel was forced to shake her head.

'Imagine it, Mum,' said Edward, who had a fair idea of what his wedding meant to Ethel, 'there'll be me, in my best Whites. I can have a Guard of Honour. Can't you see it? Bridie in a pretty dress, me in my Whites, and eight others lining the way from the church. Oh, come on, Mum, it'll be one of the grandest weddings the family's had in years!'

Ethel began to feel a little bit better. Maybe it wouldn't be a disaster after all. A Guard of Honour, eh? That'd make Clara green with envy.

'All right,' she said reluctantly. 'I'll think about it. I'm not saying as it's sorted,' she added, 'but it might be. I'll have to see.'

Unseen by Ethel, Ted winked at Edward. He leant over the table and patted Bridie's hand.

'I'm real pleased for you, love,' he said. 'Our Edward's a lucky man.'

Bridie looked at Edward. 'I'm lucky, too.'

Ted nodded. 'You two will do well together, I reckon,' he said with satisfaction.

David came running in from the street. 'I've fallen over,' he cried, showing a scraped knee.

Ethel and Bridie took him into the scullery and lifted him up to sit on the draining board while they washed the dirt off with cold water. Ethel touched Bridie's arm.

'I 'ope you don't take no offence,' she said apologetically, 'but I must speak my mind because he is my son, after all.'

Bridie hugged her future mother-in-law's stout frame. 'Ethel, he's so like you. That's what I love, the straightforwardness. I know I can trust Edward 'til the day I die, and it's you an' Ted has made him that way, because that's how you are, too. I'd never take offence, and I know you didn't mean none.'

They put a scrap of sticking plaster on David's knee.

'I suppose that convent don't do him no harm,' remarked Ethel grudgingly. 'It's improved his manners, I've noticed, and there's not a lot of kiddies you can say that for, round here.'

'That and his dad,' agreed Bridie.

Ethel looked at her questioningly.

'Talkin' of his dad,' she went on, 'when did you have in mind for this wedding? I mean, it's a bit early days yet, ain't it? ' she finished delicately.

'It's strange,' answered Bridie. 'Although we were apart so long, I still feel . . . I don't know what to say . . . like a widow, I suppose. As though Francis and me not being together didn't mean he wasn't my husband. I even miss him, in a peculiar sort of way. And David hardly knows he's gone, yet. Edward and me haven't had time to talk about it, but I don't think I'd feel ready to get married just yet. A decent time has to pass, though I couldn't rightly say why exactly. It just does.'

Ethel sighed with relief. It was what she'd hoped they'd do, and not rush into anything indecently soon.

'That's right, my duck.' She gave Bridie's cheek a smacking kiss. 'Why don't you leave me to keep an eye on David, and you two go for a walk? You've got such a lot to talk about, and he'll be gone again in a few weeks.'

And so they did. They walked arm in arm down the little byways that led to the River Lee, winding its way down to Canning Town and the East India Docks. They came to a scrubby bit of land that overlooked the wharves and cranes half a mile away at the edge of the water. In the midst of the thistles and coarse grass, there was a wooden seat facing the river. They sat down and Bridie snuggled warmly up against Edward's jacket. They talked of Ethel and her reluctance to go to a Catholic church, then of this and that, and when they'd get married, and who would come. Bridie pressed tighter against Edward's side when he asked the question she knew must come, and had been wondering how to answer. As with Ethel, she decided honesty was the only choice.

'What about your family?' asked Edward. 'You never mention them. I wondered about them, and I was going to ask you next time I wrote to you. Where are they?'

'Your mum knows about my family,' she answered after such a long pause that Edward turned and looked hard into her face with puzzled eyes. 'I told Ethel when I went to live in your house. She asked me, just like you have. So I knew I'd have to tell you, too.'

'What are you on about?' asked Edward, mystified.

'If you'd have asked me in one of your letters, I

would have told you everything, and it might have been better that way. But here we are now, and it's not a letter. Oh, Edward, I hope this isn't going to make you hate me, like it did Francis.'

Edward took her by the shoulders and turned her white face to his. 'Tell me,' he ordered. 'Stop beating around the bush and driving me mad. Tell me.'

She did. Everything.

'That's a terrible story,' said Edward at last.

'Yes,' whispered Bridie. She could feel hot tears at the back of her throat.

'What did Mum say when you told her?'

'She said something like, "Oh, you poor duck",' answered Bridie, not knowing whether to laugh or cry.

'Good,' said Edward brusquely, ' 'cause if she'd said any different, she and me would have had words.'

Bridie's pinched face lifted to his, which was deep in thought. 'Do you mean, it won't make a difference, to us? Will it still be all right?'

'All right? All right?' bellowed Edward. 'Anyone ever hurt you again, and I'll kill them with my bare hands, so help me.' His big knuckles worked at each other, white with fury.

A tear ran down Bridie's cheek and she swallowed the rest hard. 'I was so dreadfully afraid,' she admitted at last. 'It's done so much harm, and I knew I had to tell, and I didn't know what would happen after that. I thought you might hate me.'

Edward pulled her closer. 'I don't believe we could

hate each other ever, not even if one of us did do something bad. And you didn't do anything bad – the other people did. Francis sounds a monster.'

'Oh, no,' cried Bridie in distress, 'he wasn't that at all. He . . . he felt sort of deceived and he couldn't get over that. We didn't understand each other.'

'I love you enough to want to understand. Will you always tell me everything, so that nothing like that can happen to us?'

Suddenly bone weary, Bridie gave a small smile. 'Yes,' she promised. 'No secrets.'

'Then I have something to tell you.'

'A girl in every port?' asked Bridie, half anxious, half teasing.

'One or two,' admitted Edward, 'but hardly in every port, and never serious. No, it's that I used to dream about you. I had a dream that came quite often, for years. It was always the same, and I used to wake up from it sweating and shaking and afraid. When I first saw you, I couldn't believe it because there you were, the girl in the dream. I've never had it from that day to this. A kind of fear got lifted away, though I couldn't say what I was afraid of.'

'We both had something to be afraid of then,' said Bridie.

'Not any more.' Edward's warm lips on hers drove away the fears and doubts for the last time. He smoothed that unruly red hair, and vowed in his heart that he would protect her and care for her. They sat, quietly looking out over the grey river landscape, the dust making little eddies round their feet, each lost in their own thoughts.

They agreed to wait about six months. By then, Edward expected to be back again.

'If not,' he said, 'I'll apply for special leave to get married. So either way, it'll be an early spring wedding. March?'

Bridie imagined a bright crisp day, with an east wind blowing in cold sunshine. She'd have a fur wrap. She could afford it now!

'March,' she agreed.

Ethel had either overcome her objections, or was keeping them to herself. Her eyes lit up with excitement when they announced their plans. A March wedding in St Saviour's up in Stratford, and a move to Hackney.

'We thought Hackney because there's the park, and the market nearby, and a school for David, and lots of space. It's healthy down there,' Edward told Ted, who nodded agreement.

'I think it's a wise move. Property pricey down that way?'

Ted, who'd rented his small home ever since he and Ethel had married thirty years earlier, felt a bit awed at his son going out and buying a house. He swelled with pride when he told his mates over at the Market. He felt he'd taken on a whole new status. Having a property-owning son was almost as good as owning something himself.

'Yes. More than in Plaistow, because it's a much better area. I know Bridie will be sad to move away, she's ever so fond of that house of hers.'

But in the end Bridie was overjoyed with the house they found on the edge of the canal, directly over-looking Victoria Park. From the back windows, she could hear the water tumbling and sliding under the great wooden sluice gates, a hundred yards down-stream. The towpath on the far side of the canal was a riot of wild flowers. Patient horses dragged barges down to the Docks, three miles away, and then back up again to the factories over in West London, towards Windsor and Slough. The park was green. Grassy spaces lay beneath great banks of almond trees, and tall, massive chestnuts.

'It's like being in the country,' cried Bridie when the agent first showed them round. 'Oh, it's lovely, Edward.'

The house had three storeys, and all the rooms were much bigger than the ones she had at present. It was like a more modest version of Tredegar Square, which had sold in a flash for a very good price. Angus had heartily approved the sale, and had done everything he could to make it go through quickly.

'I'm delighted for you, lassie,' he told Bridie, when she introduced Edward and outlined her plans for her possessions. Her old lawyer, who had advised her so wisely, peered at her over his half-moon glasses and smiled gently.

'You see?' he said, and needed to say no more.

He handled the sale of her little house in Plaistow, and five days before Edward was due to leave for Dartmouth, and his officers' training, they stood in their own house, tired after all the rushing about and signing of forms, but completely content.

'There's just one thing missing,' remarked Edward, as they stood, arms entwined, surveying their castle.

'What's that?' Bridie asked, looking round.

'This,' he answered.

He fished in his pocket and pulled out a tiny leather box. On a velvet cushion glinted a thin gold ring with a single ruby.

'You can't be properly engaged without a ring,' Edward said solemnly, and, lifting her hand, he slipped it gently on to her ringless finger. She'd put away Francis's ring now she was to marry another man.

'There,' he said, in satisfaction. 'Now it's official!'

David, running round excitedly exploring all the rooms, wondered why his mother suddenly threw her arms round Edward's neck like that. He sighed.

Grown ups, he thought dismissively, and ran upstairs to investigate the bathroom, something he'd never remembered having before.

The days had flown by. So absorbed in each other, and with so much to do, they'd hardly seen anyone except Ted and Ethel, and Susan when she could get away from Mrs Anderson's fourth baby. So Ethel went the rounds two days before Edward was due to leave. He and Bridie and David arrived at the station platform to find not only his family, but a whole farewell party gathered together. Lizzie and Jonathan each had a twin in their arms. They were growing into bonny babies, having been a real handful for their first year. Angus stood head and shoulders above everyone else except Edward, his whiskered face alight with pleasure at the turn of events. Mrs MacDonald had a pocketful of sweets for the babies and David, and, sloping unhappily in the background but unable to stay away, was Sam Saul.

When he'd first heard the news a pain like a knife had gone through his heart. It was so many years since Sam had known tears that he hadn't recognised the stinging feeling in his nose. Then, telling Miriam that he wasn't in the office – to anyone, anyone at all – he locked his door and opened his safe. He stubbornly and systematically counted his way through its contents, and noted each amount on a sheet of accounting paper. It was past midnight, and Miriam had long gone home, by the time he finished. Red-eyed and exhausted, he sat quite still in front of the last pile of securities and listened for the pain. A faint echo of terrible loss called out of some deep part of himself. When he got home, he stopped his wife's wailing in mid sentence by saying, 'You want to go for a cruise?'

Mrs Saul's mouth worked silently. For the first time in her life she was at a loss for words.

'What?' she finally got out.

Sam gave her one of his patient looks.

'A cruise. I asked you if you'd like to go on one.'

Mrs Saul, not trusting her voice, nodded vigorously.

'All right. That's settled.'

Leaving his astounded wife, never to be any wiser, Sam took himself off to sleep in his dressing room. With his affairs in the hands of a willing but equally bemused Miriam, he departed a month later and healed his broken heart in the fresh air of the seas around Bermuda. In the second month they were away, Mrs Saul became pregnant. Her son, David Saul, was born eight months later after a difficult time, and Sam, viewing the minute scrap of a baby boy lying in his arms, at last found something else to love.

But that afternoon on the grey platform he only knew that he'd become a stranger where before he'd been a friend. It was nothing anyone said or did, it just was.

There were tears and kisses and hugs and promises of letters. Bridie and Edward wandered a little way from the others, to say their farewells.

'Go safely,' she said, smiling and dry-eyed.

'And you. Take care of everything for me.' He lifted her hand and kissed the little ring. 'I'll be back. I'll send you a telegram as soon as I know when.'

'We'll be waiting for you.'

They had one long, last kiss, then, to catcalls from the train doors where his fellow cadets had gathered in a curious bunch, craning their necks to see Bridie, he turned and laughed back at them. One last hug for David, one last gruff pat on the shoulder from Ted and a weepy wave from Ethel, and he ran to join the long train, radiating the joyful energy of a man completely happy and content with his lot.

Chapter Twenty-Five

Bridie set about taking care of everything, as Edward
had instructed her. She enrolled David at the Catholic
school in Victoria Park Road, a green and grassy walk
away, across the heart of the park. Then, though still
having to make trips to Plaistow twice a week to wind
down her business there, she had time on her hands.
One morning, after taking David to school, she called
in at Hemmingway's, the local builder's. After a good
deal of discussion, an arrangement was made for Mr
Hemmingway himself to call round at the house by
the canal. Together he and Bridie went over every inch
of it. Mr Hemmingway went away, to return two
weeks later with a sheaf of drawings under his arm.
They spread the sheets out on the kitchen table and
pored over the elegantly penned blueprints. On paper,
the house had been transformed. Scullery and kitchen
had been made one, with space for the centre-piece of
the new kitchen – a gas cooker. Mr Hemmingway
had been more than pleased to be asked to install one
of the new type of cooker.

'It's still mostly ranges round here,' he explained to
Bridie, 'though some of the big houses across the park
are putting in the gas. Not many, though. We don't

get much chance to install these, and it'll be good for the lads to have the experience, though the gasmen will be responsible for the pipes, of course.'

Then there was to be a boiler for hot water, which could be piped upstairs. Mr Hemmingway raised his eyebrows. Luxury standards. Redecoration throughout, and the building of a glass conservatory overlooking the water and trees opposite. Ambitious plans, to be completed without fail by the end of February. Mr Hemmingway sucked the end of his pencil. It was the wrong time of year to start major alterations. Weather got bad. Workmen got sick. The lady was adamant. February. Mr Hemmingway chewed his stub of pencil and decided that customers like this didn't grow on trees.

'All right, we'll have it done February. It'll put you to some inconvenience, mind.'

'As much as you like,' accepted Bridie. 'So long as it's done.'

'Right you are.'

Mr Hemmingway stomped off in his wellington boots to get his paperwork started, and Bridie got out her magazines again. She'd bought a whole armful, all telling the reader how to run, look after and decorate their homes. Brown and green were popular. For the kitchen, a lovely brown, similar to the one in Plaistow. For the back room and the hall, green. But for the rest of the house, Bridie decided she wanted something brighter and lighter, and, taking her cue from the watery colours and wild flowers outside, she chose blues and golds and greens and pinks for the other rooms.

'Unusual, very different . . . but pleasing,' was Mr Hemmingway's verdict.

While her home was in uproar, with workmen in and out and cups of tea permanently on the go, Bridie sorted out her affairs with Francis's solicitor. She wished she could transfer the whole lot to her own lawyer, whom she had come to trust completely. But Francis had left so much, and some of the investments were so complicated, that it seemed wise to stay with the man who had been in on the arrangements from the start.

'The money is mostly in stocks and shares. Some in other property, such as three small cottages down at Mile End. You have the residue – substantial, I may say – of the sale of your two houses and purchase of your present property. What do you intend to do with it?'

'What's best?' asked Bridie.

'More of the same. Stocks, bonds and property.'

'Should I leave it all where it is?'

'Your husband was a very conservative man. He liked to play safe. You could do worse than follow his example.'

'And I'd have an income from that?'

'A very substantial one, Mrs Holmes.'

Bridie leaned forward. 'I'd like to leave the capital untouched, then, but with the income I'd want to start up afresh with the moneylending business and expand – but honestly. There's them as say you can't succeed in business unless you cheat, but I know that's not true.'

The solicitor looked at her from under his eyebrows.

'I know what I can do, and I do it well. There's always a call at this side of London for that kind of trade. Not loansharking. Honest loaning. From an office where people can come easily.'

Whatever would this woman do next? The solicitor ran a hand over his hair.

'Very well. I'll continue to administer the main part of the inheritance for you. How would you like to receive the income?'

'Quarterly, in the bank.'

'A bank account?'

'Yes, Lloyds.'

'You would like me to deal with all tax issues?'

'Yes.'

'It's most unusual, what you are planning to do. Most, for a woman. My dear Mrs Holmes, you do realise you don't need to work?'

'But that's not true! I do. I love working, and I love business. I thought of all sorts of other things to do – not lending – but it's what I like to do. And I enjoy the way people need it. It may be a bit different, Mr Brown, but that don't make it wrong.'

'No, no, no. Of course not. Now, unless we have anything else to go over, will that be all for today?' He did find Bridie a little overpowering. Himself, he liked his women more retiring, not bold and blunt like this one.

Bridie got up to go, and then had another thought. 'Oh yes, there was one thing.'

Mr Brown suppressed a certain irritation.

'I want you to make a separate investment of some sort that will make sure that David has enough money to go to university, or wherever else he wants to, when he's eighteen. His teachers tell me he's clever enough, and I think he'll go to the grammar school when he's ten. I want that money to be foolproof. Invested in something that never goes wrong. Can you do that?'

'You know yourself that nothing is one hundred per cent foolproof,' replied Mr Brown, 'but some things, like property, don't make the big killings but are very sound. Very sound indeed. Or there's gold, even. That's as near as you'll get to certainty.'

'Then make it gold. Yes,' instructed Bridie, 'that's a very good idea. Please buy that.'

Mr Brown nodded. Perhaps she'd go, now.

'I'll be off then. Thanks, Mr Brown.'

He said goodbye and heaved a sigh of relief. She was not his cup of tea at all, he feared, not at all.

Chapter Twenty-Six

Edward found his front door ajar. Swinging his kit bag down off his shoulder he looked round the hallway. The house was still and silent.

'Bridie,' he called.

Nothing.

He propped his bag against the wall, which he noticed had been freshly painted a light shade of green, and walked along into the back room. What had been the back room. He stared. The wall between back room and scullery had gone. Along one side of the large room were wooden cabinets and fitted shelves, laden with neatly arranged pots and pans, plates, cups, saucers and all the paraphernalia of cooking and eating. New brown lino fitted snugly over the floor. Edward's eye ran over the new drop-leaf table and matching chairs. A stove of some kind glowed over in a far corner and, resplendent in pride of place, a brand new, shiny white gas cooker faced a metal sink and draining board, installed underneath a window that had not been there when Edward last stood here. Taking it all in, he shook his head slowly.

A thought struck him. He raised his eyes to the ceiling with some reluctance, and then, shrugging slightly to himself, he left the kitchen and went along the passage to the stairs. To the right he found the door to the front room. Pressing his lips together, he walked in. His face became expressionless. Walls painted a pale gold reflected wintry sunlight as clouds broke and scudded away. It slanted in, catching on the brown shiny fabric covering a curvaceous three-piece suite. Dark red carpet lay thick on the floor.

Upstairs Edward's face first darkened, then grew thunderous. He marched from room to room. Pink and green and gold bedrooms. Pink curtains. Carpets. Fancy furniture all over the place. At the back he found the conservatory. He had to admit, even in his by now towering rage, that it was sunny and bright. The house had been changed beyond recognition. *His* house!

'Bridie,' Edward roared. He stamped downstairs, and, finding that staying in any of the rooms simply fuelled his rage, sat down at the bottom of the stairs to wait. It was only about fifteen minutes, but with nothing to vent his rage on, it seemed forever. Finally Bridie, with an armful of early daffodils and a bag of food, pushed open the door. Dropping her shopping with a cry of surprised delight, she turned to Edward with outstretched arms. He put up a hand. She stopped and took a step back. Puzzled, she scanned his face and for the first time saw the barely contained rage, the blue eyes, usually sparkling with good humour, now sparking fire. His nostrils pinched above a jaw where she could see the muscles clenched.

'What is it, Edward?' She faltered, shaking her head in confusion.

'What the bloody hell have you been doing?' he demanded.

'What do you mean?' she put a hand to her cheek as if to ward off a blow.

'What do you think I mean, woman? What in the world have you done to my house?'

'Oh.' That was all. 'Well, I renovated it. Me and Mr Hemmingway, we . . .'

His roar of rage cut across and drowned out her words.

'Renovated.' He repeated the word with savage sarcasm. 'Renovated. Is that what you call turning my home into a whorehouse?'

'What?'

'Look at it.' He shook a furious hand at the ceiling. 'Fit for whores and queers. You'll make me a laughing stock. How could I bring my mates here now? It's a damned boudoir you've gone and made. Good God, Bridie, I'll never hold my head up in the Navy again if anyone comes here and sees this.' Out of breath, he glared at her.

'But I thought. . . .'

'No, you didn't!' he bellowed at her, so that her ears rang. 'One thing you never did was think. I'm a plain workin' man. I get my hands dirty. I have grease in my nails. Half the time I stink. I'd feel more at home in a tart's parlour in Shanghai than here in my own house.' He thrust a fist under her nose.

'Go on, look properly. They're a workin' bloke's

hands. What did you think I was else? Think? Fat lot of thinkin' you've been doin',' he finished with a humourless smile.

'What do you know about whores?'

'None of your business! I'm a sailor. I never claimed to be no angel. Grow up, for God's sake.'

Bridie whimpered.

Edward grabbed her by the elbow and half pushed, half pulled her up the stairs. 'Look at that.' He pushed her into the sitting room she had furnished so tastefully and with such love. 'What the devil's that supposed to be? For drinking tea with your pinkie waving in the air and a lot of mealy-mouthed women gossiping? Is that your idea of living round here?'

'No!' protested Bridie. 'I wanted it to be . . . oh, a bit classy, nice to live in. Different.'

Edward let out a whistling breath of exasperation. 'It's different all right. It's an 'orrible disaster. A joke.'

He pushed her away from him in frustration and she stumbled across one of the armchairs.

'If this is the kind of living you want, then you'd better look for it somewhere else. It's not me. I'm an ordinary bloke, Bridie. If you want a bloke as likes this sort of carry on, you better go out and find him. It's not me you want.'

'I wanted to give you a surprise. I would have written, but I wanted to surprise you.' Tears of dismay gathered in her eyes.

'Oh, you have. I'm astonished in fact. I never thought you could be this selfish, this . . . ignorant.'

The word hurt dreadfully.

'And whose money did you use?' The rage in his voice lashed her.

'Mine,' she whispered.

'So much for agreements. We had one, and the minute I'm away, it's out the window, is it?'

'I never meant to. You aren't being fair,' cried Bridie hotly, her own temper rising at the accusations.

'I suppose you call turning my home into a bordello being fair?'

'It ain't a bordello, it's been done up nice, that's all. I like it, an' you don't. You weren't here to ask.'

'Woman, do I have to tell you again? I'm a sailor. I'll never be here much, and if I can't trust you while I'm away, we'd better forget the whole thing.'

Bridie's face was ashen with fury.

'Well, I'd have you remember as *I* am here all the time, so I want to live in a house I like, too. You don't have no right coming along here and yelling and shouting about whorehouses. If you feel that way, and you know so much about them, you'd best get back there, where you'll feel comfortable.'

His hand shot out and caught her on the side of her jaw.

'You bastard!' she screamed, and slapped his face so ferociously that blood trickled from his nose. Edward dabbed at it with the back of his hand, amazed.

'Bloody hellcat, you are,' he remarked, almost conversationally.

'Don't you call me names.' She raised her fist again and swung it at him. The huge man, on his guard this time, caught it in one hand and laughed. Wiping his bloody nose again, he said, 'Oh no you don't,' and jerked her towards him, out of range.

She tripped and put out a hand to save herself, catching his jacket. Sobbing with rage, she tugged his jacket button off, fighting like a wildcat to get free enough to hit him. Frustrated to the point she was beside herself, she threw her head back to spit at him and suddenly his mouth was on hers, crushing her lips against her teeth. He kissed her frenziedly, picked her up with one arm and carried her through into the despised bedroom, tearing the buttons off her dress with the other hand.

Bridie's rage, in full flood, turned to excitement. She pulled his shirt free of his white officer's trousers and tried to tug at the belt. He drew his face back from hers and laughed aloud.

'You made us a whorehouse . . .' he whispered at her, grinning.

She raised an arm, but he caught it and bent it above her head.

'Would you?' he mocked, undoing his belt skilfully with one hand.

She kicked, but only to egg him on. Still holding one arm above her head, strong fist looking incongruous on the silky pillow slip, he stretched her beneath him and lowered himself over her. Bridie gave a shriek that died away to a moan of pleasure. Edward, lying still, kissed her lips, then ran his mouth down her chin and into the damp place where her neck curved sweetly down to the top of her breasts. Pushing the ruined dress gently aside, he took one hard nipple in his mouth, and caressed the other. Bridie pushed against him hard, breath coming short and fast. Edward, lifting her under him, stroked her teasingly until she begged him with little sobs, 'Oh please, oh please.'

Edward lifted his head from her breast and said, 'Say, "Sorry, next time I'll ask you first, Edward." ' Bridie shook her head violently. He lifted slowly out of her.

'No, no,' cried Bridie.

'Say sorry . . .' he stroked her neck with fingers that were trembling. 'Go on.' He stroked her again. Bridie shook her head with closed eyes. He drew a finger down, over the taut nipples, down her stomach, and raising himself slightly, down to where he lay in her. 'Say sorry.' She groaned and tried to move under him, but he was too heavy for her. He moved very very slowly in and out of her. Pleasure so intense it was like a sweet agony lay just beyond, just beyond . . . and he was holding her on the very edge, and she had to let go, let go. . . .

A long cry of surrender broke out of her, and through teeth clenched with frustration, she wailed, 'I'm sorry.'

Edward kissed her. 'And?' he asked relentlessly.

'I'll ask you another time. Now please, Edward, love me, please, please. . . .'

Edward crushed his mouth to hers and felt rather than heard her high-pitched scream of pleasure and the rapid convulsions of her body as she came to him. With a groan, he let go in ecstasy that brought blackness behind his eyes and stupor to his limbs. They lay, breathless, in a jumble of torn clothes and rumpled sheets.

Edward didn't move. He wound her hair round and round his finger, letting it go, then winding it round again. Slowly his mouth found hers, and they began to kiss, long exploring, questioning kisses. Bridie held his head between her two hands, feeling his coarse hair springy under her fingers. She felt him grow again inside her, and she stroked his broad, muscled back with hands that tensed as he began to move. This time he was demanding. He leant on his elbows, looking down at her, his eyes never leaving hers, until with whimpers and little cries, Bridie's eyes glazed and he watched her mouth draw back as he thrust faster and faster until it was over, and they held each other loosely, bodies aching and satiated and breathing as one.

Languidly Edward drew his head away from her neck and looked at her with soft, sleepy eyes.

'We'll have to fight a lot,' he said contentedly.

Bridie poked her tongue out at him and turned away hastily as she caught the look in his eye.

'I could quite get to like the whorehouse,' he remarked, 'but the rest has to go.'

She drew breath to argue, but he laid a finger on her lips. 'You said sorry, so that's that part done with. But the rest has to go,' he repeated.

Her grey eyes met his, and for a long moment they faced each other. Then she dropped her gaze, and he sighed. The issue was settled. He moved her gently from under him and put his arms around her from behind.

'You can see Hemmingway later on, and tell him to re-do all downstairs except the kitchen, and the sitting room upstairs, by the time we get married.'

'But . . .' said Bridie.

'Haven't you learned yet?' he said sleepily.

On the other side of the silken pillow a red head nodded very slightly. Yes, she'd learned.

They slept, curled up against each other, for an hour. Bridie woke to find Edward leaning on one elbow, gazing at her. As he bent towards her, she pushed him away, half laughing.

'Oh no,' she said, shaking her head at him, while her eyes belied the words. This time they made love in a slow, companionable way, high passion spent. When they finally sat up, side by side, on the bed, Edward kissed the lobe of her ear and announced that he was starving.

'What have you got to eat in this ridiculous place?' he demanded.

Bridie pushed him so that he had to grab at the sheets to stay upright. 'I'd just brought back a load of shopping when you started yelling at me.'

He remembered the bag she'd dropped in the hall-way. 'Go on, then, go and cook. I fancy a plate of eggs and. . . .' His voice was drowned in an earsplitting roar from beneath them. The floor shook and little puffs of dust rose from the bottom of the skirting board. Edward, trained to react fast to emergencies, leapt from the bed and, throwing a towel round his waist, ran for the stairs.

Bridie, shocked and bewildered, sat transfixed, eyes staring at the doorway through which he had disappeared.

'Edward?' she quavered. 'Can you see what it was?'

She heard his voice say something in answer but couldn't make out the words. A lot of noise came from below. Water splashed and objects scraped and banged in a way that made no sense. Bridie hastily got out of bed, and, dragging a gown around her, went to the top of the stairs and peered down. Clouds of black smoke were rising slowly up the stairwell. She coughed, half choking. 'Edward?' she called again, beginning to be frightened for him.

'Come and give me a hand,' he called.

She went downstairs. Holding a hand over her nose and mouth against the dense smoke, she found Edward opening doors and windows in the kitchen, coughing and cursing. Water lay in puddles where he'd thrown it at the fires that had started at several points in the room. A pile of linen waiting to be washed still smouldered. 'Got a set of spanners?' he asked, standing in the doorway breathing fresh air. Bridie nodded speechlessly. She ran to the dresser and pulled out a case of spanners from the bottom.

She handed them to Edward, who knelt down in front of the blackened heap of twisted metal that had been her gas cooker, and busied himself turning off the screw that controlled the flow of gas. The kitchen was so full of smoke they could hardly see each other. 'Turn off the gaslight,' he ordered.

Glancing at Bridie, he saw her hesitate. 'It's been blown out by the blast, but it's still pouring gas,' he said patiently. 'So turn it off, quick.'

They brought the gas under control and stood in the open doorway, breathing carefully, to survey the damage. It was a disaster. The whole room was black, and smoke filled the ground floor with dense fumes.

'What happened?' asked Bridie, awe-struck at the scale of the mess.

'Gas blew up. Must have been a faulty installation. We were lucky not to go with it. It can't have been leaking long, or the whole house would have gone up like a bomb.'

Bridie's mouth hung open silently. Her beautiful house was a ruin. They looked at each other. Edward began to grin.

'What are you finding funny?' she demanded, feeling her own tears brimming at the sorry sight around her.

Edward bent down and kissed her.

'My darling,' he murmured, 'I'm smiling at the sight of my future wife with a black face, hair on end, and the look of a small girl who's had her toy snatched away.'

Bridie wiped the filth more evenly over her face with the back of one hand and tightened her grip on her gown.

'I don't see nothing funny,' she retorted crossly. 'It's an 'orrible mess.'

'It's poetic justice,' said Edward amiably.

'What?'

'Hemmingway will have to re-do it now, won't he? The whorehouse has stayed in one piece, but, oh my word, just look at the rest!'

Bridie's eyes were round. 'You're pleased, aren't you?' she cried.

Edward shrugged. 'We'd agreed to have some redecoration, hadn't we?' he answered cheerfully. 'This just makes it a little more . . . ah . . . urgent. And,' he continued more seriously, 'that ass of a builder had better come in immediately to check for structural damage.'

Bridie looked woeful. 'My lovely kitchen,' she said tearfully.

'Come on, it's not the end of everything,' cried Edward, putting his arm round her shaky shoulders. 'You can get another kitchen, and even another gas cooker, only this time I'll make sure it's put in properly. Heaven knows what that idiot Hemmingway did. It's a new technology, gas, and you have to be careful with it . . . know what you're doing, or you get this kind of thing.'

Bridie sobbed, to be drowned out by the clamour of bells and shouts as the local Fire Brigade rounded the end of the road at high speed and clanged to a halt outside. A tremendous banging on the front door announced the arrival of a red-helmeted figure who stopped and took in the scene with practised eyes. Bridie, unnerved by yet another shock, clung to Edward and babbled in near hysteria.

'It's my fault, I didn't think, and I let Hemmingway do it all, and I never knew what a lot could go wrong. I am sorry, Edward, truly I am, and I'm sorry you don't like any of it. I'll never leave you out again.'

He laughed heartily. 'Oh, you goose,' he said, in a loving voice, and kissed her blackened lips.

The fireman coughed irritably. 'If you two love-birds could see your way to 'elpin' us check that you ain't about to get blown up fer good any minute now, I'd be glad of your co-operation, sir.' His gaze took in their state of undress and the 'sir' was said with suppressed amusement. Bridie looked up guiltily.

'Better get your men in.' Edward nodded apologetically. Four firemen picked their way through the wreckage, checking carefully for any sign of fire and making safe the gas inlets.

'I'll get over to Hemmingway right away,' said Edward as they went upstairs again.

Bridie fingered the patches of greasy black on her bedroom floor and tried to take in what had happened while Edward scrubbed himself clean in the bathroom.

'You clear up here as best you can, and I'll come back with Hemmingway, if I can find him. In fact, I won't come back until I've got him with me,' ordered Edward. 'And on no account touch anything connected to the gas, will you?'

Bridie shook her head.

Pulling on his jacket, Edward leant across the bed to kiss her. 'Never mind, it'll all get put right,' he reassured her unhappy face. 'You see, it'll look even better.'

She gave a little nod.

Edward became serious.

'Bridie?'

She looked up.

'Its as though you are my wife, now. I'd love you even if we lived in a hovel and had never heard of pink walls and gas stoves. They aren't what matter. Only you matter, for me. I don't think anything could change that, not even the whorehouse.' A smile broke out despite himself. 'And that was beautiful. The most beautiful thing. I'm half glad that Hell broke out downstairs, or I might have found it hard to come down from Heaven.'

He grinned and pulled a curl back from her cheek.

'So cheer up and get dressed. I'll be back directly, and you don't want Hemmingway gossiping, do you?'

He winked cheerfully at her and went off to look for the builder. As if the whole neighbourhood wouldn't gossip, never mind the Fire Brigade!

Bridie gazed at her ruined home, and wondered, despite Edward's cheerful words, how they'd ever get straight in time for their wedding, which had to be soon if they weren't to run out of time. Edward only had six weeks before he went back to Dartmouth, and that, sitting in what felt like a battlefield, didn't seem much to the bride-to-be. She retreated into the bathroom and emerged a long time later, pink and composed, to dress and wait anxiously for Edward to come home with the builder.

Chapter Twenty-Seven

There were a lot of sidelong glances, whispers in corners and significant little nods of the head. Bridie noticed them vaguely, immersed as she was in the job of clearing up after the explosion, and overseeing Mr Hemmingway's apologetic efforts to put things right. This time, two men in overalls came from the Gas Board to inspect the installation of new pipes. A splendid new stove replaced the one that had been nothing but a mangled heap, pulled out of the general wreckage to be added to the pile outside the back door, waiting for the dump. Next to the rubbish was a stack of bricks, for the side wall of the house had been blown out and made unstable by the blast.

Hemmingway had put up scaffolding, right up to the roof, and explained that bad weather or no, the wall would have to come down to be rebuilt from the ground up. Standing among the dust and chaos, Bridie wailed that she'd never see how they could cope with a wedding on top of it all, and finally dissolved into tears.

David added to her distress by running excitedly in and out of the ruins, helping the workmen, and showing every sign of having a thoroughly wonderful time.

Each evening his mother took down the old tin bath that had been brought back from retirement to cover the emergency created by the lack of water pipes in the house. David contentedly soaked in front of the fire in his bedroom, while Bridie distractedly tried to find a way around the problem of Edward's ever-dwindling leave. He was unforthcoming about the wedding arrangements, frustrating her with his vague 'Leave it to me, it'll be all right' remarks when she pressed him for help. He was staying at Ethel's, and came over only during the day.

Bridie started to feel miserably that everything had gone awry, and even confided to Lizzie, in a rare moment of disloyalty, that she wondered whether Edward was trying to avoid getting married, and perhaps it had all been her fault for the high-handed way she'd behaved over the house. Though, she added, the fresh decorations were being done in a colour scheme that they'd agreed on, and at the time she'd thought Edward had seemed delighted with the new plans. Lizzie looked up from spooning porridge into Oliver's mouth and gave Bridie a funny look.

'Oh,' she said, 'I should think it'll be all right. You've got a week or two yet.'

It was the same sort of unsatisfactory reply she got from Edward, and everyone else for that matter. Ethel was uncharacteristically non-committal as well. Bridie began to worry in earnest. Noticing this, Edward called a family meeting at Ethel's when Bridie was busy with the builders. It was unanimously agreed that the plan should be brought forward, even though preparations were not perfect.

Four days later Edward found Bridie listlessly putting away folded clothes in the whorehouse. He put his arms round her from behind and leant his chin on top of her head.

'You look like you could do with cheering up,' he told her reflection in the mirror.

'I'd cheer up if I knew whether I was coming or going. I'm beginning to think that you'll go away and that'll be it. I'm all muddled about what's going to happen, Edward, and you are so little help, I'm wondering if you've changed your mind.'

'It is trying, and I'm doing my best to make the arrangements,' said Edward solemnly. 'But, you know, what with here out of action, and Mum fussing about having the reception there, well, it's not easy and that's a fact.'

Bridie looked sceptical. To her ears, he sounded like a man evading the issue. She twisted the little ruby ring around her finger and eyed him doubtfully.

'Look,' cried Edward as if inspired, 'I brought you this.' He groped in his pocket and brought out a scrap of white card. It had black letters engraved on it.

'It's an invitation to visit *The Stalwart*. Cadets' Day. We bring our families on board as guests. They usually lay on a good spread, and you can see almost all over the ship. It's the day after tomorrow. Shall we go, Bridie? My Captain likes to meet Cadets' wives – and wives to be,' he added quickly. 'It'd do you good. Get a bit of colour into your cheeks. Ever since the explosion you've been looking peaky.' He looked eagerly at her, holding the white card by its corner. Bridie took it and looked at it.

'Yes, all right. I'd like to go. And David would be thrilled to bits. What should I wear for a thing like this?'

Edward appeared to consider.

'Well,' he said at last, 'it's a pretty formal sort of occasion, and the wives and girl friends all sort of try to outdo each other. It's sort of showing off. A bit silly really, but everyone has a good time.' He narrowed his eyes and grinned at her. 'I think you should dress up to the nines. Knock 'em all out. The most glamorous outfit you've got.'

'The only glamorous thing I've got is what I'm going to – or was going to – wear to be married,' said Bridie in a flat tone.

'Tell you what, then,' cried Edward, 'wear that.'

Bridie was scandalized. 'I can't do that.'

'Why not?' demanded Edward.

'You just don't. A wedding dress is a wedding dress, no matter what.'

'Ah.' Edward looked downcast. 'I suppose you'll have to come in something more ordinary, then. It's a pity, because the impression you make can mean promotion comes quicker for me. A man's family sort of reflects on him, and if you meet my Captain for the first time looking absolutely stunning, well, it sort of lingers in his mind when promotion comes up.' Behind his back Edward crossed his fingers like he used to do as a small boy.

'Really?'

'Really.' Edward nodded seriously. 'It's most important.'

'It's a stupid way to promote people,' said Bridie, considering the idea.

'Probably is,' agreed Edward cheerfully, 'but that's the way of the world. It's a pretty stupid place in more ways than one.'

Bridie gave in. 'All right, I'll wear my lovely cream silk suit, but you keep me a mile away from grease and dirt and all them bits and pieces you leave lying all over ships. I've seen them on the ferry from Dublin. A right mucky place that was.'

'A Royal Navy destroyer can hardly be compared to something that's not much more than a tramp steamer,' remarked Edward huffily. 'But I'll see you come to no harm, dress and all.'

He propped the engraved invitation on the mantelpiece.

'There you are. It'll be "Petty Officer Edward DuCane and Mrs DuCane" next time, love. Just think of that.'

Bridie had her head inside the cupboard, stacking bath towels. 'Huh,' she muttered to herself, and pushed the pile of folded cotton angrily.

'I'll leave you, then, because Mum is doing my uniform, and I have to put a bit of spit and polish on it too,' he said.

Bridie turned her head in the cupboard doorway. 'What time's all this happening?' she asked.

Edward peered at the invitation. 'Says two-thirty. Let's say I pick you and the nipper up here at half

401

past ten, to get the twelve fifteen from Waterloo. We'll be in Portsmouth about a quarter past two. That suit you?'

'Yes.'

Edward kissed her upturned cheek, and noting her distracted air, decided to leave it at that. The front door slammed after his departing figure and Bridie was left once more with the rough voices of the workmen downstairs, and a sense of loneliness. Shaking her head slowly to herself, she reached inside another cupboard and pulled out the silken suit in its paper wrapping. It didn't feel right, all this carry on, but if that's what Edward wanted, well, she'd do it. He didn't come back that evening, to look over the day's work on the house and put his strong arms round her with loving kisses. Bridie waited up until she had to admit that it was too late for him to walk over, and as she lay down to try to sleep, a tear trickled its way down her cheek.

Maybe he doesn't love me after all. The treacherous thought gnawed at her heart and she tossed uneasily in a shallow sleep.

Her heart was still heavy when she left David, smartly togged out in a sailor suit, with strict instructions to stay in the front room and look at books. Up in the whorehouse, she put the final touches to her dress. The beautiful, rich silk skirt fell almost to her ankles. Lace frothed at the neck of the long, loose jacket and she'd bought little, lacy gloves to match. Her hair was bundled into a high chignon, on top of which glossy pile perched a dark cream hat with a veil that softened her eyes and just skimmed the bridge of her nose. Downstairs, the workmen leant on their brick hods and stared in admiration.

'Blimey!' one of them was heard to mutter under his breath.

She was just smoothing down David's sailor collar when she heard the sound of a motor car outside. It instantly reminded her of that fateful night when Sam Saul had driven her to Tredegar Square, and involuntarily she shivered. Then, all dark blue worsted and gold buttons, Edward strode into the house.

'Chauffeur is here,' he called.

Bridie emerged from the front room, half puzzled, half excited. 'What are you doing?' she asked.

Edward doffed his white peaked cap. 'If Madam would care to step this way. . . .' He waved a hand towards the door.

Its grey-uniformed driver saluted her as she stood in the doorway and stared.

'Oh, Edward. Whatever are you up to?' she asked in amazement.

'We're going in style to meet the Navy. In you get, my dear.'

With delighted confusion, Bridie stepped into luxury and settled David beside her, who fidgeted and demanded to sit in the front, by the driver. The man grinned cheerfully, and said 'Why not?' So with David transferred to the front passenger seat, Edward swung himself in through the door on the other side, and, like royalty, they drew smoothly away and glided off, heading south down the long, straight road that led to the huge Naval Docks where the great ship *Stalwart* rode motionless on the still waters of the Port.

Edward's hand found Bridie's under the rug that covered their knees, and he held it tightly all the way while David squirmed with excitement and watched every move the chauffeur made, promising himself that one day he'd drive a car like this. One day. . . . The chauffeur drove fast and they drew up on the dockside by early afternoon. Several heads in peaked caps looked down at their arrival, and abruptly vanished. Bridie looked around her.

'I thought there'd be lots of people,' she remarked.

'Oh, there will. I think we're a bit early.'

The reply, along with much else, didn't make sense, but the chauffeur was opening her door and handing her down, and touching his cap respectfully. Bridie gave him a delighted smile, and, taking David's hands, the three of them began to climb the long gangplank. There was silence from the ship. Halfway up, Bridie paused.

'Are you sure we've come on the right day? Is this your ship? You're certain?' she asked uneasily.

'Think I don't know my own vessel?' grinned Edward. 'Carry on up.'

She did as she was told. At the very top there was a step down. She turned to make sure David didn't trip, and suddenly a row of men in brilliant white uniforms appeared at one end of the walkway leading to the front of the great ship. They stood smartly at attention.

A tall, familiar figure rounded the corner of the deck, and against the glare of the light from a late autumn sun, Bridie recognised Jonathan. He smiled broadly and came to meet the little party. Bridie saw in amazement that he was resplendently got up in top hat and tails. As he shook Edward's hand and turned to Bridie, the white-clad sailors moved as one, and suddenly each man had a bugle in his hand. The small, perfectly practised band swung into a spirited rendering of 'Here Comes The Bride'.

Jonathan tucked his hand under Bridie's elbow and gently urged her along the side of the ship. Emerging into full sunlight, she came upon the breathtaking sight of the ship's crew at attention, Ethel, Ted, Susan, Lizzie and her twins, Mrs MacDonald, and any number of DuCane relations and in-laws and second cousins twice removed, and so on and so forth. No-one had been left out, and Ethel was happy and proud fit to burst. Every face broke into a huge smile as Jonathan and Bridie walked, Bridie looking round dazzled, not believing her eyes, towards the white-covered table on the deck, where the Captain stood next to a priest, who wore the robes of a Jesuit over his naval blue.

Jonathan looked down and kissed her cheek, his eyes full of delight. He turned and gestured Edward to stand beside her. The three of them stood before the sailor priest, and as the last notes from the band died away he began to intone the first phrases of the marriage ceremony. Wide-eyed with astonishment, Bridie began to realise that it was really happening. She'd come to be married! She looked up at Edward, who almost laughed aloud at the expression dawning on her face. She shook her head at him, as if to say, 'Oh you. . . .' and then they both turned to attend to the priest's words.

Jonathan produced a plain gold ring from his breast pocket, and in the presence of the crew, the Captain, almost the whole of the DuCane family and her closest friends, Bridie married her Edward, while a gentle onshore breeze cooled her flushed cheeks. David, awed by the occasion, only fidgeted a little bit to go and look over the side of the tall ship, and in any case was taken all over it by a group of enthusiastic sailors when the ceremony was over.

Then there was such a hugging and a kissing, and tears and laughter and excited explanations as you never did see or hear from that day to this. The Captain slapped Edward on the back and told him he was a lucky man indeed. Ethel wept all through the playing of the Guard of Honour that escorted Edward and Bridie down through the small door that led off the deck to a long cabin below, where they drank toasts in white wine and ate little pastries handed round by grinning sailors. Bridie's eyes, brimming with joy, followed her husband everywhere, and when the speeches had been made, and the jokes laughed or groaned at, and the wine all finished up by merry guests, Edward saluted his Captain.

To the sweet high sound of the band playing a farewell, Edward handed his bride over the threshold of
the gangplank, and, leaving David to run the length
and breadth of the ship as long as he was allowed until
Ethel took him home to stay with her and Ted, they
rejoined the patient chauffeur on the dockside, and
drove the long road back, man and wife, to their now
deserted home by the canal.

Ignoring the chaos downstairs, Edward scooped up
his wife, carried her over the step, up the stairs and
into the whorehouse. Someone had placed a tray, covered with linen and adorned with red roses, on a small
table. Cold, pale wine and delicate sandwiches had
been placed alongside a small, heartshaped cake
whose white icing was decorated with a silver horse-
shoe and two elegantly piped words: 'Edward. Bridie.'

A candle burned, casting a golden circle into the
enchanted place.

The tall officer drew his wife inside. All the world
was theirs, in that small candlelit room. Edward and
Bridie closed the door. As lovers do.

More compulsive fiction from Headline:

HARRY BOWLING

Conner Street's War

Behind the grimy wharves of London's docklands lies Conner Street, where women stand gossiping in doorways, small boys play marbles on the cobbles and the dockers pop down the 'Eagle' for a quick pint. Corner shops nestle beside tiny terraced houses and two minutes away is the Tower Road market where, it's said, if you can't buy something then it's not made.

Children swap cigarette cards while the wardens hand out gas masks. And when the wail of the air raid siren splits the night all of Conner Street rushes out to the shelter . . . silly Bobbie – a bit slow since his father beat him round the head once too often; Patrick Flannagan, the genial Irishman who likes a drop and Stanley Nathan the grocer who falls for pretty Julie Brett, little guessing her dark past. Meanwhile, down the 'Eagle', Florrie the landlady tempts innocent Albert Conlin behind the blackout curtains with disastrous consequences . . .

FICTION/GENERAL   0 7472 3063 3   £2.50

LONDON'S CHILD

The saga of a turn-of-the-century foundling

PHILIP BOAST

London – a man and a city
London – the first child of the new century

January 1st 1900. A Yorkshire servant girl abandons her illegitimate son on the frosty steps of the London Hospital. A lonely nurse takes the infant home and gives him a name – Ben London – never dreaming that the foundling born in a cemetery will rise to make the city his own . . .

First Ben must endure the hardships of the Workhouse and learn to survive by his wits. It is Ria who teaches him to fend for himself – Ria, the tough and fiercely loyal slum girl who will never forget him. And it is her brother, Vic, who challenges him in such a way that Ben vows never to be powerless again . . .

But the Great War brings escape from the sordid East End backstreets and a chance to prove himself as a fighter pilot. Ben's heroism turns the tide of his fortunes and takes him into the highest echelons of European society – the beginning of an extraordinary rise that will make him owner of London's most elegant emporium. His sights set high, Ben struggles for success, fuelled by the memory of his first love – and by a desire for revenge . . .

London – a world of crime and passion where a foundling can win fame and fortune
London – a self-made man who must truly live up to his name

FICTION/SAGA   0 7472 3186 9   £3.99

Headline books are available at your bookshop or newsagent, or can be ordered from the following address:

Headline Book Publishing PLC
Cash Sales Department
PO Box 11
Falmouth
Cornwall
TR10 9EN
England

UK customers please send cheque or postal order (no currency), allowing 60p for postage and packing for the first book, plus 25p for the second book and 15p for each additional book ordered up to a maximum charge of £1.90 in UK.

BFPO customers please allow 60p for postage and packing for the first book, plus 25p for the second book and 15p per copy for the next seven books, thereafter 9p per book.

Overseas and Eire customers please allow £1.25 for postage and packing for the first book, plus 75p for the second book and 28p for each subsequent book.